D0597036

# Last Whisper

# Last Whisper

CARLENE THOMPSON

St. Martin's Paperbacks

LAST WHISPER

Copyright © 2006 by Carlene Thompson.

Cover photo © Shirley Green

ISBN: 978-0-7394-7395-5

Printed in the United States of America

St. Martin's Paperbacks are published by St. Martin's Press, 175 Fifth Avenue, New York, NY 10010.

In loving memory of Vera Gladys Biggs
A gracious lady

# Last Whisper

# prologue

Brooke Yeager flopped over on her back, put her hand on her upset stomach, and looked up at the stars on her bedroom ceiling, their iridescent paint catching the glow from the night-light that helped ward off her intense fear of the dark. Her mother had painted the stars on Brooke's ceiling six months ago. When her grandmother Greta had first viewed them, she'd clucked her tongue and declared she'd never seen such nonsense in an eleven-year-old girl's room. But Brooke had noticed the twitch of a smile on her grandmother's round face.

After her many years in the United States, *Grossmutter* Greta had not lost the German accent Brooke loved, especially when she told bedtime stories. Brooke wished she could hear one of those stories now, but Greta had visited less and less during the last two years after her former daughter-in-law, Brooke's mother, had married Zachary Tavell.

Brooke rolled on her side and pulled her knees to her

stomach. She didn't blame her grandmother for not wanting to be around Zach. He was always polite, but Brooke felt his coldness toward both her and Greta. Brooke thought maybe he was jealous of her father, who had been handsome, full of joy, and had lots of friends. Zach was quiet, only knew a couple of guys Brooke didn't like, and seemed to live in a world that included only him and Brooke's mother. How different Daddy had been! Brooke still missed him terribly, even though he'd died three whole years ago of cancer.

At the time of his death, Brooke had believed her beautiful, gentle mother, Anne, might die, too. Anne didn't eat, didn't sleep, and cried all the time. Brooke adored her girlish mother who seemed more like a sister than a parent, and she'd been frightened of losing her, too. Finally, Greta had convinced her daughter-in-law to go to a doctor, who gave Anne a bunch of pills that seemed to make her feel lots better. Then, almost before Brooke realized what was happening, her mother started dating Zachary, who had a tiny photography store where he took their picture at Christmas, and a couple of months later, Zach and Anne had gotten married. Brooke had been surprised, and not too happy, but Zach was fairly nice to her and he made her mother laugh again. At least for a while.

But eighteen months after their marriage, Zach had changed. He watched television most of the time, ignored Brooke, drank beer and whiskey almost constantly, and started bickering with Anne. Their squabbles were small and few at first, then grew louder and more frequent. Lately the arguments had become downright scary, close to physical on Zach's part, and Brooke had grown afraid of what might happen.

The fight this evening had been extra bad. Zach had thrown a glass figurine against the wall, cursed at Anne, then slammed out of the house. Anne had yelled that she was going to divorce him. Anne never yelled, but tonight her voice had been ragged with grief and anger. That's when Brooke's stomach had begun to hurt. She was supposed to go to her friend's for a sleepover, but Brooke had made up an excuse not to go. She had wanted to stay home and comfort her mother, but the more Anne cried and ranted, the more helpless Brooke had felt and the worse her stomach ached. Finally, defeated and queasy, she had retreated to her bed. With a tearstained face, Brooke's mother had whispered, "Good night, my angel," but even Mommy's affection didn't make her feel much better than she had an hour ago.

Suddenly, Brooke wondered if she might be dying like Daddy, and as much as she missed him and thought she might see him again in Heaven, or *Himmel,* as *Grossmutter* called it, she wasn't ready to die. "Please don't let me die, God," Brooke whispered. "I need to stay to take care of Mommy."

Suddenly, music began playing downstairs. Brooke jerked in surprise, then relaxed when she heard "Cinnamon Girl" by Neil Young. Her father had loved the song, played it almost every day, and often called Brooke *his* Cinnamon Girl. Neil Young was singing about running in the night and chasing the moonlight. Right now Brooke wished she could run in the night and chase the moonlight with Daddy. She wished she and Daddy and Mommy were all running far away from this small, dark house Brooke had come to hate. The fantasy was so pleasant, Brooke began to feel easier. A tiny hope grew within her that maybe this evening would improve. Maybe Zach would come home—sober—and he and Mommy would kiss and make up and tomorrow would be a brighter day.

Eventually Brooke rolled onto her back again, stared up at the shining painted stars, and fell into a light sleep. She dreamed of one of her grandmother's tales of a beautiful princess who had once lived in a castle in the Black Forest of Germany. The princess had waited for a handsome prince to come for her, but years went by and she'd nearly given up hope when her father and his servants had carried in a huge stag her father had shot with an arrow. "There is something strange about this deer," the father had told the princess. "In my heart, I know I should not have shot him. But he isn't dead. We will care for him until he is well, Daughter, and then we will release him again into the forest." That night the princess learned what was "strange" about the deer. Under her gentle care, he had gradually turned into a man, explaining to her that he was really a prince who'd been turned into a deer by a witch jealous that he did not love her. For years he had roamed the forests, waiting to meet his princess, but unable to do so until he could enter her castle and show her who he truly was. The deer-turned-prince and the princess had kissed, and then—

Brooke jerked awake. Something was wrong. The atmosphere of the house seemed to jitter and throb with tension. Brooke stiffened as her senses grew more acute. She could hear voices, but they were partially lost beneath the loud tones of "Cinnamon Girl," which her mother must have been playing over and over. Brooke strained to listen, but all she heard was Mommy's voice, full of the stridency Brooke hated. On went the music. On went the voices.

Not again, Brooke thought desperately. Please don't let them have another fight. If they did, something terrible would happen. She didn't know how she knew this, but she did. She rolled into a ball, battling the dreadful certainty that disaster was stalking a dark path to her house.

She put her hands over her ears. "Stop it; stop it!" she chanted beneath her beautiful, glowing stars, trying to drown out the cacophony of sounds traveling up the stairs. "Stop shouting. Stop fighting!"

Brooke closed her eyes. She willed herself back into her dream of the prince and princess in their castle in the Black Forest, but it didn't work. She couldn't escape the commotion downstairs. She couldn't escape the air of menace taking over the house, creeping into her soul.

And then, although she still covered her ears, she heard it—a loud sound like a firecracker going off. Then another. And another. But it wasn't the Fourth of July or New Year's Eve. No one would be setting off firecrackers in early October, especially in this quiet neighborhood. Brooke knew from watching television what she had heard. It was a gun being fired. Once and again and again.

Trembling, she took her hands away from her ears. All she heard was music. Then the music stopped and there was nothing. A terrible nothing.

She slid from her bed and crept to her door. I shouldn't do this, she thought. If I get back in bed and go to sleep, I'll wake up in the morning, the sun will be shining, and everything will be all right.

But Brooke couldn't force herself back into bed. The silence downstairs drew her as irresistibly as the fatal Sirens' song had drawn sailors in the little bit of ancient Greek stories her grandmother had read to her. Brooke slowly turned the handle and pushed open the door an inch. Still silence. Then another inch. More silence, but not a peaceful silence.

Chills raced over her although the night was only chilly and she wore flannel pajamas. But she knew she had to see what was happening downstairs, no matter how cold she was, no matter how her hands trembled, no matter how painfully her heart thudded in her chest.

Forcing herself down the hall from her room, Brooke took hold of the mahogany banister and started down the flight of stairs. Usually her mother told Brooke to stop flying up and down those stairs before she fell and broke an arm or a leg, but no one had to give her a warning to slow down tonight. Her dread grew with every step downward, but she went on relentlessly. By the time she reached the last stair, a cold sweat had popped out on her forehead beneath her blond bangs.

Then she saw it, the thing she'd feared, the thing that had caused both the chills and the sweat, the thing too awful to be fully realized with one glance.

Her mother lay sprawled in the front hall washed in cool night air seeping in from the open front door. Her slender body was twisted, the lower half turned to the left, one leg wrenched at the knee and bent outward, her upper body turned right at her waist. Scattered beneath her rested white roses—a dozen delicate long-stemmed roses Zach had brought home for her yesterday, now crushed and garishly splashed with bright, crimson blood. But worst of all, nothing was left of Anne's beautiful face—nothing except a pulpy red mass pointed right at her daughter.

And above Anne stood her husband, Zachary Tavell, holding a gun aimed at Brooke.

# one

## 1

"I can't believe someone is actually thinking of buying this house," Mia Walters said. "How long has it been since we've even shown it?"

"You mean shown it to anyone who was interested, not just someone we dragged there on a tour of other houses?" Brooke Yeager shook her head, grinning. "At least six months. Certainly not since you started at Townsend Realty."

Mia peered from Brooke's car at the late-summer dusk falling on the South Hills section of Charleston, West Virginia. "I just wish we didn't have to be showing the place at night. I had plans."

"A date?"

"No. To color my hair. My dark roots are showing," Mia giggled. "And I *insist* on keeping my hair the same color as yours. Do you realize how lucky you are to have *naturally* wheat blond hair?"

"It's my German and Scandinavian heritage." Brooke

paused, forcing herself to say brightly, "Both my parents were blond. They looked like brother and sister."

Mia, who knew Brooke's father had died young and her mother had been murdered, clearly didn't know what to say and began fiddling with the CD player. "You're listening to a country music CD? I thought you hated country music."

"Patsy Cline is in a class by herself. Besides, I do a rockin' version of 'Walking After Midnight.'"

"I've heard you singing at your desk, Brooke," Mia said dryly. "Remind me never to go to a karaoke bar with you."

Brooke burst into laughter. Mia was twenty-one and had been with Townsend Realty for only two months. The owner of the firm, Aaron Townsend, had assigned Mia to Brooke for training. The two had hit if off immediately. Brooke knew Mia looked up to her—she'd started dressing like Brooke and even bleached her light brown hair to blond—but Brooke liked the girl for her intelligence and sense of humor, not her blatant admiration. Brooke hoped that in a few more months Mia's confidence would grow and she'd begin to develop her own style.

"Aaron really should be showing this house," Brooke said of the boss she barely liked. "After all, it *is* night. Or it will be when we're trying to tour the place."

"That's why he assigned us," Mia said dismally. "He has plans. *Real* plans, not like coloring his hair. He and one of his snooty girlfriends are probably entertaining other snooty people, or going to the symphony, or eating snails or raw beef at some fancy restaurant."

"If I know Aaron, he simply didn't want to waste time showing this lost cause of a house tonight," Brooke returned. "Most likely he's home alone or with his sister watching television and drinking a bottle of those vintage wines he spends a fortune on. I don't think his life is half as glamorous as he tries to make everyone believe."

Mia smiled. "That makes me feel better. I *hate* to think of the rest of the world being out having a good time while I'm—"

"Stuck with me?" Brooke interrupted.

"I didn't mean—"

"I know," Brooke laughed. "I'm not stupid, Mia. I'm sure nothing could be more fun than spending your evening showing this nightmare of a house with me." She slowed her car slightly, peering closely as they passed a lovely one-story stone house on Fitzgerald Lane. White numbers painted on a piece of dark wood jutted from a brick post near the street: *7313*.

"That house isn't up for sale, is it?" Mia asked.

"No, I just remember it fondly. I visited there several times when I was a kid. I thought the house was beautiful and the people who owned it were wonderful, and I wanted desperately to live there. I almost did."

"You almost lived there? What happened?"

Brooke jerked her mind back to the present. "It was during the awful time after my mother's death. I won't bore you with all the details. I'm just glad to see that the house is as pretty as ever."

They turned right on Sutton Street. Although they only traveled a block, the area looked run-down and nearly deserted. Mia groaned. "Oh God, there's *our* house hulking back in the woods. Who on earth designed that place, anyway?"

"I don't know. I think the architect obliterated all mention of his name from the blueprints, then killed himself after it was built."

"Really?" Mia asked innocently.

"No, but he should have." Brooke turned into the long driveway. "I don't see a car. Looks like we beat our prospective buyer to the spot."

"Lucky us."

Brooke pulled up to the house and they both got out of the car. We look like twins, Brooke thought. She wore a tailored periwinkle blue suit with her long hair pulled up in a French twist. Mia had selected an aqua suit cut the same as Brooke's, and had pinned up her slightly shorter blond hair. The prospective buyer will think this is the Townsend Realty uniform, Brooke thought, amused. At least Mia wasn't wearing pearl earrings and stood an inch shorter than Brooke's five foot six.

"This house is *really* ugly," Mia said, gazing at its long, low, tubelike gray lines and tiny windows. "It looks like a submarine. I wonder how the owner's wife felt about it."

"He wasn't married. According to Aaron, he was extremely odd and a recluse. He bought two acres surrounding the house and some land across the street, too, so he could ensure his privacy. That's why there are no houses near it. He wouldn't sell the land."

"I doubt if he had many bids on it, anyway. Who would want to live near the neighborhood submarine? You'd think you were in an amusement park." Mia shook her head. "I guess there's no way we can avoid going inside."

"Not if we want to sell it. And please put a smile on that pretty face and emphasize all the good points to our customer."

Mia looked glum. "This house doesn't have any good points."

"Okay. You just smile, Mia, and I'll emphasize the good points. The last five years have turned me into an expert at making a disastrous house sound like a jewel."

"If you can sell this place, Aaron owes you a *very* big bonus."

When they entered the musty house, Brooke was glad they had arrived before the client. "Let's open some of the windows and air out the place," she told Mia.

"You mean those portholes masquerading as windows? Even on a breezy day not much air could creep through them."

"Then we'll open the front and back doors, too. And turn on the air conditioner. It must be eighty-five degrees in here. If Aaron hadn't just dropped this in my lap, I would have come earlier to prepare the place."

"It doesn't matter. It won't sell." Mia forced open a small window. "This house is a lost cause."

"Nonsense, young lady! Every piece of property is just waiting for the right buyer!" Brooke said with gusto.

Mia groaned. "Oh no. When you start quoting our esteemed leader Aaron Townsend, I know we're in trouble."

They prowled through the house, turning on lights, checking the cabinets and closets to make sure no vermin had gotten up the nerve to creep in and die. Decaying mice never made a good impression on a buyer, Brooke told Mia solemnly, making the girl giggle. When they'd inspected the entire house, they sat down in an ugly yellow booth in the kitchen.

"It's still hot in here," Mia complained.

"I know. We should have stopped for soft drinks on the way, but then we might have spilled them on the beautiful gravel gray carpet." Brooke glanced at her watch. "The client said nine o'clock. It's nine twenty."

"He can't blame traffic. There's hardly any at this hour."

"But he *can* blame the maze of Charleston's one-way streets. Or his unfamiliarity with the South Hills region."

"Or he might say he didn't know the Kanawha River separates South Hills from the downtown section of Charleston."

"There you go. He had trouble finding a bridge. We'll allow him fifteen more minutes for that."

At quarter to ten, Brooke looked at Mia. "Forty-five minutes late and no call on my cell phone. He's a no-show."

"So we've sat here all this time for nothing."

"Nothing! Why, I've had an enchanting evening sweating in my good suit and scouring my brain for nice things to say about the house and wishing I could slap Aaron for pushing off this ordeal on us." Brooke stood up. "I say it's time to get out of here."

"No argument from me," Mia said, then asked almost meekly, "May I drive your car? I love the feel of a new car."

"Certainly." Brooke fished in her purse and came up with the keys. "Just don't bang into anything or run us into the river. River water doesn't do much for new-car smell."

"So I've heard. I promise not to go over eighty miles an hour."

"You'll also pay for the speeding ticket," Brooke laughed. "Come on, kid. Let's abandon ship."

The moist, heavy air of a night late in August descended on them as soon as they stepped from the slightly cooled house. Brooke locked the front door, then turned to see Mia hurrying to the driver's side of the Buick Regal. Brooke would have preferred a sportier model, but the one she'd chosen was excellent for driving clients around, with its comfortable seats and plenty of legroom.

Brooke walked past the headlights a moment before Mia flashed them on bright. "Just trying to get my bearings in here," Mia said distractedly. "I don't want to flip on the windshield wipers when I mean to turn on the blinker." Brooke climbed into the car and shut the door. "Okay," Mia said gaily. "I think I've got everything located. I'll be really careful—"

The blast came just as Brooke had bent down to squash a mosquito clinging tenaciously to her ankle. Glass rained on her head. Glass and big wet globs of something. She reached up and dabbed at one.

Why, it's blood, Brooke thought calmly. Imagine that.

The second shot knocked Mia's body back. From where she still crouched, Brooke could see Mia's feet jerk above the car pedals. This isn't happening, Brooke thought distantly. This just *can't* be—

A third shot followed, slamming Mia down on top of her. Brooke's head crashed on the console between the bucket seats. She remained conscious, but before she could get out a sound, Mia's blood was pouring over her face, running into her hair, and dripping down the neck of her suit.

Brooke stayed crouched for what seemed an endless time, waiting for the fourth shot, that would finish her. But it didn't come. And finally, unable to bear not knowing whether Mia was still alive, Brooke gently tried to lift Mia off her. Light tugging didn't work, though. Finally, Brooke had to give the girl a hard shove that hurled her back against the door.

"I didn't mean to push you so hard," Brooke quavered, trying to loosen her leg and back muscles that seemed locked into place. "How bad are you hurt? Can you hear me?"

But now that Mia rested in an upright position, Brooke knew Mia could not hear her. Or see her. The beautiful, laughing girl who had just gotten into the car five minutes ago was now nothing but a lifeless husk, her left shoulder blown off, blood pouring from a wound in her neck, and the left side of her face gone. *Gone.* Just like Mommy's, Brooke thought as the world began to spin. Her face is gone just like Mommy's.

Brooke climbed out of the car, carefully closing the door behind her, walked to a line of shrubbery about thirty feet away, bent down, and threw up. She dropped to her knees and again threw up, this time so hard that the spinning world went dark for a little while. She wasn't sure how much time had passed before she awakened disoriented. She breathed deeply and touched her lips, which were moist with something the color of blood.

Absently, she wiped her hand across her mouth, tottered to her feet, and started back to the car as her mind began to clear a bit. My purse, my cell phone, she thought hazily. Then she stopped. She could *not* go near the car again. She tried to force her steps in that direction, but her body simply wouldn't obey. Mia was in there. Poor, shattered Mia . . .

Brooke's hands began to shake, and on legs that felt as substantial as water she managed to turn and began walking in the opposite direction. She knew she should do something more resourceful, but she couldn't think of anything. No other houses sat anywhere near. She saw no one else, but that didn't mean whoever had shot at the car wasn't lurking close by. For a moment, she considered turning back and scuttling into the submarine house, but the keys to the house were in the carnage of her Buick. Besides, if someone really wanted to get in that house, they'd find a way. She decided she would probably be almost as vulnerable in there as she was outside.

Brooke's body trembled. Her mind roiled, her thoughts a whirlpool of grotesque images. Only one clear phrase kept echoing in her head—Fitzgerald Lane. I need to get to Fitzgerald Lane.

And what was on Fitzgerald Lane? For a few moments, she couldn't imagine why Fitzgerald Lane was important.

Then she pictured the lovely stone house and somehow knew that inside lay safety.

But how could she get there without taking a chance on being shot out here in the open? Brooke thought, I can't. There's no other way than to walk.

Suddenly, she saw the movement in the bushes to her left. Time seemed to slow and almost stop. She sensed danger so near she could hardly breathe. She closed her eyes and touched a heart-shaped locket given to her long ago by her mother. She didn't pray. She just waited.

Then a car drove by, headlights on bright, garishly illuminating the street, the shrubbery, Brooke. She was too surprised to move. The car slowed and Brooke stood still and tall, staring at the rough-faced male driver who stared back, then stopped the car and rolled down the window. "Give you a ride there, little lady?" he called.

Brooke shook her head, but he didn't drive on. He just stared at her, then finally said, "Awful lonely here in this car." He showed her what he must have thought was an enticing grin, with long, crooked teeth. "It's nice and cool in here." He leaned over and began opening the passenger door. "Pretty lady like you don't need to be wanderin' around in the dark." He pushed his door open wider. The interior lights of the car shone on her and his smile abruptly disappeared. "Hey, is that blood on you?" His lips parted in surprise. "How'd you get blood all over you?"

"Someone is trying to kill me," Brooke said stonily. "Someone with a gun is following me."

"What the hell?" The man gaped at her. "You're . . . you must be crazy!" he blustered. Then he looked again at the blood splattered all over her. He slammed the door and roared off so fast he left tire tracks on the street. Should I have said that? Brooke wondered. Should I have gone with him? Then deep inside she knew she was safer on the street with someone possibly following her than she would have been with that man.

She ambled to the corner of Sutton Street and Fitzgerald

Lane and stood for a moment, her head pounding, her hair stiffening with Mia's drying blood. Brooke felt alone and terrified, and she was certain death hovered near, just waiting for an opportunity to snatch her. Terrified but desperate, she closed her eyes, drew a deep breath, and started down Fitzgerald Lane toward a stone house where she remembered that warmth and security had lain a long time ago.

# 2

With every step, Brooke's head hurt more, and in the humid, almost starless night mosquitoes bit viciously at her face and hands. She realized she'd begun to stumble in her high heels when finally she saw the big white numbers on the dark wood: *7313*. She'd found the house on Fitzgerald Lane.

A few small landscape lights led up a curved sidewalk to the home made of wood and natural stones, the wood painted yellow and the shutters slate blue. Pink impatiens lined the sidewalk and the lights inside glowed bright and warm.

She stood outside for a few minutes, waiting to see if anyone familiar passed the windows, but no one walked by them at all. Then she moved a bit closer to the house, abruptly afraid the people who'd once lived here had moved away.

Pain pierced her left temple and she reached up, feeling dried blood. For a moment she thought she was going to faint. She swayed just as the front door of the house opened. The form of a man stood in the doorway.

"Miss, can I help you?" Her throat had gone dry, her dizziness increased, and she couldn't answer. The man flipped on the porch light and stepped outside, "Miss, are you all right?"

Brooke forced herself to swallow the little bit of saliva left in her mouth. "I need help," she muttered. She came forward reluctantly, shakily. When the man saw her clothes, his smile morphed into a look of shock. "My God, what happened to you?"

She managed one more word. "Accident . . ."

He peered at her in the light. "You were in an accident? What kind of accident? A car wreck?"

"No. Shooting."

"Shooting?"

"Someone shot at me, but they killed Mia instead." Violent trembling overtook her and she began to sob.

Someone came up behind the man. It was another man, much older, with thick gray hair. Brooke could see them muttering. She gained control of the sobbing, lowering it almost into silence, and heard the older man saying, "If she's hurt, she needs to be brought in."

The young man looked shocked. "Bring her in! That's ludicrous! We don't know anything about her. She's covered in blood. I'm going to call the police."

"Come inside, young lady," the older man said.

"No!" The young one looked both furious and wary. "Dammit, Dad, do you know how dangerous it could be to let her in?"

The older man, however, kept smiling, ignoring the younger one's angry reluctance. "We want to help you, don't we, Vincent?"

"We'll call nine-one-one, but she is *not* coming in this house!"

The older one suddenly turned on the other. "This is *my* house, Vincent. You do not give orders here, especially to your father!" He looked at her again, squinting. "We'll call for an ambulance, miss, but you must come inside. You look like you're going to collapse."

Brooke moved toward the older man's gravelly yet amiable voice. A familiar voice. When she reached the brighter light of the porch, the older man stepped in front of the younger one named Vincent and peered at her from beneath shaggy brows. He frowned and she bit her lower lip, suddenly fearful of his deep scrutiny. She was on the verge of backing away from him, in spite of his kind voice. She didn't really know him, except that something about him seemed familiar to her, but she stood still, too weak to walk. The man finally stood about two feet away from her, studying her closely, when surprise flashed in his slightly bloodshot blue eyes.

"Dear God," and he exclaimed, "Vincent, I'm almost sure this is Cinnamon Girl!"

"Cinnamon Girl?" the younger one repeated blankly, but Brooke didn't hear him. She'd finally collapsed from terror and exhaustion into the sweet nothingness of unconsciousness.

# 3

"Dad, who is this woman?"

"I told you. Cinnamon Girl."

"That's a nickname. What's her *real* name?"

"It's on the tip of my tongue. Damn, I hate this Alzheimer's. I'm sundowning, aren't I?"

"Yes," the younger one said sternly, then more gently, "I don't think you really know her, Dad. Maybe she looks like someone you once knew—"

"No! I'm telling you, this is Cinnamon Girl!"

"Okay. Don't get upset. I'll call Emergency Services. They'll know what to do for her. I'll go in and get a blanket to throw over her."

"No. We're taking her in the house."

"Dad—"

"I do recall that there was trouble involving her. . . ."

"All the more reason for not letting her in the house."

"The trouble was not of her making—it was something she got caught up in."

"I'll call for an ambulance and get a blanket. You can watch over her out here."

"I said *no,*" the older man commanded. "If you don't help

me carry this poor woman inside, Vincent, so help me I'll shout and rave—"

The man called Vincent saw the older one's face getting dangerously red as sweat popped out on his forehead, then began running down his face.

"Okay, Dad," Vincent said in a softer voice. "I'll help you carry her inside if you promise to calm down. Your heart—"

"I'm healthy as a horse! You get her legs and I'll get her shoulders. Be gentle, Vincent, or I swear I'll—"

"You told me." The look on Vincent's face changed from anger to worry. "I'll be gentle. Just calm down. You know what the doctor said."

"The doctor is a damned fool! I'm as strong as ever. Now pick up her legs, Vincent."

"She's so slender, I can carry her into the house myself. You open the screen door for me, all right?"

The older man gave Vincent a hard look, then grudgingly clambered to his feet and managed to steady himself. Vincent watched his father teeter to the house, then picked up Brooke Yeager in his strong, steady arms.

# t w o

## 1

Brooke lay perfectly still. She'd awakened a couple of minutes ago but still pretended to be unconscious. She could tell she wasn't outside on the lawn anymore. Maybe the two men had brought her into the house. What she lay on was comfortable—probably a couch—and something soft and warm covered her. A blanket. She was scared, but the men were treating her kindly and one of them seemed to know her. And she knew him. The half-formed memory hovered on the edge of clarity. He'd called her Cinnamon Girl; somehow she knew he'd known her mother; she remembered him and his wife giving her brownies and Kool-Aid and telling her everything would be all right. . . .

"Did you call that emergency number?" she heard the older man ask.

"Yeah, I called nine-one-one. An ambulance is on the way."

Brooke opened her right eye slightly to see the older man

leaning over her, his forehead deeply creased, a troubled
look in his blue eyes.

"Vincent, she's awake!" Vincent? I don't know a Vincent,
Brooke thought. The older man leaned closer to her. "Honey,
tell us your name. I'm sorry I can't remember. I've got this
disease that affects my memory, but you're safe here. Everything's going to be all right."

*Everything's going to be all right.* She remembered the
voice, the words, the protective expression in the eyes. "Detective Lockhart!" she burst out. "Sam Lockhart!"

The man looked shocked, then smiled. "That's right. I'm
a homicide detective—"

"It's me, Detective. Brooke Yeager. My mother Anne was
killed. Murdered by my stepfather. You were in charge of the
case—" She couldn't seem to stop babbling and tried to rise
up on the couch. "Later, I came here. You talked to me. Please,
I need you now. He's out there. He killed Mia. . . ."

"Good God," Sam Lockhart breathed. "Brooke. Yes. I remember now. I haven't seen you for years. I lost touch. I'm
sorry."

"Dad," the younger man said sharply, "she said someone's out there. Someone tried to kill Mina?"

"*Mia.*" She glared at him. "Who are you?"

"Vincent Lockhart, Detective Lockhart's *son.* I thought
you knew him," he seemed to accuse.

"I do. He talked about you, but I forgot your name." Although Sam tried to push her back down on the couch, she
sat bolt upright. "Someone shot at Mia and me at that gray
house on Sutton Street. He *killed* Mia!"

"Who killed Mia?" Vincent demanded.

"I don't know, dammit! He had a shotgun or a rifle. I
didn't see him. And I'm tired of talking to you. Where's your
mother? Where's Laura?"

Vincent looked at her unflinchingly for a moment. Finally, he said, "She died of cancer three years ago."

"Died? She's dead, too?"

Vincent nodded. "It was very peaceful. . . ."

"Peaceful? Is that supposed to make me feel better?"

Brooke cried, suddenly feeling as if she couldn't stand knowing that she'd lost one more person she'd loved. She swallowed convulsively, then in a flash of wild misery, threw back
the blanket. She had to get out of here, away from Vincent's
suspicious eyes and cold attitude, away from images of death
and being surrounded by strangers. She swung her legs off
the couch before a wave of dizziness hit her again and she
half-crumpled, fighting to hold on to consciousness. Vincent
caught her and laid her back on the couch, his green gaze so
piercing it seemed to hurt. She averted her own eyes and
muttered in defeat, "I need help. I just can't fight anymore."

"Calm down, Cinnamon Girl. Help is on the way," Sam
said, his own voice abruptly strong and sure. "Vincent, get
her some water. She's passing out again."

Gunshots. White roses. Blood. Her mother bleeding into
Brooke's arms. Then her mother changed to Mia. She knew
the difference, even though their faces were gone. Gone . . .

Brooke's eyes snapped open. She struggled to sit up, but
she didn't have the strength. Trying to relax slightly, she
took shallow breaths and heard muttering coming from
nearby. Sam and Vincent. In another room? No, close by, but
not hovering over her.

In an effort to force the images of her mother and Mia
from her mind, Brooke lay still and did a quick scan of her
surroundings. She was in a living room with carpet the color
of desert sand and a huge hearth with what looked like real
logs in it. She remembered that hearth so well. She saw two
chairs, both burgundy, and marble-topped end tables, one
sporting a Tiffany lamp. It was real—a family heirloom. She
recalled Sam's wife, Laura, telling her so. In one corner sat a
curio cabinet filled with delicate pieces of glassware. Brooke
had stood in front of that cabinet many years ago, admiring
the pieces, but never touching them. She had been so afraid
of doing anything to alter the sanctity of this house. The
sanctity? She almost smiled at the word. She hadn't thought
of it at age eleven. She'd only thought of the house as her ultimate safe haven.

Suddenly, Vincent leaned over her holding a glass of water. She resisted, but he put a hand under her head and lifted it up. She took a couple of sips before Vincent pulled away the glass.

"I know you want more, but your head is hurt. At the hospital, they may want to give you an anesthetic, which they can't do if you've drunk a lot of water," Vincent said. His voice was deep and smooth, not rough like his father's, but it wasn't friendly, either.

Brooke answered defiantly, "I don't want more anyway."

"Sure you do, but you're too stubborn to say so."

"Oh, Vincent, pull in your horns," Sam snapped. Then he, too, leaned over her. "At least your lips don't look so dry, honey. Vincent, take a look at her head."

Vincent sighed, clearly not happy with playing caregiver to this stranger, but he lifted a piece of cloth Brooke thought they must have applied when she was unconscious. "Looks like the bleeding has stopped," he said.

She gazed into his green eyes. She thought they were the prettiest green eyes she'd ever seen, if only they were smiling, too, not looking back at her with near hostility. He didn't want her to be here, she thought. He didn't want her here even though she was in danger. Creep, she thought furiously. How could he possibly be Sam Lockhart's son? But he was and even though she wanted to escape his suspicious gaze and wary attitude, she knew she was physically incapable of making it out of the door.

Especially when a killer might be waiting for her.

# 2

Vincent saw Brooke jerk under the blanket as paramedics pushed her into the hospital emergency entrance, slamming open the doors with the gurney. He gritted his teeth in annoyance. This rush and shouting as they entered seemed like theatrics. They'd briefly examined her at home and knew she apparently had suffered only a bad bump on the head and some scratches. She wasn't hanging on to life, making every minute crucial. All they were doing was scaring her.

"Where am I?" she asked groggily, the noise of their arrival having awakened her.

"You're at the hospital," a paramedic snapped.

Vincent could see fright streak through her. "I don't want to be in a hospital!"

At first, no one paid any attention to her. Finally, after shouting out her condition to a nurse not ten feet away, a paramedic asked her, "Back at the house this guy"—he jerked his head at Vincent—"said he doesn't really know you. Is there anyone you want him to call?"

Brooke looked up at Vincent. "There's Robert, my boyfriend," she said vaguely. "Robert." She frowned, suddenly looking almost panicky. "No, we . . . broke up. Not him! There's my grandmother, but she's in a nursing home and I don't want her to know what happened to me tonight. I have no other relatives." Brooke's eyes grew almost wild. "I can't be left in this place alone, though. He might come after me!" She paused. "I have a friend! She lives in my apartment building. Stacy . . . Corrigan. I can't remember her phone number. But her husband's name is Jay!" She glanced imploringly at Vincent. "Please call her. *Please.*"

"All *right.*" Vincent noticed that one of the paramedics shot him a doubtful glance. No wonder, Vincent thought. Brooke acted almost afraid of him. "You don't have to sound so desperate. I wasn't going to leave you here by yourself anyway, but I'll look up the number in the phone book and call your friend. Satisfied?"

She nodded, tears in her eyes. Good God, Vincent mused. The paramedic probably thinks I'm a tyrant.

Vincent was stopped at the nurses' station. Once they learned he wasn't a family member, they brusquely dismissed him and sent him to the waiting room. Standard procedure, he knew. Besides, he didn't want to accompany

Brooke Yeager in for a full examination. He didn't even know the woman.

But Brooke had looked so vulnerable and battered that in spite of himself, Vincent felt a slight protectiveness toward her that baffled him, because he didn't believe anyone had been shooting at her and had killed her friend. Her story was ludicrous. She must have been in a car wreck.

Either that, or she was suffering from some kind of domestic abuse. She'd mentioned a boyfriend named Robert with whom she'd "broken up." The thought pulled Vincent up short. Had Robert refused to let her go? Had she ended things by stabbing him? Or, more likely, had he moved on to another woman whom Brooke had stabbed to death? Was it the blood of Robert's new girlfriend all over Brooke's clothes? Was that why she'd said with such fear, "He might come after me"? Was she referring to Robert?

Sighing, Vincent took a seat in the waiting room, hoping this incident wouldn't end up with his father learning that his dear "Cinnamon Girl" was using him to set up some kind of cover story for a murder *she* had committed.

# 3

Brooke lay rigidly beneath a thin blanket, sniffing the room full of unpleasant antiseptic smells. She hated hospitals. She hated the clattering sounds crashing all around her, intensifying her headache. And most of all, she hated feeling helpless.

Why couldn't she remember everything that had happened this evening? She'd asked herself the question at least fifty times. She, who had been officially declared to have a photographic memory when she was seven, now recalled only flashes and feelings. Jumbles. Hodgepodges. Was there even such a word?

An elderly nurse leaned over her. "What was that, dear?"

"I just wondered if 'hodgepodge' was an actual word."

A professional smile appeared. "Why, I'm sure it is if you *want* it to be!"

"And if I wish hard enough, Tinker Bell in *Peter Pan* will live."

A nice-looking young doctor leaned over Brooke. "What's this about Tinker Bell?"

"She's rambling, Doctor," the nurse said darkly.

"I'm *joking*," Brooke replied.

"She's joking when I didn't say anything *funny*," the nurse whispered portentously to the doctor.

He smiled at Brooke. "Soooo, we have a case of unprovoked joking. They're very rare. Don't think I've seen one since 1912." They smiled at each other while the nurse glowered, certain they were making fun of her. She'd decided at least half the people in this hospital made fun of her and she intended to do something about it one day. "Are you going to tell me your head hurts?" the doctor asked Brooke.

"It *really* hurts."

"No wonder. Looks like it took a severe thump. How did that happen?"

We were caught in a hail of bullets and my friend's body crashed onto me, banging my head on the console, Brooke thought. Of course, she couldn't say that. Not now. It was too fresh, too raw. "I was in a wreck," she said simply, her eyes beginning to fill with tears.

"Shook you up pretty bad, didn't it?" he asked kindly. "They always do, even if you're not seriously hurt."

"I'm not seriously hurt physically," Brooke declared. "But there's something wrong with my memory. Gaps. I couldn't remember my ex-boyfriend's name or my best friend's phone number. What if I stay like this, with only half a memory?"

"You have more than half a memory, but you'll retrieve those gaps you talk about soon. They're caused by shock," the doctor said firmly. "Psychogenic or partial memory loss is common after an upsetting experience. Just stay as calm as possible, Miss Yeager. Don't *try* to remember things. That makes the condition worse because you get agitated when you can't immediately recall something. Think pleasant thoughts—wish Tinker Bell alive or something—and we'll check you over for other injuries." The doctor smiled down at her and touched her lightly on the chin.

"Doctor, let's not forget the rules about inappropriate touching," the nurse reminded him tartly.

He rolled his eyes and purposely touched Brooke's chin again. The nurse glared and her face seemed to swell with anger as Brooke burst into nervous, uncontrollable giggles.

# 4

Vincent's vigil in the waiting room seemed interminable, especially for a restless man. A guy sitting beside him made a point of continually turning his head to cough directly onto Vincent, mouth wide and uncovered, then mutter an insincere, "Sorry."

After fifteen minutes of this, Vincent moved, sitting down beside a woman with a black eye and a split lip who immediately launched into a diatribe about her jerk of a husband. Loudly she listed all of his misdeeds, which seemed endless. But she'd never leave him, she declared to Vincent, because she'd stood in front of a preacher and vowed to God to stay with him until death do them part and a vow to God meant everything to her. Besides, if she left the jerk, he'd immediately set up housekeeping with the slut he'd been seeing on the sly. Then she'd have to kill him. Kill him *dead*. That was a promise. Maybe she'd kill the slut, too. She'd have to think on that one. She might not have the stomach for two murders in one night.

Vincent kept nodding at her in pretend sympathy until he felt like one of those bobble-headed dolls. Finally, he excused himself and went to the soft drink machine for a Coke he didn't really want.

His cell phone went off and he eagerly grabbed for it. Leaning against the drink machine in the relative quiet of the hall, he spoke to his father. "What's up?"

"That's *my* question. How's Brooke?"

"I don't know yet. She's still in an examination room and no one feels obligated to give me any information because I'm not her family."

"You should have said you were her brother," Sam reprimanded. "That would have been the smart thing to do."

"Dad, they wanted her address, insurance information, prior medical history, on and on. There's no way I could have bluffed them into thinking I was her brother." Vincent took a sip of his Coke, telling himself he *must* be patient with his father. An extremely short temper seemed to be accompanying the Alzheimer's. "Dad, why don't you tell me who this woman really is and how you know her?"

"This woman is Brooke Yeager," Sam said sharply. "You already know that."

"But who is Brooke Yeager? What's she to you?"

"Good grief, boy, weren't you listening when she was here?"

"She was babbling—"

"A little, but you've heard her name. It was a long time ago, but I'm the one with the bad memory, not you." Vincent remained silent, not wanting to upset his father any more than he had already. "When she was a child, her mother was shot to death by her stepfather. He shot her mother right in the face. The girl walked in on the scene. He would have killed her, too, if a neighbor hadn't burst into the house just in time to save her. I was the lead investigator in that case. She was so traumatized that for two days, all she'd say is, 'I'm Cinnamon Girl.' It wasn't until the third or fourth day that she started talking. She remembered every detail of what had happened." Sam finished with a note of triumph that almost completely assured Vincent that everything his father had just told him was accurate.

"Okay, she was involved in a murder case. But you act like you really know her, Dad."

"I *do*. And you would have, too, if you hadn't been away at that university."

"Berkeley. In California."

"I know where you went to school," Sam said irritably. "Anyway, afterward, the state put her in a foster home right here in South Hills because her grandmother had had a heart attack over the murder. Brooke found out where I lived and came here a few times to talk over the case. That's what she'd always say. 'Let's talk over the case, Detective Lockhart,' like a little adult. Your mother and I'd call the foster parents and tell them we'd bring her home within the hour. Usually they'd never noticed she was gone. Not much of an excuse for a foster family, if you ask me. Your mother absolutely loved her. We talked about adopting her. Good God, Son, we sent you a letter about her and I think a picture."

Slowly, memory washed over Vincent. "I remember Mom writing to me about a girl you were thinking of adopting, although she didn't go into much about her background. I don't think I even remembered her name was Brooke," Vincent said. "Mom asked me if I'd like to have a little sister. I think I said, 'Sure, whatever you want,' and didn't give her another thought." Vincent sighed. "I was pretty into myself back in those days."

"Yeah, well, most teenagers are," Sam said grudgingly. "And maybe it's better you didn't make a big deal out of it, because when Brooke's grandmother recovered, she was sent to live with her. I suppose that was best. People should be with family. But it nearly broke Laura's heart."

"And she didn't say a word to me about it." Vincent suddenly felt ashamed of himself. His mother had been aching with the loss of a child she'd almost had, and she didn't feel she could bother him with her hurt and disappointment. It had all happened a long time ago, though, and his regret couldn't help his mother now. But maybe he could help his father. "Listen, Dad, I know as a child Brooke Yeager was close to you, but you haven't talked to her for years. You don't know anything about how she's turned out, and more important, you don't really know what really happened to her tonight."

"Oh yes, I do," Sam announced proudly. "I called Hal Myers. Used to be my partner. You do remember him, don't you?"

"Of course, Dad. I actually *knew* him."

"Well, he's still on the job and he gave me all the details the police have so far. I hope I can keep it all straight. I wrote most of it down so I could remember."

"That's good, Dad. Way to go!"

"More hippie talk. You sound like I didn't spend a fortune putting you through college."

"I had part-time jobs—"

"That paid practically nothing. Never mind; that's not the subject. Okay, here's what I found out. There was a shooting nearly two hours ago at a vacant house on Sutton Street. That's only half a mile from here, but I figure between Brooke getting knocked out, then wandering around for a while before she found our house, then all the time that went by before you called me"—Vincent sighed at the jibe but said nothing—"the time lapse is accounted for." Sam paused and Vincent could picture his father adjusting his reading glasses as he looked at his notes. "Anyway, the shooting took place in a car in the driveway. The victim was a Mia Walters. Shot three times. Brooke Yeager's purse was found in the car, but there's no sign that she was the shooter. I could've told them that," Sam said as an aside. "Both women work for Townsend Realty. According to the owner of the business, Brooke and Mia were supposed to be showing the house. He also said they were friends."

"Hal is *certain* Brooke was involved in the shooting but wasn't the shooter?"

"The woman was killed by three shots from a *rifle,* Vincent, but the rifle was nowhere around."

"A rifle," Vincent said thoughtfully. "So this Mia was shot from a distance."

"Yes. And as for Brooke, if she were the shooter, why would she leave her purse in the car with all her identification? Why would she kill this woman when their boss knew they'd be together?" Sam waited through Vincent's silence, then demanded, "You're still suspecting Brooke of something, aren't you?"

"I just . . ." Vincent knew anything he said against Brooke would either upset his father or make him angry. "I just wondered if they have any idea who the shooter was or what's going on?"

"No-o-o."

"You don't sound so sure, Dad, or like you're trying to hide something. Tell me all of it."

Sam hesitated. Then he said reluctantly, "Brooke Yeager's stepfather—Zachary Tavell, who shot her mother to death—escaped from Mount Olive Correctional Center in the middle of last night. That place is less than two hours from Charleston. Wait a minute. Writing's a little fuzzy here. Okay! A car was stolen not far from Mount Olive and a gun shop was robbed." Sam paused, and Vincent knew his father was no longer reading notes. "Son, the police think Tavell is on his way to Charleston. He's probably already here."

"How did he get out of prison?"

"Hal gave me a lot of technical information about how he did it, but I'll be damned if I can remember much of it and he was going too fast for me to write it down. The important thing is that he shot Brooke's mother to death, for God's sake, and even *that* wasn't his first offense. No doubt he's the one who stole the car and robbed the gun store." Sam paused. "Vincent, Brooke is in a terrible position. This jerk could have gotten away with his wife's murder if it weren't for her being an eyewitness. Instead, he was put away for forty years without much hope of parole. Hal reminded me that Tavell was just forty-two at the time of the murder."

"Which means that forty years in prison would probably have been the rest of his life," Vincent said slowly.

"That's right. And according to Hal, the prison officials say Tavell's gotten real strange the last few years. Hardly ever talks. Just reads the Bible and writes all the time."

"Writes? Writes what? Arguments for an appeal? Stories, a novel?"

"I don't know. Maybe one of those things, too, but he

doesn't talk to people; he writes them a note. He gives notes to the other prisoners, to the guards, to everyone he comes across about whatever is on his mind."

"That's pretty strange. I mean, a lot of prisoners suddenly 'get religion,' but I've never heard of one communicating mostly through notes."

"Me, neither," Sam said. "Listen, Son, I think he wants revenge on Brooke. He's armed and sure enough a little crazy. The prison officials think he's extremely dangerous."

"No shit."

"Don't talk like that in a public place! People will hear you and think your mother didn't teach you better," Sam reprimanded sharply. "Anyway, there's only one important thing to remember, Vincent. We can't take our eyes off that poor girl or Tavell is going to kill her, just like he did her mother."

# three

## 1

After Vincent shut off his cell phone, he saw two policemen enter the emergency area of the hospital and speak to a woman at the desk who pointed them in the direction of the examination rooms. He figured they'd arrived to question Brooke. He thought about following them. He knew from being around cops all his life that their interrogation techniques could be less than gentle, especially if they thought that Brooke had killed the other woman in the car. They might be verbally forceful with Brooke, even threaten her. His father certainly wouldn't like that, considering how much he thought of the girl. But the police hadn't had time to do a thorough investigation. Besides, Vincent wasn't Brooke's family or her lawyer. He didn't stand a chance of being allowed into the examination room to observe the questioning. He could do nothing, and he wasn't sure he should try. The information his father had given him seemed to clear Brooke of any wrongdoing, but Vincent still wasn't satisfied that she was the innocent she claimed to be.

Contacting the woman Brooke had said was her friend might be his only way of finding out more about her, he decided, and he could have kicked himself for not doing so immediately. But what was her name? The drama of hearing that Brooke's stepfather, a murderer, was on the loose had completely knocked it out of his memory.

Vincent paced up and down the hall, thinking. Was the woman's name Carrie? No. Casey? No. *Stacy!* That was it! But Stacy what? Carrington? Something like that. He went to the pay phone and picked up the directory, annoyed as always by all the pages torn out. Why couldn't people just write down the phone number they wanted instead of ripping out the whole page? He found the section of Cs and began scanning. At last, he came to "Corrigan" and a bell went off in his mind. *That* was the last name! Luckily, there weren't many Corrigans. When he quickly came to Jay and Stacy Corrigan, he felt like cheering.

The first time he called, the line was busy. He waited five minutes, then tried again. On the third ring, a woman announced, "Corrigan residence."

"Mrs. Corrigan? Mrs. *Stacy* Corrigan, friend of Brooke Yeager?"

The woman laughed lightly, making Vincent realize how ridiculous he'd sounded. Then she said in a slightly deep, sensuous voice, "Yes, this is Stacy, friend of Brooke Yeager. What can I do for you, Mr.—"

"Lockhart. Vincent Lockhart. Look, I don't know you—I barely know Brooke—but she's been in . . . well, an accident." He didn't feel now was the time to go into details. "She's at Charleston General and she's asked for you."

The sensuousness vanished from the woman's voice. She spoke louder than necessary, fear edging her voice. "What was it? A car wreck? Is she badly hurt?"

"Not a car wreck. She has a head injury. I don't think it's too serious, but they're still examining her. There could be other things wrong. Internal injuries. I'm not a doctor."

"What happened?"

"I'll tell you when you get here," Vincent said quickly. He

felt that the woman was getting angry at his vagueness. "It's complicated. I'll be in the waiting room. I'm in my early thirties and I have black hair. No, wait. Go to the receiving desk and I'll catch you there. Just come as soon as you can. Brooke expected me to call you sooner, but I got busy."

The woman didn't even say good-bye. She slammed down the phone, which could mean she was rattled or that she thought he was a lunatic playing a prank. Vincent hoped that Stacy Corrigan had believed him and was on her way.

# 2

Vincent headed back for the waiting room. As soon as he stepped in, the woman with the black eye and split lip motioned vigorously to him. No doubt she wanted to continue her harangue about the jerk. Vincent didn't want to insult her—not because he cared about her feelings but because she was the type that when incensed would no doubt burst into a raucous tirade. Instead, he pulled out his cell phone, acted as if he'd just received an important call, and made a "back in a minute" gesture to her. Then he ducked into the safety of the hall, and finally out the door so he could smoke a cigarette. He'd been trying to quit, but now he felt his hands begin the slight trembling that indicated an oncoming nicotine withdrawal fit.

Outside, the soothing warm air of an August night washed over him. The air-conditioning inside had been too low for his taste. He liked the heat, which was why for the last ten years he'd been living in Monterey, California. His father's condition had prompted his unscheduled trip back to West Virginia. Although Sam Lockhart would be the last person to ask for help, his increasingly rambling letters and phone calls had alerted Vincent to the man's failing memory. Only a week ago, Vincent had learned his father had Alzheimer's.

The news had come as a shocking blow, from which Vincent still hadn't recovered.

He took a deep draw on his cigarette, wishing he'd never started smoking in the first place, yet gleaning some comfort from it anyway. He'd cut down tomorrow, he promised himself. Or as soon as he figured out how to handle his dad. The man certainly couldn't go on living by himself. Vincent had arrived home to find bills three months overdue, a refrigerator containing nothing except butter, six packages of cold cuts in various states of decomposition, a loaf of moldy bread, and two paperback books. Every old phonograph album the Lockharts owned lay scattered throughout the living room along with articles of his mother's clothing and at least thirty travel brochures collected through the years for trips the Lockharts had never taken.

Vincent knew something would have to be done soon. But what? Should he move in with his father for a few months? The idea was unbearable to him. He'd been home for only two weeks and just about all they'd done was argue. Vincent had a book deadline in a month, and he couldn't possibly finish a book around his father, who wandered and mumbled and constantly demanded attention. He could get an extension on the book deadline, but another month wouldn't solve Sam's condition.

And Vincent desperately missed Monterey. He had a house he loved, friends, two dogs, his agent. His whole world existed in Monterey. He didn't want to leave it. Dammit, he *wouldn't* leave it, he thought. Vincent loved his father and intended to help him, but he'd spent too long building his own life to have it all fall apart by his moving back to Charleston to look after a man who might be beyond Vincent's ability to help in as short as six months or as long as six years.

He tossed down his cigarette in frustration and had started to light another one when he saw a tall woman striding toward him. She had very long curly light brown hair, a lithe and obviously strong body with large breasts that looked too big to be real, and a determined look in her gray eyes.

Somehow, he knew this was Stacy Corrigan, and he approached her.

"Mrs. Corrigan?"

She stopped, giving him a steely look from those granite gray eyes. "You're the man who called me about Brooke?"

"Yes. I'm Vincent Lockhart. I came to the hospital with her."

"I recognize your voice from the phone." She looked him up and down almost accusingly. "How is Brooke and what the hell happened? Did you hit her with your car?"

Vincent was taken aback by her hostile tone. "Hell no, I didn't hit her with my car! What makes you assume *I* hurt her?"

"You wouldn't be here if you hadn't done something to her. Apparently, you don't even know her."

"If I'd done something to Brooke, I'd be in police custody." Vincent immediately felt dislike for this attractive but brittle woman. "And I don't know how she is yet. Shall we go inside and see if we can get some information?"

"Yes, let's do that," she said curtly, sweeping past him and almost letting the hospital door fly back and hit him in the face. Bitch, Vincent thought. At least he now knew one thing for himself about Brooke—he sure as hell couldn't say much for her taste in friends.

Stacy marched toward the admitting desk and asked for Brooke Yeager. As Vincent had anticipated, the middle-aged woman behind the desk said there was no news on Ms. Yeager yet. Stacy then demanded to see a doctor. "He's busy," the woman told her dismissively.

"Then tell him to get *unbusy* and come out here," Stacy nearly shouted. "I have no idea how my friend is. She could be dead for all I know. Exactly *what* does it take to get a little common courtesy around here? A scene? Because believe me, Miss Whoever You Are, I'm more than ready to cause one."

The woman behind the desk abruptly looked alarmed. Vincent almost laughed in spite of his dislike of Stacy. She might be abrasive, but her methods worked. The woman quickly answered, "I'll get some news to you immediately, Miss—"

"*Mrs.* Corrigan."

"Mrs. Corrigan. I'll just write that down." The woman had gone white and her handwriting looked jerky. "Please have a seat in the waiting room, Mrs. Corrigan, and I'll see that you get information on Ms. Yeager soon."

"See that you do, or I'll be back up here in fifteen minutes, and next time I won't just threaten a scene; I'll *make* one!" Stacy left the reception clerk openmouthed and flounced toward the waiting room, Vincent trailing in her hot-tempered wake.

With tremendous relief, Vincent saw that both the woman with the black eye and the male coughing machine had vanished. Two vacant chairs sat beneath a window. Stacy headed for one, plopped down, fished in her purse, and withdrew a cigarette. "You can't smoke in here," Vincent said as he reluctantly sat down next to her.

"Damn it! You can't smoke anywhere anymore! They treat smokers like pariahs in this country!" Stacy's voice was loud. People looked at her, then quickly glanced away, as if fearing a tongue-lashing. Vincent didn't blame them.

Stacy set her purse on the floor and folded her hands tightly in her lap, but not before Vincent had noticed their trembling. In fact, her whole body seemed to throb with tension. She crossed her legs and began jiggling her right foot nervously. Then she turned on him. "Who are you and *what* happened to Brooke?"

"I didn't hurt her, I promise," Vincent returned, startled.

"Well, all right. You don't have to sound like a little boy making excuses to his mother."

Anger flared in Vincent. "Lady, you look *way* too old to be my mother," he returned nastily.

Of course, it was a lie—Stacy looked like what the kids called *hot* or a *babe*—but perhaps an insult might dent this woman's high-handed manner, and she certainly needed to be taken down a peg, Vincent thought.

Stacy glared at him for a moment. Here it comes, he thought. An outburst. A rant. He braced himself, but she surprised him. "I'm quite sure I don't look older than your mother, but I might have deserved your sarcasm. I'm sorry I took that tone with you. I get loud and bitchy when I'm scared, and I'm fairly shaken right now. Brooke is only five years younger than I am and she feels like a little sister to me, even though I've only known her slightly over a year."

Somewhat mollified, Vincent said, "I can understand that. She seems like the kind of person you think you should take care of."

"How would you know that? I've never heard her even mention you before." She stiffened. "Are you a friend of *Robert's?*"

"Who's Robert?" Vincent asked innocently.

"Robert Eads. Her boyfriend. Ex-boyfriend. Stalker. *Nutcase!*"

"I remember her mentioning a Robert earlier, but no, I am not a friend of his."

"Then who *are* you?"

"I already told you on the phone my name is Vincent Lockhart—"

"That name sounds familiar," she interrupted, "and not because you just told it to me on the phone."

Vincent didn't want to talk to her anymore, but he knew if he didn't answer her, she'd just keep badgering him. She was the badgering type. "Maybe Brooke has mentioned a Detective Sam Lockhart," he managed to say with a modicum of civility.

Stacy frowned. "Yes, she has. A couple of times." She paused. "He had something to do with her mother's case."

"He was the lead investigator. I'm his son."

"Oh! The lead investigator in her mother's *murder?*" Vincent nodded and Stacy looked startled. "Now you're really making me feel weird. Why are you here? What do you have to do with her mother's murder?"

"I don't have *anything* to do with her mother's murder and would you *please* lower your voice?" Vincent hissed.

"I'll lower my voice if you explain this whole situation to me from the beginning."

Vincent felt like telling her to go to hell, but they'd already created enough of a scene in the waiting room. Nearly everyone was staring at them now.

"All right, but only if you don't interrupt me—I *hate* to be interrupted—and keep your voice *down*. Deal?"

Stacy narrowed her cool gray eyes at him for a moment, then said grudgingly, "Deal. Start talking."

Trying not to ignore the headache that was starting to creep up his skull from the stiffening muscles in his neck, Vincent started out with Brooke appearing in front of the Lockhart house, her suit covered in blood, her head injured, her memory fractured. "My father and I brought her inside and it turns out that she'd been to our house several times not too long after her mother was murdered. She was placed with a foster family in South Hills, not far from my father's house. She knew he was the detective in charge of her mother's case, and she'd sneak over to see him to talk about it," Vincent explained. "Her grandmother had suffered a heart attack and for a while it was thought she might not live. My parents actually thought of adopting Brooke. I was away at college at the time and never actually met her. But her grandmother recovered and Brooke went to live with her.

"Anyway, apparently she and another young woman, a Mia Walters, had been sent over to show a house on Sutton Street," Vincent continued. "I'm not sure if they were coming or going from the house, but someone opened fire on them when they were in the car."

Stacy gaped at him, her taut, high-cheekboned face going slack. "Someone *what?*"

"Shot at them. Three times with a rifle. The other woman was killed. I don't know how Brooke was spared unless the shooter thought he got her, too, and didn't hang around to find out."

"Someone shot at her with a rifle?" Stacy breathed.

Vincent nodded. "Afterward, Brooke turned up at my father's house. It's close to the place on Sutton where the shooting occurred and she seemed to remember it, although she wasn't clear about other things. She had a head injury, so we called an ambulance. My father insisted I come with her to the hospital."

"Oh my God," Stacy mumbled. "This is incredible."

"I know."

"Who would want to kill Mia?"

"I have no idea. I didn't know her at all. But I think there was a mistake and the target was Brooke."

"Why?" Stacy asked sharply.

"I've learned from my father that in the middle of the night Brooke's stepfather broke out of Mount Olive Correctional Center. The police think he has a car and a gun, and he could certainly have made it to Charleston by this time." He paused. "Brooke was the only eyewitness in his trial. Maybe he was the shooter and she was his target."

Stacy made the sign of the cross and closed her eyes. "I can't believe this! Then you think that Tavell guy thought he'd killed Brooke?"

"I don't know any more than my father could find out from the police. Dad's been retired for four years now, but he still has some sources of information."

"Maybe I can find out more," Stacy said. "Believe it or not, my husband is a detective, too. He's just second grade, but then, he's only thirty. I'm sure in a couple of years he'll be promoted to first grade. And he's just been assigned as partner to this really great detective everyone thinks walks on water, Hal Myers. Anyway, Jay has probably heard of your father." She looked at Vincent closely. "But it's not just your father's name I recognize. There's something about you. Are your eyes really that green or do you wear colored contacts?"

"I don't wear contacts," Vincent said, suddenly noticing several people peering at his face, focusing on his eyes.

"Well, your eyes are really remarkable. Sexy and not something I'd forget," Stacy went on relentlessly. "I've seen you before."

"I don't think so." Vincent pretended to look at something on his shoe and wished Stacy would lower her voice. "I live in California. Monterey."

"Do you visit often?"

"Not often enough."

"But I feel like I *know* you."

Vincent sighed. "I write books. My father wanted me to be a cop, but I didn't really want to, so now I just write about them. Maybe you've read one and seen a photo of me on the cover. . . ."

"That's it!" Stacy exclaimed. "You're a writer! Wait a minute." She scrunched up her forehead in thought. "*Murder in a Small Town!*"

"That was my first book."

"And I'm actually reading one right now! Your picture is on the flap. That's why you looked familiar to me! You have a trench coat on and a devilish look in your eyes."

"I remember the trench coat—that was the photographer's idea—but a devilish look?"

"Definitely a devilish look."

"Oh. Well . . ." So she wanted to flirt. Even though she was married, even though she was worried about her friend. Although he was annoyed, Vincent was never one to let a woman embarrass him into self-conscious verbal stumbling. "I guess I'm just naturally devilish."

"I *knew* it!" Stacy plunged on. "The book I'm reading now is *Dark Moon.*"

"*Black Moon.*"

"Of course! *Black Moon*! And my friend told me if I like *Black Moon,* I'll love *Last Good-bye.*"

"My latest. Your friend has excellent taste," Vincent said dryly.

"I can't believe it. I'm sitting here talking to the writer of best-selling books!" she exclaimed loudly.

"Yes, so you are." Vincent grew more irritated, wishing she'd quit yammering on even if she was being flattering. People in the waiting room were now glancing at him as if they expected him to do something special because he was *somebody*. That always made him uncomfortable with what he considered his small bit of celebrity. Besides, he always felt odd about his profession, probably because his father had never considered "making up stories" a manly way to earn a living.

"Does this shooting mean Brooke will get twenty-four-hour police protection now?" Stacy asked abruptly.

Vincent blinked, then realized she'd mercifully changed the subject. The flirting session appeared to have ended. "I'm not sure about surveillance. Your husband could probably answer that question better than I can."

"Yes, I guess so." Stacy abruptly stood up and walked the perimeter of the waiting room. She wore tight jeans and a skimpy tank top. Vincent guessed her to be about five foot nine, with the toned body of someone who worked out regularly. She was certainly striking, if not his particular idea of beautiful, and he noticed the male gazes following her restless pacing, most of them focused on her chest, which looked as if it had paid a visit to a plastic surgeon for enhancement. Vincent wondered if in the past she'd done some modeling.

Finally, she glanced at her watch and headed grimly out of the waiting room. She'd given the hospital staff fifteen minutes to get a report on Brooke to her. Vincent looked at his own watch. Eighteen minutes had passed by! Someone was in for trouble now, he thought with amusement.

Luckily, at that moment the harried-looking woman from behind the reception desk appeared at the waiting room door, nearly colliding with Stacy. Stacy turned and motioned for him to come. Like a dog, he thought. All she'd needed to say was, "Here, boy!"

In the hall, the reception clerk said nervously, "Ms. Yeager is in Examining Room Four. You can go in now," before quickly retreating to her desk as if she thought Stacy might do her bodily harm before she could seek cover.

They found the correct examining room. Brooke sat huddled on a table garbed in some kind of paper contraption from the waist up and a white blanket wrapped around her from the waist down to her ankles. Her pale feet with their bright red toenails dangled above the floor.

Stacy rushed to her and enfolded Brooke in her arms.

"Oh, sweetie, I'm so sorry about the shooting. This guy"—
Stacy jerked her head in Vincent's direction—"told me what
happened."

Brooke cast him a slightly vague glance, as if she didn't
quite recognize him, and Stacy looked at her closely. "You
*do* remember him, don't you?"

"Y-yes. Sure."

"What's his name?"

"Vincent Lockhart."

"He *is* Detective Lockhart's son, right?" Stacy continued.
"All he did was come with you to the hospital? You're certain he didn't do anything to hurt you?"

Vincent bristled at Stacy's suspicious tone. Did she think
he'd made up the whole tale of the shooting to cover up an
attack on Brooke *he'd* made?

"He *is* Sam Lockhart's son." Brooke's voice sounded
stronger and more definite than earlier. "He helped me. He's
been very good to me, Stacy."

"What did you think?" Vincent sarcastically asked Stacy.
"That I attacked Brooke, risked getting caught by the cops to
bring her here, then I called you and just hung around so you
could praise my books?"

Stacy gave him her narrow-eyed look, then said insin-
cerely, "I apologized. I told you I get rude when I'm nervous."

"You said you get bitchy," Vincent corrected. "It's more
accurate."

"Do either of you care how *I* am?" Brooke asked, some
of her usual feisty spirit returning. "Or would you prefer I
just keep quiet so you two can keep sniping at each other?"

Vincent and Stacy looked at her guiltily. "I'm sorry," they
said at the same time. Stacy continued, "This has just been
so upsetting."

"No kidding," Brooke returned sourly. She suddenly
wished she hadn't asked Vincent to call Stacy. Stacy was her
closest friend, but she was high-strung and not always great
at creating a calm atmosphere. At least Vincent didn't care

enough about her to cause a stir. "This hasn't been one of the best evenings of my life, either, Stacy."

Stacy's high-cheekboned face turned red. "God, here I am, thinking about myself. Jay would say that's typical."

Brooke shook her head. "No, he wouldn't. Jay adores you."

"Yeah, well, love is blind. And in his case, mute." Stacy shook her head. "Sorry for being so egocentric, Brooke. How are *you*? Any serious injuries?"

Brooke touched the bandage on the left side of her head. "A bullet grazed me."

"Oh my God!" Stacy exploded.

"It just tore the skin, but I guess scalp wounds bleed a lot," Brooke said, wincing at Stacy's loud voice. "It's nothing like what happened to Mia."

Brooke abruptly began to shudder and Stacy put her arms around her again. "I never met Mia, but I know you liked her."

"Someone shot her. Over and over and over," Brooke said flatly. "I just don't know *why*."

Stacy looked at Vincent. Clearly, she was asking if they should tell Brooke about the escape of Zachary Tavell. Vincent was surprised that Stacy had even considered his opinion in the matter. He shook his head *no*. After what Brooke had just been through, he thought the last thing she needed to hear was that the man who had murdered her mother was on the loose. She might go into hysterics, and no one, least of all him, needed that right now. Of course, Brooke had to hear about Tavell soon, but perhaps he'd ask the doctor to give her a mild tranquilizer first.

"I'll be right back," Vincent mumbled, and slipped out of the examining room door, but not before hearing Stacy ask, "Has he been nice to you or a pain in the ass?" He forced himself not to stop and listen to Brooke's answer.

Forty-five minutes later, Brooke had dressed again in her bloody suit ("If I'd known, I could have brought some clean clothes from home," Stacy had said), and the three of them traveled through the night to Brooke's apartment building. Vincent and Stacy helped Brooke up to Apartment 312 and Stacy found Brooke's key in her purse.

They entered a small but neat living room, decorated in cream and saffron yellow with an occasional splash of hibiscus pink. On one wall hung a beautifully framed excellent Degas print, and Vincent noted a wall lined with bookcases, all bulging with hardcovers and paperbacks. His opinion of Brooke rose a bit. She was obviously an avid reader like himself.

A blond dog ran toward them, a slender-boned mixed-breed, about forty pounds, Vincent guessed, and shy. Brooke bent to cuddle her. The dog joyfully licked Brooke's nose, then looked at Vincent with trepidation in her sherry brown eyes. "This is Elise," Brooke explained, kissing the top of the dog's head and rubbing her floppy ears. "I got her at the pound when she was only about six weeks old. I named her for Beethoven's 'Für Elise.' It's my grandmother's favorite song."

"I like that," Vincent said. "I'm surprised you're allowed to have a dog in an apartment, though."

"I pay extra." Brooke fondled the dog some more. "Plus she's house-trained. And *very* quiet."

At that moment, Elise let out a sharp bark. "Shhhh," Brooke said. "I know my suit smells strange, but I'll change in a minute." Her voice shook. "Actually, I'll get *rid* of the suit—"

Bark. Bark. *BARK!*

"Good heavens, what's wrong with you?" Brooke said, holding Elise's slim face in her hands and looking into her eyes. "You *never* make this much noise!"

"Maybe she senses that you're upset," Vincent said. The doctor had agreed to a Valium, and after he'd given it to Brooke, Vincent and Stacy waited about thirty minutes until it began to take effect, then told Brooke as gently as they could about Zach Tavell's escape from prison. Brooke had taken the news calmly—the calm a result of the tranquilizer or shock, Vincent couldn't tell—but she wasn't acting agitated now. Of course, dogs could sense tension in their owners that humans couldn't. They could smell heightened adrenaline. Maybe Elise was more aware of Brooke's true state of being than either Vincent or Stacy. The dog quivered, then ran over to the door and sniffed at a sheet of paper Vincent hadn't noticed when they entered.

Stacy walked to the door and Elise stood back while Stacy stooped and picked up a folded sheet of white paper.

"What is it?" Brooke asked.

"It's—" Stacy read it silently, then exclaimed, "God, I shouldn't have just picked it up! Jay has taught me better police technique than this. Is there a tissue handy?"

"What *is* it?" Brooke demanded. She stood and walked to Stacy's side, yanking the paper out of her hand. Brooke went motionless, simply staring at the note for a moment as her pale face turned even paler. Finally, she read aloud:

" 'Until We Meet Again.' "

# four

## 1

Brooke looked up with frightened violet-blue eyes. "He was *here*."

"*Someone* was here." Vincent felt his own stomach tightening at the thought that the man who had slaughtered a young woman just a few hours earlier had already invaded Brooke's home, the man prison officials said had almost completely stopped talking and started communicating in notes. He knew, though, his keeping a calm tone might prevent Brooke from spiraling into a full-blown panic attack. "The note could have been left by that guy you used to date. Robert, wasn't it?"

"Is that Robert's handwriting?" Stacy asked.

"It's printed," Brooke pointed out. "Printed in big, sloppy letters."

Stacy frowned. "How long has it been since you've seen Robert?"

"Actually *seen* him? Almost three weeks. But he's left

dozens of messages on my answering machine and two days ago he sent flowers to my office."

"You're staying with us tonight," Stacy announced to Brooke. "This is Jay's poker night, but he'll be home soon. You'll feel perfectly safe with a police detective in the apartment."

"You're allergic to dogs," Brooke said, looking at Elise.

"So the dog will stay here."

Brooke shook her head. "And howl all night for me? I don't think so."

Stacy threw the dog an offhanded look. "She'll settle down after a while."

"I want Elise with me tonight," Brooke said in a loud, firm voice. "That settles the matter."

Stacy looked surprised. "Well, you're very bossy tonight."

"And you're bossy all the time," Brooke fired back.

With what Vincent had observed to be one of her typical mood swings, Stacy suddenly started laughing. "You're right. I'm sorry, sweetie. I didn't mean to upset you."

"Well, you did!" Brooke burst out. "And I don't see what's so funny!"

"Oh, for God's sake," Vincent said, feeling as if his neck had turned to concrete and his head might burst before this horrible evening ever ended. "I agree that Brooke doesn't need to be alone tonight, even though the police are going to provide surveillance. Dad and I are dog lovers. Brooke and Elise can stay at the house with us." Stacy gave him a hard look. "We have four bedrooms. She doesn't have to share a bed with Dad or me and I assure you, Stacy, neither one of us is a rapist. Does that suit everyone?"

"No, it does not!" Stacy flared. "The idea of Brooke spending the night with *two* strange men—"

"We're not strange," Vincent said innocently.

"You *know* what I mean. Brooke doesn't know you. She'd be *terribly* uncomfortable."

"No, I wouldn't," Brooke said with unexpected calm. "I went to that house earlier because it represented security to me. It still does." She threw an unconvincingly warm smile at Stacy. "I know you're trying to look out for me, but this is really the best solution, at least for tonight."

"Good!" Vincent said, not sure if he'd offered the invitation to annoy Stacy or because he had some puzzling concern for Brooke. After all, Brooke Yeager was still an unknown quantity as far as he was concerned. Stacy opened her mouth to protest, but Vincent was determined not to waver. "Look, Stacy, we'll have the surveillance moved to our house. There Brooke will have police on the outside of a house, not a big apartment building, and two men will be inside, one of them a former cop."

Stacy sighed, then looked resigned. "Okay, kiddo," she said to Brooke. "I guess you should do what makes *you* comfortable, not what makes *me* comfortable, and I'll stop giving orders."

"Is that possible for you?" Vincent sniped.

Before Stacy could snap back an answer, someone tapped on the apartment door. Stacy, Brooke, and Vincent looked at one another blankly, as if bewildered by some strange phenomenon, until a man called out, "Hey, it's me. Harry. You got some trouble in there?"

Brooke and Stacy let out pent-up breath. "Harry Dormer," Stacy said to Vincent. "He's the combination building superintendent and handyman."

She opened the door and Harry strode in, bright yellow polo shirt stretched tightly across his fifty-inch gut, which hung over the waistband of baggy jeans. He wore filthy running shoes, a baseball cap atop gray-brown hair, and some kind of locket on a silver chain. Vincent peered closer. The locket was clear plastic and contained a gigantic black widow spider, hopefully fake. A guy had to be confident to wear that kind of jewelry, Vincent thought, trying not to grin.

"Mrs. Kelso saw you folks comin' in the lobby and said Brooke, Miss Yeager, looked kinda shook up and—" Harry's small, pale blue eyes widened. "Holy shit, Brooke, is that *blood* all over your suit?"

"Subtle, Harry," Stacy said.

"Well, jeez, she looks like she got beat half to death, except her face isn't hurt. Pretty as ever. That's a relief."

"Better for her to have a broken back than a cut on her pretty face, right, Harry?" Stacy asked acidly.

Harry feigned amazement. "She has a broken back?"

"I was in an accident," Brooke interrupted so smoothly that Vincent was slightly astonished. She sounded completely composed, almost casual. "This isn't my blood. It's someone else's, but I'd rather not discuss the details right now."

"Did somebody get killed?" Harry asked avidly.

"Watch the news tonight," Stacy quickly intervened.

"So somebody *did* get killed! Well, gosh, that's awful." Harry looked excited, not the least bit concerned. "I just wanted to make sure you're all right."

"I appreciate that," Brooke said evenly. "I'm fine. But I'll be spending the night somewhere else, and I need to get a few things together." She gave him a slightly lopsided smile. "I hope you'll excuse me . . ."—Vincent could see the search for a name behind her eyes—". . . Mr. Dormer," she finally managed, "but I'm in a hurry."

"Mr. Dormer!" Harry boomed. "Since when do you call me Mr. Dormer? I can take a hint, but—"

Stacy put a slim, strong hand on his shoulder. "One question before you leave. Was Robert here a while ago? Robert Eads?"

"Brooke's guy that can't take the brush-off? Not that I saw, but I don't stand around the lobby all day," Harry said virtuously. "I have *lots* of work to do."

"I know, and you do it very well," Stacy returned. Everyone in the room except Harry could see that she was just playing up to him for information. "Please think, Harry. This is important. Did you see anyone unusual? Not a tenant? A man who came up here?"

"No. Why?"

"It's not important."

"Then why do you keep asking me about it?" Harry peered around the room as if he expected someone to jump out from behind a drape. "You saying someone's been up here that shouldn't be?"

"We don't know. Thanks for the information," Stacy said quickly, and pushed him into the hall. "Good night, Harry. See you tomorrow." She closed the door behind him.

"I didn't know who he was at first," Brooke said desolately.

"It would have been better if he could have stayed a blank spot permanently," Stacy said dryly, then looked at Vincent. "Harry probably saw more than he's saying. He's acting like the overworked superintendent who never hangs around the lobby gossiping or just looking over all the guests and visitors. But Jay is the policeman, the one who needs to be asking Harry these questions, not me. He's intimidated by Jay. Harry doesn't act like a smart aleck with him."

Stacy continued talking to Vincent as if they were old friends, gossiping. "Harry is just sickening. He looks at every woman under fifty like he can see right through her clothes. He's especially bad about eyeing Brooke and me from head to toe, even when his wife is around. Besides, I think there's something sneaky about him."

"Such as?" Vincent asked.

"He lurks. Or he gives the impression of lurking. I sound paranoid, but Jay has noticed it, too. And his wife Eunice is a real piece of work. Always playing off sick."

"She *is* sick," Brooke said. "Her diabetes is serious and her legs swell and she has migraines."

"Honestly, you are such a soft touch for a sad story, Brooke." Stacy shook her head. "Harry and Eunice are probably harmless, but I've always felt you need to keep an eye on them."

"Which you do," Brooke said. "I think Harry's a little scared of you."

"Good." Stacy smiled. "Okay, you sit down, Brooke, and I'll pack up a few things for you to take tonight, although I still think I should just stay here with you—"

"Stacy," Brooke said warningly.

"Right. No more orders. Where's your overnight bag?"

"On the top shelf of the bedroom closet."

"Where I probably can't reach it."

Vincent headed toward what he thought was the bedroom. "I'll get it. You're tall, Stacy, but I have a few inches on you."

"It's tan with brown trim," Brooke called. "More like a giant tote bag than a suitcase." She looked at Stacy. "How could I remember that so clearly, but not Harry's name?"

"Memory is a funny thing, and you've been through a hell of a night. Don't worry about it," Stacy said, giving Brooke a pat on the arm.

Within half an hour, Brooke had packed the bag, attached a leash to Elise's collar, and reassured Stacy for the fifth time that the Lockhart house was where she really wanted to stay for the night. Tomorrow night, she would probably make other arrangements. Stacy walked the three of them to a cab and gave Brooke a quick kiss on the cheek. "If you get lonely or scared, call me. Don't worry about waking up Jay. He could sleep through an earthquake."

"Thanks, Stacy," Brooke said with genuine warmth. "I'll call you before noon tomorrow."

Vincent and Brooke said little in the taxi on the way to the Lockhart house. Brooke still felt stunned by what had happened, and Vincent couldn't think of one comforting thing to say in this situation. He had already called Sam to let him know that Brooke would be staying with them, and Sam greeted them at the front door wearing striped pajamas and a plaid robe turned inside out.

"Well, now isn't this a pleasure!" he thundered as if Brooke had stopped by unexpectedly. Vincent winced. Sometimes his father acted as if everyone around him were half-deaf. "And I see you've brought your dog. Hello there, fella!"

"I told you we were bringing the dog," Vincent said mildly.

Brooke nodded. "Her name is Elise. She's house-trained. She shouldn't be any trouble. I appreciate you letting me bring her."

"Why, honey, we always kept at least one dog until . . ." Sam looked blank. Until Mom died and her dog died one week later, Vincent thought. "Anyway, I've always had a way with dogs," Sam went on, "although this one seems a mite shy."

"She spent her first few weeks in a dog pound," Brooke said. "I think it frightened her for life."

"Well, no wonder!" Sam stooped, his knees creaking and popping, and stroked Elise on her sleek head. "She's a good dog, though. I can see it in her eyes. She's smart. And nice. And she loves her mistress. Who could blame her for that?" Brooke smiled. "How about some sardines and beer, Brooke?"

"She might prefer a glass of wine," Vincent said quickly, unable to picture Brooke wolfing down greasy sardines and beer like Sam did. "And maybe a sandwich."

"I am a little hungry," she said, almost shyly. "I can't remember the last time I ate. Elise hasn't eaten, either."

Sam peered past Brooke as a patrol car pulled up out front. "You fix everyone something to eat and I'll go talk to the guys for a few minutes." Sam could never pass up talking to another cop.

Vincent made himself smile at Brooke as he shut the door behind his father. "Dad still likes to be in on the action."

"I remember that he seemed so strong and capable when I was young," Brooke said. "He made me feel completely safe at a time when my whole world was falling apart."

Vincent nodded. "He was an incredibly strong man, and I've heard from quite a few other policemen he was the best cop they ever knew. I always wished I could be more like him."

A slow, half-ashamed look twinkled into Brooke's eyes. "You put Stacy in her place more than once today. I'd say that makes you a *very* strong man."

He couldn't help laughing and motioned for her to follow him into the kitchen as he said, "Is Stacy your closest friend?"

"Yes, although I haven't known her for long. But I don't have many friends. For a while I went through a stage of not having any. I suppose I was afraid if I cared for anyone, they'd be taken away from me."

What a sad little girl she must have been, Vincent thought, sympathy springing up in him almost against his will. First she lost her father when she was eight; then three years later her mother was brutally murdered by Tavell, a man Brooke had probably come to trust. No wonder she'd decided to keep her distance from people for a while. They did seem to have a tendency to let her down.

Which didn't mean all those losses hadn't turned her into a hostile, conniving—

"The note!" she said suddenly, startling him. "What happened to the note we found in my apartment?"

"It's tucked in an envelope in my pocket. As soon as Dad gets through gossiping with the guys outside, I'll take it to them. They'll get it into headquarters and maybe we'll get lucky and find some helpful fingerprints."

"But what if Robert left the note?"

"Then maybe knowing his note is in police possession and being checked for fingerprints in an ongoing murder investigation will scare him into backing off." He looked at her. "You wouldn't mind that, would you?"

She looked surprised. "Mind it? I'd love it! Did you think I might be enjoying his attentions?"

"I didn't know how serious you were about him," Vincent said brusquely as he opened a fresh loaf of wheat bread.

"I don't remember being serious about him even when we *were* dating." Brooke sat down at the kitchen table and Elise placed herself daintily at her feet. "He seemed to be a pleasant guy to spend an occasional evening with, but I should have known he was a nut. I always attract nuts."

"Oh," Vincent said, torn between smiling and saying something sarcastic. He opted to let the remark drop. "Would you like chicken or turkey on your sandwich?"

"How about both? I don't think I've eaten since this morning. At least I don't feel like I have."

"A girl with a healthy appetite."

"More than healthy. If my metabolism slows down, I'll be in trouble. And Vincent, could Elise have a few slices of chicken? She didn't have any dinner."

He turned and looked at the dog. He'd always been partial to dogs and had two dogs of his own being kept by friends in

Monterey. "I think we can spare some chicken for a beautiful dog." Elise's tail swished as if she understood the compliment. "Would she like turkey, too?"

Brooke nodded. "Like mother, like daughter. We both have healthy appetites, although she's as fine boned and slim as most cats, not dogs."

Vincent noticed Brooke yawning hugely after she'd eaten her sandwich and drunk a glass of milk. "I think it's bedtime for Elise," he managed diplomatically.

"Bedtime for all of us," Sam boomed from the doorway. "I have to be at work at the crack of dawn tomorrow. That damned Zach Tavell is on the loose. He murdered the mother of one of the sweetest little girls I ever met."

Vincent colored and Brooke looked at him in total confusion. Vincent hadn't yet explained to her about Sam's Alzheimer's and he couldn't imagine what she must be thinking, but he couldn't fill her in on Sam's malady, now. Instead, he tried to cover for Sam by taking Brooke's arm and nearly lifting her from her chair. "I think the guest room at the north end of the house would be best for you," he said loudly. "Nice view, although you're probably not concerned with the view right now. Double bed. Small bathroom attached. You'd probably like to take a shower after all you've been through. Plenty of room for you and Elise."

"Who's Elise?" Sam asked.

"The dog," Vincent said. "Remember that Brooke brought her dog?"

"Cinnamon Girl."

"Yes. Cinnamon Girl and her dog, Elise."

Sam looked down at the blond dog, who hovered close to Brooke's legs, bristling. "A dog," he mumbled. "A dog." Then memory flashed in his eyes. "Of *course* I remember the dog, Vincent. I'm *not* senile!"

At least they're not calling what you suffer from senility anymore, Vincent thought, but he didn't press the matter. Lately, Sam's temper had become hair-trigger, often a symptom of Alzheimer's.

Vincent and Sam walked Brooke to the guest room.

Vincent flipped on the light to show a large bedroom decorated in shades of lilac and ivory. "How beautiful!" Brooke commented.

"Mom redecorated this room right before she got sick," Vincent said. "Unfortunately, she never got a chance to have anyone stay in it."

Sam grinned. "She'd be glad you're the first guest, Brooke."

Brooke smiled. "I'm glad, too. Thank you for being so kind to me. I don't know what I would have done without you." She hesitated and looked at Vincent. "*And* you."

Vincent stared into her large violet-blue eyes, right now looking incredibly beautiful in spite of their fatigue. For a moment, she seemed to be looking back at him just as intensely. Then Sam blasted out, "Nighty night, Cinnamon Girl!" He looked down at the dog. "Good night, Bernice."

"It's *E*lise," Vincent corrected, then could have kicked himself. What did it matter if his father didn't get the dog's name right? But Vincent just couldn't bear to see his father's once razor-sharp mind growing fuzzy and confused.

Sam glared at him for a moment and Vincent braced himself for a tirade. Then Sam's expression softened and he said magnanimously, "Son, it's past your bedtime. You're getting cranky."

Relieved that Sam hadn't burst into a loud verbal dressing-down, Vincent allowed Sam to lead him down the hall as if he were an eight-year-old boy.


# 2

For a long time, Brooke lay wide-eyed and tense in the big, cool bed, staring into the dark, listening. Finally, Brooke felt her eyelids growing heavy. She fought sleep for a while, feeling she must stay up all night, alert and ready for imminent flight, but finally sleep claimed her exhausted body.

Brooke dreamed of beautiful iridescent stars shining down from the ceiling. Then she heard the voices. Her mother's, crying, saying she'd made a mistake and should never have married Zach, because Karl Yaeger had been her only love. Then Zach's sharp reply that she didn't know what she was saying. He'd saved her and Brooke. She was simply out of control. "I'll divorce you!" she was screaming. "I should have done it months ago!" And later, ominous popping sounds that roused Brooke and brought her flying down the stairs to find her mother lying on the floor with half of her beautiful face gone.

Noise woke Brooke again. But this time, she didn't hear the multiple reports of a gun. She heard a squeaking sound coming from the area of the window. Then she felt Elise pawing at her, then saw her running to the window and standing on her hind legs looking out between the draperies.

Brooke slid from bed and put her arms around the dog. "What is it, girl?" she asked, expecting the dog to have seen nothing more than an opossum or a raccoon. Instantly the squeaking sound stopped, and as Brooke became more alert she realized someone was trying to push up the window. She pulled back the drapery a fraction to see that a hole had been cut into the screen—a hole high up, close to the window lock. In a moment, she heard a man speak. "Brooke, it's all right. God sent me. Just hold still." And she did hold still, frozen by fear and shock, long enough to see the face of a man—long, pale, wrinkled, with a slightly crooked nose and hooded, exhausted dark eyes. A face that although it had grown older, she would never forget.

Zachary Tavell.

Without realizing it, Brooke began to shriek. The face darted away from the window, and Elise started barking furiously. Then someone from behind her yelled, "Brooke, what's wrong?"

She screamed again at the nearby voice, then turned to

see Vincent. "Z-Zach," she managed. "He was outside look-ing in the bedroom window."

Vincent looked as if he was trying to convince himself that Brooke had dreamed the face at the window, but Elise's vociferous barking eliminated that possibility. He turned and bounded from the room.

Brooke crawled away from the window, followed by Elise, and huddled by the bed frame, clutching the dog and trying to slow her painfully thudding heart. She hadn't seen Zach Tavell for fifteen years, yet just a glance at him had filled her with dread and terror.

From beyond the bedroom, Brooke heard Vincent talking loudly and Sam shouting. Then they quieted. She crawled from the bedroom, thinking of what an easy target she would make if she stood with the window right behind her. She slunk into the living room, which was empty, and huddled by the huge stone hearth. What seemed like minutes, which were probably only seconds, ticked by before she heard an unfamil-iar male voice yell, "Stop! Police!" Another couple of seconds ticked by before, "Police!"

And then, the gunshot.

# five

## 1

Brooke slowly opened her eyes and looked up at a graceful ceiling fan swirling slowly above her bed. She did not have a ceiling fan above her bed. She jerked up, ready for flight. Elise, too, jumped, then crept toward her, touching Brooke's nose with her own. Instinctively, Brooke ran her hands over the dog's slim, warm body, which edged comfortingly toward her own. Outside, Brooke heard mourning doves searching the grass for breakfast. She looked around the beautiful ivory and lilac bedroom. For an instant, she wondered in whose bed she slept. Then relief washed over her when she realized she was in the Lockhart house, the home once occupied by Sam and Laura, now by Sam and Vincent. She was protected. She was safe.

Still, she felt fearful. Although she wore a light gauze gown, her body was sticky from perspiration brought on by her images of Mia's and her mother's shattered bodies that had danced through her tortured sleep. Brooke got out of bed slowly, feeling every muscle ache from the strain of yesterday's attack. Or rather, two attacks. Last night, after she learned Zach Tavell had escaped the surveillance team, she had simply crawled back into this bed and shivered for the next hour; then somehow, out of sheer physical and emotional exhaustion, she'd fallen asleep.

As soon as she got out of bed, her legs gave way. She crumpled to the floor, totally alert but too terrified to stand up. She didn't call for help. She refused to give in to fear. Instead, she rested for about ten minutes, then slowly stood up, listening to birds chirping in the bright morning sun she could see through the crack where the draperies met. The sun. Light. Zach wouldn't dare come near her in the light, she thought. He always committed his murders in the night.

Someone had placed a glass of water on the bedside table, and she drank it dry. Then she headed for the bathroom. She longed for a hot shower, still imagining she could feel the stickiness of Mia's drying blood on her face, her hands, in her hair, even though she'd showered before she'd gone to bed.

After taking an unusually long shower and washing her already clean hair three times, Brooke thought she felt a bit better. She'd brought along jeans and a long-sleeved blouse to wear today, but when she took the clothes out of her suitcase, they looked too tight and binding. Her sore body simply couldn't tolerate tight denim and new, stiff Nike shoes.

Five minutes later Brooke entered the kitchen barefoot and wearing a soft silk floor-length robe. Vincent and Sam stared at her and she felt herself blushing. "In all the excitement last night, I forgot to pack a robe, and I'm feeling sort of beaten up today—too beaten up for tight clothes. I found this robe in the closet. I hope you don't mind that I'm wearing it."

"Course not," "It's lovely," Vincent and Sam said together. Then Sam continued. "That was one of Laura's robes. She always wore beautiful nightwear until the last few months of her life when she had to abandon it for flannel. I saved that one. It was my favorite."

"Oh, I'll take it off," Brooke said hurriedly. She'd guessed it was Laura's but hadn't thought of how tactless it would be of her to put on the clothes of the dead woman both men had loved. "I'm so sorry."

Sam waved his arm. "Don't take it off!" he said loudly. "You remind me of her in it, all feminine and pretty."

"Really, I can just go back and put on my jeans," Brooke protested, deeply embarrassed by her lack of sensitivity.

"Don't be silly!" Sam boomed. "Laura would love the idea of little Brooke Yeager wearing her robe."

Vincent, to Brooke's surprise, gave her an encouraging nod and smile. "It does look pretty on you and she'd probably like to know you were wearing it, instead of it just hanging untouched like a piece of clothing in a museum exhibit." He looked at his father. "And you don't have to keep yelling at us, Dad. We're right here."

"Was I yelling?" Sam asked innocently. "Damn, don't tell me my hearing is going, too."

Vincent knew Sam's hearing *was* going, but he had seemed in a good mood this morning and Vincent didn't want to depress him. "I think you're just exuberant because we have company. You always did get loud when you were happy. Or you'd had a couple of drinks. Did you make Bloody Marys before I got up?"

Sam tossed a towel playfully at Vincent's head. "I do not start off my mornings with tomato juice and vodka, although now that you've mentioned it, it sounds like a pretty good idea. But we're out of vodka. Have been for years, I think."

"Then I'll run right out and buy you some," Vincent teased back.

Sam laughed, then turned to Brooke. "Vincent and I have already polished off a pot of coffee. The new one should be just about finished."

"Good. I can't get going without caffeine in the morning," Brooke said.

"Do you want it black, or with cream or sugar?" Vincent asked.

Brooke went blank. "Cream, I think." She blushed. How embarrassing not to remember how she took her coffee.

"There's plenty in the pot," Vincent said casually. "We'll keep trying mixtures until we get it right."

"Does Denise like coffee?" Sam asked.

Brooke saw Vincent start to correct his father about the dog's name, then clamp his mouth shut. "No, dogs and caffeine don't mix too well," Brooke said. "Elise will just have some water."

"Fix her some of that fancy French stuff Vincent likes."

"That isn't necessary. Tap water will do fine."

Sam shook his head. "Vincent, get the dog your fancy water. I can't *imagine* wasting money on foreign water you have to go to the store and buy in bottles when perfectly acceptable water comes right out of the spigot in your own kitchen, but ever since he went to California, Vincent has gotten exotic *tastes,*" Sam said darkly.

Vincent rolled his eyes at Brooke, brought out a bottle of Perrier, and poured the cold water in a bowl for Elise, who acted like she'd never tasted anything so delicious in her life, licking the bowl dry and looking around hopefully for more. "See, Dad," Vincent said, smiling. "Even *dogs* like it better."

"She's just thirsty," Sam groused. "She'd like anything." He suddenly turned a sweet smile on Brooke. "You want some breakfast? Laura always said I was a genius at making omelets."

"Just coffee will be fine," Brooke said.

Vincent had just poured a cup for her when the doorbell rang. The three of them went still, their eyes widening. Elise barked, snapping them out of their trance. "Well, I don't suppose Zach Tavell has come to join us for breakfast," Sam said, rising heavily from his chair and heading for the front door. In a moment, he returned with Stacy and Jay Corrigan.

Stacy led the way, as usual. She headed straight for Brooke and gave her a hug. "Jay heard all about Tavell being here last night and I expected you to look like a ghost this morning. Instead you look ready to pose for a Victoria's Secret ad."

Brooke blushed. "I think I'm a bit more covered than the catalog's models. I forgot my own robe."

"This one is beautiful." Stacy smiled at Vincent, then introduced herself to Sam. "I'm Brooke's best friend. At least I like to think of myself as her best friend. It was so kind of you and your son to invite her to stay last night."

"It was our pleasure." Sam beamed at Stacy, who looked like a slim and sophisticated model in a pale green suit and high heels.

She turned to Jay. "I believe you already know my husband. He's a detective, too."

"I . . . I've heard of him," Sam said, barely letting his smile falter. Brooke immediately knew he had no idea who Jay Corrigan was. Jay—about five-ten, muscular, and slightly bulky, with an easy smile and heavy sandy eyebrows above bright blue eyes—looked more like Sam's son than the tall, slender Vincent with his more refined features and startlingly green eyes. Jay extended a hand to Sam. "It's an honor to meet you, sir. I don't think a week goes by that I don't hear about how Sam Lockhart cleared more cases than all of us put together." Sam made a derisive face, but Brooke could tell he was pleased. "We stopped at a bakery and bought a dozen doughnuts," Jay said, holding out a box. "I hope you like doughnuts."

Sam guffawed. "A cop who doesn't like doughnuts? Does such a being even exist?" Jay laughed along noisily with him. "You two have some coffee with us," Sam said to Stacy and Jay. "Vincent, get the coffee. Don't know if Stacy wants one of my omelets, but Jay's having coffee and a doughnut with me."

Jay smiled. "I'd love to stay for coffee, sir, if we're not putting you out."

"Putting us out? Mostly Vincent and I just quarrel in the mornings and then he goes running and comes in dripping sweat. This is like a regular party."

Vincent began pouring coffee while Sam, Stacy, and Jay sat at the kitchen table. Brooke saw Vincent slip Elise a doughnut, which she carried to a corner to enjoy in private. "I'm sure we're a bother so early in the morning," Stacy said, "but when Jay heard this morning what had gone on here last night I insisted we come over and check on Brooke. A phone call just wouldn't do it for me. I needed to see her."

"That was considerate of you," Brooke said.

"And here you are calm and pretty as a picture." Stacy looked down, leaned closer, and said softly, "But exactly *how* scared were you?"

"I'm trying not to think about it," Brooke whispered.

Stacy gave her a searching look. "You seem so . . . normal. After what happened yesterday . . . well . . . are you sure you're all right?"

"No. I think the trauma just hasn't set in yet. But for now I feel okay, and I'm going to enjoy the feeling as long as it lasts."

Actually, Brooke felt conspicuous, self-conscious, and, most important, frightened to the core. Bad dreams had torn through her bouts of uneasy sleep, and she had to force a smile and keep her hands steady. But she was determined not to look like a weakling. Ever since her mother died, Brooke had tried to prove to her worrisome and not-too-healthy grandmother that she was handling things well. She was strong. She was resilient. The act had become a habit, and she almost believed in it herself.

Stacy hugged Brooke, towering over her in her spike heels, smelling of some delicious perfume she always wore just a trace of on her neck. "You'll be fine. And I know this horrible man is going to be caught, isn't he, Jay?"

Jay Corrigan looked up from his doughnut. His smile disappeared and his blue eyes turned serious. With the sparkle gone from his eyes and without his smile, he looked closer to forty than thirty. He had a rough charm Brooke found appealing, but he was also hardy, somewhat brash and dominating. Brooke knew Stacy was perfect for him. No matter how aggressive she was, she would never intimidate this man. He loved her feistiness. A quiet, passive woman would have bored him to tears.

"We're doing everything in our power to catch Tavell," Jay told Brooke solemnly. "He's our number one priority. You should be happy to know that Detective Hal Myers has been assigned to the case. He's probably the best cop we have since Detective Lockhart retired."

"It was a *forced* retirement because of my age," Sam groused. "I had plenty of good years left in me. But thanks for the compliment, Jay. Hal is my best friend and former partner."

"I know." Jay smiled. "That's one of the reasons I was so happy to be assigned as his new partner last week."

"You're Hal's new partner?" Sam blasted. He slapped Jay on the back. "Well, good for you! You can learn a lot from him."

"I know, sir,"

"And drop that 'sir' business," Sam said, grinning. "You're Hal's partner, so I'm 'Sam' to you."

"Thank you, sir . . . Sam."

"Sir Sam. I like that," Sam laughed. "Think I'll make everyone start calling me that."

"I won't," Vincent teased, delivering mugs of coffee to the table. "Don't expect anything except 'Dad' from me."

" '*Sir* Dad' from now on," Sam answered, smiling. "Okay, Jay, since you're now one of the chosen ones, you should be privy to some information you're willing to share. Do the guys have any idea of what happened to Tavell after he left here last night?"

"Around dawn, about two blocks over, a neighbors' dog set up a howl when it went outside," Jay said. "Seems there was fresh blood on its doghouse, which the dog never sleeps in anymore. The lab has already determined that it's human blood. No doubt Tavell was injured and hid in the doghouse. That's why no one could find him last night. We have no idea how badly injured he was, of course, but nearby a guy said he heard a car with a loud muffler starting about four in the morning on the street in front of his house. He didn't get a good look at it—no license number, naturally—but it was green, small, kind of battered and at least fifteen years old. There are no reports of stolen cars, though."

Sam frowned. "That's odd."

Jay shrugged. "Maybe someone keeps it stored away and hasn't noticed it's missing."

"I'm sure Tavell didn't show up in an emergency room," Sam said.

"No. That could mean the injury was minor."

"Or maybe we're lucky and he's dead," Stacy added harshly.

Jay gave her a faint smile. "Can't disagree with you about that being a lucky break as far as I'm concerned, honey." He looked at Brooke. "He's probably *not* dead, though, so you need to be extremely careful. I'm sure I don't have to tell you that, but it doesn't hurt to remind people." He paused. "The world can be a dangerous place."

"Which is why there are brave men to protect us like Jay? And Detective Lockhart," Stacy added with a radiant smile at Sam, who smiled back with equal radiance. Brooke smothered her own smile. Stacy was a flirt, no matter what age the man. But Brooke knew her friend was absolutely loyal to her husband. Besides, Jay wasn't the jealous type, anyway.

So far, Vincent had been quiet. He'd also avoided looking at her. It's the robe, she thought. He's bothered by seeing me in his mother's robe, no matter what he said earlier. He's probably boiling inside.

But at last, he spoke. "More coffee, Stacy, Jay?" he asked, holding out a steaming and fragrant carafe.

Jay looked as if he was ready to say "yes" when Stacy answered for both of them. "No thanks. It's time for Jay and me to be off to work." Jay looked up, his hand freezing in midair as he reached for a second doughnut. "Jay gets to do all the exciting work, like you did," she told Sam. "I slave away at Chantal's downtown."

"The clothing store?" Sam popped up. "My wife Laura used to shop there sometimes."

"Really?" Stacy asked, acting fascinated. "Their clothes are very nice, but still overpriced in my opinion. And I just hate catering to some of the snobs who come in there. Not women like your wife, I'm sure. You know—the overbearing type who act like you're dirt under their feet." Stacy sighed. "I should have stayed in nursing school, but I hated being around sick people all the time. I tried college, too—English major with dreams of being a writer like your son—but I'm not the studious type. I dropped out after less than a year. What a mistake. Oh well." She smiled again and tapped Jay on the shoulder. "We've taken up enough of these people's time. Detective Lockhart, Vincent, thank you so much for taking care of Brooke last night."

"It was our pleasure," Sam said.

Stacy moved forward and hugged Brooke again. "And you take care of yourself, young lady."

"I intend to keep myself safe and sound," Brooke said, grinning.

But her grin faded quickly. Safe and sound, Brooke thought as she watched Jay help Stacy into their car like a gentleman. That's what her mother used to say to her. "I want to keep you safe and sound, my baby."

But Anne hadn't been able to keep *herself* safe and sound. She certainly couldn't help Brooke do the same.

# 2

Madeleine Townsend slowly pulled her white Lincoln into the lot of Townsend Realty, circled the lot twice, then chose the spot closest to the main door. Carefully she stepped from the car, lifted a cane from the backseat with a determined look, took a deep breath and limped toward the office.

Over the years, many people had said Madeleine was the most beautiful woman they'd ever seen, with her wealth of glossy mahogany-colored hair, large eyes like rich brown velvet, and almost perfectly symmetrical face with a small dimple in her chin. At thirty-seven, she could have passed for a vibrant twenty-seven, except for the limp that gave her an oddly swaggering walk. She thought after having lived with her twisted right leg since she was ten, she would have gotten over it, but she hadn't. Every time someone looked into her lovely face and smiled, Madeleine watched the smile fade as their gaze traveled down her slender body to her double adjustable elbow crutch and on down to the wrenched leg and foot noticeable even in the slacks or long skirts with boots she always wore. Each time it happened, pain touched her soul. She tried to keep the emotional hurt under control. She didn't always succeed.

Madeleine held her affected right leg behind her and let her strong left leg bear her weight as she ascended the three steps into the building. The day was bright but muggy, and as she entered the office she gratefully breathed in the air-conditioning. Aaron always kept the temperature a perfect seventy-two degrees. He allowed no one to tamper with the thermostat. She'd heard people grouse about what a dictator he was behind his back, but she'd never told him. She liked that Aaron had created his own private fiefdom in this office that had once belonged to their father, who in his tireless efforts to please everyone was generally thought of as pitifully spineless. Madeleine hated her father's weakness of spirit. That's why she'd always encouraged her brother to be as strong as possible, no matter how many people considered him an absolutist. He shouldn't *care* what other people thought, she told him. And he didn't, except for her. Madeleine knew her opinion mattered to Aaron more than that of anyone else in the world.

"Hello, Miss Townsend," a pretty, young girl said.

Madeleine thought quickly. What was her name? Hannah. Hannah's last name she didn't know and didn't care to know. "Hannah" was enough. "Good morning, Hannah," Madeleine said. After her accident, her parents had her home-schooled by a woman who acted with the formality of a governess in a nineteenth-century novel. Madeleine, because of overprotective parents and her own self-consciousness, had not interacted much with people her own age, and therefore modeled her speech and manners on those of her arrogant and formal mother and the equally haughty governess. She didn't sound like a woman of thirty-seven, and it was impossible for her to banter casually with people her own age. But Mother had told her to always try to say something flattering to people, and she tried never to forget Mother's lessons. After all, the elderly woman was still alive and monitoring almost every move Madeleine and Aaron made. "That's a lovely dress, Hannah."

Hannah smiled in delight. "Oh, thank you! I was afraid it was the wrong color for me, but I got it on sale."

It *was* the wrong color for her, Madeleine thought with her impeccable taste. The color made Hannah look sallow. And Madeleine immediately spotted a crooked seam in the right sleeve and shoddy rayon lining sewn in carelessly, throwing off the flow of the whole outfit. But Madeleine knew better than to openly criticize. People never appreciated it, no matter how helpful the comment. "Nonsense," Madeleine said firmly. "The color complements your . . . eyes." She smiled graciously. "Is my brother in?"

"Oh, sure. He's always here at the crack of dawn. He's not with a client, though. You can just go right in."

"Thank you, my dear." Madeleine sounded exactly like the grande dame her mother was and loved it, because it usually gave her a sense of superiority, which she felt compensated for the bad leg that made so many people pity her. She could not *stand* to be pitied or patronized or treated as if she were somehow lacking. The grande dame manner intimidated almost everyone, preventing their treating her with anything except respect or even awe.

She bestowed the imperious air on all members of Townsend Realty and it seemed to work on everyone, excluding Brooke Yeager. Brooke did not show her the proper respect, Madeleine thought as she stepped into Aaron's office. Brooke did not recognize Madeleine's superiority and acted as if they were equals. Also, Aaron always seemed to treat Brooke with maddening kindness and respect. Madeleine did not like Brooke. Actually, she couldn't stand Brooke. She was relieved the woman was not here today.

Madeleine stood for a moment, looking at her brother's dark head bent over a sheaf of papers. The hair was still thick, but strands of gray had begun to run through the dark brown. She had noticed it first on his temples about a year ago. Now the gray appeared throughout. "Good morning, Mr. Bright and Early," she said sweetly.

He looked up, his face haggard in the glaring morning light, his dark eyes slightly bloodshot. The facial skin didn't look as tight on the bones as it should at only forty years old, Madeleine thought with concern. He had lines from nose to mouth she'd never noticed before, and the tiny worry wrinkle between his eyebrows had become a definite furrow.

"Are you upset about that poor girl, Aaron?" she asked gently.

He looked at her incredulously. "Of course. Mia Walters was blown apart by a rifle last night. You haven't forgotten that she worked here, have you?"

Madeleine cringed slightly at his tone. "Of course I haven't forgotten, Aaron. Do you think I'm empty-headed?" Before he could answer, she held up a manicured hand. "What happened to Miss Walters was a terrible tragedy. We agreed I'd come in this morning to lend you moral support while you addressed the employees about Mia's death, so certainly I didn't forget, and I could hardly not care after talking to her mother for nearly an hour. The woman is crushed."

"I'm sorry for biting off your head, Maddy," Aaron said quickly, rising from his desk, slim and well toned even if his suit was not as crisp as usual. "I'm upset by this whole thing. Distraught, really. Mia was a sweet little thing and she died while on an assignment for me and . . ."

"And you're worried about how the manner of her death will affect this company," Madeleine finished for him.

"Affect the company? No! That's not why I care. I'm worried about . . . well . . ." He looked at her, his expression ashamed. "Oh, I never could lie to you, Maddy. I don't know why I even try. To be honest, I *am* worried about the firm. That's awful of me, I know."

"No, it's practical," Madeleine said with both comfort and confidence in her voice. "You're being realistic. I'm sure Mia was nice, but we barely knew her. How long had she been here—two months? I'd only met her once. Her death will be hard on her family, but they'll get over it in time. We'll see that they receive a substantial death benefit from us no matter what insurance arrangement Mia had made, which was probably none considering she was only a bit over twenty. Anyway, the newspapers will be full of this sordidness for a few days; then it will fade and people will forget it ever happened." She gave him an assuaging smile. "There's nothing to be so worried about, Aaron."

"You sound just like Mother," he said with a trace of resentment.

"And you sound all softhearted like Father. There is no room for the softhearted in business. After all, look what happened to him. He fell flat on his face with all of his empathy and sensitivity and generosity. If it hadn't been for Mother's money and strength, he would have ruined this family, ruined *our* lives. Don't ever forget that, Aaron. And that statement is not as selfish as it sounds. All the employees of Townsend Realty are counting on you. By being strong, no matter how hard it is sometimes or how insensitive it feels, you're doing them a favor by holding the business together and providing them with a future. You are standing tough for all of *them*!" She ended with a graceful hand flourish toward the staff outside of Aaron's office.

Madeleine beamed at him after this speech, and Aaron thought he felt a tad better. In fact, he felt a lot better. And stronger. More capable. No one could ever guess the courage his delicate, beautiful, injured little sister could give him now, and *had* given him most of his life.

"I suppose you're right." Worry and doubt still shone in his dark eyes. "I don't want to seem callous, though. I can't put off saying something to the staff about Mia. And Brooke."

"I agree. That's the smart thing to do in this situation, and the sooner the better. In fact, I've already gathered all the information on Mia's funeral from her family. Nothing is written in stone at this point because there will be a murder investigation"—Aaron winced—"but at least it won't seem like we're ignoring Mia. I don't know much about Brooke.

I was told she's not a patient at any of the hospitals, so I suppose she wasn't seriously injured."

"No, she wasn't. She called this morning and told me she was okay. I gave her the rest of the week off, of course. She said she wasn't staying at home, but she changed the subject when I asked where she *was* staying, because some of the people here want to call her. She said she didn't want to talk about the incident right now, even though she appreciated everyone's concern. She's very popular here."

"Not with everyone." Madeleine didn't need to mention the name Judith Lambert. The tall, once-attractive woman made no secret of her ongoing desire for Aaron, although he'd ended their relationship over a year earlier. In fact, she seemed almost obsessed with him and her appearance had suffered drastically since their breakup. She'd lost at least twenty pounds and looked ten years older than she had last year, not to mention that she'd cut her auburn hair and dyed it bright red and begun wearing flashy clothes. Madeleine thought she now looked like a hooker.

"Judith has a ludicrous notion that I broke off with her because I'm romantically interested in Brooke," Aaron said. "I don't know how she got such an idea, but she's made things uncomfortable in the office with her jibes at Brooke."

Madeleine raised her eyebrows. "Aaron, Brooke is good looking in that common, blond sort of way and you are always especially nice to her. Almost . . . respectful."

"I treat her like I do any employee who does good work. Charlie Burton, for instance, but you don't think I have a crush on him."

Madeleine laughed. "Well, he's fifty-five, weighs almost two hundred pounds, and has the most appalling comb-over I've ever seen! Really, Aaron, you *must* make him do something about his hair!" Aaron smiled and seemed to relax a bit. "But I'm not worried about Charlie. People like him. Judith, on the other hand, has *no* class, Aaron. Neither Mother nor I ever approved of you being involved with her, no matter how casually. And that was when she looked and acted with some decorum. Now she's a wreck, not to mention the fact that she bickers with Brooke in the office *in front of clients*. Robert told me. You really should let Judith go, Aaron."

"She's my top seller."

"No matter. She'll cause trouble in some way, and avoiding trouble is more important than the fact that she sells a bit more real estate than other people here do. Besides, I've always suspected that she's not above using sex to sell that real estate."

As if hearing her, Judith's head jerked up from her desk. She looked through the long glass panel in Aaron's office and fixed Madeleine with a blue laser gaze that would have made most people flinch. Madeleine merely smiled at her sweetly, then turned back to her brother.

"Maddy, I wouldn't keep Judith in my employ if I thought she used sex to sell houses," Aaron snapped. "Don't you think I have any principles?"

Madeleine took four steps closer to her brother, emphasizing her limp, and looked warmly into his eyes. "I think you are the most principled man I have ever met. It's just that you give these women so much leeway. After all, Judith is older than you and has been divorced twice—"

"She's only three years older than I am."

"She appears at least seven or eight, not to mention that she wears too much makeup and douses herself in that awful cologne and smokes cigarettes like there's no tomorrow when she's out with clients, which I know you forbid."

"How do you know she smokes when she's showing properties?"

"I've asked some of your clients. I was only trying to help, Aaron, and I will tell you that a lot of them don't like the smoking. Besides, you told me yourself last month that her sales are slipping." Madeleine paused. "And while we're on the subject of unsuitable employees, I have to bring up Brooke Yeager trailing clouds of scandal. Oh, don't give me that disapproving look. I know it's not her fault her stepfather murdered her mother, but some people do remember the murder and that awful trial, and *many* people will remember now that she's been involved in *another* murder. They won't know what to say to her."

"They don't have to say anything."

"Oh, but they'll be thinking about it and it will make them uncomfortable. They'll want to get away from her as soon as possible. And of course, they'll talk about it after they go home. The last thing any of us want—especially you—is unnecessary and unflattering attention drawn to Townsend Realty. I think you have no choice but to let Brooke go. I realize you can't fire her now. You'd look completely unfeeling and that certainly wouldn't be good for office morale or for business, if word got out. Maybe you could do it gracefully in about six months. Or she might decide to quit, just like Robert Eads did." Madeleine paused. "I've checked and he doesn't have another job."

"You checked?"

"Well, yes. I was puzzled. One day he was here doing excellent work and the two of you were friends—playing golf and racquetball together—and then he was gone."

"He just quit. Greener pastures and all that."

"Well, I guess there weren't any greener pastures like he thought there would be." Madeleine looked at her brother closely. "You're insulted that he quit. You don't want him back here, do you?"

Aaron's hand shook slightly and he said quickly, "No, I don't want him back here."

Aaron reached for something and swept papers onto the floor. He swore and stooped to pick them up. Madeleine looked at him, flustered and clumsy, and something changed behind her dark eyes. For a moment, the gentleness vanished, replaced by anger.

"Maddy, let's discuss all of this later," Aaron said edgily as he stood up, a sheen of perspiration on his upper lip. "I have this whole long damned day to get through and I didn't sleep. Let's just go out, face the masses, and get this speech about Mia over with as soon as possible."

Madeleine nodded, her eyelids lowered to hide her eyes'

unaccustomed sharpness. "You're absolutely right. I'm
sorry I've upset you. Mother always says I ask too many
questions—"

"Mother says lots of things, most of them untrue and all
of them unflattering."

"Well, you *are* in a mood!" Maddy gave him a smile.
"But I was being nerve-racking with my interrogation. Anyway, people *are* staring in at us, so we should go face them.
You say all the right solicitous things, then give me a little
nudge when you're ready for me to deliver a rundown on the
details I know about funeral arrangements." She smiled lov-
ingly. "All right?"

Aaron smiled back, relief easing the handsome, hawkish
lines of his smooth-skinned face with its aquiline nose and
high cheekbones. "Has anyone ever told you what a remarkable woman you are, Maddy?"

"Just you. Everyone else sees me for the quite ordinary
person I am. You're prejudiced."

"No, I'm not. There's not an ordinary bone in your body.
I don't know what I'd do without you."

Madeleine's beautiful smile seemed to glow. "You'll
never have to find out, Aaron. Never."

# six

## 1

The morning had gone in a whirl. After Stacy and Vincent left, Brooke quickly changed out of Laura's robe and into her jeans and blouse, even if her tight jeans seemed to bite and chafe at her sore body. Later, Sam had reminisced about his detective days while listening to the police scanner at what seemed full volume. Vincent sat in a corner trying to write and not being too successful, if the number of times Brooke saw him sigh and hit the DELETE key was any indication.

After noon, when Sam and Vincent had both picked at their lunches, Sam had retreated to his room for a nap. Vincent had told Brooke she looked tired and suggested the same for her. She'd promised she would, although after Vincent had checked all the door locks and made certain she pushed the dead bolt shut on the front door before he went for a run, "just to shake the cobwebs," she had sat down on one of the wing chairs in the living room and picked up an old photo album she'd seen Sam looking through earlier.

She felt a tad guilty, expecting to see a collection of family photographs that she hadn't been invited to view.

Instead, she stiffened as page after page of newspaper clippings about the murder of Anne Yeager Tavell seemed to jump out at her like an old, malevolent ghost that refused to leave her at peace.

Meanwhile, Vincent Lockhart jogged down Fitzgerald Lane. He'd invited Elise to go with him, but she'd merely cowered near Brooke. "She'll never go with you unless you take her on a date and show her you're a proper gentleman," Brooke had told him with mock seriousness.

Vincent had given her a tight smile and started on his run, trying to clear his head but obsessing over Brooke. He was no longer suspicious of her having anything to do with the shooting last night, but she was another complication he didn't need, not with his father in such bad shape. Still, Vincent felt grudgingly sorry for her and even a little responsible for her. After all, she'd almost been his sister.

Except she wasn't his sister. Not even close. He could never think of her that way, even last night, since he'd really looked into those depthless violet-blue eyes so full of intelligence and vulnerability and toughness mixed together, all he had done *was* think about her, which was ridiculous. It wasn't as if he were a novice with women. Just the opposite. His friends often teased him about his many affairs. "You're going to use up the supply," one of them had joked. "Just because you're the celebrity doesn't mean you can't leave some for the rest of us."

Another, more serious friend had told Vincent he was trying to prove something. "You think your father is disdainful of what you do for a living, so you believe you'll impress him with the number of women who are so dazzled by what you've made of yourself, you can seduce them without even trying." Vincent had told the guy to keep his pop psychology bullshit to himself but actually had given the words some somber thought. It *was* true that most of the women he dated didn't really mean much to him. And he didn't think he really meant much to them, either. They liked the fact that he was a best-selling author and an okay-looking guy. A "gorgeous" guy, they said, a compliment that Vincent took with a grain of salt.

But most of those women had at least been flashy. Guys looked twice at them in bars and restaurants. The women looked great and had looked great on his arm when the paparazzi took photos at premieres of movies based on Vincent's novels. Brooke wouldn't draw that kind of attention, although on close inspection she was naturally prettier than most of the highly groomed, salon-addicted women he dated in California. In fact, he'd hardly been able to take his eyes off her this morning when she wore that filmy blue robe. Her long hair had hung loose and wavy and her face had looked nearly flawless, almost luminous, even without makeup.

But Brooke seemed a little shy. Vincent didn't like shy. He didn't like serious. He liked fun. He wanted to be with a fun woman, a woman who was carefree and lighthearted, with a great sense of humor without being bawdy or loud, certainly a woman who didn't come with a lot of baggage, like a murdered mother and a killer stepfather. No, Brooke Yeager was definitely not for him.

Not for him? Vincent almost stumbled. His thought seemed to indicate he was even considering her as a romantic interest. She was a seemingly nice girl who needed help. That's *all*.

And yet . . .

# 2

Brooke stared at the first page of the album. Each page had been covered with a page protector, keeping the newspaper clippings underneath in excellent condition even though they were fifteen years old.

I should close the album cover right now, she thought

when she realized she was looking at a collection of newspaper material about her mother's murder. *I should just put the album back where I found it, turn on the television or listen to music or . . .*

Right hand shaking slightly, she turned a page, unable to stop herself from facing a recap of the horrible events of fifteen years ago. The first thing her gaze fell upon was a newspaper headline:

YOUNG MOTHER MURDERED IN HER HOME

Accompanying the story beneath the headline was a studio picture of a beautiful, smiling Anne taken only two months before her death by, of all people, Zachary Tavell. In the photo, Anne looked delicate and classic, a Grace Kelly lookalike. Only Brooke would have noticed that her mother's eyes didn't sparkle with true happiness the way they did in photos taken of her with Brooke's father, Karl.

Brooke turned the page. The next article nearly screamed that Anne Yeager Tavell had been shot three times two hours after neighbors had heard her arguing violently with her husband, Zachary Tavell. Tavell, the article claimed, had been found standing over his wife's body holding a chrome-plated .38-caliber Smith & Wesson revolver registered in his name.

Another article revealed that patrolmen had been the first to arrive on the scene, but within thirty minutes veteran homicide detective Samuel Lockhart had been called in and assigned the case. By this time, reporters and photographers had begun showing up. One photographer had managed to sneak past the police barricades, and the powerful lens of his camera had picked up an image of Anne's mutilated body.

Brooke cringed when she saw the old photo of her mother lying twisted on the floor, half of her face nothing but a pulpy mass lying on a cluster of blood-covered roses. The reporter who'd written the accompanying article had labeled this "The Rose Murder," and the name had stuck to the case. In the photo, near Anne had huddled a stunned eleven-year-old

girl everyone had forgotten in the surrounding uproar—
Brooke, rigid, with a stark white face and hands clutched to
her ears. She looked small in her flannel pajamas—much
smaller than an average eleven-year-old girl—and stunned,
almost glaze-eyed. Brooke looked closely at the photo and
tried to remember what she'd been thinking at the time, but
nothing came to her. Maybe shock had simply closed down
her mind just the way it had yesterday when Mia had been
shot and lay across Brooke's body, pouring blood onto her
hair and into her eyes.

Brooke shut her own eyes for a moment, forcing herself
to relax a bit, and turned the page.

This article stated that Zachary Tavell, who was supposed
to be in Columbus the night of the murder, claimed he had
come home because he was upset over the earlier argument
with his wife. According to Tavell, when he walked into the
house two men had already entered. One held Anne at gun-
point while another was apparently ready to burglarize the
home. Tavell said he'd grappled with the man holding the revolver, which had gone off three times during the struggle
before Tavell had been able to grab it away from the shooter.
The two men had run out the back door just as eleven-year-
old Brooke had come down the stairs to see Tavell standing
over her mother. At that point, Tavell said, a neighbor had
rushed in and, mistakenly believing Tavell had shot Anne,
lunged at him. Tavell swore that in a combination of panic
and desire to catch the man who had shot his wife, he'd run
for the back door. By this time, another neighbor had arrived, and the two men caught up with Tavell, jumped on
him, and brought him to the ground in the backyard.

Subsequent articles revealed that over the next two days,
six officers visited the crime scene, looking for further evidence. They discovered the lock on the front door had not
been jimmied. Either the door had been unlocked or someone had entered with a key. Also, rain the day earlier had left
the ground soft and police found no footprints in the backyard that did not match those of Tavell and the two men who
had wrestled him to the ground. Finally, only Tavell's prints

were found on the Smith & Wesson revolver and Tavell's right hand bore gunshot residue.

The last article Brooke forced herself to peruse stated that when Tavell was twenty-one he had been arrested for assault on a girlfriend. The girl had suffered a broken arm and slight ligature marks on her throat, but she had dropped the charges against Tavell, saying she might have mixed him up with another one of her boyfriends.

"Sure you did," Brooke said bitterly, closing the album. "You dropped the charges because you were afraid of Zach. He went free, so he could assault God knows how many other women who were afraid to press charges. And finally, because no one stopped him, he ended up murdering my mother."

Her hands shaking, her stomach in a knot, Brooke laid the album down beside the chair, wishing she hadn't looked at it yet somehow perversely glad she had refreshed her mind on all the details of that awful time. Her grandmother Greta had shielded her from most of the details of what had happened that night when Brooke's mind had gone blank after she saw her mother's mutilated face, the night she'd referred to herself only as "Cinnamon Girl" and really remembered only one person—Sam Lockhart, who had seemed capable and so protective. He had symbolized safety to her that night, and the symbolism had been so profound, her subconscious had driven her right back to him after Mia's murder.

Brooke took a deep breath, forcing the tightness from her chest, then stood up and reached for the ceiling. Every muscle in her body felt rigid. She closed her eyes, counted to ten, then decided to fix a cup of chamomile tea. She'd never had much faith in the claims made by herbal teas, such as weight loss for green and calming for chamomile, but she at least liked the taste.

As Brooke headed for the kitchen, the doorbell rang. She stopped, her gaze shooting to the closed, windowless door as if an army stood behind it. Sam was asleep. Vincent was out jogging, and although he'd locked all the doors before he left, he'd certainly taken a key with him. Of course, the Lockharts probably had neighbors, some of them friends.

The doorbell rang again. Brooke crept to the front window, parted the sheer draperies, and peeped out. A police surveillance car sat directly in front of the house. Behind was parked a van bearing the name Flowers for You. Someone had sent flowers?

Finally, a young deliveryman, certainly no more than a teenager, headed back to the van. Brooke opened the curtains a bit wider and caught the eye of one of the policemen. He nodded and smiled at her. He must have checked the delivery and seen nothing dangerous about it.

The van was pulling away from the curb when Brooke finally flipped the dead bolt, unlocked the door, and opened it. On the porch sat a glass bud vase holding a perfect white rosebud.

Her stomach clenching again, Brooke slowly bent and picked up the vase. Attached to the side with a delicate pink ribbon was a card bearing a message:

*Say hello to your mother for me.*

# seven

## 1

"You're here to protect her!" Vincent blustered at the patrolman. "How the hell could you let that flower be delivered to her?"

The young policeman, who didn't look over twenty-one, climbed out of the patrol car, his dark eyes contrite. "I'm sorry, sir. So sorry. I stopped the delivery guy, saw that all he had was a rose, and I read the message. 'Say hello to your mother for me.' That didn't sound threatening to me."

"Even though you know the murderer of Miss Yeager's mother is now trying to kill *her*?"

"All I knew was that my partner and I are trying to keep some nut from breaking into the house. I didn't know anything about roses and messages with hidden meanings." The young man's indignant expression almost immediately dissolved into one of devastation. "Look, man, I messed up. I admit it. But there's nothing I can do except apologize. That and ask if Miss Yeager is all right."

The young cop looked so remorseful that Vincent couldn't force himself to make the guy feel worse. "Yes, she's all right. Remarkably calm, actually, considering the circumstances."

And she was. Brooke had looked at the card, set down the vase without touching the message because the card was handwritten and there might be fingerprints, walked straight into the kitchen, and taken a can of beer out of the refrigerator. She was sitting on a chair taking long gulps when Vincent unlocked the door into the kitchen and walked in, dripping with perspiration from his run. He'd taken one look at her chalky face and asked in alarm, "What happened?"

"He sent me a rose," Brooke said calmly. Then she burped from the beer. "Zach sent me a rose and told me to say hello to my mother."

"Good God!" Vincent exploded. "Where's the rose?"

"In the living room on an end table. It's in a glass vase that was delivered by a floral company named Flowers for You. Don't touch the card. Fingerprints, you know." She burped again.

Vincent dashed into the living room, stared balefully at the vase, rushed into the kitchen, and flung open drawers until he found a box of plastic bags, then returned to the living room. In a moment, he stood in front of Brooke holding up a Ziploc bag with the card, bow and all, inside. "I only touched the top edge of the vase with a tissue," he announced. "We'll give this to the police."

"We'll give what to the police?"

Vincent and Brooke looked up to see Sam standing in the doorway, his thick gray hair askew, his eyes heavy-lidded after his nap.

"Tavell sent Brooke a rose," Vincent told him. "It arrived with a note reading, 'Say hello to your mother for me.' The note is in here." Vincent held up the plastic bag. "I didn't touch it. Did you, Brooke?"

"I picked up the vase from the porch where the delivery boy left it and I touched the card," she said, taking another gulp of beer. "Yes, indeed I did. So sorry, sir. I prob'ly screwed up all kinds of evidence."

Vincent frowned. "How many cans of beer have you had?"

"Three in about the last ten minutes," she slurred. "I think I'll have another."

"I think three is enough." She glared at him. "At least give that third one a chance to settle. You don't want to get a headache."

"My head is fine," Brooke announced, then hiccupped.

"Let me see that card," Sam said suddenly, as if he'd just snapped out of a stupor, his eyes alert, his voice strong. Vincent handed over the bag. Sam read the card through the plastic, then looked up, his expression ferocious. "How did Tavell manage to get this to Brooke when we have surveillance on the house?"

Vincent absently rubbed a paper towel over his black hair, now curly rather than wavy because it was wet. "I already talked to the guys outside, Dad. They're very young and inexperienced and knew practically nothing about the case. They checked the delivery and saw only a white rosebud with what to them seemed like a harmless message. I guess it's not fair to get angry with them."

"It's fair to get angry with their lieutenant for not filling them in on the particulars of the case," Sam announced loudly. "Does he think they're mind readers? Or does he just not rate the stalking of a young woman by an escaped murderer high on his list of priorities? In *my* day—"

"Things were a *lot* different," Vincent interrupted, his voice weary, his expressive eyes revealing even through Brooke's slightly beer-blur-induced gaze that he was trying to stem a mantra he'd heard a hundred times. "Should I give this bag to the guys outside?"

"No," Sam said firmly. "I'll call Hal Myers. They've assigned him to this case, thank God, because he knows what the hell he's doing. I'll ask him to pick it up and see that the evidence is logged in properly. I'll also tell him to have a talk with the lieutenant, set him straight about a few things!"

Sam strode toward the phone in the other room and Vincent muttered, "I'm sure the lieutenant would appreciate being reprimanded by one of his men."

"This Myers person won't actually do what your father tells him to, will he?" Brooke managed. "You know, piss him off so bad he won't do anything?"

In spite of the circumstances, Vincent had a hard time not smiling at Brooke's suddenly earthy language. "Will Myers be stupid enough to tell off the lieutenant? No. But he'll hear chapter and verse from Dad about what he *should* say and do. Hal Myers is a good guy, though. He's also an excellent cop. I'm glad he's on this case. He's one of Dad's oldest and best friends. He's incredibly patient with Dad. A lot more patient than I am, I'm afraid." Vincent sighed, then stooped down in front of her. He was still wet with perspiration, but the smell was merely strong, not in the least foul. His cheeks were reddened by the sun, but the slight lines around his beautiful eyes looked deeper as he frowned up at her. "Are you sure you're all right?"

"I am perfectly fine, as you can see."

"Yes, you've only slid halfway out of your chair. I shouldn't have left you here alone."

"I wasn't alone. Your father was here."

"Asleep."

"And two policemen."

"Who didn't know what they were doing."

Maybe it was a loosening of inhibitions by the three beers she'd drunk with record speed, but Brooke, who rarely touched people except to lightly shake hands with customers, reached out and stroked the side of Vincent's worried face, running her cool fingers from his flushed temple to his chin. "It was a *rose,* Vincent, not a *snake*. Nothing bit me. The rose didn't let out a puff of anthrax. I didn't touch a card dipped in poison. Let's see, what kind of insecticide is it that's so deadly upon touch? Par'fion."

"Par*athi*on, and that's good, because I'm the one who put the card in the plastic bag," Vincent said.

"And you got no signs of twitching, nausea, or ca'vulsions. In fact, you look like you're just blooming with healf."

"You know, I've never dreamed of women finding me handsome or sexy. I've always wanted them to think I look *blooming* with health."

Brooke smiled. "I meant it as a comp'ment. *I'm* all right, Vincent. The note just shook me up for a minute. I haf myself under control again."

"Thanks to your own strength and three cans of Budweiser beer." Vincent grinned. "You know, you're an awfully ladylike-looking young woman to let out such resounding burps. Were you on a burping team in college?"

Brooke's face went pink, but she laughed. "Oh, I forgot the burps."

"Good old carbon dioxide rushing out."

"I'm sorry," Brooke said, smiling shamefacedly. "They were pretty loud?"

"Well, yes, they were. I thought that second one was going to crack one of the windows."

Brooke bent over laughing. "Oh, lord, my grandmother and mother wanted me to act like a lady. If they ever heard me burp like that, much less knew I'd done it in front of a young man . . ." She shook her head.

"Oh, I don't think they'd be too horrified under the circumstances." He hesitated, then told her the truth. "Besides, you're usually such a lady, almost prim, I thought seeing you burping to beat the band was kind of cute."

"Oh yeah, just darling. I think I'll start burping around clients at the office. Aaron will fire me in a heartbeat." She stood up, weaving slightly but still smiling. "You're right. I don't need another beer." She headed for the bedroom. "But I do think I'll lie down for a little while."

"Okay. Some rest would probably do you good *and* make your head stop spinning, which I know it is by now. Meanwhile, I desperately need a shower. How about if I order in a giant greasy pizza for dinner?"

"Oh, lord, that sounds absolutely heavenly!" she yelled in a slightly slurred voice.

Vincent couldn't help but break into a grin. For the first

time, she didn't seem like a vulnerable little creature *or* a nuisance. She seemed like the strong kind of sassy chick with a sense of humor and a less-than-perfect demeanor Vincent had always liked.

Plus, she looked great. Brooke's back was turned to him, but she raised her hand in a little wave. Her jeans were cut low and tight on her firm body, she wore a metallic belt with a semitransparent gauzy blouse, her blond hair was slightly tousled and hung halfway down her back, reminding him of old pictures of Brigitte Bardot, and Brooke was barefoot, her toenails painted a bright, saucy red.

Maybe having her around wasn't so bad after all.


## 2

After the rose incident, the young surveillance team nearly frisked and shone bright lights in the eyes of the pizza delivery boy who arrived three hours later. Brooke caught a glimpse of them at the front door when Vincent paid him. The guy couldn't have been more than eighteen and looked terrified. I'll bet he never delivers pizza to this address again, she thought in amusement.

Brooke and Vincent dived into the pizza while Sam slowly ate his chicken hoagie. "Chicken," he said, giving the sandwich a baleful look. "Used to be I never had to give cholesterol a thought. Now mine stays high no matter what I eat."

"Just a little above normal," Vincent corrected. "It would go through the roof if you started eating all the wrong foods."

"But I'd feel satisfied at the end of a meal."

"And you'd end up in the hospital having spear-tipped tubes run through your arteries to unclog them." Brooke and Sam both winced at the exaggerated image. "Besides, Dad, you loved chicken until you were told you should eat it instead of beef." Vincent turned to Brooke. "Ready for another piece of pizza?"

"One more."

"How about a beer?" Vincent teased. "I got a whole twelve-pack for you."

She grinned. "That was terribly considerate, and I do usually drink at *least* twelve beers with my pizza, but tonight I think I'll stick with Coke."

Half an hour after they'd straightened the kitchen and Sam retired to the living room to watch his favorite television show, Vincent passed by the guest room and looked in to see Brooke packing her tote bag. "What's going on?"

"I'm going home."

"Going home!" Vincent's eyes widened. "Why?"

"Because I need to be in my own place. I'm a disturbance here."

"A disturbance? What gave you that idea?"

"Seeing how upset your father was after the flower arrived. He hasn't stopped talking about it and he barely touched his dinner."

"When he gets excited, he says the same thing over and over. It drives me nuts, but it doesn't mean he's upset. And he was just carping at dinner because he couldn't have pizza."

Brooke looked at Vincent reprovingly. "Those were what my mother used to politely call 'fibs.' Nice try, Vincent, but I have eyes. I can tell my presence and all the uproar surrounding me is making your father nervous. And you, too, for that matter."

"I'm *not* nervous!" Vincent burst out. Elise barked in fear of his loud voice and drew nearer to Brooke, who raised an eyebrow at Vincent.

No, you don't sound a bit nervous, he thought. You've been cool as a cucumber all day—unable to write, yelling at those policemen outside, treating that delivery boy as if he were dropping off a bomb instead of a pizza.

"Okay. I *am* a little hyper today. But after all that's happened, I think there would be something wrong with me if I *were* 'cool as a cucumber,' as you put it." Vincent stepped into the room. "Brooke, you aren't safe in your apartment."

"I'm not safe anywhere." Brooke folded her nightgown

and stuffed it into the tote bag. "Last night a message was left at my apartment, so I came here. And who should wake me up in the middle of the night looking in my window? Zach Tavell. Then he had a rose and another message delivered *here*."

Vincent would expect himself to put up an argument—he wouldn't want to see any young woman put in jeopardy. But he recognized that he was deeply upset at the thought of Brooke leaving—more upset than he would have believed possible even this morning. He should just cool it and let her do what she wanted, he told himself. After all, she was an adult. And who said he knew what was best for everyone? He was acting stupid and it was time to stop, to back off, to let her do what she damned well pleased. But he couldn't stem the words of protest streaming from his mouth.

"Brooke, in your apartment, you're alone. Here, you're with two men."

"One of whom is . . . not up to peak capacity; the other I've known for twenty-four hours. It's unfair and selfish for me to expect you to protect me." Brooke stopped packing, looked at Vincent, and sighed. "You don't know how much your concern means to me, especially since you hardly know me. And I'm not being polite—I'm being totally sincere. But you have your father to look after. Good heavens, he's why you came home in the first place. As for me, I'm a lot tougher than I look."

"You just think you are."

"Don't contradict," Brooke said firmly. "Look, Vincent, I lost my father when I was eight, my grandmother wasn't well even then, and my mother was emotionally immature—far too immature to be taking care of a child. God, on a whim she married a man she knew nothing about, a man with an assault record, a man who *killed* her when I was only eleven!"

Brooke hated the tears she felt rising in her eyes and quickly blinked them away. "Vincent, I am not a little girl, even though I seemed like one yesterday after Mia's murder. I am levelheaded, strong, and able to take care of myself in ways you probably can't even imagine." She looked

unflinchingly into his deep green eyes. "I am largely responsible for Zach Tavell getting a life sentence in prison. He's
going to pay me back for that. If I run, he'll just follow me.
So, instead, I'm going home, to go on with my life and let
him *try* to destroy me. And I do mean *try* because he can't
do it. Somewhere deep inside, I've always known this time
would come. And I've prepared for it. But I've prepared to
fight the battle *here,* in Charleston, on *my* turf." She paused.
"Vincent, I won't let Zach win again."

Vincent stood quietly for a long moment, staring at a female he'd thought of almost as a vulnerable girl until five
minutes ago. Now he realized she was a woman, and a forceful one at that. Still, he was certain she was getting carried
away with her strength. But she wasn't in the mood to take
orders, especially from a near stranger.

"Okay. I can see that arguing with you is useless. I just
hope you win this battle, Brooke," he finally said in a calm
voice, although inwardly he was more disturbed than he could
have imagined. "I hope more than anything that this time, you
win."

# 3

Elise seemed happy to enter the familiar apartment
and ran immediately to her doggie bed to squeeze one of her
squeaky fuzzy toys. Vincent was obviously not so happy. He
commented that the apartment door felt flimsy, the window
locks looked small and inadequate, and from the corner of
one he could see the fire escape, which was close enough for
a stalker to break in without breaking a sweat or pulling a
muscle.

"This is my home and I'm staying in it," Brooke told him
firmly, never flinching from his disapproving gaze.

"Do as you please. I'm not saying anything."

"You've just made several criticisms of the place and

you're looking at me like I'm a dope for coming back here."

"I'm not looking at you like you're a dope."

"Yes, you are."

He sighed gustily. "Have it your way."

"She should stay here if she wants to," Stacy said from the doorway. "Did you miss this place, Brooke?"

"I thought my coming back was best for several reasons."

"And Vincent doesn't agree."

Vincent gave Stacy a long, cold look. "My opinion wasn't solicited by Miss Yeager because, as she has told me in no uncertain terms, she does what she pleases." He glanced at both of them. "Good night, ladies. Enjoy your evening."

He slammed the door behind him. Stacy looked at Brooke and grinned. "Looks like you've made quite an impression on the world-famous writer."

"A bad impression."

"Oh no. A very good one or he wouldn't be so upset that you've deserted his presence." Stacy frowned. "That's what makes me worry about him. He just met you yesterday and already he's obviously attached to you. I'm afraid you've attracted another Robert."

Brooke dropped her tote bag on the couch and shook her head. "He's not at all like Robert, Stacy. I sensed something off about Robert's *romantic* interest in me from the beginning, which is part of why I could kick myself for continuing to date him. I should always listen to my instincts. But I don't sense anything from Vincent except concern."

"And attraction."

"I didn't notice any particular attraction to me on his part."

"Then you'd better sharpen up those instincts, kiddo." Stacy walked toward her, arms crossed over her substantial chest. "So why *did* you decide to come home tonight if it wasn't to get away from Vincent?"

"Because his father has Alzheimer's and my presence was disturbing the routine that helps keep him on course. Besides, Zach Tavell knew I was staying at the Lockhart house anyway. Last night he was at the window, and today he sent a rose and a message."

Stacy's arms dropped and her eyes widened. "What rose and what message?"

Brooke turned back to her tote bag and began unpacking. "Oh, a florist delivered a white rose today," she said casually. "Flowers for You was the name of the shop."

"The *message*, Brooke. What did the message say?"

" 'Say hello to your mother for me.' "

Stacy's jaw dropped. *"What?"*

"Zach wanted to freak me out."

"And did he?"

"I was a bit shaken at first," Brooke returned offhandedly, determined not to mention her craven flight to the refrigerator for a beer-gulping episode after reading the note. "But when you think about it, the message wasn't particularly clever."

"It *wasn't*?"

"No. It didn't show a whole lot of imagination."

"Well, either you're a good actress or you have a cooler head than I do," Stacy said. "I would have been a wreck if I'd gotten that note *with* a rose."

"Jay would have calmed you down."

"My husband is strong and smart, but he's not omnipotent." Stacy paused. "At least I really know him, though. Vincent Lockhart, however, is an unknown quantity. When you think of the kind of books he writes—"

"Which you love. And you're certainly too bright to think that if people write about murder, they want to commit it." Brooke stifled a yawn. "I'm tired although I've done exactly nothing today. I even had a nap."

"It's the strain. You need a good night's sleep in your own bed with Jay and me nearby. As a matter of fact, I hear Jay opening our door now, finally home from work." She patted Brooke on the cheek. "I'll get out of your hair. You do whatever it is you do to relax and I'll bet you're having sweet dreams in a couple of hours."

But at midnight, after Brooke had taken a long, soothing bath and a couple of aspirins for a headache that had thumped dully ever since the flower delivery, she lay wide-awake listening to sounds floating up from the street. Traffic was light for a warm, dry summer night. She heard a couple of teenagers yelling at each other on the sidewalk until a man opened a window and told them to shut up or he'd call the police. After the shouting stopped, Brooke rolled onto her side, tensed, waiting to hear her front doorknob turning or stealthy footsteps on the fire escape, or an evil little peck at her bedroom window. When the phone rang, she nearly screamed.

Brooke looked at the caller ID readout: *White Willows Nursing Home 555-7333*. She picked up the handset on the extra base by her bed. "Hello?"

"Miss Yeager?" Before Brooke could answer, the familiar voice of Mrs. Camp, a registered nurse at White Willows, rushed on. "It's your grandmother. She's just had a stroke. I happened to be passing the room, thank goodness. She's alive, but I don't know how severe the stroke was. We're rushing her to Charleston Area Medical Center as we always do when a patient suffers a serious incident. You need to get there *now*."

Brooke jumped out of bed, stripped off her nightgown, and slid into jeans and a T-shirt. She grabbed her purse and keys to her rented car, stepping into the hall, and dropped everything with a clatter. As she scrambled on the floor gathering the contents of her purse, running her hand around a shadowy corner where her keys seemed to be purposely eluding her, Stacy's door opened. Jay stood tall and formidable, wearing only pajama bottoms, his short, sandy hair sticking straight up. "What's going on, Brooke?" he asked sleepily.

"My grandmother has had a stroke. She's at Charleston Area Medical Center. I'm on my way."

Jay grew instantly alert. "Not by yourself. Come in here and wait. I'll throw on some clothes and be ready to take you in five minutes."

By now Stacy had appeared, half-dressed. "I heard what you said to Jay."

"My keys," Brooke said on the verge of tears. "I dropped them. I don't trust that flimsy door lock, and I can't shut the dead bolt from the outside without them."

"Go in our apartment and sit down for a minute," Stacy said firmly. "I'll find them and lock up. Then I'm going with the two of you."

"It's late and you both have to work tomorrow—"

Stacy stepped into the hall, took hold of Brooke's arms and pulled her to a standing position. "You are not going to go out by yourself and Jay and I can each make it through tomorrow without a full night's sleep. Now take a couple of deep breaths, stop thinking the worst, and wait for us to drive you to the hospital. That's what friends are for."

After what seemed to Brooke like an eternity, they traveled through the nearly empty streets of Charleston, wound through a tangle of hallways at the hospital, and finally arrived at Greta Yeager's room. Jay insisted on standing outside the hospital room while Stacy waited at the nurses' desk. A nurse had said she would get the doctor immediately, but according to Stacy, "You can't let up on these people for *one* minute or they'll leave you waiting here half the night. You go see your grandmother and I'll keep nagging until I get some action." And so she would, Brooke thought with amusement in spite of her anxiety. These nurses had no idea exactly how maddeningly relentless Stacy Corrigan could be.

Brooke entered her grandmother's room slowly, her heart pounding, her forehead damp with perspiration. Greta lay motionless on the narrow hospital bed. Brooke had expected to see her wired to a tangle of tubes and wires, but only a clear tube leading from a saline solution bag had been inserted into her arm. Her white hair was brushed back from her round face, that had always been healthily pink until the last stroke, three months ago, which had left it almost as white as her hair. Her breathing was shallow, and Brooke saw that tonight's stroke had drawn down the left side of her face.

She took her grandmother's cool hand. "Grossmutter," she said softly. "It's me. BAnI."

Her grandmother's right eye opened slightly and shifted toward Brooke. She squeezed Brooke's hand with her right hand. Apparently her right side had been unaffected by the stroke. "BAnI Brooke," she managed in a slurred voice.

"Yes. BAnI. Bunny Brooke. Are you in pain?"

Greta slurred out another word that apparently started with an *n*, which Brooke accepted with relief as "no." "I'm so sorry this happened," she said lamely.

Her grandmother muttered a few unintelligible words, then shut her mouth and her eye from the strain. Brooke squeezed her hand again as she felt tears pressing against her own eyes. She would not cry, she told herself. If Grossmutter opened her eye to see the tears, they would only alarm her. Holding back her grief and fear was hard, though. Greta had suffered several strokes over the past two years, and even to Brooke's untrained eye, this one appeared worse than the others had.

At last, Jay walked in and hovered above Brooke. "Stacy just told me the doctor would be here in a minute. She's raised so much hell he's afraid *not* to come as soon as possible." He gave Brooke a tiny, tentative smile. "You know how tough my girl can be."

"I'm so glad both of you came with me," Brooke said. "I don't think I could have handled this alone."

"Neither of us would have dreamed of letting you come alone, even if there weren't all this Zach Tavell business—"

Greta's right eye snapped open. The right side of her face—the mobile side—jerked and contorted. Her hand gripped Brooke's. "Z-Zhach," she muttered in agitation. "Zhack Ta . . . Ta . . ."

"Jay was talking about Zach Tavell, Grossmutter, but Zack isn't here," Brooke reassured Greta.

The right side of Greta's face twisted into a grimace. "No, not . . . h-here. Nurshing home."

"No," Brooke said. "Zach wasn't at the nursing home."

*"Was!"* Greta insisted, her right eye filled with terror, her grip strong. "Come to my r-room. Zhack. Never forget him. *Teufel!*" Brooke ran through her rusty German vocabulary. *Teufel*—the Devil. "S-shaid . . . s-aid he come for you, BAnI," Greta ground out. She gulped air and finally managed, "S-said he want *you!*"

# eight

## 1

Zachary Tavell had managed to break into White Willows Nursing Home to get to Greta, darling Greta who took care of me since I was eleven, and even before, Brooke thought. He'd done it to threaten me again, and look what he did to Grossmutter.

Brooke took a shaky step away from the bed. I am so frightened, she thought. I cannot allow myself to get so frightened. I might faint, whimper, or do something further to upset Grossmutter, who's barely holding on to life. I must lower my horrified eyes, force my hand in hers not to tremble, and keep my voice steady. "I think you had a dream, Grossmutter," Brooke said kindly.

That awful, fierce look blazed into Greta's right eye again. "N-no. No d-d-dream. Real." Saliva trickled down the right side of her chin and Brooke gently wiped it away. "Zhach real. *Real!*"

"Okay, okay," Brooke said robotically. "He was real. Is that what made you . . . sick?"

A tear ran across the creases on Greta's cheek. That was definitely a "yes."

"Well, you're not at the nursing home now," Brooke said soothingly. "You're in a different building with people all around. Even a policeman. The man standing beside me is Jay Corrigan. Do you remember him? My next-door neighbor, the detective? You can't get much safer than having a detective in the room by your bedside. You just close your eyes and rest. We won't leave you. Not for one minute."

Slowly Greta's grip on Brooke's hand relaxed. Brooke took two steps back from her grandmother and turned to Jay. "Zach caused her stroke," she said softly but urgently. "He was in the *nursing* home!"

Jay frowned. "Not necessarily. At White Willows do unfamiliar visitors have to sign in at a reception desk?"

"No. They lock the doors at eight in the evening. If anyone tries to enter or exit *any* one of the doors, an alarm goes off."

"Do they conduct a bed check at night?"

"Yes. Even if a patient is well, they look several times an evening, and always around eleven, when it's time to turn off the lights. A nurse just happened to be passing my grandmother's room around twelve thirty and saw her having the stroke."

Jay glanced at his watch. "It's ten minutes 'til one and your grandmother was rushed here immediately. If the doors were locked at eight, someone checked on her at eleven, and she was obviously fine. Do you think Zach managed to hide in the nursing home from before eight until after midnight when that nurse saw Greta having the stroke?"

"He must have. Jay, they have a large and vigilant staff at White Willows, but Zach is a clever man. For heaven's sake, he escaped from the penitentiary days ago and the police haven't been able to catch him, even though he's right here in Charleston. He came to Sam Lockhart's house, and they *still* lost him!" She paused, realizing her voice had risen with her agitation. She said in what she hoped was a calmer tone, "Jay, I'm certain my grandmother *did* see Zach!"

"I wouldn't be absolutely certain she saw anything," said a slight, balding man entering the room, Stacy hot on his heels. "I'm Dr. Morris and I assume you are Mrs. Yeager's granddaughter," he said, extending a hand to Brooke.

"Yes. Brooke Yeager. And this is Jay Corrigan. He's a homicide detective with the Charleston police. And the woman behind you is—"

"Stacy Corrigan. She informed me three times while I was at the nurses' station," the doctor said dryly.

"Well, you were needed in here and you were just standing around," Stacy returned tartly.

"I was not just standing around, Mrs. Corrigan," the doctor said edgily. "I was filling out charts and I do not move with the speed of light." He looked at Brooke. "I'd like to talk to you about what we know of your grandmother's condition at this point. Would you prefer to do so privately?"

"No. Stacy and Jay are good friends. There's nothing they can't hear."

The doctor looked disappointed. Brooke could tell he wanted to get away from Stacy, who obviously set his teeth on edge, but he nodded resolutely. "Let's go into the hallway. We don't want to disturb Mrs. Yeager."

He doesn't want to say anything that might agitate her in case she's only pretending to be asleep, Brooke thought, depressed. Maybe this doctor always looked solemn, but Brooke had a strong feeling he did not have good news to deliver.

The hallway seemed unusually cold to Brooke and she wrapped her arms around herself before the doctor began in his toneless, professional voice. "As I've already said, we haven't had time to run all the tests we need to on your grandmother, Miss Yeager, so I don't have a lot of information to give you at this point."

"I understand," Brooke said, feeling Stacy lightly place her own sweater over Brooke's trembling shoulders.

The doctor cleared his throat and looked at her expressionlessly. "The stroke appears to have taken place on the right side of her brain. Oddly enough, the part of the body that is affected by the stroke is the opposite side of the brain from which the stroke occurred. For instance, if the stroke happened on the left side of the brain, the right side of her body would be affected. In your grandmother's case, the opposite has happened. I'm sure you noticed that the left side of her face is drawn down, and she speaks through the right side of her mouth."

"She held my hand with her right hand, too," Brooke said.

"Exactly. So far, she hasn't experienced any seizures. That's good. However, she suffers from reduced mobility, reduced reflexes, and incontinence."

She's incontinent, Brooke thought inanely. How humiliating her immaculate grandmother would find this condition. "Is there any chance for a full recovery?" Brooke asked.

The doctor looked at her sympathetically. "Your grandmother wasn't in good health before this last stroke. Unless you believe in miracles, she will never be well again—not even as well-off as she was *before* the stroke."

"Is she in pain?" Stacy asked.

Dr. Morris frowned. "I don't think so. Of course, it's always hard to tell, but she appears to be sleeping. Her blood pressure is up, so we're raising her dosage of medicine to keep it from climbing farther. And we've noticed some bladder problems, which I think we can alter without too much trouble."

"Well, none of that seems too bad," Jay said, trying to sound hearty.

"No," the doctor answered neutrally as it passed through Brooke's mind that the three of them really had no idea how bad off Greta was. Doctor Morris was either telling the truth or merely trying to calm her.

"Doctor, have you heard of an escaped convict named Zachary Tavell hanging around this area?" Brooke asked.

The doctor paused. Then he nodded slowly. "Yes, I believe I have."

"He was in my grandmother's room at the nursing home tonight. I think that's what brought on this stroke."

Dr. Morris's face froze and he suddenly looked as if he

were dealing with a possible lunatic. He seemed to think that if he held perfectly still and adopted a wooden smile, he would be safe. "Really? What makes you think that, Ms. Yeager?" he asked tonelessly.

"Zach Tavell is my stepfather. He killed my mother. He broke out of prison two nights ago and he's come here to kill me. But Grossmutter, I mean Grandmother, said he'd been in her room."

"At White Willows?"

"Yes."

"I see." The doctor continued to look at her warily. "I don't believe that's possible, Ms. Yeager."

"Why not?"

"Well, the security, for one thing. White Willows has very good security. Besides, well . . ." The doctor looked at her helplessly. "If this escaped convict is after *you,* as you say, why would he risk getting caught by going to your *grand-mother's* room?"

He had a good point, Brooke thought. Still . . . "My grand-mother was adamant about his being in her room at White Willows."

The doctor looked at her steadily, and Brooke could see him marshaling a calming tone and composed manner. "Ms. Yeager, I'm sure your grandmother *did* sound convincing, but one of the symptoms of a stroke is altered thought process."

"But she sounded so *sure.*"

"I'm certain she did. But often a patient who's suffered a CVA, or cerebral vascular accident, as your grandmother has, also shows signs of impaired thinking ability. She can be utterly sure she saw this man, but I really think it's highly unlikely."

Yes, it did sound unlikely. Zach would have been taking a great risk to break into White Willows Nursing Home. And for what reason? To scare Greta? She'd never done anything to hurt him. She wasn't the reason he'd come to Charleston. Brooke was his prey.

"I suppose you're right," Brooke finally said, feeling

foolish because she'd pushed an issue whose answer seemed obvious. "What comes next?"

"More tests." Dr. Morris gave her a small, professional smile, only slightly less unnatural than the last one. "We'll know more by tomorrow afternoon. Right now, your grandmother appears to be getting some rest, and I recommend that you go home and do the same."

"I can't just leave her!" Brooke exclaimed.

The doctor said calmly, "I understand you feel as if you're deserting her, but you're not. You can do nothing medically for her, though. What you can do is preserve your own strength. She might need it tomorrow. Let's hope she doesn't, but just in case . . ."

Brooke knew he was merely giving her a rehearsed speech, one he'd probably delivered a hundred times, but that didn't make its contents false. Greta needed tests. Greta needed professional care. Brooke could do neither. Her continued presence at the hospital was just a drain on stamina she might need later, not to mention a burden on Stacy and Jay. "All right. I'll go home for now," she told the doctor. "Is there anything I need to do, first?"

"Stop at the admitting desk in Emergency and make sure they have all of your grandmother's insurance information, all paperwork pertaining to her case from the nursing home, and any phone numbers at which you can be reached, such as your friends', if they don't mind."

"Of course we don't mind," Stacy and Jay said simultaneously. Everyone let out tinny little false laughs and the doctor forced one last minuscule smile before heading quickly away to see another patient.

"Let's go to the desk," Stacy said immediately. "They should already have the paperwork, but you know how these places are. Monuments of inefficiency."

"Now Stacy," Jay said mildly. "You think no one can do anything right except you."

Stacy grinned at him. "You're right. Me and my ego! But I *am* efficient; you have to admit it."

"Most efficient person I ever knew," Jay said proudly. "Wish we had you working down at headquarters."

"Darling, you know how much my job at Chantal's means to me," Stacy teased with false sincerity. "I'd never dream of giving up selling overpriced clothes. It's *always* been my desire." She looked at Brooke, her smile fading. "We'd better get you home. You look tired enough to drop."

"I feel guilty leaving like this."

Stacy took her hand. "Sweetie, there's nothing you can do. Like the doctor said, you need to get some rest so you'll be strong for tomorrow."

In the backseat of the Corrigans' car, Brooke could hear Stacy and Jay talking softly as they drove back to the apartment building, but she didn't pay any attention to what they were saying. This is my fault, she thought dismally. What happened to Grossmutter is my fault. I didn't warn anyone at White Willows about Zach.

Jay glanced at her in the rearview mirror. "You're feeling guilty, Brooke."

"I didn't know you had ESP."

"I do. Stacy keeps trying to get me to leave the police force and open a carnival act." He gave Brooke the feeble grin his weak attempt at humor deserved. "You're mad at yourself for not telling the people at White Willows about Zach's escape, aren't you?"

"Yes. You *do* have ESP."

"No. I've just been at this job long enough to know how people's minds work. For some reason, all the good people want to take the blame for everything the bad people do. The bad people blame everyone else."

"I should have warned them, Jay."

"Why? Who in the hell would have thought Zach would go to White Willows? For that matter, who told him Greta was there?"

Brooke stiffened. He was right. Who would have told Zach? Certainly not her. She had no other close relatives, and even distant ones wouldn't have had any communication with

Zach. "Could he have a source on the outside?" she asked.

Jay nodded. "Lots of prisoners do. Some wackos even keep up a correspondence with these guys. It gives them a feeling of power. But like the doctor said, even if someone had let Zach know Greta was in White Willows, why would he have taken the chance of going there? Certainly not to find you around midnight. Remember what the doctor told you. People who have a stroke can suffer from . . ."

"Impaired thinking process," Stacy filled in for him, then turned in her seat and smiled reassuringly at Brooke. "She must have dreamed it, Brooke. Or gotten today's events jumbled up with events from a long time ago."

"Yes, I guess so," Brooke said without conviction.

When they reached the apartment building, Harry Dormer lingered in the lobby, another garish T-shirt stretched over his growing belly, a baseball cap on his badly cut salt-and-pepper hair. "You folks are out late tonight. Anything special going on?" he asked curiously.

"Brooke's grandmother had a stroke," Jay said.

"Is that right? Well, what a shame. Is she alive or did this one do her in?"

Stacy glared at him. "She's alive, thank goodness, and will you *please* work on your tact?"

"I don't have good tact?"

"You have *no* tact," Stacy snapped.

"Oh, *no* tact. Gosh, I feel awful," Harry drawled. "I might not have tact, but I got something else."

"A social disease?" Stacy asked as they headed for the elevator.

"Information."

The three of them stopped dead and looked at him. He looked back, smirking. Then Jay said sternly, "Okay. Out with it." Harry seemed to waver. "I mean it, Harry."

"All right. I was gonna tell you." He looked at Brooke. "Miss Yeager, your ex-boyfriend, that Eads guy, was here about an hour ago lookin' for you. My wife says he's handsome, but I don't see it myself. Too much of a pretty boy.

Anyway, he didn't look pretty tonight. He looked scared and tired and . . . well, sort of like a truck hit him. The guy wasn't in good shape at all."

"And that was an hour ago?" Jay asked.

"Give or take a few minutes."

"Did he say what he wanted?" Stacy demanded.

"Nope. He just went flyin' up to Brooke's apartment, pounded on her door, then went dashin' out the front door again. I said hello to him, but I don't think he ever even saw me." Harry shook his head. "Something had that guy worked up. *Real* worked up. Something to do with you, Brooke."

The elevator doors opened and Stacy nearly shoved her inside. As soon as the doors closed, Stacy put her arm around Brooke. "Don't pay any attention to Harry. Robert probably wasn't acting any different than usual. Harry simply likes to get attention."

"Maybe Robert knew something about Grandmother. . . ."

"How could he?" Jay asked. "I doubt if White Willows called your old boyfriend to tell him your grandmother had a stroke. You never even took Robert to see her, did you?"

"No."

"Then Harry's just being dramatic," Stacy said in disgust. "He's such a toad. I absolutely can't stand him. I don't think anyone in the building likes him."

"Except his wife," Brooke said.

Stacy waved away the idea of Eunice's love for her husband as if she were brushing away a gnat. "She's just too homely to get anyone else. And she depends on him. She can't hold on to a job, so he provides a paycheck. She's even too much of a coward to give herself her own insulin shots. Harry has to do that for her. I can't stand cowards."

"Third floor, ladies," Jay said as the elevator doors opened again.

"You go on home, honey," Stacy said to Jay. "I'm going to get Brooke settled for the night."

"Sure you don't need anything I can provide, Brooke?" Jay asked. Stacy raised an eyebrow at him and his face turned red. "Well, I didn't mean *that*! God, Stacy, you're acting as possessive as Harry's wife."

"Compare me to Eunice Dormer again and you'll be sleeping by yourself for a week," Stacy said, but her eyes twinkled at Jay.

When they walked into the apartment, Elise nearly hurled herself into Brooke's arms. The jolt sent Brooke back a couple of steps, but she laughed. "That kind of stuff was cute when you weighed five pounds, but you'll have to cut it out now that you're up to forty."

"Maybe you should send her to obedience school," Stacy suggested.

"For being glad to see me? I don't think so."

Stacy offered to fix Brooke tea or hot milk, both of which sounded revolting, then literally tucked her into bed. Brooke felt ridiculous, but she knew Stacy meant well. "Sleep well, although I think you'd sleep better without the dog in the bed with you."

"No, I wouldn't. Thanks for everything tonight, Stacy. And thank Jay, too. I couldn't have made it without you."

"Sure you could, but at times like these, friends can make things easier. See you in the morning."

After she'd gone, Brooke turned on the bedside light, her childhood fear of the dark returning. The apartment seemed twice as large as it really was and full of shadows. Elise lay down and pressed against her chest. Brooke wrapped her arms around the dog's warmth, thinking.

The doctor had said people who'd suffered strokes often experienced confused mental processes. In other words, Greta might have merely imagined that Zach was in her room at White Willows. But Brooke knew her grandmother better than anyone else did, and she'd seen the fierceness in the woman's clear blue eye.

Zachary Tavell had gotten into Greta's room tonight, Brooke thought. He'd gotten in and told her he was coming after Brooke.

# 2

Vincent Lockhart marched back out to the curb, looked up at Brooke's lit window, and climbed into his silver Mercedes roadster, the car his father never stopped calling inconvenient, overpriced, and pretentious. He took one last look at the window, then spun away from the curb.

Vincent wasn't sure if he was angry or worried, so he decided to be both. True, the Lockhart house hadn't proved to be the sanctuary for Brooke that he'd hoped, but she was safer there than in her apartment house. She didn't care that her murder would devastate his father. It would even bother him. But she wouldn't listen to reason. That's what made him mad. She hadn't even given him time to present half of his arguments against such a move. Actually, she hadn't given him time to *think* of all his arguments against the move.

He put in a CD, turned it up loud, and tried to put her out of his mind, but he couldn't. Brooke Yeager was obstinate, headstrong, and intractable. Vincent realized he'd used three words that meant the same thing. He'd try again. "Obstinate" was good—she wouldn't listen to reason. She was also foolhardy, leaving even though she knew better security could be provided for her at the Lockhart home than at the apartment house. Finally, she was naïve, thinking she could escape someone like Zach Tavell. What had her exact words been? "I've known this time would come. . . . I've prepared to fight it on *my* turf!" Something like that. God! Had she been watching too many shows like *Xena: Warrior Princess*? Was she spouting dialogue she'd heard on *Buffy the Vampire Slayer*? She sounded childish and ridiculous.

He took a deep breath and told himself to calm down. Why was he getting so worked up over this woman anyway? Was it because his parents had been so fond of her they'd thought of adopting her? Maybe *they'd* been fond of her, but he'd never even seen her except for the old photograph his mother had taken and a couple of grainy newspaper photos of the little girl involved in "The Rose Murder." Was his overconcern for her because she was so pretty? Hell, California was full of pretty girls. He'd certainly dated his share. Beautiful women. Sexy women. He'd come close to marrying twice. He was now glad neither of those engagements had ended in an actual ceremony, but the ex-fiancées had been glamorous, sophisticated women. Women who were savvy and worldly-wise, not ingenuous, inexperienced young ladies like Brooke Yeager, who obviously thought she was a superhero or something equally absurd.

That kind of thinking was going to get her killed, Vincent thought with conviction. And for some reason he couldn't fathom right now, he knew if that happened, he wouldn't be able to forgive himself for letting her go back to that apartment house.

Even if she *was* a reckless fool.

# nine

## 1

The alarm clock went off like an air-raid siren. Elise burst into a volley of startled barking and Brooke, hanging on the edge of the bed, rolled facedown on the floor.

"Good grief," she moaned, touching her nose to make sure it wasn't broken. Luckily, it wasn't, but she knew she'd hit hard enough to cause some darkening around her eyes. "People will think you beat me up in the night," she told Elise, who'd jumped down to lick her cheek. "I'm okay, baby," she told the dog, then looked up at the clock. Six A.M. Why was she up so early?

Greta. The memory of her grandmother's stroke washed over her. Grossmutter could have died between the time Brook left the hospital last night and now. She could have died, alone, while Brooke slept.

Shaken by the thought, she headed for the phone. A call to the nurses' station on Greta's floor assured her that her grandmother was alive, but the nurse refused to give details about the woman's condition. "That's up to the doctor," she said crisply. "He makes rounds between nine and eleven in the mornings. You'll have to come in and wait for him."

Brooke hung up the phone and groaned. All she knew was that her grandmother was alive, not whether she was better or worse. The hospital staff acted like the woman's condition was a state secret, to be kept even from her own granddaughter. But Brooke knew getting frustrated over stupid rules was useless. She would simply go to the hospital and be waiting for the doctor when he drifted in between nine and eleven. If he didn't show up until late afternoon, she would still be waiting.

Brooke passed down the long hospital corridor to her grandmother's room. She was glad she'd thrown on a light sweater. Even though it was in the midseventies outside, the hospital thermostat seemed to be set on sixty degrees. Over the years, Greta had spent a lot of time in hospitals, so Brooke had known what to expect.

Behind her walked one of the policemen charged with her surveillance. Brooke wished he would walk *with* her, but he insisted on marching along at least two steps behind, constantly looking left and right, like a Secret Service man guarding the president. He made Brooke feel conspicuous and silly.

Greta lay still as a corpse in her sun-washed room. Oddly enough, Brooke would have been reassured by seeing tubes and monitors attached to her grandmother. Brooke knew the sight would have given her the feeling the equipment was helping sustain Greta's life. But the woman had experienced a stroke, not a heart attack. She didn't need the impressive paraphernalia. Brooke had learned this when her grandmother had suffered her last two strokes over a period of fifteen months.

Brooke leaned over the bed and kissed her grandmother's cool forehead. Greta's skin looked and felt like white clay. Brooke's heart seemed to jump when Greta's blue eye snapped open. The woman blinked rapidly three times before she apparently recognized Brooke. "Hello, Grossmutter," Brooke said, forcing a smile at the frail woman on the bed. "I've been up for ages, but I had to wait for visiting hours before I could come and see you."

"Eyes," Greta said in a dry, raw voice. "You . . . eyes."

"Eyes? *My* eyes?" Brooke remembered her tumble out of the bed. "I fell out of bed this morning like I always did when I was a kid. No one hurt me. My eyes are just darkened by the fall. I meant to put on concealer, but I forgot. The shadows will fade by tomorrow. Thank goodness I didn't break my nose like I did when I was thirteen!"

"B-blue eyes. Like mother."

"Yes, my eyes are the same color as Mom's. Daddy's were darker." A tear ran down Greta's cheek. Brooke pulled a tissue from her pocket. " 'Thistle-colored eyes.' That's what color Daddy always said Mom's eyes were," she said as she dabbed the tear away from Greta's dry skin. She pulled her chair closer to Greta's bed, then removed a small bottle of lotion from her purse and began gently applying it around Greta's cheeks and forehead. "Mom always said her eyes were Dutch iris. She thought that sounded prettier."

"Remember," Greta said almost clearly.

Brooke finished with the lotion, put some lip balm on her grandmother's wrinkled lips. "Do you need another blanket?" she asked, taking Greta's hand.

Greta shook her head and squeezed Brooke's hand. "Z-zhack. Find him?"

"Not yet, but they will soon. He was wounded the other night. He's likely to get treatment. Every hospital, clinic, and private practice in the area has been alerted about him. He can't stay on the loose much longer."

The right side of Greta's mouth quirked. Brooke hoped it was her attempt at a smile. She continued to hold her grandmother's hand and chattered about everyday things for half an hour. Then she couldn't resist asking, "Grossmutter, are you *sure* you saw Zach in your room at White Willows? I don't mean to doubt you, but the police seem to think it was impossible for him to have been there. I wondered if maybe after you've had more time to think about it, you realized you'd seen an orderly or a janitor or—"

Before she could finish, Greta squeezed her hand with tremendous force, given her condition. She wrenched the right side of her face into a grimace. "N-*no*! Zhack!"

Brooke squeezed her grandmother's hand in return. "You're *sure*."

"Y-yes." Greta's right eyebrow drew toward the middle of her forehead. "M-ole."

"Mole?"

"M-mole. His mo-mouf."

"A mole near his mouth?" Brooke looked away from Greta at the window. Suddenly, Zach's face flashed in front of her. Zach Tavell had a small mole beside his mouth. Through the years, Brooke had completely forgotten it.

She leaned over her grandmother. "The man who came into your room had a mole?" Greta blinked rapidly. She might remember a mole even if I didn't, Brooke thought. But is that all she remembered? Brooke pointed her finger at the upper left side of her own mouth. "It was *here*."

Greta grimaced again. "N-no." Slowly, she raised her right arm and, after several jerking attempts, put her finger on the lower right side of her mouth—exactly where Zach's mole had been.

The doctor seemed convinced Greta hadn't seen Zach Tavell. He'd spoken of her altered thought processes, but for someone with impaired thinking processes, Brooke thought grimly, Greta certainly had an amazing memory.

An hour later, Brooke entered the beautifully maintained grounds of White Willows Nursing Home. As she drove over the curved driveway leading up to the main building, she looked around at the perfectly kept beds of pansies, petunias, marigolds, and impatiens.

In the middle of the grounds spread a large pond full of ducks, many of them the common white ducks, quite a few the vividly colored wood ducks and the male mallards with their beautiful emerald heads. And everywhere were white willows, for which the nursing home had been named. The few people Brooke had brought to the nursing home to visit

Greta, such as Stacy and Jay, had commented on the beauty of the willows in summer. They'd been surprised when Brooke told them that salicin used in aspirin was derived from the bark of the willow. Stacy had actually laughed about the wit of the founder who'd named the nursing home after the tree that supplied ingredients for one of the most common drugs used in the place.

After Brooke left the hospital, she'd decided to stop by the nursing home to speak to Mrs. Camp, the nurse who always seemed to pay the most attention to Greta and the one who might know more about the possible entrance of Zach Tavell into Greta's room than anyone else. After all, it was Mrs. Camp who had been on duty and called Brooke when Greta had the stroke.

Brooke entered the double doors and stood for a moment in the sunny foyer. To her right spread a large room filled with furniture covered in vinyl that looked remarkably like leather sitting on thick blue carpet. A bay window allowed sun to spill over well-tended plants, a white brick-faced fireplace, and a rack filled with recent magazines from *Vogue* to *Field & Stream*. A number of elderly people sat around talking with friends and family. In the corner, two men who looked to be in their late eighties hunched close to a television, squabbling about whether to watch the news or a game show with a sexy hostess.

Two administrative offices with doors closed sat on Brooke's left, and straight ahead stretched the long admittance desk. She approached it to see four people talking while they worked on forms and answered phones. A young brown-eyed woman looked up at her.

"Hi," she said, beaming. "May I help you?"

"You're new," Brooke blurted, suddenly suspicious of any employees who were unfamiliar.

The young woman looked slightly taken aback but said smoothly, "Yes. I'm Miss Johnson. Rhonda. I just started yesterday."

"Oh. Well, I was looking for—"

She broke off when Mrs. Camp walked up behind Rhonda,

looking concerned. "Hello, Miss Yeager. Were you looking for me?" Brooke nodded. "How is your grandmother?"

"Holding her own so far. May I speak with you privately, or are you too busy?"

Mrs. Camp smiled. "Lucky for you, I'm on my lunch break. Let's go to the cafeteria for some of their elegant cuisine."

Fifteen minutes later, Brooke sat in the incredibly loud cafeteria with a piece of overcooked fish, peas as hard as BB pellets, and a cup of tapioca in front of her. "They give the good food to the patients and save the dregs for the staff," Mrs. Camp said, the wrinkles around her hazel eyes deepening as she laughed. During the four years Greta had been in the nursing home, Brooke had never seen a drop of makeup on Mrs. Camp's middle-aged face or a sign that she'd done anything except wash her curly salt-and-pepper hair. Her hands looked dry and reddened, as if they'd been scrubbed a dozen times a day for years.

The first thing Mrs. Camp wanted to know was everything the doctor had said about Greta's condition. Brooke repeated it all as accurately as possible. "Her left side is paralyzed," she added. "Do you think there's a chance the paralysis could improve?"

She couldn't help noting how absorbed Mrs. Camp became in chasing one of her peas to the edge of the plate. "There's always a chance," the nurse said. "After spending over twenty years in this field, I've learned there are few absolutes in medicine."

Brooke waited for the woman to meet her gaze. After ten seconds, she said, "Mrs. Camp, I'm not a great believer in miracles. I have a feeling you aren't, either, no matter what you say to the families of the sick people. All I'm asking for is *your* opinion, not a pronouncement carved in stone."

Mrs. Camp dallied with her tapioca, then finally looked at her. "I think Greta is reaching the end, Brooke. You should prepare yourself, not over the next year, and not over the next few months."

"Over the next few weeks."

"Yes." Mrs. Camp hesitated. "Or sooner."

"Days."

The woman nodded, then added, "But I could be wrong. I don't have all the answers. I can't predict—"

"She's going to die within days." Brooke's voice was dull with hopelessness. "You really didn't have to tell me. I felt it. I *knew* it—" She placed her hand over her heart. "I knew it here."

Mrs. Camp seemed to retreat behind her hazel eyes as if she was searching for something comforting to say.

"Don't feel bad," Brooke uttered. "I didn't come here for reassurance about my grandmother's health that you can't possibly give. I came to question you about what caused her stroke. Or rather, *who* caused it."

Mrs. Camp's expression morphed from guarded to shocked. "*Who* caused it? You think someone at White Willows did something to throw your grandmother into a stroke?"

"Not someone from White Willows." Brooke ran the tip of her tongue over her suddenly dry lips. "You know my family history. You know about my mother's murder, my testimony at my stepfather's trial, his life sentence—"

Mrs. Camp reached across the table and patted Brooke on the arm. It was then Brooke realized her voice had begun to tremble.

"I know all about it, dear. You don't need to go into details."

"Do you know that my stepfather, Zachary Tavell, has escaped from Mount Olive Correctional Center and come to Charleston?"

"I knew he broke out and came to Charleston—it's been on the news, although I made certain Greta never saw any of the newscasts and that no one mentioned Tavell's escape to her—but I didn't think he'd *stay* here. There must be a massive police hunt for him. It seems he'd want to get as far away from Charleston as possible."

"There is a police search, but they don't think Zach has left Charleston. He was wounded when he tried to get to me at a friend's house night before last, but he still escaped and he hasn't shown up for medical treatment. Apparently he's not only elusive; he has a strong physical constitution," Brooke said sourly. "Yesterday, he used a Charleston florist to send me a flower. A white rose. He gave my mother white roses. She died with her blood spilled all over a dozen of them. That's why the case became known as 'The Rose Murder.' "

Mrs. Camp's hand fluttered to her throat. "My God, Brooke! How awful! I know about the blood on the roses when your mother died. Greta talked about it sometimes. But I had no idea Tavell had sent a rose to *you*. That's despicable!"

"He's a despicable human being. He hasn't stopped with the murder of my mother or the torture of me. *He* caused my grandmother's stroke. Literally. Mrs. Camp, he was here, in Grossmutter's room."

Mrs. Camp's mouth opened slightly; then she vigorously shook her head. "No. That's not possible."

"I think it *is* possible. I just wanted you to help me find out how he managed it. After all, you're closer to my grandmother now than even I am. You see her every day. You take special care of her."

Mrs. Camp colored slightly. "I try to treat all the patients equally, but I have to admit I've always had a soft spot for Greta. I probably spend more time with her than I do with other patients. But that doesn't mean I know how anyone could have gotten in here and scared her into a stroke. My goodness, Brooke, the doors automatically lock at eight. Afterward, no one can get in or out of here without setting off an alarm. I saw your grandmother having the stroke around midnight. That means Tavell would have needed to get in here before eight o'clock and spend the whole night until the doors were unlocked the next morning."

"Which isn't impossible."

Mrs. Camp hesitated. "No, I guess it isn't."

"What I want to know is if you saw anyone or anything unusual that night, before or after my grandmother's stroke. An orderly who didn't look familiar? An ambulance attendant? Even a doctor?"

Mrs. Camp looked down at the table and frowned in thought. Finally she sighed and shook her head. "Nothing.

I can't remember anything that seemed wrong. I'm sorry I can't be of any help, but I just don't remember anything odd about last night."

"That's all right," Brooke said, unable to mask the disappointment in her voice. "It's not your fault."

"Brooke, I know I shouldn't interfere, but don't you think you should leave Charleston until this man is caught?"

"Yes, I should leave, but I can't. Or rather, I *won't*. My grandmother means more to me than anyone in the world and I don't believe she'll survive this stroke." She smiled thinly. "It's another one of those things I feel in my heart. I won't leave her to die alone, Mrs. Camp. I would never forgive myself."

"Brooke?"

She looked up to see Vincent Lockhart standing over her. His black hair glistened under the harsh fluorescent lights and his intense forest green eyes seemed to see only her. He wore dark slacks, a pale green shirt, and a perfect golden tan. Brooke thought he looked jaw-droppingly handsome, and the gaze Mrs. Camp fastened on his face told Brooke the nurse thought the same thing.

"What a surprise," Brooke finally got out, dumbfounded by his presence.

Vincent held up a steaming Styrofoam cup. "I was just taking a tour, asking a few questions, and I felt like I needed a jolt of caffeine."

"The coffee in the place will give you more than a jolt," Mrs. Camp said. "Sometimes I think it's pure caffeine with a little brown water mixed in."

Vincent looked at the nurse and smiled. She smiled back. Brooke watched them intently for a moment, then jerked back to reality. "Oh, I'm sorry. I didn't introduce you." Brooke could feel her face getting pink and she sounded rattled. "Eileen Camp, this is Vincent Lockhart." The two barely had time to exchange a greeting before Brooke rushed on. "Mrs. Camp has been a nurse for over twenty years and came to White Willows three years ago, just about the same time as my grandmother. Mrs. Camp, Vincent is from California. He's an author."

Mrs. Camp raised her straight eyebrows. "An author? How exciting! I'd like to be able to say I've read your books, but I stick to category romances and you don't look like a romance writer to me."

Vincent smiled. "No. I write true crime. It's not everyone's cup of tea."

"Maybe not, but it's quite impressive. I read the little romances because they don't take a lot of concentration." She abruptly rose from her seat. "Well, time for me to get back to work. I enjoyed the company, Brooke, if not the food. So nice to meet you, Mr. Lockhart. Wait until I tell my family I talked to a real author today!" She nearly tripped trying to escape and leave the two good-looking young people alone. "Bye, everyone!" she called, rushing out the door still holding her tray, which was supposed to be deposited on a conveyor belt that took it back to the kitchen.

"May I sit down?" Vincent asked Brooke, smiling slightly at Mrs. Camp's flight from the cafeteria. Brooke wondered if the woman would slink back in with her tray or hold on to it until she and Vincent had left the room. She looked at Vincent and nodded.

He sat down and glanced at her fish. "That looks delicious."

"I'm sure it would have been last week when it flopped up on the riverbank and died of old age." She put down her fork and picked up the cup of lukewarm coffee. "What brings you to White Willows?"

"I'm not following you."

"The thought never crossed my mind."

"Sure it did." Brooke colored. It *had* crossed her mind as soon as she'd seen him. "I'm here because of Dad," Vincent said.

"He's all right, isn't he?"

"Actually, he's sharp as a tack this morning, which makes me feel guilty for being here. But he's only sharp half the time. The rest . . ." He shrugged. "He can't live by himself much longer, and he'd never tolerate having a caregiver, some *stranger* messing around in Mom's house. So, I'm checking out places for him. I put White Willows first on my list because you said your grandmother was here and you seemed satisfied with her care."

"I have been."

"I guess you're here visiting her today."

Brooke paused. She'd already pulled this near stranger more deeply into her life than she had anyone for years except Stacy and Jay, but she heard herself opening up to him almost before she realized what she was saying. She told him all about Greta's stroke and the woman's claim that Zach had come into her room last night, telling her he intended to "get" Brooke. "She says that's what caused her stroke," Brooke said. "All the medical professionals seem to believe she was dreaming or the stroke jumbled her thoughts, but I believe her," she ended firmly.

Brooke focused on Vincent's eyes, waiting to see the first glimmer of doubt, the first desperate struggle for something insincere yet comforting to say. Instead, she saw in them only surprise and deep thought. Finally he said, "They already explained the security system to me on my tour. Now how did Tavell hang around in here unseen all night until the doors were unlocked and the alarm turned off?"

"You're not going to tell me Grossmutter dreamed it or her thoughts are jumbled?"

"No. You know her intimately and something she said convinced you that she's not mixed-up. That's enough for me."

Brooke felt a wave of relief and gratitude wash over her. She'd expected him to put up an argument, to tell her Greta had just imagined something and frightened her when she was already agitated. Instead, he had simply taken her word without explanation. He believed in her, and for some reason, she felt almost exultant. She was being silly, she told herself. Silly from nerves and anxiety. Maybe he was just one of those people who never rationalized bizarre explanations.

"What's wrong?" he asked. "You look like you're disappointed that I believe you."

"I just didn't expect you to. I don't think anyone else does."

"I'm not just anyone else." Vincent reached toward his

pocket for a pack of cigarettes, forgetting he'd decided to quit three weeks ago. Thanks to nicotine patches, he hadn't really wanted one until right now. He remembered he wasn't allowed to smoke in the nursing home, and he picked up his cup of execrable coffee to keep his hands busy rather than longing to hold a long, menthol cigarette.

"Brooke, you know I write books about true crimes," he began. "When I first started interviewing murderers, one of the things that shocked me was their desire to keep the game going, for a better phrase. Not all of them, of course, but quite a few. Many aren't satisfied with having taken a life. They want to keep their adrenaline flowing by torturing the families of their victims. It gives them a rush."

"That's a hell of a way to get excitement," Brooke said sadly.

"I agree, but these aren't normal people. They're sociopaths and psychopaths. Take Tavell, for instance. He could kill you without the frills—the rose, the notes. But just killing you wouldn't give him the gratification that mentally torturing you does. He's probably decided that if you hadn't appeared from upstairs the night he killed your mother, you wouldn't have distracted him, slowed him down, and he wouldn't have gotten caught. And he certainly hasn't forgiven you for your testimony in court. So, in his mind, it's your fault he's been suffering in prison all these years. Now it's your turn to suffer, and for him, suffering means torturing your grandmother, whom he knows you love so much, as well as torturing you." He paused. "I'm sorry. I didn't mean to deliver a lecture. It must be all the caffeine in this coffee."

"Then keep drinking it, because you just made perfect sense."

Vincent grinned. "I *do* make perfect sense sometimes, but not very often. According to my father, rarely."

"Your father is proud of you. He just doesn't know how to show it."

"You're sure about that?" Vincent asked lightly but with an undertone of doubt.

"Yes. I can see it in his eyes when he looks at you."

Vincent raised his eyebrows. "Are you trying to bolster my confidence, Miss Yeager?"

"No, I'm just observant. Besides, I don't think your confidence really needs bolstering. Deep down, you know your father is proud of you."

"Deep down, I'm not sure of that at all." He gave her a slightly lopsided smile. "But let's get back to the important subject—Zach Tavell. I don't know why everyone you talk to seems to think it was impossible that he came in before the doors were locked, hid in a storage room for a few hours, came out to terrorize Greta, then returned to his hiding place or found a new one." Vincent drained his coffee, looked at Brooke with an expression of a comrade. "So, we proceed with the assumption that Tavell *was* here."

We, Brooke thought. Vincent had said "we proceed," which meant unlike everyone else, he believed her. Suddenly, she didn't feel so alone. Suddenly, she didn't feel quite as frightened as she had just an hour earlier.

# ten

## 1

Eunice Dormer leaned back in her recliner, propping her swollen house-slippered feet on the battered ottoman, and listened to the supposedly heart-stirring music that introduced her favorite soap opera. She'd been a fan of the show for almost twenty years, but the last few months, her interest had begun to flag. Over half of the characters seemed to be under eighteen, and the show's vixen was not only in the midst of ending her eighth marriage but also, even worse, showing her age everywhere except her forehead, lately frozen by Botox.

As the first scene opened, a fifteen-year-old couple sat on Astroturf edging an impossibly clear pond while they whined about their parents not understanding their undying love. Eunice sighed in annoyance and reached for one of her clove cigarettes. She smoked them partly because she craved their pungent, sweet taste and smell but also because she thought smoking them gave her an air of the exotic. Let other women puff away on their ordinary Vantages or Virginia Slims.

Long ago, Eunice's beautiful mother with her many boyfriends and sexy clothes had smoked clove cigarettes. She'd gotten Eunice started on them when she was ten. Liz, as she insisted on being called instead of Mom, had thought a ten-year-old girl smoking clove cigarettes and sipping single-malt scotch was hilarious. Her boyfriends had, too, before they shooed away Eunice so they could have some private time in the bedroom with Liz.

Liz had died long ago, but Eunice's addiction to cigarettes and scotch lived on, although Harry had allowed her to continue buying clove cigarettes only if she compensated by drinking a cheaper scotch. A much cheaper scotch. Harry had been a disappointment to Eunice, but being uneducated, plain bordering on homely with her equine features, a diabetic, and an alcoholic, she'd had to take what she could get. Twenty years ago, Harry had been the only man even vaguely interested in marrying her, and that was because she was pregnant with his child. The child had lived only until age three, when it died of leukemia, but the marriage had drudged on for another seventeen mind-numbing years. They had nothing in common, but Eunice was an excellent cook and Harry was good at giving her the insulin injections she couldn't bear to give herself. Also, both knew that other partners weren't lining up for either of them.

After her child's death, Eunice had slipped into a deep depression that lasted for several years. Some men would have left her, but Harry rode it out, although she knew he'd turned to other women to "help him through the bad time." So, she'd stayed with him, even though their marriage made her feel as if her own life had turned to gray, with no excitement, no closeness, no passion. Just tolerance. At first, Eunice had tried to add a bit of excitement to her life by taking an interest in the tenants of the apartment buildings at which Harry was superintendent. Her interest was casual for a while, but over the years living vicariously through the tenants had become more intense, and during the last two years it had become an obsession for Eunice.

In fact, that obsession was tightening its grip on her.

Right now it was becoming intolerable. Eunice knew she was too nervous to sit quietly in her apartment one more minute. But she didn't want to take a walk. The day was hot and humid. Even if it had been cooler, though, she wouldn't have been tempted. People on the street weren't interesting or diverting in the way she knew she needed to be diverted now. People in public knew they were on view, being observed. Only people who thought they had total privacy enthralled Eunice. Poking into people's lives preoccupied her and, luckily, she had the perfect means to accomplish her goal—Harry's set of master keys to the apartments. The set of keys represented the gateway to a dozen worlds full of people with captivating surprises and intriguing secrets.

Harry had caught her in an apartment one afternoon last winter and given her hell, telling her that if the couple came home and found her, he'd lose his job, like she didn't already realize that possibility and hadn't been careful to choose the apartment of a couple who'd gone to Pennsylvania to visit family for Christmas. She'd solemnly promised never to do such a stupid thing again. She'd laid low for a while, which had been pure misery, but Harry hadn't remained vigilant for long. Since February, when he'd dropped his guard, she'd invaded apartments at least a dozen times, but she'd been more careful to do so only when she'd been certain Harry would be out of the building for at least a couple of hours. Fortunately, Harry wasn't any more heedful about always taking his keys with him than he had been about keeping his eye on her.

Eunice stamped out her cigarette in the ashtray beside her recliner, got up, and moved in slow motion to the pantry, where Harry's master keys hung on the Peg-Board. She hoped if she walked sluggishly enough, she could talk herself out of her desire for "exploration" by the time she reached the pantry, but her halfhearted try at self-control failed. Five minutes later she climbed the stairs to the third floor, clutching the key ring, forcing herself to maintain her usual leisurely gait, trying not to let her eyes dart around furtively. By the time she reached her goal, her heart pounded and her mouth had gone dry. But she'd made it to the apartment she'd always wanted to invade but never dared to enter—Stacy Corrigan's.

Eunice had taken an instant dislike of Stacy the first time she saw her striding across the lobby with her tall, lithe body, big breasts, long curly hair, and air of ultimate confidence. Stacy wasn't beautiful like Eunice's mother, Liz, had been, but she had that same aura of self-pride and tremendous self-confidence. When Eunice had told Harry she thought Stacy was a bitch, he'd snapped at her that she was jumping to conclusions when she'd never even talked to the younger woman. Besides, didn't Stacy always smile and say hello to Eunice when they ran into each other in the lobby and hadn't she even asked how Eunice was feeling a couple of times, instead of ignoring Eunice like old Mrs. Kelso? And after all, Stacy was Brooke Yeager's best friend, and Eunice liked Brooke. So why would Brooke be friends with a woman who was a jerk?

Harry had almost convinced Eunice she was wrong about Stacy until suddenly Eunice realized Harry's defense of her had been a bit impassioned. And he stared at Stacy even more than he did at other pretty women in the building, like Brooke. Also, he'd been gone on mysterious fix-it jobs around the building more than usual lately. Eunice was certain Harry was having an affair, and she'd begun to think it was with Stacy. Maybe Stacy hadn't actually given in and slept with him, but she was probably taking advantage of his interest. The more Eunice mulled it over in her mind, the more she became convinced this was a definite possibility. She just had to know for sure.

Eunice didn't think Brooke had gone back to work, but she'd passed her in the lobby this morning and Brooke had said hello, asked about Eunice's health, because she never forgot about Eunice's diabetes, then said, "I'll be back this afternoon. If any flower deliveries come for me, please see that they're left in the lobby." Flower deliveries? Harry had told her how upset Brooke had been about a note being in her apartment a few nights ago, but she didn't know anything about a flower.

Brooke must have given Robert Eads a key to her place and he'd left the note, Eunice decided. Robert was great looking and polite, but Eunice had always gotten an odd feeling from him the few times she'd run into him with Brooke. Eunice had told Harry that Robert didn't look at Brooke the way a man should look at a pretty woman. Harry had asked if she thought she was a psychic like those crazy people on television who claimed to know all about you by just hearing your voice on the phone.

One of the bulbs had burned out in an overhead light, making the hall dimmer than usual. Harry would have to replace it this evening, but right now Eunice was glad for the added concealment of shadows. She slipped the key in the apartment door lock. It turned easily; she opened the door about a foot, then slipped in and silently shut the door behind her. She took a deep, relieved breath and looked around.

As Eunice expected, the apartment was immaculate. Moss green and chocolate brown furniture sat on the tan carpet, and the few lamps and knickknacks were arranged with precision on end tables. Eunice far preferred the splashy colors of Brooke's apartment and the air of casual comfort with a few magazines tossed around, a couple of houseplants, some CDs and DVDs piled beside the entertainment center. Brooke's apartment was full of life, Eunice thought. Stacy's had a stillness, an air of waiting, that made Eunice jumpy. She wondered how the exuberant Jay felt in here. Stiff and uncomfortable in his own home, probably, but he'd put up with anything for Stacy. Eunice could tell he was wildly in love with her.

Eunice crept across the living room to the bedroom. Here she found the same tan carpet, a double bed covered with a moss green spread and pale green decorative pillows, a gleaming maple dresser and chest of drawers, and matching bedside tables. Both tables had lamps, but only one bore a book. Eunice hurried over and picked it up. It was a hardcover called *Black Moon*.

She flipped over the book again. *Black Moon* by Vincent Lockhart. Vincent, she thought. That was a nice name.

Lockhart. Eunice Lockhart. "Mrs. Eunice Lockhart," she said aloud like an adolescent girl trying out the name of a boy on whom she had a crush.

With a jolt, she thought of fingerprints. She'd left her fingerprints all over the book and Jay was a policeman! Then she relaxed. Certainly Jay didn't check the room for fingerprints regularly. Of course, even if he did, he wouldn't do it himself. He'd call in a crime scene investigation unit. Eunice knew about these things. She'd learned from watching television. And a CSI unit wouldn't search the room unless there had been a crime here, and there hadn't been. She let the trapped air of fright out of her lungs but quickly laid down the book, pulled up the bottom up her dress, and wiped it over both sides of the novel's jacket, just to be safe.

Eunice turned away from the bedside table, her gaze falling on Stacy's jewelry box—a large, square maple piece holding about ten drawers with gold handles. The box was obviously a nice piece, which had probably cost nearly a hundred dollars. Eunice thought of her old, skinned pink box—not even half the size of Stacy's—and felt furious. Of course, she didn't have much to put in her box. Harry wasn't one to give jewelry for presents. At least to her. Maybe Stacy was a different matter.

I swear, if he said I couldn't have a new microwave oven because he spent money on jewelry for that silicone-enhanced floozy, I'll kill him, Eunice thought in a rage. She marched over to the jewelry box and jerked a drawer so hard it flew out of the box and the contents fell on the floor. Eunice crawled to pick up each piece and place it neatly in the drawer just like she thought it had been originally. As she did, she looked at everything and saw that it was all delicate and sophisticated. The very few times Harry had given Eunice jewelry, it was large and gaudy, which he thought was beautiful. No, Harry definitely hadn't picked any of this tasteful stuff, Eunice thought, half-glad, half-disappointed. So far she had no evidence of an affair between Stacy and Harry.

Eunice moved on to the double closets. Jay's held three suits of fairly good quality, two pairs of khaki pants, four pairs of jeans, dress shirts and T-shirts, and four pair of shoes, the running shoes looking in desperate need of replacement, as did his jogging suit. Stacy's closet was more interesting. For one thing, not one piece of clothing was out of place. The sweaters all hung together, the blouses together, the dresses together, the slacks together, the jeans together. And clearly Stacy had a penchant for shoes. Eunice counted twenty-one pairs, all placed in a large shoe organizer.

Eunice knew Jay couldn't afford so many fine clothes, but Stacy got a discount at Chantal's, where she worked. It must be wonderful to be around such finery all the time, Eunice thought. She stroked a soft cashmere sweater, then couldn't resist taking it out of the closet and holding it against her flat chest. She'd never had a cashmere sweater in her life and it felt like heaven, even if she didn't have to glance in the mirror to know it wouldn't look as good on her as it did on Stacy. Eunice had a sudden urge to steal it, which she quickly quelled. Somehow, Stacy would know who'd taken her sweater and all hell would break loose. Harry might even leave Eunice, and then what would she do? She hadn't even finished high school. She could try working at a fast-food restaurant, but her legs always swelled and gave out after two hours of standing. No, she *had* to hang on to Harry. He wasn't much, but she wouldn't let Stacy or anyone else take him away from her.

A framed eight-by-ten color photo sat on the dresser. Jay and Stacy posed against a background of heavily wooded mountains. He was sitting on a large rock, wearing a pale blue shirt under a red sweater. His sandy hair was mussed and his cheeks ruddy. Behind him stood Stacy, her curly hair long and wild, her arms crossed over Jay's chest. They both beamed, looking like the happiest couple in the world. Of course, people could fake smiles, Eunice reasoned, but their smiles seemed real.

She sighed. She would have been frantic if she'd found any sign that Harry was involved with Stacy. At the same time, she couldn't stifle her disappointment that she'd been wrong. Of course, just because Harry hadn't dared to pursue his infatuation with Stacy in this apartment—the apartment of a woman whose husband was a police detective—didn't mean there was nothing going on between them. But Eunice couldn't imagine Harry springing for a motel room or Stacy meeting him at one for a passionate afternoon tryst. Actually, now that Eunice had satisfied her curiosity about Stacy's apartment and seen the photo of her with Jay, she felt silly for even thinking that young, shapely, pristine Stacy would have anything to do with overweight, sloppy Harry.

Eunice glanced at her cheap watch and saw that she'd spent more time in the apartment than she'd intended. Harry would be back in half an hour, maybe sooner. If he caught her up here . . .

Eunice hurried across the living room and had her hand on the doorknob when she heard a footstep in the hall. Oh God, she thought, her eyes darting around the room. Where could she hide? The pantry in the kitchen? The closet in the bedroom? She nearly fainted when someone banged on a door. Then, slowly, she realized the banging was on Brooke's door, not Stacy's. After a moment, someone pounded again, this time even harder. "Brooke, I know you're in there!" Robert Eads, Eunice thought. He was just a notch below shouting.

If I was in there, I sure wouldn't open the door, Eunice mused. But she wasn't in there, thank goodness, and neither was Brooke. It wasn't usual for Eunice to feel protective of anyone besides herself, but Brooke had taken time to inquire about the seriousness of Eunice's diabetes, to offer to do anything she could to help, and to inquire after her health at least once a week. That made Brooke okay in Eunice's mind. Even Harry didn't show that much concern, although he was good about giving her insulin injections, even if he grouched about it sometimes.

Robert pounded on the door again and then let out a full-fledged yell: "Brooke! Dammit, open the door!"

Eunice cringed. Robert was a big man—at least six foot two—and muscular. Could he actually beat down the door? He wouldn't find Brooke, but God only knew what damage he might do to her apartment. And that sweet little dog was probably in there. Eunice liked Elise, who was gentle and always licked her hand. Plus, the longer Robert stood out in the hall, the longer Eunice stayed trapped in Stacy's apartment, and Harry would be coming home soon.

The phone on an end table rang and Eunice literally jumped at least two inches off the floor. Apparently Robert heard the ringing, too, because he stopped shouting and pounding. Another ring. A third ring. Then the answering machine flipped on. Stacy's slightly husky voice cooed, "Hello there. This is five-five-five one-two-two-two. We're not in right now, but if you'll leave your name and number, we'll get back to you just as soon as we can. Have a simply *fabulous* day."

Robert remained silent, although Eunice knew he must have realized he wasn't listening to Brooke's machine. "Lila?" a man's voice asked. "Lila, you know who this is." Lila? Oh great, Eunice moaned inwardly, a wrong number. A violent wave of frustration washed over her. Now she'd be trapped in here even *longer* because of a stupid wrong number. "What you're doing is wrong." The male voice took on a plaintive note. "You're doing it out of pain." Eunice frowned. Was the man crying? "Lila, I do love you. I didn't realize how much because I was a fool. But I've learned things, had time to think. . . ." He trailed off pathetically and Eunice thought with relief he was going to hang up. Then he said in an incredibly strong voice, "But my love for you doesn't mean I'm just going to leave you alone like you want." The line went dead.

Robert was still quiet outside. Eunice knew the voice had been loud and he'd been just as riveted by the words as she. No wonder, Eunice thought. The guy on the phone sounded as frantic as Robert. He was obviously another spurned lover, just like the man beating on Brooke's door. God, why hadn't she ever met any of these crazy-in-love guys? Because I don't look like Brooke or Stacy, she thought, or probably the unknown Lila, either. And probably neither one of them appreciated what it was like to be desired. They took it for granted, not knowing what it was like to be plain and unwanted like

Eunice was. The thought made her mad, but only a little. Over the years, the hurt of being what she was had dulled for her. Still, Eunice wondered if Lila, whoever she was, would be moved by the words of the man who loved her. I'll never know, Eunice reflected, because I have no idea who Lila is, and Lila will never get that message, anyway.

Eunice hoped after the phone call Robert would leave and she could escape. Instead, she heard more footsteps coming up the hall toward Brooke's apartment. "Damn!" Eunice whispered. She didn't want Brooke coming face-to-face with Robert. On the other hand, Brooke might let Robert inside and then Eunice could make her getaway.

Her hope of imminent freedom died when she heard another man's voice. "Robert, what are you doing?"

He sounded older than Robert Eads, Eunice noted. Older and angry.

"What's it look like?" Robert snapped. "I'm trying to talk to Brooke, but she won't open her door."

"Did you happen to notice her rental car isn't in her parking space? Or were you so hell-bent on seeing her that you didn't notice anything else?"

"She could have parked the car somewhere else. She didn't come to work today, did she?"

"No, but I gave her the week off. I told you that."

*I* gave her the week off? Eunice frowned. The man talking to Robert must be Aaron Townsend, who owned Townsend Realty, where Brooke worked.

"I *have* to talk to her," Robert said, pain edging his voice.

"You already tried that. She doesn't have anything else to say to you. I'm telling you, Robert, leave her alone. Quit harassing her before there's trouble."

Mr. Townsend sounded really hot, Eunice noticed. He wasn't giving advice. He was making a threat. What was the deal? Was Aaron Townsend in love with Brooke?

"*Before* there's trouble?" Robert repeated. "There's already been trouble. She saw us. Then you got that call and that letter about you and me. They were from Brooke. She's heartbroken. I know it. But if I could just *reason* with her, then maybe . . ."

"Then maybe what? She'll suddenly understand how you deceived her? Women aren't made that way, Robert. If you keep up this behavior, you'll just make her more furious." Mr. Townsend's voice had softened. He was cajoling Robert, trying to work him into a better mood. "Come on, Bobby. Let's go get a nice lunch. I promise you'll feel better after a glass or two of wine. Forget Brooke Yeager. She's not worth all this uproar, darling."

*Darling?* Eunice almost repeated the word aloud. Had Aaron Townsend just called Robert *darling*?

"Okay." Abruptly Robert sounded like a little boy.

"Excellent!" Footsteps sounded as the two men retreated down the hall. "We must go somewhere with a good wine list!"

As she heard them headed for the elevator, Eunice could have gotten down on her knees and thanked God if she'd had time. She waited two minutes, counting out the seconds, opened Stacy's door a crack, and saw that the hall was empty, then flew out of the apartment, making sure the door locked behind her.

By the time she reached the lobby, Stacy Corrigan walked in. Sweat popped out on Eunice's forehead and her heart felt like it was going to explode through her ribs. Stacy glanced at her, then strode in her direction. Eunice thought she was going to faint until Stacy asked nicely, "Are you all right, Eunice?" Eunice was so surprised at Stacy's tone, she just stared. "You're white as a ghost and you're sweating. Did you eat lunch?"

"I . . . I don't know. No. I guess I forgot."

"You could pass out if you let your blood sugar level drop too much."

"Yeah, I know." Eunice wished she could get her breath. "I'll go eat something right now."

"Do you need help back to your room?"

"No!" Eunice nearly shouted. "I'll be fine."

Eunice almost shrieked when Harry walked in the front door. Two close calls in less than five minutes had nearly unhinged her. She fled to her apartment, feeling as if guilt and terror followed her like two little loud, laughing demons.

# 2

Robert had drunk too much wine at lunch. After he'd parted company with Aaron and headed home, he'd had another glass just because it seemed to relax him even more. He'd dozed for a while until the phone awakened him. The caller was his father. His father the minister. Oh God, Robert thought. Why today of all days was Dad calling?

"Hello, Robert," Reverend Eads said in the strong, mellifluous voice that rang out over his congregation each Sunday morning. "I haven't seen you for almost a month. I was beginning to worry."

"I called you a couple of weeks ago."

"Hearing your voice over the phone isn't the same as seeing you, Bobby."

"I'm sorry I haven't been to church, but—"

"You're busy. I know. And I've accepted that during this time in your life, religion isn't one of your priorities." There was no rebuke, no sarcasm, in Rev. Eads's voice. Only kindness. "I wondered if I could talk you into coming to Sunday dinner. Your mother is planning a special meal."

"Would it be just the three of us?"

"Well, I might invite another parishioner. Or two. No more." One of the parishioners will be a young female Dad hopes I'll fall in love with and marry, Robert thought. They'd been through this dance a hundred times. "I'm not sure, Dad. I have some work I was going to catch up on. . . ."

"You can't spare us just a couple of hours? It would mean so much to your mother and me, Bobby."

Robert had always thought if there were really angels

who walked the earth, they would be like his father. The man was never demanding, manipulative, or selfish. Even now there was no note of pleading or whining in his voice, and Robert knew if he declined his father's invitation, the man would not be resentful or angry—just disappointed. And disappointing his father was something "Bobby" Eads could not bear. "I'll be there, Dad. What time?"

"Wonderful! One o'clock, in case some parishioners linger to talk."

"Do you want me to bring anything? Maybe a cake or . . . a bottle of tequila?"

"Tequila only if it has a worm in the bottom. I've always thought a dead worm lying in a drink looked so delectable." Rev. Eads laughed. "No, Bobby, you don't have to bring a thing except your charming self." He paused. "Oh, by the way, Brooke dropped by this week."

*Brooke!* Robert felt as if a car had landed on his chest. Stabbing pain. Then numbness. He could only get enough air in his lungs to gasp out a breathy, "Oh?"

"Yes. She came by to bring back those books I loaned her the last time you two came to dinner."

"Books?" Robert croaked.

"Yes. The biography of George Herbert and the one on Chinese porcelain. The book about porcelain is so big, I guess it would have cost her a fortune to mail it. Of course, when I loaned the books to her, I'd hoped she'd return them the next time you two came to dinner." Robert went blank and his father asked quietly, "Bobby, why didn't you tell me you two had broken up?"

"I . . . I don't know." Robert could feel the pulse pounding like a jackhammer in his abdomen. "I guess I didn't think you'd be that interested."

"You didn't think I'd be interested? My word, Son, I was quite impressed with Brooke. I'd hoped . . . well, you know what I'd hoped. You've always been elusive where girls are concerned, but—"

"Elusive!" Robert burst out. "What the hell does that mean?"

"Robert, your language! My goodness, I only meant you've never seemed to have a serious girlfriend."

"But I have. *Lots* of them!"

"Well, I guess you've been keeping them a secret, then."

"Secret? I don't have any secrets!"

"Son, what's gotten into you?" Reverend Eads asked, his voice sounding genuinely concerned as well as baffled. "Are you feeling all right?"

"I'm fine. I'm perfectly fine!"

"You're sure? You sound overwrought. Is it grief over your breakup with Brooke?"

Grief? Terror was more like it. And she'd gone to his parents' house? Spoken to his *father*? Had she implied something about their breakup?

Robert closed his eyes and forced himself to say casually, "Did Brooke say why we'd broken up?"

"She said something rather evasive and seemed a tad embarrassed. I thought that must be because *you* had broken off the relationship. But it was kind of her to make sure I got back the books."

"Yeah, kind."

"She only stayed for a few minutes. Didn't even come in the house. She said our house was on her way to another house she was showing. It was clear she hadn't come here to talk to me about you, if that's what you're worrying about. I'm quite sure Brooke isn't the type who would enlist me and your mother to help her win you back."

"No, she wouldn't," Robert said weakly.

"So you just show up for dinner and after you've had a fine meal, we'll have a good, long talk. If you're upset over Brooke, perhaps I can help."

"Oh, I doubt it."

"We'll see. In any case, I'm looking forward to Sunday dinner. I've missed seeing my son's handsome face."

"Yeah, well, bye, Dad."

Robert hung up slowly, depression pressing down on him until he felt as if he were going to hit the floor. He'd been in his early twenties when he'd finally admitted to himself that he was homosexual, but he'd vowed that his father would never know, not because he would turn his back on Robert, but because Reverend Eads would find homosexuality wrong, deeply wrong, and he'd be crushed. He also would be desolate that his only child would never produce the traditional family. The reverend would pray for compassion and acceptance, but he would be ashamed, especially knowing how many of his parishioners felt about the subject. Robert would shame his father, the man he'd looked up to, almost idolized, all his life, and that Robert could not bear.

He thought back to just a few weeks ago, when life had seemed smooth and good, at least as good as his life could be considering the amount of guilt that had taken root and bloomed within him for the past ten years. He'd been working at Townsend Realty, where he'd met Aaron and their affair had begun shortly afterward. Worried that others in the office might catch a stray, revealing glance between them or an irresistible caress of hands, Robert had decided he must start seeing a female. He also wanted to make sure everyone knew he was *involved* with this woman, which to him meant not just talking about a woman he was dating but actually having people see him with her, particularly the people at work. After all, hadn't Aaron done the same thing with Judith Lambert until their heated breakup last year? It was a good plan, sans breakup.

Aaron didn't often make mistakes, but picking Judith as his "beard" had been a blunder. Robert intended to be a bit savvier and choose a woman neither so possessive nor as unrefined as Judith. He had known Brooke Yeager since before her mother was killed, and Brooke's family had attended his father's church. Robert had always liked Brooke, even when she was just a kid, and she'd grown into a fine woman—the kind of woman his father would be thrilled Robert was seeing. She was young, attractive, and classy. He'd even recommended Townsend Agency to her when she was looking for a job. She'd seemed the perfect choice for a "girlfriend." They'd dated for three months and gotten along well, even if their relationship had remained on the passionless side. Brooke didn't seem to mind.

And then she'd returned to the office late one night to pick up some papers she'd forgotten and found Robert and Aaron half-naked on the leather couch in Aaron's office. Everyone had simply frozen, eyes wide, mouths open, stunned into complete silence and immobility. Finally, Brooke had said in a tinny voice, "Sorry. I didn't know anyone was here," and vanished out the office door. Robert had tried to call her later that evening, but she hadn't answered.

She appeared at work the next morning, looking as calm and put-together as usual. She'd made no sign that there was trouble between them, thanking him politely when he brought her coffee and a doughnut, managing stiff little smiles for him throughout the day. No one who didn't know them well would have guessed anything was wrong. And later, when he'd attempted to talk to her, to explain his situation, to apologize for hurting her, she'd simply said mildly, "Robert, there's no need to say a word. I understand, now, from the beginning of our relationship until that night I saw you with Aaron. I don't appreciate being used, but maybe everyone uses someone occasionally. At least we had some good times together. Let's just remember those and let the matter drop for now."

Let the matter drop for *now*? That phrase had frightened Robert to the core. What did she mean? Did she intend to do something later? That's what it *must* mean, because he'd been certain she was in love with him. She must be crushed. Heartbroken. *Furious.* He would have understood if she had screamed and cursed at him. It was her silence that scared him, that made him certain she was planning some kind of revenge. And then Aaron had gotten a weird call last week. He claimed the voice was unfamiliar, but Robert was sure the call had come from Brooke, disguising her voice as she asked, "Been seeing anyone new lately?" The words terrified Robert because he thought Brooke meant not only to blackmail Aaron but also to tell everything about Robert, especially to his father. Next Aaron had received a letter—a letter taunting

Aaron about his relationship with Robert and "wondering" what Mrs. Townsend and Reverend Eads would think.

And now Brooke had "dropped by" to see Rev. Eads. "Oh God," Robert moaned. She couldn't just have been returning books. He *knew* it. There was a deeper reason. Her plan, whatever it was, had begun. She was trying to torture him.

And she was doing a good job of it.

# eleven

## 1

"So where would you like to have lunch?" Vincent asked as they walked out the nursing-home front doors.

"Oh, anywhere."

"You must have a favorite restaurant."

"I have several, but you don't have to take me anywhere nice, Vincent. Fast food will be fine."

"Absolutely not. Name a restaurant. I insist." He tilted his head, a glint in his dark green eyes. "I will not stop harping on you until you give me the name of a *real* restaurant, and I assure you, Miss Yeager, I can be even more relentless than Stacy Corrigan."

"Dear lord, *that's* a frightening thought!" Brooke laughed. "Okay. Tidewater Grill. It's in the Town Center Mall."

"I ate there the last time I visited Dad. Great choice," Vincent said as he took her elbow and guided her to the left. "Let's just take one car. We'll cut down on air pollution, do our part for the preservation of the ozone layer, and not clog up the highways. I'll bring you back here afterward to pick up your car."

"Well, I can hardly argue with those good reasons for taking one vehicle." Vincent stopped her at a silver Mercedes convertible. "Wow!" Brooke exclaimed. "The book business must be doing well."

"I splurged. I'd always wanted a convertible. Dad had a fit when he saw it. First he told me I'd flip it and turn my head to mush. Then he kicked all four tires. Then he asked how much it cost. I'll admit only to you—I lied about the cost."

"Lying was probably your best option," Brooke giggled. "*I* happen to know approximately how much a car like this does cost. Your father would have had a heart attack." She ran her hand along the silver side. "I, on the other hand, have never even been in a convertible and I don't give a damn how much it cost." Vincent's laugh rang out in the clear midday air. Brooke opened the passenger's door. "Dark red leather seats. How racy." She slipped into the car, leaned back her head, and let out a sigh of pleasure. "Ohhh, I'm in love."

Vincent shuffled his feet and ducked his head. "Oh, Brooke, I know I'm irresistible, but this is so sudden—"

"With the *car,* Mr. Ego. I'm in love with the car." Brooke wondered why Vincent was being so nice to her. He was acting, well, not only human but also flirtatious. He was looking at her questioningly, clearly aware of her puzzlement, which she covered by nodding at the police cruiser not far away. "We have to let them know where we're going. I know having surveillance trailing you everywhere is a drag."

Vincent shook his head. "In the writing business, mine is a household name. I can never go anywhere without a full phalanx of security," he said with mock seriousness. "I'm used to it."

"You mean you're full of it," Brooke shot back, making Vincent laugh again.

Five minutes later the gleaming Mercedes, followed by the police cruiser, pulled away from White Willows. Brooke let out a sigh. "You know, as nursing homes go, White Willows is wonderful. The building is lovely, the staff is great, they bring in entertainment regularly, always trying to keep the residents happy and stimulated, and yet—"

"It's still a nursing home," Vincent finished for her. "I'm sure at least half of the residents would rather be in their own houses following their own routines."

"Yes. My grandmother didn't protest when I told her the doctor said she should be in a place where she could get round-the-clock care. Even a full-time caregiver has to sleep, and that's when a lot of people get up and wander—you know, go outside, fall, and get hurt. Sometimes they get lost."

"Hence the locking of the nursing-home doors at eight o'clock," Vincent said. "I heard about that on my tour, along with the alarm system in case there's an escapee. In some ways it's like a prison. Yet you didn't have any choice except to put your grandmother in there. And I'll have to put Dad either there or a place like it. He can't go on by himself anymore, and he wouldn't want me living with him. I know he loves me, but I get on his nerves with my odd working hours—sometimes I write all night and sleep most of the day—and he cannot stand taking orders from me, even when it comes to taking his medication. If I tell him it's time for a certain pill, he refuses it out of pure stubbornness. He will *not* be bossed around by his son." Vincent shook his head. "My moving back to West Virginia and into the house with him is definitely not the answer to our problem. Maybe a place like White Willows will be."

The day was dazzling, the sun a stunning daffodil yellow in a soft blue sky. Brooke put on her sunglasses, then leaned back her head, letting the wind blow her long hair as they sped toward downtown Charleston. Vincent looked over at her. "Thank God you're not one of those women who wrap a scarf over their heads and clutch at their hair, trying to hold some complicated, gelled-up style in place."

Brooke laughed. "I'm afraid my hair has never been touched by hair gel. At work I usually wear it up so I'll look more businesslike, but I really like to leave it loose. And I love the feel of wind blowing through it."

"That's because you know you look so good with wind blowing through your golden tendrils."

"Golden tendrils?" Brooke asked dryly. "I hope you're not going to start talking like some nineteenth-century poet."

"Why, sweet maiden? Don't you care to hear about your rosebud mouth and eyes as blue-violet as wisteria drenched with beads of the sweet morning dew?"

"Oh, good grief," Brooke moaned. "That visit to the nursing home knocked you for a loop, didn't it? Or did you sustain a blow to the head you didn't tell me about?"

"Actually, I'm just hungry. I always go off on poetic tangents when I'm hungry."

"Then let's get to the restaurant," Brooke said, grinning. "And *hurry.*"

They found a spot on the third level of the parking building, then walked into the large, bright mall. "It always seems so cheerful in here," Brooke said. "Sometimes when I feel down, I like to come and just window-shop and people-watch."

"You're a Peeping Tom?"

"I don't peek in the windows of homes, Vincent," Brooke said with dignity. "I sit on a bench and watch people in a public place."

"Oh. You're just a voyeur."

"And you're impossible. No wonder you get on your father's nerves. We need to get some food in you so you start acting normal again."

Brooke had always enjoyed the casual ambience of the Tidewater Grill with all its wood, tile, hanging plants, dim lighting, and length of mirror behind the bar. The waiter seated them beside the expanse of windows looking out on Quarrier Street. Beyond the windows, which were decorated with heavy wooden blinds, hung an awning over more tables in a street café setting. Brooke often opted to eat there, but today the breeze had grown brisk and they agreed they'd be more comfortable inside.

When the waiter appeared, Brooke impulsively ordered a piña colada and Vincent requested the same. "I usually have scotch and soda, but today I'm in the mood for something frivolous," he told her.

She nodded. "Something to get our minds off ailing loved ones and nursing homes. But I'm only drinking one, Vincent."

"Did I say you had to have more?"

"No, but you probably expected it after my beer-drinking display at your house the other day."

"Well, I did wonder if that was normal behavior for you," he said solemnly. "I just wondered how you got away with it at work. Oh, I know it's easy to down a quick beer in the restroom, but that burping afterward!"

She tossed a toothpick at him, her cheeks growing pink. "You're never going to let me live that down, are you?"

"Never," he said. Then they both looked at the table. *Never?* That sounded like they'd be seeing each other for quite some time, when clearly whatever they were enjoying today—friendship?—would be short-lived.

"I think I'll just have a salad."

"I'm having a full meal."

They'd spoken at once in a moment of discomfort. Brooke grabbed for her drink and sipped with gusto. "A salad?" Vincent asked. "Certainly you're too hungry for just a salad."

"They have a Salad Nicole with chicken that I love. Coleslaw comes with it and fresh rolls. That's what I want."

"Okay," Vincent said. "The lady shall have what she wants, even if she'll be hungry in a couple of hours."

"I won't."

"Bet you will."

"You're as bossy as Stacy."

Vincent rolled his eyes. "I don't think anyone is *that* bossy. You two seem so different. How did you get to be such good friends?"

"Living next door to each other was the initial step. I moved in first. She and Jay came about a month later. I helped them unpack—Harry tried to help, too, but you can imagine how efficient he is. Stacy and I kept giggling about how he was crashing around and ogling us. After Jay came home and Harry left, we all had a big pizza and ended up spending another couple of hours talking." Brooke lifted her shoulders. "I've never had a lot of friends, but I just felt I knew Stacy almost right away."

"That seems strange."

Brooke smiled. "I know on the outside Stacy and I seem different. She's extroverted, even brash, and I'm self-contained. At least most of the time. But underneath, we're remarkably alike—stubborn, even tough."

"You're not as bossy and pushy."

"Maybe I'm just more subtle about it than Stacy is," Brooke laughed. "And Jay is a sweetheart. Not a pushover by any means, the way he sometimes seems around Stacy. He's a man to be reckoned with, especially on the job. He's a good friend. And he adores his wife."

Vincent dug into the large tossed salad that came with his meal. "I'm glad you have a cop living right next door under the circumstances, and the fact that Jay seems to be moving up the ladder so quickly lets me know he's got a talent for the job."

"He might grow up to be another Sam Lockhart!"

Vincent smiled. "I hope so, but I'm afraid there's only *one* Sam Lockhart. I swear, I think he was solving cases by age five."

"You mentioned a friend of his—Hal Myers, I think. Is he as good a cop as your father was?"

"I'd say he's a close second." Vincent took a sip of his piña colada, then a second. "I might start having 'girlie' drinks more often. Just in places like this, though."

"I hope word doesn't get back to California and ruin your reputation." Brooke smiled, then said, "I wondered if any of your father's friends had come up with any information about my case."

Vincent immediately became serious. "As a matter of fact, one did. It's about the rose you received at our house, the one with the message 'Say hello to your mother for me.'" We already knew it came from Flowers for You. Hal Myers, who you know has been put in charge of this case, said an assistant at the store claims the order was phoned in. She barely remembered the voice, but said it sounded 'kinda deep.' She couldn't be sure if it was a man or a woman. Those are the kind of vague witnesses cops love. Anyway, the rose was charged to a card belonging to a woman named Adele Webster."

"Adele Webster?" Brooke repeated blankly.

"It turns out she's about sixty-five, married to a prominent lawyer, has no idea who you are, has not ordered flowers for at least six months, *and,* here's the good part, her credit card has not been stolen." Brooke looked at him. "She didn't lose her credit card, Brooke. Someone managed to get her credit card number. There have been no other bogus charges on that card."

Brooke leaned back in her chair. "How could someone do that?"

"A dozen ways. All anyone would have to do is get a look at her credit card and either write down or manage to memorize the number. Mrs. Webster says she rarely carries more than twenty dollars with her and uses the credit card constantly. That, of course, will make it even harder to figure out who might have used her number."

"Wonderful," Brooke said glumly. "Of course it was Zach who used the number. I guess he just has all kinds of talents—memorizing credit card numbers, entering and leaving nursing homes with the stealth of a phantom, breaking out of a maximum security prison, and eluding capture for days."

"But not forever."

"How do we know that, Vincent? Maybe Zach will never see prison again. In fact, I have a very strong feeling he won't."

"On what do you base that feeling?"

"I don't know," Brooke said, her voice rising. "I just have it!" Their waiter threw them a quick look, then glanced discreetly away. "Maybe it's just fear talking, Vincent," she went on, lowering her voice. "Maybe I'm just *afraid* the police will never catch him and I'll be running from him until one of us finally drops."

"Well, you're a lot younger than he is," Vincent said casually, "so he'll probably drop first. That should give you a few peaceful years during your old age."

Brooke saw that he was only trying to lighten a dark situation, to make her laugh when she was letting nerves get the best of her. "You're trying to make me think you're one cool guy."

"I *am* one cool guy. The coolest, baby."

"You're going to think you're the coolest if you ever call me 'baby' again."

"What would you prefer? 'Sugar lump'? 'Sweetie pie'? 'Tootsie Roll'?"

" 'Miss Yeager,' if you don't stop acting like a dope."

Vincent bowed his head slightly. "Yes, ma'am. Sorry, ma'am."

Brooke burst into laughter and the rest of the meal went calmly, even enjoyably. She even broke her own rule and they each had a second piña colada.

A bit giddy from her two drinks and cheered by the bright, carefree atmosphere of the mall, Brooke suggested they not leave immediately. "I feel like I've been a prisoner for days," she told Vincent. "I think even though I know we have surveillance following us, a turn around the *real* world might do me good. Would you mind keeping me company?"

"It would be my honor to escort you," he said.

She tilted her head up at him, her blue-violet eyes sparkling. "To hell with escorting me. Just hang out with me like we're two eighteen-year-olds without a care in the world."

"Now *that* sounds like fun." Vincent smiled.

First, she dragged him into Waldenbooks, with its prominent display of his novels, and loudly introduced him to the manager, staff, and any customers lucky enough to be around at the moment. His embarrassment was smothered by the obvious fun she was having as people crowded around him, asking for his autograph and praising his work.

After they emerged from the bookstore, Vincent took over and led her to a kiosk where they sold Godiva chocolates, buying a big box for her and one for his father. Vincent then nearly pushed her into a dress store filled with youthful, colorful fashions. "Vincent, this stuff is too young and sexy for me," she protested.

He frowned. "Nonsense! You're eighteen, remember? Not a care in the world? Now go forth and shop!"

They emerged half an hour later, Brooke with a bag holding a frothy flowered chiffon skirt and a matching sequined tank top. "I don't know where in the world I'll wear this," she said, acting baffled that she'd bought it, although Vincent had told her she looked breathtaking in it as she twirled in front of the mirrors, and two other guys had winked at both of them in approval.

"You'll wear it dancing," Vincent said.

"I never go dancing."

"You mean Robert never took you to any clubs?"

"Robert?" Brooke giggled. "Robert's idea of a good time was a rousing night at the symphony and a quiet glass of wine afterward, during which we could discuss the conductor's interpretation of the piece."

"Then you definitely need to be taken dancing. And not to the kind of music my father listens to. There were a few rock clubs in town when I lived here. There must be at least one left."

"There is," Brooke said. "Tourmaline. Very hot."

"Tourmaline?"

"Tourmaline is a pink gem."

"I *know* that. I just didn't expect any place in Charleston to be named Tourmaline."

"What did you expect? Hernando's Hideaway?"

"Olé! And don't laugh. That was one of my mother's favorite songs."

"She sang it to me once!" Brooke laughed. "She played it on the piano, very dramatically, got up and acted out parts of it, and made me smile for the first time since my mother was killed. I'll never forget it. Or her. I really loved your mother, Vincent."

He smiled wistfully. "So did I. I just wish I'd told her

more often, but when you're young, you think your parents will be around forever." His smile froze. "God, Brooke, I'm sorry. Your parents died so young. I'm an insensitive—"

To his surprise, she touched his lips with her fingers. "You're not insensitive. Just natural. Mine was an odd case. Very odd, thank goodness. As for you not telling your mother often enough that you loved her, stop worrying. She knew it. One time she showed me your picture and started talking about you. Of course, she told me a lot of fabulous things about you that I'm sure were highly exaggerated"—she winked at him—"but she also said, 'Sam and I have been very blessed to have a son like Vincent. He's not only handsome and brilliant; he loves us, *really* loves us, although he never says it.'"

"Moms always brag on their sons," Vincent said offhand-edly, although Brooke saw the rims of tears at the base of his eyes.

"Your mother wouldn't want you to mourn her," Brooke said, pretending not to have noticed his emotions. "Your mother would want you to be happy. I know that sounds clichéd, but it's true. She knew you wanted to be a writer, and that's what she wanted for you. If she could have seen all those people gathered around you in the bookstore—" Brooke sighed, smiling. "Well, all I can say is that she would have been one enormously proud mother. And your father is proud of you, too. He's just too cantankerous to show it."

"You might be right about my mother, but not my father."

"I'll tell you a secret. One of those times when I'd slipped away from my adoring foster parents over to your house, your father read aloud a paper you'd written in college and sent home. He glanced at your mother, then at me with a look of wonder on his face, and said, 'Can you only *imagine* having the talent to express yourself that way? It's God-given; that's all I can say. God-given.'"

Vincent stared at her in surprise for a moment, then abruptly got up. "I have to go to the restroom."

Brooke sat down on a bench, waiting. The mall seemed

unusually crowded, almost as filled with people as it was at Christmas. As she casually gazed around her, she became aware of one person standing, looking at her. A few people passed between them and then she saw Judith Lambert from work. The woman wore a skirt just short enough to show her bony knees, and a short-sleeved jacket over a chemise that should have been covered, not that Judith's tiny breasts were exactly overflowing the cups. Brooke didn't know the exact time, but it was certainly after two o'clock, not Judith's lunch hour. Maybe Aaron had given her some extra time off, Brooke thought, then decided the matter was none of her business. She gave Judith a brief smile as the woman continued to stand stock-still, staring at her.

Brooke looked into the bag with the chocolates, almost overcome by a craving for *just* one, when someone said, "Grieving for your lost friend, Brooke?" Brooke glanced up to see Judith standing over her, a look of outrage on her bony face. "According to Aaron, you were so upset, he gave you a few days off. And here you are—shopping your little heart out."

"Judith, I just happened to run into someone—"

"Yes, I know you're here with a man, what else?" Judith's cheekbones seemed even sharper under the harsh lights of the mall. "I'll be sure to tell Aaron I saw you and your escort having a lovely afternoon. I'm certain he'll be *delighted* you're making such a fast recovery."

"Judith, if you'd just let me explain . . ."

"Explain what?" Brooke went blank as Judith glared, her eyes like shards of aqua glass. "You're so pretty and you seem so sweet. You always get what you want while robbing the rest of us of what *we* should have." Judith shook her head slowly, as if just coming to an important realization. "Nature isn't fair," she said slowly. "That's why sometimes it's up to man to correct the mistakes."

Judith whirled and strode away so fast Brooke didn't have time to say anything else, not that she would have known what to say. The idea that she was having a grand old time right after the death of Mia was ludicrous, but Brooke had to admit she'd enjoyed her two hours at the mall, and that awareness immediately brought on feelings of guilt. But what on earth had Judith meant about man needing to correct nature's mistakes? Was she merely trying to say something dramatic, or was she saying what she truly felt? Or worse, *meant*?

When Vincent emerged from the restroom, he looked a tad redder around the eyes and nose, but Brooke didn't call attention to his altered appearance. She knew her words about his father had affected Vincent deeply and there was no need for more conversation on the topic. Still, she was mainly thinking about Judith, feeling both angry and shamefaced at the same time.

Vincent gave her a bright smile that dimmed when he looked at her more closely. "What's wrong?"

"Nothing much."

"You saw Zach?" he asked in alarm.

"No. I'll tell you later. Right now I'd just like to leave the mall." Without thinking, she took his arm almost as protection. "How would you like to meet my grandmother?" she asked.

"You want me to go to the hospital with you?"

"Yes, unless you hate hospitals."

"I don't. I just didn't think you liked me well enough to invite me to meet the person you love most in the world."

"Oh, don't get too carried away with yourself," Brooke said airily, trying to recover her good mood. "I just like riding in your convertible."

"How could your grandmother think I look like your uncle Heinrich when he had light brown hair and blue eyes?" Vincent asked as they spun back to White Willows to pick up Brooke's car three hours later.

"Because she had you mixed up with her uncle Thomas, who had black hair and green eyes."

"Well, then, don't you think—"

"That she got mixed up last night and saw an orderly instead of Zach bending over her bed?" she finished for him. "No, I don't. She hasn't seen Heinrich and Thomas for forty years. She also described the mole on Zach's face; then she pointed on my face to the exact place where Zach's mole was located. And she said he'd said he'd come for me. She didn't even know Zach was out of prison, Vincent."

"At least we think she didn't. I know the staff at White Willows tried to keep her shielded from the news, but couldn't some of her friends have seen the news and told her?"

"I thought you believed me, Vincent," Brooke said quietly. "I thought you were the one person who believed that Grossmutter really had seen Zach."

He was quiet for a moment, negotiating a tight turn on the way up the hill to White Willows. Then he said, "Brooke, I *do* believe you. It's just that I know that if you're determined to make the police believe that Zach got into that nursing home, they'll be asking you tougher questions than I have been. I'm only trying to get you prepared."

"Okay. As long as *you* believe me."

"Why do you care if *I* believe you?"

She looked slightly flustered for a moment, then said, "I'd just like to know that *someone* believes me."

No, I care if *he* believes me, Brooke thought with a burst of annoyance. What Vincent Lockhart thought shouldn't matter to her at all. But, much as she hated to admit it, she did *care.*

When they pulled up beside Brooke's car, she glanced at her watch. "Good heavens, it's five thirty!"

"Think we're too late to catch dinner in the White Willows cafeteria?"

"Let's hope so," Brooke said dryly. "Vincent, thank you for lunch—"

"Save the speech for two minutes. I'm going to open your car door and help you in like my mother taught me to do."

"Vincent, I'm not an old lady."

"I'm doing this for my mother."

"Oh well, as long as it's not for *me.*" Brooke sighed, amused in spite of herself, then allowed Vincent to get out, go to her car, open the door, and hand her in with a flourish. "May I adjust your seat belt?"

"I think I can manage that, and you don't fasten women's

seat belts unless you want to get the reputation of being a letch."

"I *am* a letch."

"Your mother wouldn't like that."

"Then I'll leave your seat belt alone." He stepped back and smiled. "I had a nice afternoon, Brooke," he said through her open window.

"Me, too."

"Thanks for taking me to meet your grandmother. She seems like quite a lady."

"She liked you, too. She didn't say much, but I could tell by the look in her eyes." Brooke fumbled with her keys, suddenly self-conscious. "Tell your father hello for me. And thanks again for the day. It was just what I needed."

"Good. Now I've heard what I've done right for the day. Next I'll go home and hear from Dad everything I've done wrong."

Brooke laughed. "You two love arguing and you know it. Good night. Sleep tight."

*Sleep tight?* she thought as she drove away from White Willows. That was the kind of thing you said to a child, not to mention sounding a bit intimate. Actually, sounding a bit strange, when you thought about it. What was the opposite of sleeping tight? Sleeping *loose*? What would that entail? "Brooke, you need to go home and have a quiet evening," she said aloud. "After all that's happened lately, you need to wind down like an old clock."

## 2

Robert decided to go for a long drive through the summer evening with its tranquil, fading colors. The only problem was that the evening was neither tranquil nor colorful. By seven o'clock the sky had turned a flat shale gray and wind tossed around tree limbs, gently at first, then with more force. A storm was coming. Robert had hated storms ever since he was six and lightning had hit their house, setting it on fire. No one had been injured. The incident had locked itself in Robert's memory, however, and during storms he had crawled under his bed until he was twelve and became ashamed of seeking this haven, although sometimes he still longed for its safety.

Tonight Robert didn't care that Charleston lay in the path of a storm. Bolstered by almost unbearable nervous tension and the remnants of the three glasses of wine he'd consumed at lunch and three more at home, he felt strong and reckless. A little lightning and thunder weren't going to scare him, by God.

Robert thought about going to Aaron's but quickly rejected the idea. They'd had a long lunch and Aaron had been supportive and charming. But Robert had sensed that Aaron was playing him, speaking with a lack of sincerity, trying to "jolly" him into a better mood. Robert hadn't let Aaron know he'd sensed the counterfeit manner, but he knew something dark lay under Aaron's wide smile and something hostile hid behind his ebony eyes.

Actually, he'd seemed wary of Robert. Aaron's attitude hurt Robert. It also made him angry. He couldn't understand why Aaron refused to acknowledge the threat Brooke posed to both of them. After all, Aaron's violently homophobic mother actually owned Townsend Realty, not Aaron. If she had any idea that Aaron was gay, she'd jerk the business away from him before he knew what hit him. She'd write him out of the will, and if Robert knew the old witch as well as he thought he did, with her considerable influence she'd poison every well in the local business world against Aaron.

As he drove, Robert kept catching himself gripping the steering wheel and sitting with his back stiff as a board. He would draw a deep breath, let his back curve slightly, and loosen his hands on the wheel. Two minutes later, he'd be rigid and clutching again. He even began grinding his teeth, which he hadn't done since he was ten.

He wasn't sure how long he'd cruised around town before

he ended up at Brooke's apartment building. He orbited the block twice, immediately seeing the police surveillance car parked out front. That quashed the idea of bearding Brooke in her den. If he cared to humiliate himself like he had this afternoon by pounding on her door, she'd sic the cops on him in a minute. But even if he had the chance, he wouldn't try talking to her like that again, he decided. Reasoning was useless with a woman in love, a woman bent on revenge. Still, even as he told himself these things, he was parking half a block away from her apartment building, determined to see her and give talking with her, begging if necessary, one last try.

When Robert got out of the car, rain began to fall. Getting back in the car and simply driving away never occurred to him. He just turned up the collar of his trench coat, lowered his head, and circled the block on foot. Once he glanced up and thought he saw Aaron's BMW parked on the other side of the street but couldn't see the license plate. Oh well, Aaron wouldn't be sitting around in his car on a middle-class street in the rain. I'm just jumpy, Robert told himself, and I have to calm down if I'm going to do this.

He approached the apartment building from behind, being careful to walk like an innocent man simply trying to hurry out of the rain as he passed the second surveillance car parked behind the apartment house. Suddenly the rain picked up and before the cops could turn on their windshield wipers, Robert quickly darted into the alley running between Brooke's building and the one next to it.

He sidled closer to the brick structure and walked to where he could look directly up at a third-floor window he knew was Brooke's. A fire escape crawled up the side of the building, passing within a couple of feet of her window. How easy it would be to pull down the lower section of the ladder, climb up to Brooke's bedroom window like an aging Romeo, and enter the apartment. If the window was locked, he wasn't above breaking the glass near the lock to open it. He'd pay for the damage later. Brooke would probably scream when she first saw him. He could tell from the dim light in the bedroom that she was in the living room. He thought he could even hear music. Something classical. Maybe if she was drinking wine, she'd be calm and not go berserk when she saw him.

Robert's hands had begun to tremble. He'd always been "the good boy," the one who followed all the rules, the kid who had never skipped school or even gotten a traffic ticket. Yet here he was planning to climb a fire escape and break into a woman's apartment. But all he wanted to do was talk to her. Abruptly his father's face flashed in front of his eyes, a face full of pride and love slowly changing into one of shame, even revulsion, if he discovered his son was homosexual. Yes, Robert would just talk to Brooke. Unless it took more than just talking. . . .

He moved closer to the building, inching closer to the fire escape. He passed the Dumpster, the smell rising up to greet him almost as a warning that he was doing something dark and dirty and foul. Something deep within him told him not to continue, but he couldn't stop himself. Fear raced through him like it had when he was a little boy and a storm raged outside. But if he didn't make sure Brooke would keep his secret, he would face another storm—a storm of the soul when he lost his father's love and respect.

Robert had reached the fire escape. The bottom rung hung about ten feet above the alley to prevent people from climbing up the steps to do exactly what Robert was planning to do. Although he was six foot two, the bottom rung was still far above Robert's head. He'd played basketball in high school, though. How many times had he jumped up and touched the ten-foot-high rim of the basket? That was over seventeen years ago, but he'd stayed in good shape. He could probably grab that bottom rung, pull down the lower section, and easily climb the ladder.

The rain had picked up. He fumbled with the collar of his designer raincoat Aaron had bought him for his birthday, but rain still crept down his neck, wetting his shirt. His brown hair plastered itself to his forehead, the ends getting into his eyes. He brushed it aside, leaped, and caught the wet rung. Before he could clench his hands, though, he slipped loose.

His feet slid on the slick pavement and he fell, painfully smashing the back of his head about an inch from a puddle. God, how embarrassing, he thought, lying in a wet alley like a drunk. He should just forget this ridiculous plan and go home. But Brooke had gone to his home and talked to his *father.* What would she do next? Tell him everything? Robert had to see her tonight, and this seemed to be the only way.

Robert opened his eyes against the pouring rain, tried to stand up, and lost his footing again on the slick pavement, this time landing on his left side. With a groan, he turned his head, and for a heart-stopping moment he saw a face looming over him. Then it hit him—a piercing, excruciating jab in his back. He made a choking sound, the air pushed out of his mouth by the torturous pain ripping through him. He reached around to the right side of his mid-back. For an instant he felt something metal and sharp-edged before it vanished. "What?" he muttered as pain ripped through him again. This time he tried to scream, but the sound was weak and mewling. Blinking furiously against the rain, once again he saw a form above him, but only for an instant.

Vaguely he thought he should get up, fight off his attacker, run if he had to, but the pain was too great for him to fight and he could feel blood gushing from his back. My kidneys, he thought vaguely. Someone stabbed me in the kidneys.

He felt rather than saw a person kneel beside him, place two hands on his midsection, and turn him over. His face landed in a puddle, water coming to the tops of his ears. He closed his eyes tightly, but he could do nothing about the filthy water running into his ears and creeping beneath his eyelids. He tried to lift his arms, to get his hands on the pavement so he could push up and attempt to rise, but he just didn't have the energy. From somewhere deep in his brain a fact from a high school physiology class flashed into his memory: The kidneys receive a quarter of cardiac output. One-fourth of the blood that flowed through him every time his heart thumped went straight to his kidneys. And now, straight *out* of his body. Blood that he needed. Blood he would die without.

This thought registered with him just as another unbearable pain seared his back. Someone sure wants to make sure I never leave this alley, he thought with one last flash of macabre humor.

Miraculously, he managed to lift his head out of the puddle so he could draw a gasping breath. Blinking away the tears and the rain, he saw a figure beside him. The face, a pale blur, was only inches from his. Then Robert saw the right arm rise, stiffening for another vicious strike with a glinting metal blade. "Please, not again," Robert muttered at the black holes masquerading as eyes that seemed to burn in the white blur of a face. "I'm already dead."

# twelve

## 1

Warm air flowed over Brooke's face. A long, stiff hair brushed across her upper lip. A slightly damp nose caressed her cheek. Keeping her eyes closed, she murmured, "That has to be Antonio Banderas or"—she opened her eyes—"Elise!"

The blond dog trampled joyfully over the bed, darting up to give Brooke a lick on the nose. Brooke hugged her, feeling the dog's heart beating strongly beneath her ribs, and ran her hands over Elise's soft, short hair. She'd had Elise for only two years, but now she couldn't imagine life without the energetic, happy little creature. Elise was always ecstatic to see her, always ready to snuggle when Brooke was feeling down, always eager to go for a walk or a run when Brooke got out the leash, and had a habit of rolling into a ball on the couch beside her mistress and snoring loudly through some of Brooke's favorite late-night movies.

"I'll bet you need a trip outside," Brooke said. "Give me ten minutes."

They emerged from the back door of the apartment building to see the morning surveillance shift. Brooke wore a navy hooded knit jacket and stretch pants with silver stripes down the sides so she and Elise could take a short run in the clear morning air. Elise pulled on her leash until they reached her favorite bathroom stop. Afterward, Brook ambled down the road behind the apartment building, hearing the surveillance cruiser starting up to follow them. When they reached the end of the building, Elise turned away from the road and pulled toward the alley. "Wrong way, girl," Brooke said. "There's nothing down there except the smelly old Dumpster."

Usually Elise was completely obedient on the leash, but today she kept pulling toward the alley. Brooke gave the leash a gentle tug, but Elise jerked back, determined to investigate the alley. "Oh, all right," Brooke sighed. "Every day you go where I want. Today I'll let you take control."

Elise trotted down the alley, her curled tail in the air, daintily stepping around puddles with her slender paws and sailing over rain-soaked boxes with her sleek body. She sniffed various "interesting" objects, but without her usual concentration. Brooke had the strange feeling that Elise was on a mission, searching for one particular smell that intrigued her more than any others, and she wasn't going to be stopped until she found it.

Puddles from last night's rain reflected the clear, cloud-studded sky. Elise pulled closer to the Dumpster. Brooke was always amazed by how many people just threw refuse *at* the Dumpster instead of *in* it. The heavy metal container sat like an ancient gray behemoth surrounded by Styrofoam cups, dark trash bags torn by rats and spilling garbage, beer cans, a shattered wine bottle, and a fast-food hamburger container. Flies buzzed above and around the Dumpster.

"Come on, Elise," Brooke said. "Thank goodness they empty this thing tomorrow, because it is getting *rank.*"

Elise continued to pull stubbornly forward, finally stopping at a pile of wet, mud-splattered clothing. The clothes lay over a mound. Elise nosed around the heap, then began to whine. The dog rarely whined unless she was really frightened or upset. Brooke took a couple of steps closer to the dirty heap of clothes. She saw what looked like a trench coat with a large brownish-red stain on the back. Farther down she saw a shoe—a shoe with a foot inside.

"Elise, get back!" she yelled, feeling as if her blood had turned to ice. "Back!"

But as Brooke jerked at the leash, dragging Elise away, the dog slipped out of her collar and returned to the body. She whined again and then howled—a long, mournful sound that sent shivers through Brooke. The dog pawed determinedly at the body, and finally took a piece of the trench coat between her teeth and pulled hard. To Brooke's horror, the corpse slowly rolled over and Robert Eads's beautiful blank eyes stared up at the azure sky.

# 2

Brooke would have expected herself to scream for all she was worth. Instead, she stood still and stared at Robert and the dog, whose howling had turned into whining. Robert's affection for Elise was tentative because he was frightened of most dogs, but Elise was so gentle and quiet around him, he hadn't seemed afraid of her. He'd always patted her on the head and called her "pretty girl." He would never call her that again, Brooke thought.

Feeling as if she were in a dream, Brooke walked to the back of the alley, strode to the police cruiser, and said calmly, "There's a dead man beside the Dumpster. It's Robert Eads." Then she staggered. She would have fallen if one of the cops hadn't jumped out of the car and grabbed her.

Brooke was hardly aware of the sudden flurry of activity. Police spoke urgently on radios, more police cars arrived, and someone blocked off the alley. While Brooke sat on the curb, one of the policemen slipped Elise's collar and leash back on and brought her to Brooke. The two of them sat huddled together beside a police cruiser when a balding man arrived and bent over her. "Hello, Miss Yeager. I'm Hal Myers, Sam Lockhart's friend." He smiled at her with his long hound-dog face and slightly crooked nose. "I've heard a lot about you from Sam."

"Yeah, I'll bet," Brooke returned without a trace of humor. "Look for a murder and you'll find Brooke Yeager nearby."

"He's said only good things about you," Myers said kindly. "What makes you think Robert Eads was murdered?"

"What?" Brooke looked at him blankly. "You mean he wasn't?"

"I didn't say that. I just want to know what made *you* think he was."

"When we found him—Elise and I—he was lying face-down. There was blood all over the back of his trench coat and holes in it. Holes like stab wounds. He *was* stabbed, wasn't he?"

"Yes."

"Oh." Brooke closed her eyes. "I hope the first . . ."

"You hope the first?"

"I hope the first stab wound killed him. I mean, I hope he wasn't alive, feeling the pain of being stabbed over and over." She placed a hand on her abdomen. "I'm afraid I'm feeling nauseated."

"It's understandable. Don't be shy about throwing up."

Brooke bent her head down, drawing deep breaths, swallowing the hot water running into her mouth. Elise drew near to her, and she put her arm around the dog, squeezing her tightly. Finally, Brooke raised her head and opened her eyes. "I think I'm okay, now. At least as far as being sick, that is."

Myers smiled again. He had jowls and deep nasal-labial folds. His face looked comfortable, like an old piece of furniture, but his dark eyes were sharp as diamonds. "Good. But if you feel like—"

"I'm fine. Really." Brooke wondered what made her so determined to convince Hal Myers she felt fine when she didn't feel fine at all. She felt sick—sick physically, sick emotionally.

"Okay. Miss Yeager, did you touch or move the body?"

"*I* didn't. Elise did. The dog. She led me down the alley straight for Robert. We used to date, so Elise knew his scent. When we reached him, all I saw was the trench coat and a shoe. I tried to pull Elise away, but she seemed particularly strong and pawed at him, even took hold of his coat in her teeth, until she turned over . . . the body. I saw it was Robert."

"Did you see him last night?"

"No."

"Where were you last night?"

Brooke knew it was a routine question, but she stiffened anyway. "I was in my apartment. Alone."

"Did he come to the door?"

"No."

"You said the two of you used to go out."

"Yes. We broke things off about a month ago. He's been calling me a lot, though, even following me."

"So *you* broke up with *him,* but he wanted you back?"

Brooke hesitated. "I ended our relationship, but he didn't want me back."

"It sounds like he did."

"I know, but he didn't."

"Did you end it because you were seeing someone else?"

"No. Things . . . just weren't working out." It would have been so easy to tell this gentle-voiced man the truth, but Brooke knew how important it was to Robert that his homosexuality be kept secret. She'd been surprised when she found out the truth, but not horrified. She hadn't even been hurt. She'd only been angry that he'd used her to cover up the truth, a truth she didn't want to betray even now, even though it couldn't hurt him anymore. "Our breaking up was a mutual decision," she said, surprised that she'd lied and immediately regretting it.

"That's not what you said before."

"Well, there was a lot of back-and-forth, you know how those things go, and I guess I'm the one who actually suggested we just not see each other anymore, and he agreed to the suggestion."

Hal Myers frowned. "If he was so agreeable to it, why was he phoning and following you?"

"Uh . . . he wanted to talk to me."

"About what?"

"Just . . . I don't know." She was starting to breathe faster, well aware Myers knew she wasn't telling the truth. "Maybe he wanted to apologize."

"For a mutual breakup?"

Brooke sighed. "Oh, hell. I've been lying." She looked into Myers's face. It was serious. There was no humor in his dark eyes, but he didn't look angry. Yet.

"I broke off things with Robert because I found out he was gay. He didn't want anyone to know, especially his father, because he adored his father and thought he wouldn't understand and wouldn't love him anymore. . . . I don't know. . . . I've met Reverend Eads and I think he might have been surprised and confused, even hurt, if he found out the truth, but he would never have stopped loving Robert and he would have eventually come to understand, at least I believe he would have, but Robert didn't believe it and he was frantic that I was going to tell, so he kept after me, begging me not to tell anyone, which I wouldn't have done anyway, and—"

"You're running out of breath and you're going to pass out," Hal Myers said calmly. "I get the picture. Take a breath, then tell me why was Eads so certain you were going to tell his big secret?"

"I don't know. I honestly don't know, but he was convinced. He did say something about a call that had been made to . . . his lover, and he also mentioned a threatening letter. I guess he thought I made the call and sent the letter. Of course I didn't. I tried to tell him that, but he wouldn't believe me. He even offered me money to keep my mouth shut, for Pete's sake."

"Hold on now, Brooke. Someone called the lover. Who *was* Eads's lover?"

"Oh God, please don't make me tell that, too."

"Miss Yeager, we are talking about a homicide case here. Murder." Myers's voice had become stern. "This is not the time for secrets, no matter how well-meaning. After all, considering the murder weapon . . ."

"What about the murder weapon?" Brooke asked sharply.

"You go first. Who was Eads's lover?"

Brooke sighed. "Aaron Townsend of Townsend Realty. I work for him. That's how I found out about Robert. I went back to the office late one night to pick up some papers I'd forgotten and I found them together."

"What did you do?"

"I was shocked. I said something—I don't remember what, but it certainly wasn't threatening—and I left."

"But you weren't furious?"

"Furious?" Brooke shook her head no, then decided absolute honesty was the only way to go now that Myers had already caught her in one lie. "Yes, I guess I was furious, but not at that moment. Later. It wasn't fury over losing Robert, though. It was fury over his using me as a smoke screen." She frowned. " 'Fury' is too strong a word. If I'd loved Robert, I might have been furious. But I didn't love him. I thought he was a nice guy—I've known him since I was a child and we went to his father's church—but as a boyfriend, he was actually kind of boring. No wonder. I wasn't the person he wanted to be spending evenings with. I was already thinking of ending things, although I probably would have let them drift for a while. It wasn't as if I was unhappy dating Robert or anything. We got along fine. There just weren't any sparks, if you know what I mean."

She stopped abruptly and groaned. "I'm babbling. All I can say is that I didn't hate Robert. And although I was getting tired of his recent harassment, especially when it was so unwarranted, I wouldn't have done anything to him to stop it, except maybe get a restraining order or something if he didn't quit." Brooke took another deep breath. "All right. I've told *you* everything I know. Now you tell *me* what you meant about the murder weapon. I don't even know what it was. Why did you think mentioning it would frighten me into telling you the truth?"

Myers paused a moment, looking at her closely as if

sizing her up. Even though the morning was comfortably cool, Brooke felt sweat pop out on her—sweat caused by fear of the unknown.

At last, Myers said, "The murder weapon was lying right beside Eads. It was a silver envelope opener—shiny and very sharp." Brooke stared at him, baffled. What did a letter opener have to do with her? She didn't even own one.

"I don't get it," she said flatly.

"Are you sure?" Myers asked coolly. "Because the opener was engraved with the letters *ALY* on one side and 'I love you' on the other side. I've studied a lot of Sam's notes from your mother's case, Brooke. I know—"

Brooke didn't hear the rest of what Hal Myers was saying as her mind spun back. She could see her mother sitting at a small desk, her beautiful mother with the sun shining on her blond hair and glinting off the silver letter opener given to her by her husband Karl, a letter opener engraved with the letters *ALY*—Anne Lindstrom Yeager.

# 3

Brooke sat in a wooden rocking chair beside the stereo, Elise at her feet, listening to *Lakmé* by Delibes. She stared straight ahead, but she didn't see her cheerful saffron yellow chair or hibiscus pink embroidered pillows or the violets growing at the window. All she saw was a trench coat covered with rust-colored stains and Robert's soulless eyes staring up at the beautiful sky.

She didn't know how long she'd been sitting in the cherrywood chair her father had made until someone knocked lightly on the door, then opened it. Vaguely, Brooke saw Stacy standing in front of her, kneeling down and covering her cold hands locked on the chair arms with her own strong, warm ones.

"Brooke? Brooke, look at me." Obediently Brooke looked, but she didn't really see. "Brooke, it's Stacy."

"I know."

"Then look like you know it." Stacy's words were firm but not harsh. "Honey, snap out of it."

"Stacy, you should have seen him."

"I'm glad I didn't, and you shouldn't have, either. I know all about it. Jay's down there now, talking with some other detectives." Stacy stood up and looked around. "First, we're going to turn off this unbearably depressing music. Robert gave you this CD, didn't he? I've always hated it." She snapped off the CD player. "And now I'm going to fix you something to drink."

"I don't want anything."

Stacy was already in the kitchen. "I'm putting on a pot of coffee." In a moment she was back, handing Elise a dog biscuit. "No matter what the tragedy, you can always count on Elise to drown her sorrows in beef-basted biscuits."

For some reason, this struck Brooke as funny, and she started to laugh. And laugh. Louder. Harsher. Then Stacy was shaking her. "Don't make me slap you, Brooke Yeager, because you know I will."

"And enjoy every moment of it."

"Damned right."

Brooke almost immediately calmed down, tears starting to flow, the awful laughter stilled. "I'm sorry."

"Don't apologize. I'm used to it. Jay cries all the time. Sometimes I have to slap him senseless."

Brooke smiled through her tears and Stacy smiled back. "Feeling better?"

"Not better, but not hysterical."

"Well, that's a start." Stacy handed her a tissue. "I don't mind tears, but your nose is running."

Brooke blew, wiped, accepted a fresh tissue from Stacy to dab at her dripping eyes, then tossed the tissue in a nearby wicker wastebasket. "What a way to start out a morning."

"It's nearly noon," Stacy said, looking at her wristwatch. "But I'll bet you haven't had a thing to eat."

"I'm not hungry."

"Okay, I can understand that. But you're having coffee, whether you want it or not."

Brooke heard cabinet doors opening in the kitchen. "Have you forgotten where the coffee cups are?" Brooke called.

"No." In a few moments Stacy reappeared with a gigantic mug with a rooster painted on the side. "Christmas present from Harry last year. Remember?"

"How could I forget?" Brooke took a sip of the steaming liquid, winced, then smiled. "Now I know why you were opening all those cabinet doors. You were looking for the brandy. Exactly how much did you pour in here?"

"Enough to put you back on your feet."

"Or send me straight to bed."

"Either one will do you good. But while you're still conscious, do you mind talking to me a little?"

"I don't mind. I *need* to talk."

Stacy sat down on the floor, almost at Brooke's feet. She didn't seem to care how close she was to Elise, although she was allergic to dogs. "I know from Jay that you found Robert stabbed to death beside the Dumpster. I also know the section of the fire escape that leads practically to your bedroom window had been pulled down."

Brooke's eyes widened. "I didn't notice that."

"They're dusting for fingerprints, but God knows how many people have touched that thing, even though it's high. Kids jump up there all the time trying to grab it."

"But it was down, and Robert was only a few feet away." Brooke looked at Stacy. "Do you think Robert pulled it down? That he was planning to break in here?"

Stacy shrugged. "We were home and we didn't hear anyone banging on your door. Did he phone you?"

"No. No one came to the door and no one called. I read all evening."

"And listened to that awful music. We could hear it."

Brooke managed a faint smile. "I'm sorry if I had the stereo on too loudly, but *Lakmé* isn't awful. You just don't like classical music."

"It's depressing. Anyway, my taste in music has nothing to do with this murder." Stacy frowned. "Jay says the murder weapon was a letter opener with initials engraved on it."

Brooke nodded, this time taking a gulp of the brandy-laced coffee. "The initials were *ALY*. Anne Lindstrom Yeager. On the other side was engraved 'I love you.' My father had it made for my mother because she was always so particular about her nails. She had long red nails. She always complained about opening envelopes tearing her nails or chipping her polish."

"How can you be sure it's the same letter opener?"

"How many letter openers of exactly that description do you think are floating around out there? Besides, my grandmother mentioned in the police report after my mother's murder that the opener had gone missing shortly before her death. The detective in charge of the case now, Hal Myers, had read the report. He remembered the opener."

Stacy looked at her blankly for a moment. "How did Robert get your mother's letter opener?"

"I don't think he did. It would have been too much of a coincidence if he'd come across it somewhere." Stacy kept looking at her in confusion. "I remember that a few days, maybe a week, before Mommy was killed, she was looking all over the place for her letter opener. She accused me of taking it. Of course I didn't. I wasn't even allowed to touch it. She kept it in a felt wrapper that was supposed to prevent tarnish and she didn't want *anyone* touching it. One time she caught Zach handling it and she had a fit."

"Because it was a gift from your father."

Brooke nodded. "Zach was jealous that she was so possessive of something given to her by Daddy. I remember he threw it on the floor and stormed out of the house. By then, their arguments were getting fairly regular, but my mother cried over that one. She didn't see me watching her, but she wiped the letter opener over and over, as if to get every trace of Zach's handprint off it, then wrapped it again and hid it in a bookcase. A couple of days later, she couldn't find it."

"Zach took it."

"Probably. And her wedding ring from Daddy. It had a tiny diamond in it and on the inside was engraved 'Anne and Karl.' She kept it in a small blue felt jewelry box in her lingerie drawer. When she found it missing the same time as the letter opener, she was nearly hysterical."

"The ring disappeared the same time as the letter opener?"

"Yes. At least, my mother discovered that it was missing the same day. The ring could have been gone for several days or even weeks before she noticed it, but I don't think so. I have a feeling Mommy looked at that wedding ring almost every day."

Stacy tapped her fingers on her thigh, as if thinking. "The ring aside, Zach couldn't have kept a letter opener all this time he's been in prison."

"No. He must have had it hidden somewhere."

"Why wouldn't he have just thrown it away?"

"Stacy, I have no idea. Zach Tavell was always a mystery to me. Even though I was only nine when my mother married him, I couldn't understand why she did it. They'd known each other less than three months. He was completely different from my father—serious, quiet, almost gloomy."

"It must have been a rebound relationship for your mother."

"That's all I can figure out, not that I understood such a thing at the time. I just remember I wasn't happy about the marriage, although I tried to pretend I was because I thought it made my mother happy. But it didn't. I'm sure she would have divorced him." Brooke almost choked on a humorless laugh. "But she didn't get a chance because he killed her first."

"Drink some more of your coffee," Stacy said briskly, obviously afraid Brooke was going to burst into tears or worse. "Just remember, they aren't sure the letter opener was the murder weapon."

"No, it just turned up after fifteen years next to a man who'd been stabbed God knows how many times."

Stacy sighed. "Okay. Let's say that Zach has had this letter opener hidden someplace for fifteen years. Why would he kill Robert with it?"

"He had it with him. It was a weapon of convenience."

"I repeat, *why?* Why would Zach Tavell kill Robert?"

"Because Zach has been following me. Therefore, he must have seen Robert following me, too. When he saw Robert trying to break into my apartment last night, he killed him."

"To protect you?"

Brooke drained her cup, then gave her friend a grim smile. "No, Stacy. Because *Zach* wanted to be the one to kill me."

# thirteen

## 1

Aaron Townsend's doorbell rang. He looked out the window, saw his sister's car, and hurried to the door. When he opened it, he smiled when he saw her elegant black pantsuit accented by the mandarin collar and French cuffs of a white silk blouse. "Maddy, you look stunning."

"I'm not sure that's the proper compliment for funeral attire, but I'm glad you approve." She smiled. A gust of cool breeze blew her shining black hair across her beautiful face. "Maybe I should have pulled my hair into a French twist."

"No. I hate it that way. It looks like Mother's," Aaron said. As his sister walked ahead of him, Aaron asked, "Maddy, are you feeling all right?" She looked at him questioningly. "It's just that—"

"I'm limping more than usual," she finished for him. "Aaron, you have to stop being so squeamish about mentioning my leg. My limp is worse because I took a tumble out the back door day before yesterday. I tripped over the cat. I'll be all right by tomorrow."

Aaron ushered Madeleine into the foyer of his large stone house. "Mother said you should get rid of that cat."

"I live in Mother's house and I obey all of her rules except that one. If Shadow goes, so do I, and Mother knows it. Besides, it wasn't Shadow's fault; it was mine."

"Whatever you say. By the way, she's not coming to Mia's funeral, is she?"

"Shadow?" Aaron smiled. When the brother and sister were together, all traces of formality on Madeleine's part vanished. "Oh, you meant Mother. Well, much to your disappointment, no. She said she didn't even know the girl. Besides, she claims her sciatica is acting up."

"She has extremely convenient sciatica," Aaron said dryly. "It always acts up when there's an event she doesn't want to attend."

"You disrespectful boy!" Madeleine looked Aaron up and down. "That silk robe is beautiful, but do you plan to wear it to the funeral?"

"I was waiting for you to get here to help me decide which suit looks best—the navy blue Joseph Brooks or the charcoal Perry Ellis."

"The charcoal has always been one of my favorites."

"Tie?"

"Solid black. It's stylish yet appropriate for a funeral. You'll look extremely handsome." Madeleine frowned. "Although you're very pale. Are you ill?"

"I'm exhausted after the conference yesterday. In fact, I could use a cup of coffee before I start getting dressed. Want one?"

"Sure." Madeleine followed him into the large kitchen fitted with stainless-steel appliances. She loved the marble countertops and the off-white cabinets that seemed to glow in the light pouring through the skylight. The room was so different from the huge old-fashioned cavern of a kitchen in her mother's house. Madeleine sat on a stool at the maple butcher-block-topped island in the center of the room, slipping her arm from her cane, which she leaned against the next stool. "I thought you weren't going to that conference in Cleveland yesterday."

"I thought I wasn't, too, but at the last minute, I decided it wouldn't look good if I didn't show up." He handed her a delicate teacup and saucer, the cup filled with a fragrant exotic blend. "Normally I would have spent the night and come back today. Instead, I headed back around eight."

"Which means you didn't get home until midnight."

"Well past midnight. There was a wreck involving a semi-truck that tied me up for at least forty-five minutes. And my head was killing me. God, those conferences are boring."

"I spent the day with Mother. She insisted she felt horrible and we went to the emergency room. I think they did every test known to man—"

"And didn't find a thing wrong?" Aaron asked in mock surprise.

"How did you guess?" Madeleine laughed.

"I know Mother. She probably enjoyed all the attention immensely, not to mention having the thrill of wasting your day."

"Thank heavens I took a novel with me. *Anna Karenina.* It's about ten thousand pages long and I almost finished it."

Aaron smiled, sipping his coffee. "So we both had fabulous days. I tried to call you on my way home, but I had bad cell phone reception."

"You don't have to report in to me, Aaron."

"I wasn't. I just wanted a little witty repartee. I can't stand the radio and I was sick of every CD I'd taken with me."

Madeleine beamed. "I'm glad you consider my conversation witty. Mother certainly didn't."

"She wanted to spend her time telling the doctors and nurses in minute detail about each of her aches, about how truly terrible she feels *every single day of her life,* but how she soldiers on, a model of strength and dignity in spite of her bone-wrenching agony."

Madeleine burst into giggles.

"Well, I'm sure she managed to hear that blasphemous outburst, so I'll probably drop dead in the cemetery."

"If you do"—Madeleine grinned—"at least you'll be well dressed."

Aaron put down his cup. "Not if I don't stop gabbing with you and put on some clothes." Just as Aaron rose from the stool, the doorbell rang. He glanced at the clock. "Eleven fifteen and the funeral is at one. Who the hell can this be?"

"Do you want me to answer it while you get dressed?" Madeleine asked.

"It's my house, it'll be someone for me, so I might as well go," Aaron returned sourly. "But of all times . . ."

Aaron tied the sash of his paisley print robe tighter around his waist and walked to the door. He looked out the peephole to see two unfamiliar men standing on the low stone porch. Neither looked the least bit tentative, as if they might be at the wrong house. In fact, they each looked almost severe. For a moment Aaron thought about calling for Madeleine—men usually acted more polite and milder in her presence—but he then decided it would be cowardly to hide behind his little sister. He swung open the door. "May I help you?"

"Aaron Townsend?" the older, balding one asked.

"Yes."

"I'm Detective Myers and this is Detective Corrigan. We're from the Charleston Police Department. We'd like a moment of your time."

The Charleston Police Department? For a moment, Aaron's stomach clenched. His great-uncle had been the police superintendent many years ago. Aaron had always hated the harsh-voiced, hook-nosed old man. "Of course." He paused. They stared at him, then at his colorful robe, which until just this moment Aaron had loved. Suddenly he thought it looked prissy. "Won't you come in?" he asked in a voice slightly deeper than normal. At least I can sound manly even if I don't look it, he thought.

Aaron led the men into his living room with its floor-to-ceiling windows offering a view of the woods and the flagstone patio with a gas grill and green-patterned chair and chaise longues. The walnut flooring in the living room felt cold under Aaron's bare feet and he was glad to step onto the large flax rug in the middle of the room. He motioned the detectives to a long cream sweep of couch in front of the windows while he sat on a stark black chair next to the huge stucco fireplace.

"What can I do for you gentlemen?" Aaron asked, and realized he'd gone from sounding manly to chirpy.

The detective called Myers said, "We're here about Robert Eads."

Aaron felt himself flush. He tried to keep his expression casual, but there was nothing he could do about the rush of blood to his face. He swallowed, tried not to let his foot jitter the way it did when he was nervous, and said pleasantly, "Yes? What about him? I hope he's not in any trouble."

"He's dead," Myers said flatly. "He was murdered night before last."

"Oh." To his horror, Aaron felt himself smile. He couldn't stop smiling. It was a nervous reaction, but a horrible one. They looked at him quizzically and he was afraid he was going to burst into laughter.

"Robert Eads?" he finally croaked, trying desperately to get himself under control. "M-murdered?"

"Yes," Myers said slowly. Aaron noticed that although Myers's remaining hair was mostly gray, the shadow of a black beard lay beneath his tanned skin. And his eyebrows were black. Coal black with a strong arch. What a stupid thing to notice. "We called you yesterday but got no answer."

"I attended a conference in Cleveland. I got caught behind a wreck coming home and didn't arrive until around midnight. But why did you want to question me about Robert's murder?"

Myers looked at Aaron steadily, his dark eyes revealing absolutely no emotion. "We had reasons."

"Well, I assume so, but I didn't even know Robert had been murdered until this minute!" Aaron heard his voice rising as if it belonged to someone else. He tried to swallow again, couldn't, and insisted, "I didn't know anything about . . . the tragedy."

Myers raised those arched black eyebrows. "You didn't know?"

"I . . . no . . . uh . . . when?"

"When what?" Myers asked.

"When was Robert murdered?"

"We believe around thirty-six hours ago."

"Oh. Well, why am I just finding out?"

Myers took on a patient tone. "Eads wasn't found until yesterday morning. You said you were out of town all day yesterday." He frowned. "But didn't you hear it on the news?"

"I didn't listen to any news. Not in the car. Not when I came home. I just went straight to bed. No television."

"I see." Myers paused, his dark gaze fixed intently on Aaron's face. Finally he asked, "You knew Robert very well, didn't you, Mr. Townsend?"

Aaron abruptly became aware of his bare feet, which seemed like blocks of ice. In his silk robe and thin silk pajama bottoms, he felt naked and vulnerable in front of these two expressionless men, particularly Hal Myers with his thin lips, deeply creased forehead, and relentless stare. The man never seemed to blink.

"Robert Eads worked for me for three years." Aaron wondered if the detectives heard the slight tremor in his voice. "He quit around a month ago."

"Why?"

"Uh . . . Robert was very ambitious. He thought he could do better elsewhere."

Myers frowned. "Townsend Realty is the biggest realty office in the city, and it's my understanding he was doing well at your firm."

"He specialized in commercial property and he was quite successful."

"Then why did he quit?"

Aaron cleared his throat. "I believe he wanted to open his own firm."

"I see." Myers made a temple of his fingers and rested his chin on it. Aaron noticed the man's wedding ring, which looked too small. He didn't know this intimidating man in front of him had not taken off the ring once in his thirty-five years of marriage. Aaron also didn't know that the detective had four children and seven grandchildren, all of whom called him Papa Bear because when he was with them, he acted like a huge, cuddly bear in the cartoons. "He didn't come from a wealthy family, did he?"

"Robert?" Aaron asked in surprise. "No. Why?"

"Well, you said he'd only worked for you for three years. He was in his twenties, so he hadn't had time to build up much savings. In fact, we've checked his bank accounts. They are surprisingly low considering the money he made with your firm. Perhaps he had some expensive habits. In any case, he couldn't have qualified for the substantial loan a new agency would have required and his family couldn't have given him the money, so it doesn't seem as if he was going to open his own business. Was he going to work for someone else?"

"Well, maybe. I really don't know." Aaron could feel perspiration on his face although the rest of his body was cold. "Detective, Robert Eads simply resigned from my firm saying he was going to open his own business. I don't think quitting Townsend Realty with so little money was a good idea, but his loss was . . ." He started to say "my gain," but that sounded awful. And suspicious. ". . . was his loss."

"But you said you thought he was going to open up his own firm."

"He said that to me one time. It stuck in my mind that he might surprise me with his talent and give me some real competition." Aaron immediately thought of how bad that sounded and went to work repairing it. "I'm joking. Not about Robert's death, of course." Oh God, he thought, feeling as if he were in quicksand. Why couldn't he say anything right? Aaron adopted a somber expression and vocal tone. "Gentlemen, it takes time to build a firm like Townsend and we have an excellent reputation. Even if Robert had the money and the talent to start his own business, he wouldn't have been a threat to me. He didn't have enough experience or contacts. He probably would have failed, which would have been sad. But he could be . . . overconfident." Aaron paused. "Of course, perhaps he didn't plan to open his own firm. He might just have been trying to impress me."

"So you really don't know what he planned to do."

"No. I was simply his employer. Nothing more. We weren't close friends."

"Really?" Myers asked slowly. "Because I've heard you *were* close friends. *Very* close."

Aaron felt as if all the air had been sucked out of him when Madeleine suddenly appeared in the living room, her face beautiful in the sunlight, her limp even more pronounced than usual, drawing the detectives' attention and obviously their compassion, her voice soft and innocent. "Hello, gentlemen. I'm Madeleine Townsend, Aaron's sister. I'll bet he didn't even offer you coffee, did he? Would anyone care for some? We have a pot of an excellent Malaysian blend."

Oh, thank you, Maddy, Aaron thought, feeling slightly dizzy. He knew she'd been listening just beyond the living room and heard, even felt, his tension. The detective called Corrigan smiled for the first time and Aaron realized he'd seen the man before, although he could not remember where. Reddish-brown curly hair, freckles, clear blue eyes . . .

"No thank you, ma'am," both detectives said.

Myers continued, "We've both drunk more than our share of coffee this morning." He smiled. "Did you know Robert Eads, Ms. Townsend?"

"Barely. He worked for my brother. I met him at an agency Christmas party and an agency picnic." She looked fondly at her brother. "Aaron gives the agency at least two parties a year. More if someone is getting married or is close to having a baby. He's very good to his employees."

"Robert quit the agency almost a month ago, but your brother says he doesn't know why."

"Well, I would have no idea," Madeleine replied casually. "I don't know much about the business, but I do know that people come and go and don't always offer explanations." She shrugged and gave the men her dazzling smile. "But why is there all this interest in Robert Eads? Has he done something wrong?"

"You don't know that he was murdered night before last?"

Madeleine's hand flew to her throat. "Oh no! How awful!"

"You didn't hear about it on the news, either?"

"I was at the hospital all day yesterday with my mother."

Corrigan finally spoke up. "They have televisions at the hospital, Ms. Townsend, and the murder topped every broadcast."

"I didn't watch television. I read." She glanced at her pale, silent brother and asked the detectives quickly, "Do you know who killed Mr. Eads?"

"No, ma'am, not yet," Myers said.

"May I ask why you're questioning Aaron about him?"

"Because Eads worked for your brother until fairly recently. We thought Mr. Townsend might know something about Robert's habits."

"Habits?" Aaron snapped in a strained voice. "What kind of habits?"

"The kind of habits that could get him killed," Myers said equably.

"Like drugs?"

"That's what I'm asking *you*," Myers returned. "You knew him. I didn't."

Aaron began to jiggle his foot. "I told you I *barely* knew him. He was just an employee. He didn't confide in me. Why are you asking about drugs? Did you find drugs in his system?"

"Actually, *you* mentioned drugs, not us. Besides, we don't have all the tests back yet," Myers said.

"Well, I don't know anything about his personal life, but I never saw any evidence that he did drugs when he was at work," Aaron said. "He was very . . . efficient."

Aaron noticed Myers relax a bit. Maybe they were satisfied and ready to leave, he thought, almost leaping from his chair to show them to the door. Then he saw Corrigan lean forward and realized the two detectives were just taking turns.

"Eads was involved with someone at your firm, wasn't he?" Jay asked. "Romantically, I mean."

"Involved? *Romantically?*" Aaron heard his voice rising and did his best to lower it. "I don't know what you mean."

"He dated Brooke Yeager for a while, didn't he?"

Jay had meant Brooke, Aaron realized. Thank God. "Oh yes," he said, forcing himself to sound offhand. "I don't meddle in my employees' private lives, but I believe someone did mention to me that Brooke and Robert were seeing each other. As long as it didn't interfere with their work, I didn't care what they did. Together, that is, although they weren't right for each other."

Aaron had no idea why he'd made that last statement except that secretly he'd always felt jealous when he saw Robert with Brooke, even though Robert had assured him the relationship was a sham. At the moment, though, his subconscious seemed to be doing his talking for him.

"You thought they weren't right for each other?" Corrigan asked. "Why?"

Both detectives were looking at him with intense interest, and even Madeleine had given him a sharp glance. Aaron scrambled for an answer. "When couples work in the same office and break up, there are bad feelings, and it makes for an uncomfortable workplace. That's all I meant."

"Oh. Then weren't you going against your own policy when you dated Judith Lambert last year?" Corrigan asked.

"Well, yes, I was. I'm afraid that was a case of my asking her to accompany me to a formal affair because I was between girlfriends. Judith took the invitation wrong, thinking it was more serious than it was. I should have stopped seeing her immediately, but I stupidly let the relationship drift for a while because she *could* be good company. When I finally ended it, she didn't take it well." He laughed far too loudly. "That's why I don't like for my employees to date. Personal experience."

"I see what you mean," Corrigan said, then abruptly added, "Since you didn't even know Robert Eads was dead, I'm sure you didn't know his body was found by Brooke Yeager."

"Oh, my!" Madeleine uttered in distress. "How . . . shocking for her! Where was the body?"

"In the alley beside her apartment building beside the

Dumpster. Actually, it was her dog who found it. Apparently it picked up Eads's scent."

"Oh dear," Madeleine went on. "Poor Brooke. She must have just been horrified!"

"Naturally she was upset, although she'd been having trouble with Eads." Corrigan addressed his comments to Madeleine. "Apparently Mr. Eads didn't take their breakup well. He kept calling her and following her, even coming to her apartment and pounding on the door, insisting on seeing her. She said she was thinking of getting a restraining order against him."

"Really?" Aaron uttered a laugh that sounded like a squawk.

Madeleine quickly broke in. "Yes, Aaron, but you've always said Brooke *could* be rather paranoid." He looked at her and blinked. He'd never said any such thing. But the detectives were looking at her, not him, and that was a blessing. "Of course, I'm sure you know all about her background—her mother's murder, her testimony that helped put her stepfather in prison, and now his escape," Madeleine continued. "And Mia's murder could only add to Brooke's emotional problems. Yes, I can definitely see Brooke cracking under the least bit of pressure, even if it was just a few calls from an ex-boyfriend."

"Cracking under pressure?" Jay asked harshly. "Are you implying that Miss Yeager killed Robert Eads because he was annoying her?"

"It sounds as if he was doing more than annoying her, but I certainly didn't mean to imply she would hurt Robert. My goodness, *no,*" Madeleine protested.

Aaron looked at Jay. Although the detective's face was expressionless, Aaron saw something in the man's eyes. Suspicion? And not of Brooke. Suddenly, Aaron felt as if he could not sit and talk to these men for one more minute without exploding with the truth about him and Robert. Aaron had no idea where the urge came from—maybe from some childish fear that used to force him always to tell authority figures the truth—but the urge was almost overpowering.

"Gentlemen, I hate to be rude, but you must know that the funeral of Mia Walters is at one o'clock. I haven't even show-ered and dressed yet. I'm afraid I have to start getting ready, and since I can't be of any help in the matter of Robert Eads . . ."

"You'd appreciate us leaving," Myers said. "Certainly, Mr. Townsend. We understand. And we thank you for your time." Aaron followed the two detectives to the door on shaking legs. Madeleine stuck close behind him, as if she thought he might swoon into her arms. He felt like a fool. Myers turned and smiled at Madeleine. "So nice to meet you, Ms. Townsend. Maybe next time we can have some of that wonderful coffee you offered us."

Next time? Aaron thought in dread.

"All you have to do is let me know about the coffee and I'll be glad to make some for you," Madeleine said smoothly. "Aaron has tons of it and it really is delicious. Good-bye, gentlemen."

As the detectives neared their car, Aaron closed the door and looked at his sister. "Well, that was bracing," he said, his voice tinny and thin.

Madeleine looked at him for a long moment, her expres-sion grim and her gaze searing. "Yes, it certainly was," she said finally, and then, "Aaron, they didn't believe a word you said. They know there was more—much more—going on between you and Robert than you're willing to admit." She paused again, her beautiful eyes narrowing slightly. "And so do I."

Outside, Hal Myers took the driver's seat and waited for Jay Corrigan to get in. When he did, Myers asked, "Well, what did you think?"

"First of all, I've known Brooke Yeager for a while now and I can tell you she isn't paranoid, even after all that's hap-pened to her."

"Interesting," Myers said. "Anything else?"

"I noticed that neither one of them claimed to even know about the murder, which I find a little coincidental." Jay stared straight ahead, a tiny crease forming between his eyebrows. "I also noticed something else." He looked at Hal. "Neither one of them asked *how* Eads had been killed."

"No, they didn't, did they?" Slowly, Hal smiled. "They told me you were good, Corrigan. I think I'm going to enjoy having you for a partner."

## 2

Brooke slipped a sleeveless black linen dress over her head, and nearly pulled a muscle reaching for the long zipper running up the back. "Perfect, at last," she breathed as the zipper finally ran up to the neckline. She rummaged through the closet until she found a waist-length white and gray jacket with short sleeves that gave the dress the proper air of formality. She was just struggling to fasten a dainty freshwater-pearl necklace when someone knocked on her door.

Elise stiffened and barked at the door, a new trait she'd developed since all the trouble had begun and she'd sensed Brooke's tension. No wonder, Brooke thought. A stranger breaking in to leave a note, Robert pounding on the door, finding a corpse by the Dumpster . . . The already timid dog was probably on the verge of a nervous breakdown.

Brooke went to the door but made no move to open it. "Who is it?" she called.

"Vincent."

"Vincent?"

"Vincent Lockhart, ma'am."

Brooke opened the door, smiling. "You didn't have to give your last name."

"I'm not sure about that. You acted like you'd never heard of me before."

He wore a navy blue suit, which somehow made his eyes

look even greener. "Why are you all dressed up?" Brooke asked.

"Because I'm going to Mia's funeral with you. I don't think you should go alone." He paused. "You were going alone, weren't you?"

"Well, with my police escort, but not a friend."

"Then here's a friend at your service."

Abruptly, Brooke's smile faded. "Your father made you do this, didn't he?"

"No, Miss Yeager, it was *completely* my idea."

Brooke's smile returned. "Well, how kind of you."

"I have been known to be capable of kindness upon occasion."

"Oh, I'm sure you have. And I really didn't want to go alone, especially under the circumstances. Stacy would have gone with me, of course, but she has to work today. I really can't thank you enough."

"Yes, you can."

"How?"

"By letting me in the door."

"Good heavens! I guess that shows the state of my nerves today. Come in, please."

He stepped in and Elise trotted over to him, holding up her narrow head to be petted. She never did that with Robert, Brooke thought. And Robert never stooped down, took her face in his hands, and told her what a beautiful girl she was. Elise wagged her tail so ecstatically it was almost a blur.

"You said you were a dog lover."

"I sure am," Vincent said. "At home in Monterey I have an Irish setter named Rusty and a black long-haired mixed-breed named Lady Blackwell." He sighed. "I miss them."

"Are they in a kennel?"

"No, they're with friends who have children. The dogs love the kids so much, they probably don't even want me to come home."

"I doubt that," Brooke said. "*You're* their master."

" 'Fraid not. They are *my* master and mistress. They just

let me hang around the house as long as I don't get in their way."

"Gee, I wonder how they got so spoiled?"

"No idea," Vincent laughed. Then he ran his gaze over her. "You look very nice."

"Thank you. But I'd give anything not to be going to this particular occasion. Mia was so young, so ebullient, so bright. Dying young is a tragedy, but knowing she died in *my* place is almost more than I can bear. Zach was aiming for me, Vincent, not for poor Mia."

Vincent stepped forward and almost tentatively put his arms around Brooke. She stood stiff and embarrassed for a moment, then relaxed, moved closer to him, and laid her head on his chest. "I'm not going to cry on your suit," she said, as tears began to spill down her chest.

"Do you want me to take it off?"

Brooke giggled, crying at the same time. "I don't think that will be necessary. I'll just be careful."

His arms tightened. "Don't be careful. Cry all over it if you want to. It's not my best suit."

"I'm glad to hear that, because you already have tears on your shoulder. And mascara, too, I think. I'm sorry."

"You should be," he said gently, putting his hand under her chin and tilting back her head. "I think you're awful."

His kiss was slow and soft, and Brooke didn't want it to ever end. Her arms twined around his neck and her hand ran through his curly, amazingly soft black hair at the base of his neck. He smelled so good—fresh like a clean mountain morning—and his body felt strong and powerful, as if he could protect her from anything. The kiss deepened and Brooke sighed without really sighing, feeling as if she wanted to melt right into him. Her dress was probably getting wrinkled, her makeup smeared, but she didn't want to let go of him. Not ever.

Then Elise barked sharply. They both jumped and the dog barked again. Slowly they pulled apart and looked at her, standing on a chair, glaring at them as if they were two teenagers locked in a forbidden embrace. "Is she going to attack us?" Vincent murmured, still kissing Brooke along the forehead.

"No. She's upset because she's jealous."

"She doesn't want anyone kissing her mother?"

"No. She doesn't want her mother kissing *you*. I think she's decided she's in love with you."

"The curse of my fatal charm," Vincent muttered, then placed his lips on Brooke's again. But she stepped back. "Vincent, we can't do this."

"Because of Elise?"

"Because we're going to the funeral of my friend who died in my place. I have no right to be . . . to be . . ."

"Happy?"

"Yes, happy," she said meekly, then burst out, "Yes, happy. Attracted. Aroused. *Alive!*"

"You have every right to be alive," Vincent said quietly.

"Not in Mia's place. Not because the sweet young thing was trying to look like me and it was dark and I have a step-father who wants to murder me!"

Vincent stepped closer to her but made no move to hold her. He only gazed into her eyes, his own so mesmerizing she couldn't look away. "The key word in what you just said is 'stepfather.' *You* didn't do anything to Mia or to your mother. Zachary Tavell did. He's the one who bears the guilt, Brooke, not you."

Brooke finally managed to shut her eyes, causing more tears to roll down her face. "Intellectually I know that. But emotionally I don't. I couldn't help Mom, but if Zach had gotten me, too, then—"

"Then *Mia* would be alive now. Good God, Brooke, is that what you've been torturing yourself with?"

"It's true."

"It's a possibility. That's all. Hell, if Mia hadn't been killed that night, maybe she would have stepped in front of a bus the next day or crashed in a plane the next week. Maybe it was her time to die."

"Her time to die? Vincent, I've been around you long enough to know you're not a man of faith, someone who believes everything happens because it's predestined. You don't believe all those people you write about were predestined to be viciously murdered. You believe they were in the wrong place at the wrong time, or they met the wrong person. And for Mia, *I* was the wrong person."

"Brooke, stop it," Vincent said quietly. "Just stop it. You do not know what I believe about fate versus coincidence. You're attributing your own beliefs to me, and I'm sorry to say this, but your beliefs are more than a little skewed by all that's happened to you in your short life."

"Well, thank you very much for telling me I'm crazy!"

"I didn't say anything about you being crazy." Vincent closed his eyes, drew a deep breath, then took a small step toward her. "You're not crazy, but you've gotten the idea that you're a magnet for misfortune. It's why a beautiful, intelligent, warm, basically joyous woman has so few friends, has dated such a little bit, and when she does settles for someone like Robert, who didn't give a damn about you except as a mask for someone he *did* love. You think you don't deserve anything good in life and if something good does come your way, you'd better shun it before you inadvertently destroy it."

Brooke raised a defiant face to him. "Well, aren't you just full of psychological insight today!"

"As a matter of fact, I am." Brooke glared at him. "Brooke, baby—"

"Do not *ever* call me baby. Or babe. Or any of those other stupid endearments you use on your adoring California airheads!"

Vincent rolled his eyes. "Okay, Miss Yeager, I'll watch my language from now on. And may I say that not every woman in California is an airhead. Talk about stereotyping!"

Brooke breathed heavily for a moment, looking away from him. Finally she said, "You're right. I *was* stereotyping."

"Is that all I was right about?"

She looked away again, wiped a hand over one damp, streaked cheek, then glanced at Elise, who sat quietly in the chair quivering with nerves over the controversy playing out in front of her. Elise. Brooke loved Elise. But who else had she loved in the last few years? She counted. Of course, Grossmutter. And the memory of her parents. And she cared for Stacy and Jay. And . . . and . . . and no one except for Mia, whom she barely knew.

Reluctantly, she said, "Maybe you weren't *entirely* wrong."

"Under the circumstances, I'll take that as a ringing endorsement of my theory."

"I don't know that you should go *that* far."

"Okay. An endorsement that doesn't ring true?"

Brooke couldn't help relaxing a bit. "A *partial* endorsement that doesn't ring true."

"Well, that's better than nothing."

"It's a helluva lot, seeing as you just showed up here uninvited in your designer suit spouting theories about how I think I'm a disaster magnet."

Vincent grinned. "Yeah, I guess it is. I'll accept it as a compliment." He looked at her seriously for a moment. "Do you want me to leave so you can go to the funeral by yourself?"

She pretended to think it over. "No, I guess not. I mean, you're already dressed up and everything."

"And so are you, although at the risk of offending you again, I'd suggest you do something about your face. The smeared mascara is giving you a Goth look that isn't really your style."

"Oh God!" Brooke exclaimed, covering her face and rushing to the mirror. Vincent was right. Her eye makeup had not only smudged into big circles around her eyes, but her mascara had left long, bizarre streaks down her face. She went to the bathroom and began wiping off all her makeup. "This shouldn't take long," she called. "I'll just do a little touching up. . . ."

"I'll read this copy of *Vogue* while you're working. I should have just enough time to finish it."

Ten minutes later Brooke emerged from the bathroom looking fresh-faced, her subtle makeup as expertly applied as it had been when Vincent arrived. "Better?" she asked.

"Beautiful," he said, laying down his magazine and scooting Elise off his lap. "But I could use a lint brush."

The blond dog had left her mark on his navy blue suit. Brooke quickly found the brush, and while he worked at removing the hair, Brooke inserted her pearl earrings. *The same earrings I wore the night Mia was killed,* she thought, considering changing them for another pair, then remembering how much Mia had liked their slight dangle. "I've dropped hints to my family like crazy, but if no one gets me a pair like that for Christmas, I'm getting them for myself. If it's all right with you, that is," Mia had said. "I'd be flattered," Brooke had returned sincerely.

Her eyes started to fill with tears again and she quickly blinked them away. She and Vincent certainly didn't have time for her to complete another makeup job if they were going to make the funeral on time.

Mia's parents had picked their tiny Methodist church for the ceremony rather than a mortuary. As Vincent looked for a parking place, Brooke noticed that most of the group trailing into the church looked grief-stricken. Mia had obviously been loved. The people were also dressed simply, so plainly that Brooke guessed they were wearing their Sunday best, which was subdued. Mia had not come from a prosperous or stylish family. Brooke remembered when she'd first started at the agency and her clothes had looked cheap, almost frumpy. After two weeks, she'd worn an outfit that looked amazingly like Brooke's. After that, her emulation of Brooke's style had begun, growing over her two-month employment. *Growing until it got her killed,* Brooke thought with a pang.

"Are you all right?" Vincent asked.

"Sure." She looked around and noticed that they'd parked. "You won't mind if I cry a little during the service, will you?"

Vincent reached over, took her hand, and brought it to his lips. "Cry all you want."

"Even if my makeup smears?"

"This isn't a fashion show, Brooke. And who gives a damn what I think, anyway?"

I do, she thought, startled. I care a lot.

"Let's go," he said, nearly jumping out of the car to rush around and open her door. "The service is supposed to start in five minutes."

They hurried down the street and up the steps into the cool dimness of the church. Someone was playing "Amazing Grace" on the organ. Brooke caught a glimpse of the oak coffin with a blanket of pink carnations beneath the pulpit. Mia hated pink, she thought. Didn't her own family know that?

A man Brooke barely saw stepped up, handed her and Vincent each a program, and said, "Welcome. The family appreciates your attendance." He pointed to a gilt-edged book on a wooden stand. "Would you sign the guest register, please?"

As Brooke stepped forward to sign the guest book, she noticed a girl of around sixteen hovering near the stand. She was extremely slender and had long blond hair and cornflower blue eyes. She looked enough like Mia to be her sister. The girl smiled at Brooke, then looked down and watched her sign her name. Abruptly the girl vanished down the hall and into one of the back rooms.

"Someone you know?" Vincent asked softly.

"No, but someone who wanted to know who I was. The way she watched me sign my name . . ."

Vincent raised his eyebrows. "Yes?"

"Oh, I don't know. It just seemed odd. She looked so much like Mia. Or me at that age." Brooke shook her head. "Never mind. I'm just edgy."

Vincent scribbled his name, took Brooke's elbow in his hand, and began to lead her into the main room. That's when the girl appeared again, carrying a large vase of white roses. She stopped in front of Brooke. "You *are* Brooke Yeager, aren't you?" she asked in a young, innocent voice.

Brooke nodded and the girl handed her the vase of roses. "This was delivered about an hour ago. The deliveryman said you wanted to carry them in yourself and place them at the head of the coffin and that he wanted *me* to give them to you." She smiled. "They're very pretty, Miss Yeager."

"Yes, they are," Brooke said vaguely, an uncomfortable tickle of fear touching her neck. "But I didn't—"

"There was a card with them," the girl interrupted. "I took it loose from the flowers so you could look at it first. I didn't read it, though, honest." She shyly held out a small envelope, which Vincent took. Then he looked at Brooke.

"Read it," she said flatly.

Vincent removed the card from the envelope and glanced over it, his expression hardening. "I think we should leave now."

"Just read it, dammit." The young girl's eyes widened and Brooke felt a grim dread flowing through her like a poisonous creeping vine.

Vincent paused, then read softly: " 'Dear Mia, Thanks to you, I have kept myself from the paths of the destroyer. Love, Brooke.' "

Everyone turned to look when Brooke dropped the vase of beautiful white roses with a loud crash and ran from the church.

# fourteen

## 1

"It's biblical," Brooke said.

Jay Corrigan and Hal Myers stood in front of her as she sat rigidly in a chair, clutching the arms. She hadn't stopped shaking since she'd fled from the church, Vincent chasing her, the police surveillance team following them back to Brooke's apartment, then calling Myers and Corrigan.

"What's biblical, Brooke?" Jay asked.

"The message on the card. 'Thanks to you, I have kept myself from the paths of the destroyer.' It's biblical."

" 'Thanks to you'?" Jay asked. "That doesn't sound like the Bible to me."

Brooke rose on trembling legs, walked to the bookshelf, and pulled out the Yeager family Bible. "Grossmutter is very religious. She used to read the Bible to me. Frankly, I was bored to tears, but I remember parts. Unfortunately, not accurately. If you'll just let me look, I'm sure I can find it."

"Look all you want," Vincent said, guiding her back to

the chair. "But sit down before you fall down. You're as pale as a ghost. Do you want something to drink?"

"Something cold. Anything. Look in the refrigerator," Brooke mumbled distractedly as she flipped through the large, old Bible that had been in the family for generations. "Certainly it's not in Genesis. Or Revelation."

"How about the New Testament?" Jay asked, wishing he'd paid more attention in Sunday school instead of concentrating on trying to be the class clown to impress an ugly, haughty little girl named Patty Lou. "Could it be in there?"

Brooke shook her head. "No. Not the New Testament. I don't know how I remember that, but . . ." She trailed off, still furiously flipping through the book as Vincent brought her a glass of iced tea. She sipped it absently, grimaced, and asked him if he'd added sugar to already-sugared tea, to which he admitted. He was on his way back to the kitchen for a fresh glass when Brooke cried, "Here it is!"

Everyone stiffened, as if she'd just happened on something potentially dangerous. "It's Psalms 17:4: 'I have kept myself from the paths of the destroyer.' Grossmutter had it marked, maybe because of Zach."

The three men stared at her.

"Is that it?" Jay asked, looking deflated. "Just that one line?"

"Yes. Why do you look so disappointed?"

"I just thought the quote might give us more of a clue."

"A clue about what?" Brooke asked.

"About Zach's intentions."

"You mean a guide about what he intends to do to me next?"

"No, I . . ." Jay blushed and Hal stepped in.

"Miss Yeager, was Zach Tavell a religious man?"

"Religious? He murdered my mother," Brooke said incredulously.

"Many religious people—not truly religious, of course, fanatics—feel they're committing crimes in the name of God. Following God's will. Was Tavell that type?"

"Absolutely not. In fact, he didn't even like for my mother to take me to church after their first few weeks of marriage. Sometimes he let my grandmother take me, but only about once a month."

"That was fifteen years ago," Myers said mildly. "It's not uncommon for prisoners to 'find the Lord,' as they put it. They repent for what they've done to get themselves thrown in prison and become extremely religious. It could be that Tavell was that type. He might have been reading the Bible all these years."

"He could have," Brooke said bitterly. "But what does that have to do with anything? This quote certainly wasn't written to give me comfort. It was written to make me feel guilty."

Vincent nodded. "I have to agree, Detective Myers."

"Of course it was," Myers said. "But if Tavell wasn't religious, he had to do a lot of reading to find the perfect quote for the occasion."

"Which proves exactly what?" Brooke demanded.

"Maybe that he's had some kind of breakdown. Or he means to torture you and he's been planning it for quite a while."

"I'd say it was the latter," Brooke said dourly. "If he had a breakdown, it seems it would have been years ago when he murdered my mother. Or before that. Even though I was a child, I knew there was something wrong with him. I could tell my grandmother did, too. She was extremely uneasy around him. Only Mom seemed to think he was great. At least at the time she married him. After the first year, even I could tell she was having second thoughts."

"Well, they tried the insanity plea at his trial, but it didn't work," Myers said. "No ethical psychiatrist was willing to testify that Tavell didn't know right from wrong."

"Oh, he knew right from wrong all right," Brooke snapped. "He knew killing Mom was wrong. He never even claimed that it wasn't."

"I guess you have to give him some credit for that," Jay said before Brooke shot him a withering look.

Myers stepped in. "I think we've learned all we can from Miss Yeager, Corrigan. We need to get back to the church and find out more about who left those flowers."

Brooke nodded. "Flowers left specifically for me with a teenage girl."

"You said she also looked like Mia," Jay said.

"And that is possibly dangerous for her." Fear replaced disgust in Brooke's expression. "Find her quickly and protect her."

"Count on it, Brooke," Jay said. "Stacy will be home in a couple of hours. She'll come over. You don't need to be alone this afternoon."

"She won't be alone," Vincent said. "I'll see to it."

After the detectives left, Vincent closed the Bible, lifted it from Brooke's lap, and returned it to the bookshelf. "Can I get you something besides that tea?"

"How about a bottle of Valium?"

"Sorry. I don't have one with me today."

"No beer, either?"

Vincent looked at her, then at Elise, and smiled. "You don't need tranquilizers or alcohol. You need fresh air and some fun."

"Fun? *Today*?"

"Yes, Brooke, it *is* possible to have fun today. I'm going home, check on Dad, and change clothes. In the meantime, you leave a note for Stacy telling her you're with me and safe, get out of that nice dress and into jeans, preferably tight ones, and find a leash for young Elise over there. The three of us are going to have an adventure." He opened the door to her apartment. "Lock this as soon as I leave. I'll be back in forty-five minutes."

"Okay, but I'd still like to know"—the door shut—"where we're going."

Brooke locked the door and pushed the dead bolt into place. Then she turned to Elise. "I don't want to go anywhere, but he seems to be determined, so I guess we'd better suit up for whatever he has planned. I can't remember where I put your leash this morning—"

In a flash, the dog scrambled into a corner, pawed through her wicker basket of toys, and triumphantly pulled out the leash. "Well, aren't you the sneaky one? Is that where you hide the thing when it's raining and you don't want to go outside?" Elise looked up at her like the most innocent dog in the world. "Well, the jig's up. Now you'll have to find a new hiding place."

Almost an hour later, someone tapped on Brooke's door. "It's me," Vincent said.

Brooke opened the door, holding up her arm and taking a long look at her watch. "You are eight minutes late."

"Traffic."

"That's what they all say."

"All of whom?"

"All men who are always late. Elise and I were ready to go without you."

"You don't even know where we're going," Vincent said.

"We have our own favorite spots. However, since you *finally* showed up, I guess we'll give you another chance."

Vincent stepped into the apartment, eyeing her low-rise jeans and scoop-necked turquoise top. She'd even added a pair of chandelier earrings, supposedly very hip these days with informal wear.

"You look great."

"Thanks. You don't look so bad yourself. Please tell me you didn't pick out a particularly snug black T-shirt to show off your muscles."

"Oh, do they show?" Vincent asked innocently.

Brooke quirked an eyebrow at him. "As if you didn't know you look all tan and ripply."

"Ripply," Vincent repeated. "I like that, although it isn't really a word."

"Excuse me. You're rippling with muscles that would set any girl's heart aflutter."

"It was really Elise's heart I was after." Vincent grinned.

"Well, judging by the way she's panting, I'd say you've won it." Brooke picked up her purse and Elise's leash. "All right, Mr. Lockhart. You promised to show us some fun. Let's see how well you do."

When they walked out of the building and Brooke saw Vincent's silver Mercedes convertible, she suddenly thought of the dog. "There's no place for Elise to sit."

"How about on your lap?"

Brooke frowned. "You know how timid she is and she's never been in a convertible before. Vincent, riding in this car might just totally freak her out."

Five minutes later, as they spun east along Kanawha Boulevard, Elise sat straight and tall on Brooke's lap, her ears flapping, her tongue lolling, a look Brooke interpreted as pure rapture on her slim face. "Yeah, she's freaked out all right," Vincent drawled. "You'll probably never get her in a car again."

"You mean I'll never get her in *my* car again. She's going to insist I buy one like yours, and I'm afraid it's out of my price range."

"Maybe we could arrange a couple more excursions for her," Vincent said. "That is, if you don't think they'll make her too nervous."

Holding tightly to the dog, Brooke closed her eyes, leaned back her head, and let her long blond hair blow wildly in the wind. Vincent's CD player blasted "Livin' on a Prayer" by Bon Jovi—"a favorite from my misspent youth," he'd told her—and before long she found herself singing along with Jon and wishing she could play the guitar like Richie Sambora.

Vincent looked over at her. "May I ask what's responsible for your remarkable change in mood in the last hour?"

"Will power. I decided I could sit in the apartment, cry over Mia, and let fear for my own well-being freeze me into a living death, or I could just let go. After all, it was my decision to stay in Charleston. I couldn't expect Zach to give up on me after two thwarted attempts. He's going to keep after me." She looked back at Vincent. "But he's not going to get me, physically *or* emotionally."

Vincent gave her a small, tight smile. "I'd like to say,

'Good for you, Brooke,' and mean it, but I still think you're taking an unnecessary risk. I'm afraid you're one of those people who think they're invincible."

"I know quite well I'm not invincible, but I'm not a coward, either." Brooke paused. "And I am *not* leaving Grossmutter, Vincent, because I know in my bones she won't be alive this time next week. She has spent most of her life taking care of me. I'm not going to abandon her to die alone. Now, we're going to change the subject."

"Yes, *ma'am*," Vincent said, although the troubled look didn't leave his eyes. "Did you have a particular subject in mind?"

"The capitol building," Brooke returned as the sun bounced off the dazzling gold-leaf dome. "I'll give you a dollar if you can tell me exactly how high it is."

Vincent frowned, ran his gaze up and down the dome, tapped his fingers on the steering wheel, sucked his lower lip between his teeth, and just when Brooke was about to burst into a triumphant laugh, shouted, "It's two hundred and ninety-three feet tall, five feet higher than the United States Capitol dome!"

"Oh, darn!" she cried. "Why did you lead me on so long?"

"Because you looked so smug. Where's my dollar?"

"I'll give it to you later."

"But I need it now. We're just about out of gas."

"And you were planning to fill up on a *dollar*?"

"No. I lied."

"Figures. Where are we going, anyway?"

"It's a surprise."

They began climbing a hill, the powerful engine of the Mercedes purring with confidence, Vincent smiling, Brooke watching Elise look around in fascination. They came to a fork in the road and Vincent turned right. Onward they climbed until at last they came to Coonskin Park.

"I haven't been here for over ten years," Vincent said.

"Then you'll be surprised at some of the changes they've made."

"Including all those 'Dogs on Leashes' signs?"

"I don't remember quite so many of them from when my grandmother used to bring me up here, but then I didn't have a dog. It was just the two of us, rattling up here in her ancient Volkswagen. I always wanted to listen to the radio, but she insisted we sing German songs she'd learned when she was a kid." Brooke looked at Vincent. "They were awful and so was Grossmutter's voice. I was always *so* relieved when we finally reached the 'family center' and got out of the car."

He laughed. "My family took a few expeditions up this way, too. Dad always had to be in command. Mom would say, 'Oh, Sam, let's stop here for a family picture!' and he'd say, 'I know a better spot,' which of course he never found. After I hit fourteen, coming up here with my parents was one of the most embarrassing things in the world to me. They thought I should go with the other 'children' for a pleasant little hike, and I wanted to join some kind of tough gang and really explore the place and do something daring."

"I didn't know they had tough gangs up here," Brooke said.

"Oh, they probably didn't. They were a figment of my already overproductive imagination, but I was sure they existed and as soon as they saw me standing alone, looking all cool and tough like Clint Eastwood in those Italian Westerns, they'd appear." He threw her an abashed smile. "Stupid, wasn't I?"

"Creative, with a strong desire to be as strong and commanding as you imagined your father to be."

"Imagined?"

"We all have weak points, Vincent. Even Sam Lockhart."

"Yeah? Well, they didn't show. Not back then, at least."

They drove past a meandering stream with arched wooden bridges and scenic spots where cars were pulled over, some adult taking photographs of a child playing on a slope. Finally, Vincent slowed down. "Ah, the famous 'family center' is in view! And it looks a helluva lot more impressive than it used to."

"Watch your language in front of Elise," Brooke said. "Let's look at the ducks on the pond."

They parked in front of a large log building in which Brooke knew there was a restaurant and led Elise to the pond. White and brown ducks floated calmly on the sparkling water. Elise barked at them, whether as a threat or just as a hello Brooke didn't know, but the ducks ignored her. "No respect," Brooke said.

"They see that she's on a leash."

"They probably also know that she doesn't like to get her paws wet. Notice how she stands at the very edge of the water. Not one toe actually goes in."

They walked around the pond, looking at the tennis courts, beyond to the lush golf course, and at all the colorful playground equipment placed nearby. Elise stood mesmerized, watching a boy on a skateboard do a heart-stopping flip on the ramp.

"Did I tell you how terrific you look today?" Vincent asked.

"Yes, but I'm wearing jeans and a T-shirt. How terrific could I possibly look? Besides, I think stress has caused a zit on my chin."

Vincent took her chin in his hand and tilted it up toward him. "I'm looking at you wearing barely any makeup in harsh sunlight and I can't see one flaw." He paused. "Except a few freckles across that perfect nose, and they aren't flaws. They're cute."

Brooke blushed, which made her furious with herself. "Are all California guys ladies' men? Do you get a seduction manual when you cross the state line?"

"No," Vincent said solemnly. "Not until you reach the extreme West Coast and pay ten dollars for your official playboy badge."

Brooke gave him a light shove, laughing. The sun, the gentle warmth of the afternoon, the laughter of children and adults, the sight of Elise galloping along in spite of her leash, the presence of Vincent Lockhart—Vincent Lockhart telling her she looked terrific. All of it almost wiped out the horror of receiving the vase of white roses at Mia's funeral. Almost.

Vincent looked up at an airplane soaring above them, its

silver body gleaming in the sun. "Another jet leaves Yeager Airport," he said. Then he frowned. "*Yeager* Airport, named after General Charles Yeager, first man to fly faster than the speed of sound. No relation to you, I suppose."

"Third cousin."

"No way!"

"Yes, way."

"Have you ever met him?"

"Of course, Vincent."

"What's he like?"

"Confident."

"No kidding," Vincent said. "Wow. If I'd known you were Chuck Yeager's cousin . . ."

"Yes?"

"I would have been a whole lot nicer to you the day I met you."

"When you didn't want your father to let me into the house?"

"A lapse in judgment on my part."

"I'll say. A *major* lapse."

"Major. General. What's the difference? I apologize." Vincent looked up at the disappearing plane. "Yeager Airport is on the next hill. Would you mind if we took a jaunt over to watch a few planes take off?"

"Don't tell me—you wanted to be a jet pilot when you were young."

"Exactly. How did you know?"

"You're the type."

"And what type is that?"

"A closet thrill seeker," Brooke laughed.

"Come on, Brooke. Maybe General Yeager will just happen to be around."

"You know we're probably wearing out those poor surveillance cops who've been assigned to follow us everywhere."

"Nonsense. I'm sure they're having a ball."

"Whatever you say." Brooke tugged on Elise's leash. "C'mon, girl. We're off on another adventure."

# 2

"Vincent, I'm really not very hungry," Brooke protested as Vincent ordered the giant barrel at Kentucky Fried Chicken.

"You didn't eat any lunch and I'll bet you didn't eat breakfast, either."

"No, I didn't, but still—"

"A large container of coleslaw," he went on to the girl behind the counter, "six orders of French fries, at least twenty hush puppies, two orders of hot wings . . ."

Brooke looked outside at Elise sitting on the lap of one of the surveillance cops. Her front paws were firmly planted on the dashboard, her gaze fixed on Brooke, who'd placed herself in full view of the dog. Elise looked only slightly anxious. The cop whose lap she sat on looked intensely annoyed. The one behind the wheel was laughing.

"Vincent, we really shouldn't have pushed Elise off on that guy. His clothes are going to be covered with hair."

"And one pecan pie and one cheesecake," Vincent ended.

The girl behind the counter smiled. "One piece each, sir?"

"A whole pecan pie and a whole cheesecake. And lots of strawberry syrup for the cheesecake." He turned to Brooke. "Can you think of anything else?"

"Is this dinner for two or are we feeding a third-world country?"

He turned back to the girl at the counter. "She's thin, but believe me, she could eat a horse."

The girl smiled uncertainly at Brooke and turned away, handing the order sheet into the kitchen. Brooke glared at Vincent. "She's going to think most of that is for me."

"We'll give some to Elise."

"Either you're crazy or you're planning something I don't know about."

"You have about twenty minutes until we get back to your place. Then you can decide."

Brooke turned away, self-conscious, but admitting to herself she was famished. Vincent was right—she hadn't eaten a bite all day. It was now almost seven in the evening and Brooke could feel that at any moment her stomach was going to let out a ferocious growl.

Twenty minutes later they climbed out of Vincent's car, each carrying bags of food, Brooke leading Elise, who seemed to have a new spring in her step after her wonderful day.

As soon as they entered the lobby, Harry Dormer descended upon them. "Hey, whatever you got in those bags smells great! Havin' a party? Me and Eunice are free tonight, no big plans."

"We're not having a party," Vincent said pleasantly. "We're just hungry."

"Damn, you must be! Looks like you got enough stuff for ten people in there. Do I smell chicken? Kentucky Fried, I bet. I *love* Kentucky Fried chicken!"

He stood by, throwing them his most charming smile, which wasn't saying much, but each politely ignored him. "Did anyone stop by to see me today, Harry?" Brooke asked.

Seeing that he wasn't going to be invited to dinner, Harry immediately turned surly. "Wouldn't know. I'm *not* the doorman. I have important stuff to do all day besides watch who comes and goes."

"I understand," Brooke said, pretending not to notice his sulky look. "How's Eunice today?"

"Same as usual, I guess." He gave the bags of food one last longing glance. "Guess I better go give her an insulin shot. Looks like after all these years, she could manage it herself."

"She probably just feels more confident with you giving it to her," Vincent said. "Steady hands, unflinching in the sight of blood. You know how women admire that kind of thing."

"Yeah," Harry agreed, somewhat appeased and only a bit suspicious that Vincent was patronizing him. "She can't get along without me, but she can be a real millstone around your throat."

"Neck," Vincent said.

Harry's eyes narrowed. "What?"

"A millstone around your neck. That's the saying."

Harry shrugged. "I don't fool around learning literary sayings," he said dismissively. "Well, have a good time with *all* that food."

"We will," Vincent assured him cheerfully.

"He's going to be seething all evening," Brooke muttered as they got in the elevator.

"He probably is anyway. I get the feeling Harry's not too happy with his life."

"Eunice thinks he has a mistress."

Vincent burst out laughing. "One who looks like Catherine Zeta-Jones and has the mind of Einstein, no doubt. Eunice doesn't know how lucky she is Harry doesn't run off with this dream woman."

"I don't know how accurate the word 'lucky' is."

They stepped off on the third floor and walked down the hall. As they passed Stacy and Jay's door, Vincent kicked it lightly twice, his arms full of food, and yelled, "Dinner's here!"

Immediately the door flew open and Jay stood there, grinning. "Thought we'd starve to death before you got here."

"What's going on?" Brooke asked.

"When we left the airport and you went in the hospital to see your grandmother, I called Jay and asked if he and Stacy were up for a real Saturday night blowout with a couple of wild spirits like us."

"And it took me about two seconds to say yes," Jay laughed. "Hey, Stace, they're here! Bring the margaritas." He looked at Brooke. "She made a whole pitcher."

A party, Brooke thought, touched. Vincent was determined to entertain her all day to keep her mind off the fright she'd suffered at Mia's funeral. It was sweet. It was romantic. It was scary.

Ten minutes later Brooke and Stacy were busy unpacking what seemed like an endless amount of food and putting it on plates while the men watched a cop show in the living room, each already holding a margarita. "I had no idea Vincent was arranging this," Brooke said to Stacy.

Stacy grinned, adding a hot wing to what she'd deemed would be Jay's plate. "I think he's smitten, Brooke."

"That's silly. He's only known me a couple of days."

"Jay and I fell for each other in about twenty-four hours. We had a date, stayed up all night talking, called each other back and forth throughout the next day, and by that evening, my fate was sealed. I knew I'd be Mrs. Jay Corrigan within the next month, and I was right."

"You're impulsive, though," Brooke said. "I'm not."

"Then maybe you should loosen up a little bit," Stacy said, handing her a margarita with one hand and picking up Jay's plate with the other. "Virtue is *not* its own reward, no matter what they say."

"Stacy, I just *met* him! Besides, I thought you were suspicious of him."

"I changed my mind when he brought us dinner. Besides, he's got a cool car."

"You are *so* deep."

"You have no idea," Stacy said, sounding a tad serious in spite of her grin. "Honestly, maybe he isn't such a bad guy to have a fling with, especially after Robert. But I'd still watch myself with him, Brooke. He's extremely attentive for a guy who's just met you, coincidentally on the day when you were shot at."

"You're not saying you think he tried to kill me!"

"No, I don't think he tried to kill you." Stacy paused. "I'd just watch myself around him, if I were you. He's damned attractive and successful and charming—"

"So what's he doing hanging around me?"

Stacy rolled her eyes. "Are you trying to pick a fight?"

"No, but you just seem so amazed that he's 'attentive' to me, as you put it."

"I'm not amazed. You're a beautiful woman. It's just that he writes about famous murder cases. 'The Rose Murder' wasn't exactly on the level of the O. J. Simpson case, but now that Zach Tavell is out and apparently after you, your appeal for Mr. True Crime Writer out there might have grown." Stacy closed her eyes. "I'm sorry. I'm saying this all wrong. It's coming out like an insult, and I certainly didn't mean it that way. I'm just telling you—"

"To watch myself around him. You already said that."

"I wouldn't want you to get your heart broken, Brooke."

"I won't." Brooke lifted her chin slightly and said with spirit, "I'm not even all that attracted to him. He's simply a nice change after Robert. He's lively and fun. And like you said, he's got a cool car."

Stacy laughed. "That's a girl! Just have a good time with him. And when he goes back to California—"

"I'll look for an equally attractive, successful, charming man. They're all over the place."

"They *are,* if you'd just stop being such a recluse. After all, I met one." Stacy smiled at her affectionately. "Never mind me, kiddo. I just want the best for you. And maybe this guy is as sincere as he seems to be. I certainly hope so. A romance between you two would be fantastic, just what you deserve."

Brooke couldn't remember a time when her apartment had been filled with so much noise and gaiety. Ever since she'd moved in, she'd lived quietly. Although she'd dated some, Stacy and Jay had never joined her and a boyfriend for an evening.

Elise had been given so many scraps of chicken, she'd eaten herself into a stupor and fallen asleep in her doggie bed after her wildly adventurous day. She kicked and whined a few times in her sleep. "She's dreaming of chasing rabbits," Jay said with assurance.

"Why do people always say when dogs make noise in their sleep they're dreaming of chasing rabbits?" Brooke asked. "I don't think she's ever seen a rabbit in her life."

"It's genetic memory," Vincent said in mock seriousness. "She had an ancestor who saw a rabbit. The vision was so terrifying, it passed through generations to Elise."

"You've had too many margaritas," Brooke laughed. "Jay, he's cut off."

"Nonsense. We have enough tequila and mix for another pitcher."

"Oh, lord," Brooke moaned. "Do you know what we're all going to feel like tomorrow?"

"Better than you did this morning," Stacy said. "I heard about what happened at the funeral."

"Stace," Jay said reprovingly.

"Well, not talking about it isn't going to make her forget it. Why don't you tell her what you found out today?"

Jay looked reluctant, but Brooke pressed him. "Jay, please. I won't let it get to me; I promise."

Jay took a deep breath. "Okay. I understand you not wanting to be kept in the dark. I'm afraid we didn't find out much and with Myers on the case, you know it's not for lack of trying. The vase of flowers came from City Floral. Different floral shop than the flower you got at the Lockhart house, but the same MO. Someone called in and ordered the flowers using a credit card. Not the same number, obviously, since the card used before has been canceled. The person who took the order was an older woman who unfortunately doesn't hear too well. She wasn't sure if the voice was a high-pitched man's, or a low-pitched woman's."

"Great," Brooke said in disappointment.

"The woman said she did think it was odd that the caller specified a vase of white roses, not a funeral wreath, and that the vase be delivered to and left in the minister's office, not put out with the rest of the flowers around Mia's casket."

"What about the teenager who brought the flowers to Brooke?" Vincent asked.

Jay shrugged. "We don't know a thing about her. We checked with everyone who attended the funeral. No one claimed to have brought a girl of that age and description with them. The minister didn't even see her. His wife did, but she said she was so busy greeting people and getting them seated that she didn't pay much attention to the girl except to notice how pretty she was. She didn't ask her name."

"Did you talk to Mia's parents?" Brooke asked. know if she was a friend of Mia's?" they

"The parents couldn't help, either. You know th, still lived at home, yet after we gave them a description, ia claimed they'd never seen the girl and they didn't notice, at the funeral."

"So she was sent there specifically to give those flowers to me," Brooke said vaguely, then added, "I have to speak o Mia's parents after that awful scene I made. It was so disrespectful."

"They were already seated in the main part of the church and you were in the entrance," Jay told her. "They said they heard some kind of noise, but with the organ playing and the murmur of people behind them, they didn't really think much about it. They did wonder why you weren't there. Apparently Mia had talked a lot about you."

"I was supposed to have dinner at their house this weekend. It would have been the first time I met them. They must think I'm awful."

Jay smiled. "I'm sure they don't. They got your funeral wreath, and they know what you've been going through."

"Which means they know their daughter was killed in my place. Yes, I'm sure they think I'm wonderful," Brooke said bitterly.

"All right, enough about the flowers," Vincent said abruptly. "You said you weren't going to let what Jay told you get to you, and here you are looking like you're going to cry. Finish your cheesecake."

"I don't think I can," Brooke said waveringly.

Vincent reached for her margarita glass and handed it to her. "Then finish this." He turned to Jay and Stacy, both looking at Brooke with a mixture of concern and helplessness. "Did she tell you about downing those three beers in record time at our house?" Vincent asked. "I'll tell you, drinking beer fast makes this woman burp. I mean, *really* burp. You should have heard her!"

"Brooke burps?" Stacy asked, playing along by looking amazed. "I thought she was too ladylike."

"Good heavens, Stacy, I'm human," Brooke managed.

"I know, but *burping*? And you were a guest? I can't believe it!"

"Oh, you'd better believe it all right," Vincent said. "Scared Elise half to death. Rattled the windows. I think one actually cracked."

The banter went on for another couple of minutes until Brooke's imminent tears had vanished, although her feelings about Mia's parents hadn't. Did they want to hear from her under the circumstances? Would they be offended if she kept her distance, or would they be insulted, even hostile, if she approached them face-to-face with her sympathy? She'd decide later, she thought. At one time she would have asked her grandmother, who always gave the right advice, but now Brooke was on her own.

The phone rang and Brooke jumped, sloshing part of her drink into her lap. She grabbed for a napkin and began wiping at her jeans while the phone rang a second time.

"I'll get it," Stacy said, setting aside her own drink and reaching for the phone on the end table beside her. Without glancing at the caller ID, she picked up the main base before Brooke's message played on the fourth ring. "Yeager residence," Stacy said briskly.

Brooke had dried most of the margarita from her jeans before she noticed Vincent and Jay looking at Stacy, whose face had grown stiff as her hand tightened on the receiver. Her lips narrowed and she slammed the handset back on the base. Then she drew a breath, looked around at all the staring faces, quickly adopted a weak attempt at a smile, and announced loudly, "Wrong number!"

"Stacy, that wasn't a wrong number," Brooke said.

"Sure it was." Stacy's voice had taken on an unnatural firmness. "I've been getting them all the time. Some pitiful-sounding guy wanting 'Lila.' I keep finding these rambling messages from him on the answering machine. There's another guy, too. And some old lady who thinks she has her grandson's number and just gives him hell."

An equally false smile appeared on Jay's face as Brooke

saw Stacy, sitting beside her husband on the couch, give him a light jab in the ribs. "Yeah, we get a lot of wrong numbers," he agreed.

"*I* don't," Brooke said.

"You have an unlisted number."

Brooke asked tautly, "Stacy, I can tell when something is wrong. Who was that?"

Stacy sighed. "I *really* don't know. Just some guy."

"Just some guy who said what?" Stacy took a sip of her drink. *"Stacy."*

"Oh, all right!" Stacy snapped. She breathed deeply, looking at Brooke unwillingly. "He said, 'You shouldn't have ruined such a beautiful vase of roses, Brooke.'"

# fifteen

## 1

"What was the number on that call?" Jay asked abruptly as Brooke sat frozen, her mouth slightly open.

"I don't know," Stacy said. "I didn't look."

Jay reached across her to the phone. "I'll scroll back through the calls she's received," he said. "The last call was five-five-five four-four-three-three. Now all I need is the phone directory."

"Jay, the Charleston phone book doesn't have a reverse directory," Stacy reminded him.

"Damn," Jay muttered, then picked up the receiver. "I'll have to call headquarters. Don't worry, Brooke. We'll know in a few minutes where that call came from."

"Great," she said stiffly.

"It *is* great!" Stacy exclaimed. "Now we've got him!"

"I wouldn't count on it," Brooke said glumly. "Zach is too smart to call from someplace you could hone in on in minutes and go after him."

Vincent touched her hand. "You don't know that for sure, Brooke."

They sat in near silence for ten minutes until the phone rang again. This time Jay glanced at the caller ID before he picked up the phone. Brooke watched the hopeful look on his face fade. Then he hung up and glanced around the room. "The call came from a phone booth half a mile away."

"I told you." Brooke's voice had gone completely flat. "Zach wasn't about to call from some cozy motel room where you could locate him and pick him up in twenty minutes."

After a moment, Stacy burst out, "Jay, why can't you people find this nut? He was shot, for God's sake. He had to get medical care. Haven't you even questioned staff at hospital emergency rooms and private-practice doctors?"

"Certainly we have," Jay returned, sounding slightly ruffled. "Do you think we're idiots? But maybe Zach frightened someone into silence. There are doctors who don't have the greatest scruples in the world. They'd be willing to take a big fee to patch up old Zach and keep their mouths shut."

"Where would he get that kind of money?" Stacy demanded.

"Robert Eads's wallet was missing," Vincent interrupted. "People have said he always carried quite a bit of cash. Zach could be using that money." He looked at Jay. "Sorry. Hal told Dad this stuff and sometimes I can't keep my own big mouth shut."

"It's all right," Jay said mildly. "The police weren't trying to keep any of that quiet."

Vincent frowned. "But I just jumped in like a know-it-all—"

"Oh, for Pete's sake," Stacy said impatiently. "Will you two stop being so polite and trying not to step on each other's toes? No one cares who said what. We only care what the police know, which seems to be nothing except that Tavell is really good at getting people's credit card numbers. I'd like to know how he does that."

"People drop copies of credit card receipts in the trash all the time," Jay said. "They should always tear them up or, better yet, take them home and destroy them, but they get careless. Then the thief sidles up, picks out the receipt, and voilà—he has the number. And remember, these flower orders have been phoned in. No one has placed an order in person."

"We're always being warned about how easy credit card number theft has become," Brooke said. "I'm not careful with my receipts, either."

"All right, enough with the credit card receipts." Stacy looked almost annoyed. "Haven't you found *anything* else, Jay?"

"No, we haven't." He ignored her impatient tone. "We don't even know how he's getting around town. Obviously he has a car, but no cars have been reported stolen. We're assuming he knows someone who lets him use their car—maybe an old friend, the person who kept Brooke's mother's letter opener for him all these years."

Brooke shook her head. "Zach didn't have any friends."

"None that you know about. You were only eleven when he was arrested," Jay pointed out. "Or he could have stolen a car that no one has reported."

"Why wouldn't someone report a stolen car?" Stacy asked.

"Maybe they don't know it was stolen," Jay said. "He could have taken an old car tucked away someplace like a shed or garage that's rarely entered. The only trouble with that theory is guessing how Tavell would know where to look. He may have just stumbled across something. . . ."

"That may be the case, but I doubt it. Too coincidental." Vincent suddenly looked excited. "I was thinking of a case I wrote about nearly five years ago. A guy took a car out of long-term parking at the airport. We were just there today. That's what made me think of it. In the case I studied, the owner had one of those magnetic hide-a-key things stuck under the wheel well, and the airport lot ticket was inside on the dash. All the thief had to do was pay the parking fee and drive away. The owner didn't return for a couple of weeks and didn't even know his car was missing. Tavell might have pulled the same trick."

Jay stared off, thinking. "The parking lots at the airport keep an inventory of license plate numbers. We can check cars present in the parking lot against the inventory. If one is missing, even if it hasn't been reported . . ."

"Then *bingo!*" Stacy exclaimed. She looked at her husband. "At this point, I have only one question, Jay. Are the police always so slow in catching someone like Zach Tavell?"

Brooke saw Jay flush. He took Stacy's remark as a slight on the expertise of the police, and Brooke was fairly sure that was how Stacy meant it, although she was rarely critical of Jay. Stacy seemed unaware of how her remark might be interpreted, though. She gazed at Jay steadily, without an ounce of apology in her expression.

"Tavell was the first person to break out of Mount Olive, a maximum security prison," Jay said evenly. "He's an extremely bright man, Stace."

"And a dangerous man," Stacy persisted.

"I'm well aware of that," Jay answered. "So is the rest of the Charleston police force as well as the state police. We're doing the best we can, but we're not miracle workers."

"It just seems—" Stacy started to continue, but Vincent cut her off.

"It seems everything is being done that can be done, Stacy. I've known Hal Myers all my life. He's as good, or almost as good, a cop as my father. In the past ten years I've interviewed some of the best, and believe me, Hal can hold his own with any of them. As for Jay, he wouldn't have reached the level he has or be working with Hal if he weren't on his way to reaching the same heights." Jay didn't look at Vincent, but Brooke noticed the tiny gleam of appreciation in his blue eyes.

Brooke also heard the slight hint of dislike in Vincent's voice when he talked to Stacy. He'd been put off by her when they met, Brooke thought. He was trying to like Stacy, but he still had reservations, just like she did about him. They were wary of each other, and an evening of sharing chicken and margaritas wasn't going to fix anything. "I know you care about Brooke, Stacy. We all do," Vincent went on. "But it seems to me everything is being done for her that can be done. Of course, if she wouldn't be so damned stubborn and would leave Charleston—"

"Out of the question," Brooke said brusquely. "I'm staying, but I'll be careful."

"She won't be careful alone." An inflexible look crept into Stacy's gray eyes. "I'm spending the night here. That phone call gave me the creeps. I can imagine what it did to Brooke."

Brooke raised her eyebrows. "What about Elise? I'm *not* sending her over to your apartment so she can howl all night and keep Jay awake."

"I'll just take some antihistamine," Stacy said. "Besides, I have so much tequila in me, I think I've become immune to allergies."

Jay smiled. "I don't think that's possible, honey."

"We'll see. And if it is, I'll write an article, get it published in *The New England Journal of Medicine,* and then we can take that trip to France with my royalties."

Jay looked hopelessly at Brooke. "She's definitely had too much tequila."

"I think we all have." Vincent gave them a forced smile, then glanced at his watch. "Ten o'clock. I'd better get home and check on Dad. I just hate leaving you here, Brooke."

"I have two surveillance policemen parked in back and two in front of the building. I have a detective next door. I will be sleeping with my best friend, who is in very good physical shape, I might add."

"When she's not drunk," Jay muttered.

"I am not drunk," Stacy fired back. "Just mellow."

Brooke looked at Elise sound asleep in her doggie bed. "And I have a vicious guard dog."

Vincent rolled his eyes. "Sure. Whatever you say."

Brooke got up. "I'll walk you to the door."

Jay and Stacy began to talk quietly as Brooke opened her front door.

"Be sure to lock these doors behind me."

"Vincent, you tell me that every time you leave. Besides, I always lock the doors at night."

"And be sure the window near the fire escape is locked."

"Yes, sir. Any further orders?"

"Yes." He gently touched her cheek, bent his dark head slightly as if he were going to kiss her, then looked over at Jay and Stacy. Instead, he tapped Brooke gently on the lips with his fingers. "Have a good night, Cinnamon Girl. I'll talk to you tomorrow."

Half an hour later, Stacy had gathered her nightclothes from her own apartment and slipped into bed beside Brooke. The situation felt awkward, and for a while Brooke lay perfectly still on her back, instead of curling into her usual fetal position. She listened to street noises. She listened to Stacy breathing. And then she realized that Stacy hadn't moved, either. They lay on the double bed like two mannequins on display.

"Are you asleep?" Brooke finally whispered.

"No. I'm not the least bit sleepy."

"I'm not, either, but I don't want to get up and watch TV or anything."

"I don't, either." Stacy rolled over, propping her face on her hand and looking down into Brooke's. "Let's pretend we're teenagers having a sleepover."

"Okay," Brooke said. She felt silly, yet there was something comforting about the game, as if their sleeping together were just part of a fun young-girl ritual, not the product of fear of one woman being terrorized. "Did you have many sleepovers when you were growing up?"

"No. How about you?"

"A few. Grossmutter always seemed sort of irritated by having young girls squealing and giggling all night. Before she took me in after my mother died, sleepovers were out of the question with Zach." Brooke didn't like to think of the regimented life they led after Zach's arrival and the way she'd tried to make herself as unobtrusive as possible because she knew Zach really didn't want her around. "You never talk much about your family life," Brooke said. "What was growing up at your house like?"

Stacy went quiet for a moment, then shrugged, although Brooke had the feeling she'd just adopted a nonchalant pose to hide something that really hurt. "My dad left when I was pretty young. I think there was another woman. I never knew for certain."

"He never came to see you?"

"No. Out of sight, out of mind, I guess. Anyway, Mom was crushed. She dated some, but it was always casual. At least I never had to worry about the same experience you had, but she was as lost to me as Dad. She grew more and more distant." Stacy paused. "And then she died," she said abruptly. "No big illness—she just died."

"When you were a child?"

"No. I was eighteen."

"I'm sorry," Brooke murmured. Having heard the phrase a hundred times herself, she knew how empty it sounded, but she couldn't think of anything else to say.

"I think she was glad to die and just get it over with. At least she didn't have to think about Dad anymore."

"And that's why you grew up the tough girl."

Stacy looked at her for a moment, then smiled. "You think I'm a tough girl?"

"That's how you seem."

"Yeah, well, I guess that's how I am. You had your grandmother, who adored you. I wasn't quite so lucky."

"Until you met Jay."

Stacy laughed softly. "Yes, until I met Jay. I guess I *was* lucky, wasn't I?"

"You both were."

"Spoken like a loyal friend."

"Spoken like a highly observant woman who can see how much he loves you."

"Warts and all."

Brooke drew back in mock horror. "You have warts and you're in *my* bed?"

Stacy laughed appreciatively, then said, "Don't worry. You only get them by handling toads. In my younger years . . ."

"Oh, I don't want to hear it," Brooke groaned. She shifted

her position slightly, noticing that she didn't feel quite as tense as she had a few minutes ago, and asked abruptly, "Do you ever get the feeling someone has been in your apartment?"

"Definitely."

"It's weird, isn't it?"

"No, because someone *has* been in our apartments."

"Toads," Brooke returned, thinking Stacy was still teasing her.

"Almost as bad. Eunice."

"*Eunice!* Eunice Dormer?"

"None other."

"Why?" Brooke asked.

"To snoop."

"Oh, Stacy, I don't think so," Brooke said. She'd always rather liked Eunice, or at least felt sorry for her. "What makes you think she snoops?"

"I've smelled her cigarettes in my apartment."

"You think she comes into your apartment to smoke?"

"No, silly, she simply reeks of those awful clove cigarettes she smokes all day. You can smell her coming twenty feet away. Her clothes and hair are saturated with the smell, which lingers. *And* she has access to Harry's master keys."

"Do you think she steals?"

"No, she's too smart for that. People would complain and Harry would be on to her in a minute. He's just looking for some excuse to be rid of her. I think he's absolutely sick of her, desperate to be free, and she knows it."

"Don't tell me she's confided in you, too, that she thinks he's having an affair."

"No, she doesn't confide in *me,* but she doesn't have to tell me what she's thinking," Stacy said. "She watches him like a hawk whenever he's talking to a female. She actually likes you, so I think she's ruled you out as the possible mistress— she thinks you're too ethical to do such a thing as steal her man. I, on the other hand, am still under suspicion."

"Oh, really," Brooke giggled. "She can't possibly think you would betray Jay for *Harry!*" The thought of Harry with his big gut, dirty clothes, stupid remarks, and downright general distastefulness sent them both into fits of laughter. "I mean, I know you like to flirt, Stacy, but I thought you had limits."

Stacy adopted an accent. "I swear, Brooke, I seen Harry in that sweaty T-shirt with that fine spider locket of his'n and his stained ball cap, and I listened to all his witty talk, and I was just natcherly drawed to him. Couldn't help myself."

"I guess I should have seen it before," Brooke said seriously. "You two have so much in common. It's a match made in Heaven."

"For that, I will go home and leave you to sleep here all alone," Stacy returned with mock sternness. Then she added, "But Eunice *does* snoop. Look around every now and then and you'll notice things moved—little things like pieces of jewelry or books."

Brooke said dutifully, "From now on, I will be ever-vigilant."

Feeling somewhat comforted by Stacy's presence, Brooke finally went to sleep, dreaming with sweet sadness of her mother's last whisper—"Good night, my angel."

## 2

Brooke felt warm breath on her face. She opened her eyes slowly to see a round, black nose and clear, sherry-colored eyes looking back into hers not two inches away. "Elise?" she murmured. The dog licked her nose. "Elise, where's Stacy?"

Elise had nothing to say about the matter, so Brooke rose, noticing a bright sun pouring in between a crack in the curtains, and immediately spotted a note on the nightstand. She picked it up and read:

Woke up at dawn with sniffles (so much for my tequila as antihistamine theory). Couldn't go back to sleep, so I went home as it was almost morning and you were still safe and sleeping soundly. Talk to you later.

Stacy

"She probably didn't have sniffles at all," Brooke told Elise. "I'll bet she just missed Jay. Maybe we'll find true love like that someday."

Elise darted forward and kissed her fervently three times on the nose. "Well, not with each other!" Brooke laughed as she tossed back the covers, climbed out of bed, and parted the curtains farther. The sky was a beautiful periwinkle blue, the sun a bright marigold yellow. She glanced at the clock. Nine forty-five. She hadn't slept this late for months. She felt completely rested, clearheaded, and, best of all, calm.

The phone rang and she hesitated. Would this be another anonymous call, something to frighten her, to ruin this beautiful Sunday morning? She approached the phone slowly, then looked at the caller ID: *Samuel Lockhart 555-8988*. She closed her eyes in relief. Vincent.

"Hello, Mr. Lockhart," she said, picking up the handset.

"You certainly sound cheerful this morning. Did you and Stacy hit it off as bedmates?"

"I'm not going to touch that remark!" Brooke laughed. "As a matter of fact, when I woke up, she was gone. She left a note saying she'd left around dawn because of a case of sniffles she blamed on her allergy to dogs."

"Is Elise insulted?"

"Hardly. She just took Stacy's place in the bed and woke me up with a kiss."

"That is *so* romantic," Vincent cooed.

"Oh, be quiet. To what do I owe the honor of this early-morning call?"

"It's hardly early morning, at least not for me."

"Me neither. I have a job that starts at nine, you know."

"Well, you don't have to work on Sundays, so I had an idea," Vincent said. "Well, when I was but a young and inquisitive lad, I went to the planetarium at Sunrise Museum.

Of course, the museum has been moved to the Clay Center, but I've heard the new planetarium is great. Have you been there yet?"

"No. Robert was never interested and Stacy says places with planets whirling around her give her the creeps—"

"That would mean Earth gives her the creeps," Vincent said dryly.

"I think she was referring particularly to planetariums, not the planet on which she lives," Brooke returned tartly. "Anyway, I've never been there. I just never wanted to go alone."

"Great. How about seeing it with me this afternoon?"

"This afternoon?"

"Did you have something else planned? Not that it's any of my business, but the next-door neighbor's wife has left him—"

"Oh, how sad," Brooke interrupted.

"Don't waste your sympathy. The husband is a nice guy but a fool where his wife's concerned. Anyway, she pulls this act on a regular basis. She leaves, supposedly forever, then returns home in a couple of weeks when he's offered her an opulent gift, and all is well for another year. Anyway, the pining jerk is coming over to watch a baseball game with Dad this afternoon, so I have hours and hours of freedom, and I just thought—"

"I would love to go," Brooke said.

"Lunch first?"

"A light lunch. We ate *way* too much last night."

"It's early. The show at the planetarium doesn't start until two o'clock. We'll see how hungry you are around one. I'll pick you up at twelve thirty. Bye," he said quickly, almost as if he was afraid she'd change her mind if he gave her a chance.

Brooke looked at Elise. "Looks like I'm going to the planetarium for the first time in about eighteen years." She frowned. She pulled her hair back in a ponytail, slipped on jogging shorts, a tank top, and sunglasses, and attached Elise's leash. "Time for our morning run. And this time, young lady, we're not going down any alleys," she said, thinking of finding Robert's body crumpled pitifully beside the Dumpster. "We're staying in full view of our police surveillance team and we're going to enjoy this beautiful morning. After our run, we'll stop at the outside café down the street and I'll buy us each a croissant."

As she was locking her door from the outside, Jay opened his. "Off for the morning run?" he asked. He was wearing a sweat suit but no shoes, and his sandy hair stood almost straight up. Brooke thought he looked tired, almost haggard.

"Yes. Not a long run, but Elise and I have to keep our figures. Are you in the mood to go with us?"

"God, no."

"Too much tequila?"

"Remarkably, no. I just had trouble sleeping. Stayed up half the night watching TV and prowling around. Stacy's fussing that I messed up the desk drawers."

"I should have her come over and clean up my place. It's a wreck compared to yours. However, I'm not the neat freak she is."

"Sometimes it's good not to be so neat. I remember my good old bachelor days when I was a complete slob." Jay grimaced. "Well, maybe they weren't so good. I never could find anything except week-old pizza under a pile of newspapers."

"Ugh."

"Yeah. Being a slob is highly overrated." He smiled. "Stacy's fixing some blueberry pancakes and sausage. Want to fuel up before you take off?"

"All that sugar and cholesterol would be defeating the purpose, Jay. Besides, we're kind of in a hurry this morning. Vincent is coming by later and we're going to the planetarium."

"Vincent, huh?" Jay gave her a rakish grin. "He's keeping you busy, isn't he?"

"I think he's trying to entertain me so I don't worry so much about Zach."

"Oh yes, I'm sure that's why he keeps asking you to go places with him," Jay said drolly. "Altruistic chap."

"Chap?"

"The English say it, and I'm very continental. It's what attracts Stacy to me."

"I think there's a little more to her attraction to you than your vocabulary," Brooke laughed. "Well, we're off. Enjoy your pancakes. And tell Stacy thanks for staying last night. She *did* make me feel more comfortable, not so alone. I appreciate it, even if she did get the sniffles."

Elise's nose twitched madly at all the fresh morning scents. She took off like a rocket and Brooke had to work hard at keeping up with her. Brooke was aware of the surveillance car trailing them, but she tried to ignore it, hoping the few other people out on this beautiful morning didn't notice them, either. Of course, if the purpose of the car had been treacherous—say they were potential kidnappers—she would have been out of luck, Brooke thought. No one looked twice at them. People were either naïve, uninterested, or unwilling to get involved. Unfortunately, none of those adjectives spoke highly of the human race.

Elise seemed particularly full of energy. Brooke, however, was growing tired and sweating more than usual. Too much food and liquor last night, she thought. It was a good thing she didn't make a habit of drinking or ignoring her diet or she'd be out of shape quickly. She wasn't one of those lucky women like Stacy who never seemed to pay any attention to exercise or what they ate, yet managed to stay slim and taut.

As she'd promised, Brooke stopped with Elise at a small café, where she bought a cappuccino and two croissants, one for her and one for Elise. The two of them headed for a single table outside shaded by a bright umbrella. Elise, as usual, ate daintily and much slower than Brooke. Then she licked her front paws to make sure she got every crumb of the delicious treat.

"Sorry I'm not much of a cook," Brooke told the dog. "Otherwise, I could make these at home. But maybe that wouldn't be as much fun as 'dining out' after a brisk run on such a pretty day."

Elise lay quietly by her feet as Brooke sipped her cappuccino. The day seemed incredibly bright. Birds hopped importantly from branch to branch of a tree growing beside the café. In the yard next to it, two little boys of around five played Frisbee, laughing uproariously every time they managed to catch it. Then one boy missed, the Frisbee hit him in the head with insignificant force, and he began screaming as if he'd been attacked with an ax.

In a moment, the mother appeared, scooped him up in her arms, kissed him passionately, murmured loving words to him, then ordered both boys into the house with the voice of a fishwife. Brooke couldn't help laughing, knowing the child wasn't really hurt, mostly just mad that he'd missed the Frisbee. She reached down and rubbed Elise's head. "Nothing to worry about," she said. "I guarantee he'll recover in about three minutes." The dog looked satisfied and began gazing up at the birds again. What a perfect day, Brooke thought.

And then she felt it. A tingle along her arms, a tickle at the back of her neck, the creeping feeling that a gaze was crawling over her. It wasn't the scrutiny of the surveillance cops. She'd grown used to that sensation. This was entirely different. Curious, yes, but also guarded. A secret appraisal.

Brooke set down her cappuccino and casually glanced around her. None of the children was looking at her, but then, she'd known she wasn't feeling the gaze of a child. The few adults on the street were focused on children or each other. She even turned around and looked in the window of the café. Vaguely she saw the owner making a sale to a well-dressed woman who was sharply watching him put her pastry in the bag as if she thought he might try to short her.

Next Brooke surveyed the cars parked along the street. A black SUV. A dark green Cavalier. A silver Taurus. A red Firebird. Each car appeared empty.

No one she could see appeared to be watching her, but someone *was* taking in her every move. She noticed the tremor in her hand and immediately forced it still. She would not betray nervousness. She would never let the person who watched her know she was frightened.

"Okay, girl, we've dawdled long enough," Brooke said to Elise. "Time to get home for a shower. Vincent will be coming to see us soon."

On the walk home, Brooke wondered if she should have approached the surveillance car and told them she felt someone's gaze on her. Then she decided that it would have been impossible for them to spot anyone in the crowded neighborhood. She also didn't want them to feel she was growing into the nervous type, crying "wolf" over everything. If they lost faith in her judgment, she could lose her life if they weren't quick enough to believe her when she was absolutely certain something was wrong.

As Brooke and Elise entered the apartment building lobby, Eunice Dormer darted at them, wringing her hands. She wore one of her flowered housedresses that all looked alike and house slippers over a pair of white socks. Her mousy hair had arranged itself in thin, limp curls around her damp, flushed face. And Stacy was right, Brooke thought. The woman *did* smell of cloves. "Have you seen Harry?" Eunice demanded.

"No. Elise and I went out for a run and we just got back. Eunice, are you all right?"

"My insulin shot is overdue. Two *hours* overdue. That makes me nervous and Harry *knows* it makes me nervous."

"Can't you give it to yourself?" Brooke asked.

For once Eunice gave her a hard look. "No, I cannot. I suppose you think that makes me a fool."

"Well, no, it just seems that if you really need it and you can't find Harry—"

"I can't do it. I could inject air into a blood vessel. Do you know what that could do to you?"

"I think it would have to be a major vessel, Eunice, and what are the chances—"

"I don't take chances with my health!" Eunice burst out. "Besides, a needle going into my skin—I can't even *look* at it, much less do it myself. And don't you offer to give it to me, because I know you don't know any more about giving shots than I do!"

"I wasn't going to, Eunice. I was going to suggest you go to the hospital."

"Hospital!" Eunice looked horrified. "Do you know what they'd charge just to give me this stupid shot? And I'd be around all those sick people with their flu germs and God knows what else. They haven't found a cure for Ebola, you know!"

"I don't think Ebola is really going around here," Brooke said faintly.

"I want Harry!" Eunice looked like she was going to cry. "This is Harry's job. He knows how to do it fast and so it doesn't hurt. Where *is* he?"

Brooke paused, thinking. She had a good idea that Harry, miraculously, *had* found a mistress and was simply spending the morning with her, losing track of time. But, of course, Brooke couldn't say this to Eunice. "I don't know what to tell you," she said truthfully. "Is your car in the parking lot? If not, he could have run out on an errand and had a flat tire."

"You're right! I'll bet anything that's what's happened," Eunice pounced, although Brooke saw the doubt in her eyes. She was thinking the same thing Brooke was about another woman. Nevertheless, Eunice was darting toward the rear parking lot, thankfully before Brooke had to offer another possible excuse for Harry's absence.

"She's absolutely desperate not to lose him," Brooke muttered to an oblivious Elise. "Even though he's a creep, having her so dependent must be a drag for him. I almost feel sorry for the guy. Almost."

Upstairs, Brooke tried to decide on an appropriate outfit for the planetarium. Casual slacks, or a sundress? She decided on a pale blue sundress paired with high-heeled white sandals and a necklace with a shell pendant cut into the shape of a flower. She pulled her hair up over her ears so matching earrings could show and twirled in front of Elise. "Too formal? Skirt the right length? Any price or size tags showing?"

She took Elise's silence as an approval of the outfit, and as Brooke was gathering some toys for the dog to play while she was gone, as if Elise couldn't choose her own toys, some-one knocked on the door. "It's me," Vincent called. "Ready for a space odyssey?" Brooke unlocked the door and flung it open. Vincent's eyes widened. "Wow! If any aliens saw you, they'd keep you! You look fabulous."

"Thank you, but I didn't know aliens were interested in fashion."

"Oh yes," Vincent said seriously as he stepped into the apartment. "That's why they return so many of their ab-ductees. The humans were dressed *so* badly the aliens didn't want to keep them on board."

"Vincent, you should be writing science fiction," Brooke said.

"I've given it serious thought. I think my ideas are highly sophisticated."

"Or maybe you should stick with true crime."

"Was that an insult?"

"Only to your sophisticated science-fiction theories. You won't be spouting any aloud at the planetarium, will you?"

"I'm afraid only someone like Stephen Hawking could understand me."

"Yes, well, you go right on dreaming if it makes you happy, Mr. Lockhart." She glanced at his khaki pants and ca-sual green shirt with long sleeves rolled up to his elbows. "You're looking pretty spiffy yourself, today."

Vincent rolled his eyes. "My father thought I should wear a suit."

"To the planetarium?"

"It's Sunday."

"Oh. I didn't know he was that religious."

"He didn't, either, until about a month ago. He seems to recall that earlier in his life—like ten years ago—he was a deacon in his church. I don't remember his ever belonging to a church."

Brooke smiled. "Well, my grandmother *was* religious and I had to be in Sunday school and church every week, and I also sang in the choir. I remember the day I sang solo. Grossmutter was so proud, I was afraid she was going to stand up and throw flowers after my performance."

"You must sing well, then."

"No, I just sang better than anyone else in the choir, which isn't saying much." She picked up her purse. "Ready to go?"

"Aren't Jay and Stacy coming with us?"

"No. Did you expect them to?"

"I thought because they live right next door, you might feel obliged to invite them," Vincent said.

"I don't. Besides, Stacy left here at the crack of dawn claiming she couldn't sleep because of her allergy to Elise, and when I saw Jay in the hall briefly this morning, he looked worn out."

"Do you think there's been a break in the case?" Vincent asked.

"If so, Jay wasn't inclined to tell me. I don't suppose Hal Myers called your father with any news."

"Not that I know of." Vincent shrugged. "Maybe we just wore out poor old Jay and Stace last night. They aren't party animals like us. And Elise." She wagged her tail at him. "Sorry to leave you, girl, but—"

"She understands about unfair segregation practices when it comes to dogs in public places," Brooke said. "She'll be fine with her toys and her chew bone. She already had a nice run this morning. She'll probably take a nap."

The Avampato Discovery Museum, housed in the beautiful new Clay Center, wasn't too crowded when they arrived at a little after one. They wandered around the museum, their shoes clicking against the lovely dark blue, burgundy, forest green, and gold tiles of the flooring. First, they climbed to the Juliet Museum of Art on the second level. Although the entire museum contained nine thousand contiguous square feet of space, a separate gallery space was dedicated to nineteenth- and twentieth-century art. Brooke was particularly fascinated by the huge photos of Andy Warhol, Edie Sedgwick, Natalie Wood, and Leonard Bernstein.

"Thinking of sneaking one of these out of here?" Vincent whispered close to her ear. "You look like you're plotting something, and that museum guide is watching you very closely."

"He's probably just staring at you disapprovingly because you're not wearing a suit," she returned. "But I would like to take Natalie's photo with me."

"A Natalie Wood fan?"

"After the movie *Splendor in the Grass*? Are you kidding? She loved Warren Beatty *so* much and then later when she went to visit him and he was married and she had on that gorgeous white dress and white portrait hat and gloves and—"

"Okay, I think you're going to cry," Vincent said, moving her along gently. "If you tell me you had a crush on Andy Warhol, I'm dumping you right here."

"He was . . . different."

"That's an understatement."

"I didn't have a crush on him."

"And that's a relief, because I don't look a thing like him and women have a tendency to be attracted to a certain *type*."

"Is that so?" Brooke answered, ignoring his innuendo about wanting her to have a crush on someone who looked like him. "And men don't?"

"Oh no. We just take women as we find them. No preconceived notions of what we want. It's usually just a woman with a forgiving heart who's a great cook and housekeeper. We don't care a fig whether or not they're attractive."

"That's a good one, Vincent. Did you just come up with it or is it a tried-and-true line?"

Vincent answered, but Brooke didn't hear him. From the corner of her eye, she'd just spotted impossibly red hair worn short and spiky. "Oh God, there's Judith," she said, stepping closer to Vincent and looking intently at her museum pamphlet.

"Who's Judith?"

"Judith Lambert. She used to date my boss, Aaron Townsend. Stop looking around—she'll see you!"

"I don't even know what she looks like."

"Horrible flaming red hair done in spikes," Brooke whispered. "She used to be so attractive. She and Aaron dated for about nine months. Then he dropped her. She says it was the other way around, but no one believes her, partly because Aaron went on just as before, while Judith lost a lot of weight and did something drastic to her hair. I think the bit with the hair was sort of like flipping the whole world the bird."

"Ah, you're a psychiatrist, too."

"Well, I do think so. Anyway, she finally came to the conclusion that Aaron had broken up with her for me. I learned that through office gossip and I was flabbergasted." She lowered the pamphlet slightly and peeped at Judith and her companion. "You know what you were saying about people always being drawn to the same *type*? Well, maybe you're right, because the man she's with looks sort of like Aaron, only much tackier. Bad haircut, shirt about ten years out-of-date."

Judith's eyes flashed at them as if she'd heard the last remark, and Brooke quickly retreated behind her pamphlet again. "What if she comes over here to talk to us?" she hissed.

"Then we'll talk to her," Vincent returned calmly. "But I don't think you have anything to worry about." He glanced at his watch. "It's almost time for the planetarium show. The guy at the desk told us not to be late for it because people start lining up fairly early."

Brooke had expected there to be more children in line than adults for the ElectricSky. She was mistaken. There were twice as many adults, but all acted as excited as children, some murmuring, a few giggling, one older woman fretting to her husband, "Things move around on the walls in there and you feel like you're right in the midst of some big, swirling mass. Mildred told me. I hope I don't get dizzy."

"Mildred thinks she's seasick at the swimming pool," the woman's husband snapped. "She's a kook. You won't get dizzy if you just concentrate on *not* getting dizzy."

She gave him a murderous look. "Oh, you and your mind-over-matter crap! It's *nonsense!*"

"Young love," Vincent muttered in Brooke's ear, making her hide her smile from the woman, who was looking right at her.

The planetarium's double doors opened and everyone went totally silent and solemn, as if they were boarding an actual spacecraft destined for Mars. They walked down a long, dark hall lined with tiny floor lights, then up a curving staircase, and entered a large amphitheater. Brooke's eyes seemed slow to adjust to the darkness. She stumbled along, transported by the haunting music coming from all around them and gazing at the coral pink lights appearing to shimmer from everywhere. Vincent guided her into a row and nearly pushed her down into a theater seat. "I *love* this!" she murmured.

"So I gathered," Vincent whispered with a trace of humor. "You're acting like a three-year-old. Close your mouth before something flies into it."

The narrator started. Brooke learned that the dome was sixty-one feet from side to side and contained Dolby Surround Sound projectors. He also informed them that the projector in the middle of the area was jokingly called the Death Star. He warned the audience that the dome made all sounds travel, and requested that people not talk or even murmur, because all noises would be exaggerated.

"Remember the scene in *Rebel Without a Cause* where James Dean and Natalie Wood are at the planetarium?" Brooke whispered softly to Vincent.

"*Shhhhhhh!*" a woman behind them hissed, sounding like a large, infuriated poisonous viper about to strike. "He said to be quiet!" Brooke turned to glare at her, considering that *she* had made more noise than Brooke.

That was when Brooke saw the girl sitting right across from them. Shoulder-length straight blond hair tossed behind her ears, narrow shoulders, and a long, graceful neck. She looked like the girl at Mia's funeral who gave Brooke the vase of white roses. Brooke closed her eyes for a moment, then looked at the girl again.

Almost as if feeling her gaze, the girl turned and stared

back at Brooke. What could have made me think that was the same girl? Brooke wondered. Her blue eyes were heavily lined in black, and the lids shimmered with some kind of glittery powder. Berry red lipstick emphasized her full lips, and four hoop earrings of varying sizes dangled from her left lobe. She wore ragged jeans and a wildly patterned extremely low-cut T-shirt, and chewed gum as if her life depended on it. She looked at least eighteen, not sixteen like the girl at the funeral home. And yet . . .

She turned her gaze away from Brooke with boredom, slid down in her seat, and propped her sandaled feet on the back of the seat in front of her. The hems of her jeans were frayed and even from a distance looked dirty. Her companion, an ill-kempt boy with greasy black hair and a tattoo on his neck, also looking around eighteen, laughed out loud at something the girl muttered, drawing a dagger stare from the woman behind Brooke and Vincent. Brooke had a feeling the woman knew better than to "shush" those two, though. They had a rough look, as if they'd like nothing better than to curse her out or maybe even worse.

Brooke turned her attention away from the girl for a moment and spotted Judith and her companion. Judith was trying to show how wildly involved they were. Unfortunately, the image was ruined as he sat almost rigid in his chair while her long, skinny arms seemed to multiply and flow all over him. Brooke had the sudden image of the poor man being captured by an octopus.

"What's wrong?" Vincent whispered.

"Nothing. I'm just people-watching."

"I'm going to tell both of you one more time to be quiet," the woman behind them nearly snarled.

Vincent and Brooke both turned. The husband's face looked swollen with the blood of anger and embarrassment, but he said nothing. He probably never got a chance to say much of anything, Brooke thought.

Vincent gave Brooke's hand a squeeze, and after they both turned around again, she relaxed, immediately enthralled as the story of the galaxy began to unfold. All around her spun the images of stars, planets, meteors, and fire. The sound *did* surround her, and she could easily see how someone might get dizzy in this lifelike chamber full of color and drama. She caught herself gripping Vincent's arm, just as she used to grip Daddy's arm when he took her to the planetarium a lifetime ago when she was a child. Vincent covered her hand and squeezed, smiling although he didn't look at her. He seemed to know she was having a good time, and the expression on his face told her that her pleasure was giving him just as much.

"Everything's spinning around," the woman behind them announced loudly. "I think I'm going to vomit."

"Then leave," her husband said absently, mesmerized by the show.

"Alone? Without *you*?"

From across the room came another loud, *"Shhhhhh."*

"Well, I never!" the woman exclaimed as if she hadn't done it herself fifteen minutes earlier.

Seeing that her husband had no intention of trailing after her from the dome, the woman controlled her desire to throw up and went silent, although she did make a great show of burying her head in her hands. That husband is going to catch hell when they leave here, Brooke thought. The wife didn't act as if she were used to rebellion on her husband's part.

Although Brooke was riveted by the show, by the spectacular representation of meteors blasting against planets and the moon with spectacular bursts of light, she couldn't rid herself of the feeling that someone watched her. At first she was certain it was the nauseated woman behind her, glowering at the back of her head in pure resentment because Brooke obviously wasn't sick, but when she glanced back, the woman still had her eyes covered, letting out an occasional pitiful moan while her husband completely ignored her. Finally, Brooke glanced around the dome. All eyes seemed fixed on some point of the drama unfolding in front, above, beside them. She even looked at the blond girl, whose head was bent toward her grungy boyfriend's as they giggled, paying no attention what-soever to the show. Or to Brooke. I spooked myself, Brooke thought. I got nervous because I imagined that slut looked like the angelic girl at Mia's funeral—the girl who gave me a vase of roses from Zach.

It seemed to Brooke that the show ended in about five minutes. She would gladly have sat through it again, but Vin-cent was nudging her to get up. They stepped sideways out into another one of the dark halls lined with tiny white lights, this time climbing up toward the exit, not down the way they had come. Suddenly, people Brooke had not been aware of seemed to come to life. People babbled, men held their wives' arms and told them to watch their steps, and children dashed past them, laughing and chattering. They'd certainly followed the narrator's instructions and kept quiet throughout the show, Brooke thought approvingly. Except for the woman behind her, she hadn't heard so much as a whisper.

Suddenly, Brooke felt something like a spray of moisture followed by a pinprick on her lower back just above her hips. Had she been perspiring? Had her zipper pinched her damp skin? She reached around just as she felt another sharp, stinging jab. "Ouch!" she burst out as pain spread over her lower back. "Darn it! What—"

The pain grew more intense. She felt as if someone were holding a kitchen match to her lower back. Either that, or they'd managed to drop acid on the tender skin below her thin dress. "Vincent—"

He grabbed her arm. "What is it?"

"My back." The pain flared, raw and burning. "It hurts!"

Brooke knew someone hadn't brushed up against her with something that accidentally caused the smarting feel-ing seeming to eat through her skin. She'd been attacked, stealthily, minutely, maliciously. But how seriously?

Brooke instinctively looked around her in the narrow hall for the blond girl. At first Brooke saw no one except strangers

# sixteen

## 1

People parted around them and hugged the walls, staying as far away from Brooke as possible. Typical, Brooke thought. People never want to get involved.

Vincent wrapped his arms around her shoulders and held her tightly. "What is it, Brooke? What's wrong?"

"I don't know." Tears ran down her face as the burning on her back became worse. "I was just walking along and I felt something wet on the back of my dress and then something like a pinprick. It stung. Then there was an actual *jab* right in the middle of the wet spot, and the stinging got much worse."

Vincent ran his right hand down her back and drew it back sharply just below her waist. "Damn! That smarts!"

Brooke squirmed. "Vincent, what *is* it?"

One of the surveillance police ran up to them, kneeling beside Brooke. "What happened?"

"We were walking out and Brooke felt something sharp and wet on her back. Down low. It stung. Then she felt it again. I ran my hand over it and my skin is burning."

The policeman immediately pulled out his cell phone and dialed 911, giving them the address of the Clay Center and Brooke's symptoms. The two men bent her over, staring at the large wet spot on the back of her thin sundress. One policeman looked at Vincent's reddening hand. "It's some kind of corrosive," Vincent told him.

"My partner and I got separated from you on the way out. Who was near you?" the cop asked.

"I don't know." Vincent looked down at Brooke. "Did you see anyone?"

"Whoever did this was behind me, obviously. The only person I saw in there I knew was Judith Lambert. Oh God, how long will it take for the ambulance to get here?"

"We'll help you to the front doors," one of the cops said. "The ambulance will be here in about five minutes."

Five minutes turned into ten minutes. While they waited, Vincent sat down on the front steps of the Clay Center, placed Brooke beside him, turned her back toward him, and pulled down the zipper of her dress. People glanced at the blonde with her dress hanging below her waist and only a lacy strapless bra covering her chest, but she hurt so much, she didn't care. Vincent looked at her lower back. "There's a spot about the size of a fifty-cent piece, red as fire and beginning to blister. She's also bleeding."

"Oh great, more blood?" Brooke moaned.

"It's not a *lot* of blood."

"That's so comforting. Can't you do something?"

Vincent fumbled in his pants pockets. "I have one of those moist towelettes—Dad never lets me leave home without one, like I'm six or that detective on TV—but I'm afraid the chemicals in it might do more harm than good."

A small, round man rushed out of the building carrying a wet cloth. "I heard what happened and I doused my handkerchief in the water fountain. Maybe this will help."

Vincent immediately applied the handkerchief, and the pain eased slightly. "Oh, thank you," Brooke said to the man, tears still running down her face. "I hate to be such a baby, but the pain—"

"You're not being a baby, ma'am." The man smiled. "I'm glad it helps a little. Is there anything else I can do?"

At that moment the ambulance pulled up. "I think we're in good hands, now," Vincent said. "Thank you, sir."

An hour later Brooke sat up on a bed in an examination room. A doctor had thoroughly cleaned her wound, given her a mild painkiller, greased her with what seemed like half a tube of antibiotic ointment, and placed a thick bandage over the injury for protection against pressure. "The lab will identify the chemical on your dress," he said in his beautiful Pakistani accent. He'd already told her he'd come to the United States from Kashmir seventeen years earlier. "Hopefully, we'll soon see what we're dealing with. What a nasty thing to do to such a pretty girl."

"Thank you for the compliment, but it was a nasty thing to do to anyone," Brooke said. "You've been very kind."

Vincent came into the room, briefly conferred with the doctor, then walked slowly to the bed. "This wasn't quite the afternoon I had planned for you, Cinnamon Girl," he said apologetically.

"I know," she said gently. "I also know who did this to me. That girl—the one who was at Mia's funeral."

Vincent frowned. "The girl at Mia's funeral? What are you talking about?"

"The pretty girl who handed me the vase of roses was at the planetarium, only looking extremely different. Lots of makeup, hair tossed back so you could see four earrings in one lobe, cheap come-and-get-me clothes. She looked at least eighteen, not sixteen like she did at the funeral."

"You didn't say anything about her."

"I wasn't sure it was her at first. I wasn't really sure until after this happened."

Vincent looked at her seriously. "Brooke, it was dim in there."

"Not while the show was going on. At times it got really bright."

"And you looked at her then?"

"A couple of times."

"Did she look back?"

"Once. It was just a glance and she acted like she'd never seen me before. She turned right back to her boyfriend—"

"She was there with a guy?"

"Yes. About the same age. Longish, sort of greasy black hair. A tattoo on his neck. He had that same trashy look she did. They couldn't take their hands off each other."

"And you're sure *this* was the girl at the funeral?"

Brooke got impatient. "Yes, Vincent, I *am*. After all, no one at the funeral knew who the girl was. She gave me the flowers from Zach. Don't you see? He *planted* her there, just to give me the flowers. He probably found her on some street corner and, in spite of her striking outfit and makeup, noticed her resemblance to me, my mother, Mia. He thought the whole plan with the flowers would scare the hell out of me, which it did. All he needed was for her to clean up and to buy her a sweet, innocent-looking dress and—"

Vincent held up his hand. "You could be right."

"You're not going to argue with me?"

"I can hardly ignore that both times this girl no one knows has been around, something bad has happened to you." He grinned. "Do you think you have a dumb boyfriend or something?"

Boyfriend? Had he called himself her *boyfriend*? It sounded so adolescent. So presumptuous. So foolishly wonderful.

"But Brooke, don't forget that Judith Lambert was there, too, and you said she doesn't like you."

"Yes, but she hasn't liked me for a long time and nothing has happened to me."

"Maybe she was biding her time."

"Maybe," Brooke said reluctantly. "But I can't get that blond girl out of my mind."

"Okay. The police will want you to confer with a sketch artist," Vincent said. "We both helped with the first one after the church incident, but you're on your own with this one, because I didn't see her."

"I remember her perfectly. But the sooner I talk to the artist, the better, so I don't forget any details."

"Want to go to headquarters now?"

"Not quite yet. While we're here at the hospital, I'm going up to see my grandmother," Brooke said quickly.

"Are you going to tell her what happened?"

"Heavens, no! The last thing she needs is something else to worry her. Does my face look okay? I mean, not like I've been crying or in pain or frightened?"

"You look beautiful, as always," Vincent said.

"Yes, well, that's debatable." Brooke's voice was crisp, but only from embarrassment. He'd sounded tender and admiring. "Do you want to go with me?"

"I think I'll stay in the waiting room, if you don't mind. I'm not as good at hiding my feelings as you are. Your grandmother is still sharp, Brooke. If you don't want her to worry, don't let her get a good look into your eyes. She knows you too well."

"Better than anyone does," Brook answered. "Well, if you'll remove yourself from the premises, I'll get dressed."

Vincent grinned. "The police took your dress so they could identify the chemical."

"The whole dress?" Brooke burst out. "The doctor told me a lab was going to run tests to see what the liquid was, but I thought they might have just cut a little piece out of the dress."

"Cops are thorough, Brooke. They took the whole thing."

"Well, what am I supposed to do? Wear this hospital gown home?"

"It looks like an expensive designer gown, Brooke," Vincent said seriously. "I don't think they'll just let you take it."

Brooke glanced down at the thin gown with its ugly blue, unidentifiable pattern against white. "Yes, I'm sure it's a designer gown. It must have cost five whole dollars. What am I supposed to do? Go up to see Grandmother in my bra and panties?"

"And shoes. They left your shoes."

"Wonderful. This couldn't be coat weather, could it? That would give me something to wear."

"If it had been coat weather, your back would have been protected," Vincent said.

"Oh, quit being so reasonable," Brooke snapped, knowing none of this was Vincent's fault, but annoyed with him anyway just because he was the only person around. "Please call Stacy. She'll bring me something to wear."

"Will do, ma'am. But what if she's not home?"

"Just call her," Brooke said. "If she's not home, I'll think of another solution."

"I liked the bra and panties idea."

Brooke gritted her teeth. Now that Vincent was certain she wasn't seriously injured, he was getting too much enjoyment out of this situation. "Just call her, dammit."

Twenty minutes later Stacy arrived carrying an A-line dress in a paper sack. "Vincent said for me to bring something without a waistline. You have mostly suits and I finally had to look in my closet. I found a dress, but it will be longer than you like since I'm taller than you." She looked at Brooke in anxiety. "Vincent said something about a burn on your back. Let me see."

"It's covered with a bandage, Stacy."

"Oh. Well, how bad a burn? How did you get it?"

Brooke slid out of her attractive hospital robe and reached for the gray silk shantung dress. "We went to the planetarium. As we were coming out, walking down that dark hall, someone jabbed me with something."

"Jabbed you?"

"Yes." Brooke went into details as she slid on the silk-shantung dress and reached for the zipper. "The doctor says I'm suffering from some kind of chemical burn. The police took the dress to a lab for testing."

Stacy was right. The body of the dress was only a bit loose, but the hem hung three inches below Brooke's knees and made her feel like a little girl dressed in her mother's clothes. She said nothing, though, and stepped back into her high-heeled sandals.

"I'm sorry for dragging you down here with something for me to wear, but since the police took my dress—"

Stacy waved away her apology. "Jay's watching some base-ball game—I hate baseball—and I was restless. Vincent's call caught me just before I left for a walk. I'm not a big fan of soli-tary walks with only my thoughts to keep me company, so you did me a favor, made me feel useful."

"You are *extremely* useful. First spending the night with me, then bringing me clothes at the hospital. What would I do without you?"

"Sleep alone and be naked."

"You take gratitude so gracefully, Stacy."

Stacy grinned. "It just makes me feel silly. Ready to go home?"

"No. I'm going up to see my grandmother first. You can go, though. You don't have to wait for Vincent and me."

"I'd prefer to wait," Stacy said, then with a wink, "I want to make sure you two goofy kids get home safe and sound. I also want to make sure I get my dress back."

"You are just a riot, Stacy," Brooke said, smiling for the first time since they'd left the planetarium.

# 2

Vincent drove Brooke home, then stayed at Brooke's only long enough to drink a glass of iced tea. He didn't like the idea of leaving her alone, but she seemed oddly calm as well as tired. Perhaps the pain medication she'd been given was affecting her, he thought. Anyway, she didn't argue with him when he said he should be going, although it was fairly early in the evening. He had a feeling she just wanted to go to bed, if only to rest. Thinking she might not be as alert as she should be under the circumstances, he checked all the win-dow locks, then listened from the hall for the door lock and dead bolt. He hoped Stacy would offer to spend the night again; then he drove home.

When he walked in the house, all the lights were off. Sam

never went to bed this early, and when he did go to bed he always left on a lamp in the living room, just as Vincent's mother had insisted on doing when she was alive. Frightened, Vincent called out, "Dad!" a couple of times, stumbled over to a lamp, turned it on, and readied himself for a search of the house.

The lamp near the door nearly blinded him, the bulb in it much too bright, and after blinking a couple of times, Vincent saw Sam sitting in his favorite chair, an album on his lap, staring straight ahead. Vincent looked at the man's unblinking blue eyes. "Dad?" he said softly, almost fearfully. Sam was rock still, still staring. "Dad?"

Suddenly Sam blinked, looked at Vincent, and said, "Well, at last, Son. I told you not to keep the car out past dark. Your mother's been worried sick."

Vincent realized he'd been holding his breath. He let it out slowly and said, "I'm sorry about the car, Dad. I got held up—"

"Now, those excuses don't work anymore," Sam said firmly. "You're supposed to be in by eleven."

"But Dad, it's not eleven yet." Vincent realized he'd fallen into the same tone he'd used when he was sixteen. He pulled himself together and said in an adult voice, "Something *did* happen, though, or I would have been home earlier."

Abruptly, Sam looked alarmed. "A car wreck?"

"No, not a car accident."

"Is anyone hurt?"

"No. Everyone is fine. Well, almost fine."

Sam's white eyebrows drew together. "Almost fine. What does that mean?"

"It was Brooke." His father's frown deepened. "She's all right. I just dropped her at her apartment."

"Apartment? Doesn't she live here?"

Alarm filled Vincent. Had his father forgotten most of what he knew about Brooke? "No, Dad, Brooke is twenty-six now and she has her own place."

Vincent watched his father closely. He saw something move behind the older man's eyes, and he suddenly looked more alert. "Sure she has her own place. I don't know what's wrong with me."

"Sometimes your memory just . . . takes a break."

Sam started laughing. "Takes a break. That's a good one! But you always were good with words, Vincent. Straight As in English. Not so good in math, though."

"No, I wasn't. I'm still not, which is why I'm a writer, not a nuclear physicist."

"But you're a good writer. Everyone says so. Your mom was proud as punch of you."

"Well, that's what publishers always want to hear—that your mom likes your writing. They can't snatch up a book fast enough when they hear that one."

Sam frowned again. "So you're fine. But Brooke isn't."

"No, Dad, she isn't. She needs to get out of Charleston, but she won't because of her grandmother. We stopped by the hospital this evening. After seeing her grandmother, Brooke looked awful. She finally admitted the doctor told her Greta is failing and probably won't live more than a few days. I told Brooke her grandmother would want her to get out of danger. After all, she's tried to keep Brooke safe all her life. But Brooke is stubborn. I have to say, her courage is one of the things I admire about her, but at the same time, it frustrates the hell out of me."

Sam smiled. "She was a plucky little girl. That's one of the things Laura and I loved about her." He slanted a look at Vincent. "One of the things I think you love about her, too."

Vincent flushed. "Love? Dad, I just met Brooke a few days ago. I like her. I respect her. I have fun with her. But love? That's ludicrous."

"Yeah, well, whatever you say, Son." Sam grinned in a way that made Vincent want to protest more about how he certainly did not *love* Brooke Yeager, but he knew his father. Once he got an idea in his head, there was no shaking it loose, no matter how much you argued. He'd just let Sam think what pleased him. But *love*!

"We *have* to get Tavell," Sam began again, his grin fading. "The son of a bitch managed to break out of prison and he's after my Cinnamon Girl. After all these years, when she got into trouble, she came to me. And what have I done? Exactly nothing, because I'm just an old, useless man now." He wiped at his eyes. "Sorry, Son."

"Dad, you're not old and useless," Vincent said softly, feeling his own throat tighten.

"Yes, I am. Pretty much. I think your mother's death finished me off. Mentally, that is. Not that I'm blaming her. She was the best woman who ever lived. I never understood why out of all the men she could have had, she chose me."

"She loved you."

Sam nodded. Then his eyes clouded. "She did indeed. I felt it every day. And I've felt her absence every single minute of the last three years."

Vincent nodded. "I miss her, too, Dad."

"Seems impossible that she's gone," Sam went on. "I was sure she'd be alive long after I was dead. I used to fret about that. Who would have taken care of her if I wasn't here?"

"I would have," Vincent said.

Sam patted him on the hand. "Yes, you're a good boy. Always were, except for those few wild years you went through. I was concerned about you then."

"Because I tried to be in a rock band and rode my friend's motorcycle?" Vincent smiled. "You thought the next step was robbing jewelry stores? Dealing heroin?"

Sam grinned. "Silly, wasn't I? But you never stop worrying about your kids."

"That's good to know. Some of us never need for you to stop worrying."

"Not you. You've got the world by the tail. Brooke is another matter. Tell me what happened to her today."

"Sure you're not too tired to sit up and talk with me for a while?"

"I'm not a toddler. It's barely dark. Get us each a beer and I'll talk your leg off."

Vincent got them the beer, turned on a couple of dimmer lights, then told his father what had happened at the planetarium. "Is Brooke all right?" Sam asked.

"Yes. I think she has a first-degree burn, but it's small."

"And you believe this girl Brooke spotted—the one that looked like the girl who gave her the roses at that funeral—is responsible." Vincent nodded. "How?"

"The hallway was dark and crowded. I got separated from Brooke. The girl could have come up and sprayed something caustic on Brooke, then stuck her in the back a couple of times with a needle. The lab will let us know soon what it was." Vincent leaned forward, rolling the can of beer between his hands. "What I'm wondering is who this girl is and why she's working for Zach."

"The *why* is easy," Sam said. "Money. Who she is, well, that's another matter. But you said she looked about eighteen."

"At the funeral home I would have said sixteen tops. I didn't see her at the planetarium, but Brooke said she looked about eighteen. Of course, at the funeral home she was wearing a white dress, very demure, no makeup, straight hair. Brooke said at the planetarium she had on heavy makeup, tight grungy clothes, a lot of cheap jewelry."

"But Brooke is certain it's the same girl."

"She's about ninety percent certain. The clothes and makeup could easily make the girl look a couple of years older. And she was with a guy. I wonder if Zach hired both of them? There's a reward for Zach's capture. If he did, though, I'd think he'd be worried about messing with a couple of money-hungry kids just so he can scare Brooke. After all, both you and Brooke have told me Zach was smart. Cagey. Using that girl doesn't sound like the act of a smart man to me."

"Fifteen years in prison might dull a man's wits, Vincent. Besides, they said at the prison he'd gone a little crazy lately. Something's not quite right with his mind. He's not as sharp as he used to be, they said."

"Tavell? Good God, he broke out of a maximum security prison and has stayed free during a huge manhunt, not to mention killed Robert Eads almost right under the nose of two surveillance teams."

"Maybe not Eads," Sam said slowly.

"What do you mean?"

"Hal was here earlier today. He said he's not so sure Eads's boyfriend didn't have something to do with Eads's murder. That young partner of his feels the same way."

"Jay Corrigan?"

"Yeah. Hal seems to think the boy's got a lot on the ball. Anyway, they interviewed that real estate guy—"

"Aaron Townsend."

"Townsend, right. He acted nervous as hell. Tried to make it seem like he and Eads barely knew each other. But he made a couple of slips."

Vincent leaned back in his chair. "Why would Aaron Townsend want to hurt Eads?"

"Hal says Townsend's mother controls the family fortune and she doesn't think too much of homosexuals. He thinks she doesn't know about her son and he's frantic to keep her from finding out because if she does—" Sam broke off and took a deep drink of beer. "Well, she'd probably cut him out of the will, to say the least. Hal said young Corrigan found out all about the mother from Brooke. How controlling she is, how nervous Townsend gets when she comes to the office, that kind of thing. She says people that work for Townsend think he's afraid of his mother."

"I still don't understand why Townsend would be a suspect in the Eads murder. Eads wasn't going to run to Mrs. Townsend with the news that he and her son were lovers."

"He wouldn't have let her know on purpose, but Hal says Eads sort of fell apart after Brooke found out about him and Townsend. Eads kept following her, making scenes—you know all that. He and Corrigan think maybe Townsend was afraid Eads would lose it altogether and accidentally blow the big secret sky-high, so he decided to shut up Eads."

"With a letter opener that belonged to Brooke's mother and hasn't been seen for over fifteen years?"

"Yeah, well, there's the fly in the ointment with that theory," Sam said in disgust. "That letter opener leads you right back to thinking the killer must have been Tavell."

"Who has held on to a letter opener for fifteen years and

just happened to have it with him one night when Robert Eads was hanging around Brooke's apartment building?"

"Son, Tavell could have hidden that letter opener a hundred places after he stole it from Anne. And there's no proof he meant to use it on Robert Eads." Sam suddenly sounded like his old self, the detective everyone in the department had admired. "Tavell might have been on his way up to Brooke's apartment himself, planning on killing her with the letter opener, when he ran into Robert lurking around. Tavell's face has been all over the news for days. Eads would have recognized him if he saw him. What could Tavell do? Just let Eads walk away?"

"No," Vincent said thoughtfully. He took another sip of beer. "I wonder where he's kept that letter opener."

Sam shrugged. "Like I said—a hundred places."

"But not with friends. What would he have said to them fifteen years ago? 'My wife's first husband gave this to her and I'm jealous so I stole it and I'd like for you to hold on to it for God knows how many years'? Besides, Brooke said Tavell didn't have any friends."

"She was just a little girl. He could have had dozens of friends she didn't know about."

"Maybe *she* wouldn't have, but the police would. Especially later, after the murder, when you investigated his background."

"Sure. We found out a lot. There were police files on the case, but I had a whole box of personal files of my own. I kept those files here at the house all these years." He suddenly looked exultant. "I finally found that box of files in the basement today and spent the whole evening going over them after that moron next door went home."

"He wasn't supposed to leave until I got back."

"Well, he got all jittery, scared that excuse for a wife of his might call, so he took off."

"Jerk." Vincent leaned back in his chair, grinning. "Still, way to go, finding those files, Dad." Sam shrugged. "How much information did you have in them?"

"Lots, and I remember most of what I read. What I

don't"—he leaned down and tapped a box beside his chair—
"is right in here."

"I'm absolutely dazzled, Dad. So, are you going to share
what you know?"

"You couldn't shut me up if you paid me," Sam said lightly,
then turned serious. He was quiet for a moment, then began
slowly. "Tavell's father left when he was young. His mother
didn't pay much attention to him. Former teachers described
him as 'especially bright but unmotivated.' I don't know why
that phrase sticks in my mind, but it does. Tavell dropped out
of high school without a degree. He worked odd jobs. Stayed
the longest at some auto body shop. Can't remember the
name. It's probably not even in business anymore."

"Did he get married?"

"Before Anne? No. I was sure of that even before I looked
in my files."

"But Zach didn't marry Anne until he was forty. There
must have been girlfriends."

"Several, as I recall. One in particular. I can't remember
her name right off the bat. She had a kid, or maybe a couple
of kids—have to check the files again for that information.
Anyway, he stayed with her for quite a while. Then he just
took off. She ended up a junkie." Sam squinted as if he were
seeing a face in the shadows. "Nadine! That was her name.
Nadine . . . can't remember her last name. Have to look in
the files again."

"I'll do it later," Vincent said.

"Good. She was still alive at the time of the murder and
we questioned her. I actually remember her. She was a pa-
thetic thing and not much help. She was too far gone on the
drugs. . . ."

"What happened to Nadine's child? Or children?"

"That's not in my files, but I know any child would have
been taken away from her."

"Is Nadine still alive?"

"I have no idea. But if she is, don't get any big ideas about
tracking her down. You won't get any information from her,
Vincent. I told you. She was a wreck fifteen years ago. I just

can't imagine she could still be alive, much less have any sense left." Sam sighed. "Anyway, a few years after Tavell left Nadine, he started working for a photographer and then he opened up his own studio. That's how he met Anne. She brought Brooke in for photographs—Christmas or something. Two or three months later, they were married. Anne's friends were all shocked. We interviewed a few of them. None of them liked Tavell. He was cold, standoffish—just the opposite of her first husband, they said. And he didn't like her socializing with them. Eventually, he cut her off from just about everyone."

"Do you think he did that out of jealousy?"

"That's what most of them thought. Makes sense, but I also made a notation to myself that maybe he didn't want her finding out too much about him."

"I guess he wouldn't," Vincent said. "I glanced at that album of newspaper articles you have by the chair."

"Oh yeah," Sam said abashedly. "I saw it today, too. I guess I got it mixed in with our family albums. I hope Brooke didn't see it."

"I'm sure she didn't," Vincent assured his father, although he had a bad feeling she had. "Things get misplaced. It's just part of life. Anyway, one of the articles mentioned that an assault charge had been made against Zach by a woman when he was in his twenties. It was dropped, but I wonder how many other crimes he committed between then and the time he murdered Brooke's mother, crimes he got away with?" Vincent shook his head. "God only knows what we're really dealing with here."

"Not us, Son," Sam said grimly. "Cinnamon Girl. After all, she's the one he wants to kill."

# seventeen

## 1

"I know how unprofessional this sounds," Jay told Hal Myers, "but I really hate having to interview Robert Eads's father."

"Because he's a minister?"

"Because we have to talk about his son being gay."

"Maybe he knew."

"I don't think so," Jay said as they walked toward the Eads home. "I knew Robert, remember? He definitely wasn't out of the closet. I met his father once, too. Nicest guy you could ever run into, but traditional and clearly hopeful there was something serious going on between Robert and Brooke." Jay paused. "Brooke thought an awful lot of Reverend Eads. She'd known him for years. I guess he really tried to be there for her after her mother was murdered. Anyway, from things she said about him and the way he struck me, he just wouldn't understand homosexuality at all. He's probably not a homophobe—just a guy who wanted his son to get married and love his wife like he loved his own and give them lots of grandchildren."

Hal nodded as they passed a riotously colored mass of yellow, pink, and lavender petunias in beds around the porch. "Do you think Brooke realized he was homosexual before she walked in on him and Townsend?"

"I don't know. Stacy was pretty sure about it. She's really keen about picking up on stuff like that. But she never said if she mentioned her suspicions to Brooke or if Brooke acted like she might have her own doubts. I remember once saying I wondered if Robert and Brooke would get married, and Stace laughed and said, 'Don't bet on it.' I asked her what she meant, but she said something vague like she always does when she doesn't want me to know something."

"Does she keep a lot of secrets from you?" Hal asked.

"Oh, I didn't mean she was keeping secrets. Maybe she was just covering up for something Brooke had said about Eads in the lovemaking department, you know, like old Robert was a real dud in the sack—"

At that moment a tall, thin man who looked like an older version of Robert swung open the door, obviously heard Jay's remark, and chose to ignore it by smiling as he said stiffly, "Hello, gentlemen. May I help you?"

Jay's face flamed. Feeling the young man was beyond speech with embarrassment, Hal quickly stepped in. "Hello, Reverend. I'm Detective Myers and this is Detective Corrigan."

"I remember you."

Hal held up his badge anyway. "We wonder if you'd mind answering a few questions for us."

"About Bobby?" Hal nodded. "Certainly not," Rev. Eads said. "Please."

He motioned them into the house. Myers entered with ease, but Jay felt as if he were a crab scurrying along the beach looking for a place to hide, suddenly deciding that crabs felt ashamed of themselves. Maybe it was just the look in Rev. Eads's eyes—the forgiving, serene, almost not-of-this-world look that made Jay feel little and piteous.

They walked into a small living room crowded with furniture that looked like it had come from the 1950s, the chairs and couch swathed in brightly flowered slipcovers, the tables covered with framed photos and knickknacks, the windows shrouded with flounced net over limp satin draperies. Jay wasn't crazy about Stacy's Spartan sense of home decoration, but he knew he'd die in a busy, smothering room like this one.

Rev. Eads indicated that the men should sit on a ruffled pale pink couch, then asked if they would care for anything to drink. When they declined, he then arranged his tall, slim frame in a giant armchair wrapped carefully in a slipcover bearing carriages and horses and flowers and birds and children. Jay thought the children were supposed to be playing in a park, but it was really hard to make anything out of the frantic mess.

"Have you come up with any 'leads,' as they say on television?" Rev. Eads asked Hal.

"Nothing significant, I'm afraid." Hal took out a notebook. So did Jay, although there was no reason for them both to take notes. However, Jay didn't know what to do with his hands and feared he'd accidentally knock over one of the twenty doodads on the table right beside him. "I can tell you that your son's body will probably be released day after tomorrow. I thought you might like to begin making funeral preparations."

Rev. Eads nodded slowly. "It seems like such a long time that poor Bobby has lain in that cold, sterile place."

"The ME's office," Hal supplied.

"Yes. I understand that the conditions of Bobby's death called for his body to be . . . studied. . . ." He swallowed hard. "It was just hard waiting. Especially for my wife. She's lying down right now. Before Bobby's death, she was a whirlwind of activity all day long. Now . . ." He raised his shoulders. "It seems all she wants to do is sleep."

"She's on medication, no doubt," Hal said.

"Yes. I refused it for myself, but my wife is more fragile. I insisted she take something when she couldn't stop crying. This has been the worst blow of her life. Of course, losing a child is the worst blow of any parent's life."

Jay thought back to the children he'd seen abandoned, abused, even killed by their parents and wished what Rev. Eads had just said were true of all parents. Unfortunately, the world was a crueler place than Eads realized, or maybe cared to realize or dwell on.

Hal leaned forward. "Rev. Eads, did Robert have any enemies? I know we asked you this earlier, but I thought something might have come to mind in the last couple of days."

"I'm afraid not. Bobby had no enemies. He was a good boy—rather quiet, very private, but a fine human being. He was extremely polite and considerate, not the type to make enemies."

"Robert and Brooke Yeager knew each other for a long time, didn't they?" Hal asked.

"Since they were children. Brooke's family attended this church. Robert was a few years older than Brooke, but they met in vacation Bible school and struck up a friendship. Oh, not a close one until lately, that is. They dated for a while. I was quite happy about that, and just as unhappy when their relationship ended."

"Do you know why they broke up?"

Rev. Eads frowned. "No. Bobby was quite closemouthed on the topic. I saw Brooke a couple of times after the breakup, but I didn't ask questions. I felt it wasn't my place."

"I see." Hal wrote nothing, but Jay took notes assiduously. "Mrs. Yeager attended your church with her first husband, right?"

"Anne and Karl?" Rev. Eads smiled briefly. "Yes. They seemed to be such a happy family. They were all beautiful—just beautiful, like a family out of a magazine. Karl was a ray of sunshine. Such a confident, joyful man, who adored his wife and daughter. We were all so shocked when he learned he had cancer and he passed so quickly. Poor Anne was deeply depressed and angry with God. The latter is common but, of course, unfair. Anyway, I was extremely concerned about her. Then she perked up. Quite abruptly actually. It seemed like a miracle."

"I think the miracle was due to tranquilizers and antidepressants," Hal said gently.

"Maybe. I didn't know she was taking medication. I was simply relieved she seemed to be coming back to life. And then, just like that"—he snapped his long fingers, causing Jay to mess up a word—"she married Zachary Tavell. I performed the ceremony."

"Did you approve of Anne marrying Tavell?"

"It wasn't my place to approve or disapprove."

"But what did you think of Tavell?" Hal persisted.

The minister went silent for at least twenty seconds. Jay finally looked at him, partly out of curiosity and partly because he hoped Rev. Eads had forgotten his faux pas at the door about Robert's prowess as a lover. The man's head was cocked slightly to one side as if he were thinking. Jay remembered seeing Eads about three months ago with Jay and Brooke. He now looked ten years older, his brown hair laced with gray, his cheekbones so prominent it seemed as if they could pierce his sallow cheeks. Even his lips seemed thinner. Only the eyes looked the same—large, a darker gray than Stacy's, and almost unnervingly steady. The man looks noble, Jay thought. Righteous and *noble*.

Rev. Eads said slowly, "Frankly, Detective, I never expected to see Zachary after the wedding ceremony. I was surprised to spot him in the congregation each Sunday for the next few weeks."

"Why were you surprised?" Hal asked.

"Because he didn't strike me as a religious man. He was uncomfortable even during the marriage ceremony, and it wasn't the usual wedding jitters. I've seen those a hundred times. He kept looking around—how can I put it? Almost fearfully, as if he felt he didn't belong in the house of the Lord. When I first saw him in the congregation, I thought he might attend a couple of times to please Anne, then disappear.

Imagine my surprise when he showed up in my office at the church one evening. He said he needed to talk."

"Talk about what?"

"Detective, I know the rules of confidentiality don't apply to me as they do to a Catholic priest who has heard a confession, but I still feel I can't answer that question unless forced. The man expected the conversation to be kept private."

"Can't you even give us a hint?" Jay burst out loudly.

Rev. Eads blinked quickly three times, startled. Hal Myers looked slightly amused. Jay could have bitten his tongue, but there was no taking back the question, which even to him sounded childlike, not to mention boisterous.

"Zachary was a troubled man," Rev. Eads said carefully. "Apparently, he'd done some things in his youth he regretted. When he married Anne, he felt he'd completely changed. About a year after the marriage, though, he began having doubts."

"About himself or about the marriage?" Jay asked.

"About both, but mostly about himself."

Hal intervened. "Did he doubt that he hadn't changed enough? Or at all?" Rev. Eads simply stared blankly at him. "Reverend, did you get the feeling that Zachary Tavell was afraid he might do something to harm Anne?"

"Oh *no*. If I had, I would have warned Anne. I simply thought he was troubled, unsatisfied with himself, feeling guilty about something in his past. But certainly not that he was afraid he was a danger to Anne or Brooke."

Jay said, "But after the murder, you knew you were wrong."

Rev. Eads seemed to retreat behind those grave, steady eyes. "I still have trouble believing he murdered Anne."

"You don't *believe* it?" Jay asked incredulously.

"I said I have trouble believing it. It might be a form of denial on my part. Maybe I don't want to admit I didn't sense trouble coming, and that perhaps I could have stopped it." The minister looked down at his hands, which Hal noticed were trembling slightly.

"How did Robert react to the murder?" Hal asked.

"Unfortunately, he was fascinated by it."

Hal raised his eyebrows. "Fascinated?"

"Yes. I didn't like for my son to be intrigued by a murder. It didn't seem . . ."

"Healthy?"

"Productive. Good for him. I wanted him to be a happy boy, not one who dwelled on murder. But the incident did receive enormous publicity. It's all anyone in this area could talk about. 'The Rose Murder,' they called it. I believe the newspapers came up with that phrase. And, of course, Bobby knew the family."

Jay stopped writing. "I know Robert knew Brooke and Anne, but did he know Zach, too?"

Rev. Eads looked startled. "Well, yes. Bobby was just a teenager and Zach was around forty, but I used to see them talking sometimes. I got the feeling Zach liked Bobby."

"And how did Bobby—Robert—feel about Zach?"

"He liked Zach, maybe because Zach didn't treat him like a child as some of my other parishioners did. Bobby told me one time that Zach had promised to take him fishing and I know they played a few games of basketball together. I'm afraid I never excelled at sports. But Bobby didn't discuss Zachary, and I didn't ask what they found to talk about. I regret that now."

Hal sat back and let Jay take over. "How did Robert react when he heard that Zach had murdered Anne?"

"At first he didn't believe it. For several days he kept saying there must be a mistake. Then, as the evidence mounted, he stopped defending Zach. But it was quite a while before he lost interest in the case." Rev. Eads frowned. "I don't see what any of this has to do with Bobby's murder."

Jay ignored the comment. "Do you think Robert started seeing Brooke Yeager because of his interest in 'The Rose Murder'?"

"No! Certainly not!"

"Do you think Zach Tavell could have murdered your son?"

"*What?*" Eads's face went white. "Zachary murder Bobby? Why would he?"

"Because he thought Robert meant to do Brooke harm. Robert *has* been stalking her ever since they broke up."

"Bobby stalking Brooke? That's ridiculous!"

"It's true," Jay maintained. "I live beside her. I've heard him banging on her door and shouting for her to open it and talk to him."

Rev. Eads's face went from white to red. "That's ridiculous! I mean, you must be mistaken. Maybe there was a problem with the acoustics in the hallway . . ." Rev. Eads seemed to realize he was floundering, took a deep breath, then said firmly, "Detective Corrigan, their breakup was a mutual decision. Bobby told me so and he didn't lie."

"Then why was Brooke considering getting a restraining order against him?" Jay asked.

"A restraining order?" Rev. Eads's eyes darted around as if he might find a reason somewhere in the room. "As I said, there must be some kind of mistake." He trailed off weakly. "Bobby would never harass . . ."

"He did."

Eads abruptly became agitated. "Why on earth would Bobby be stalking Brooke?"

"Because he was afraid she was going to tell people, particularly you, why they broke up."

"What do you mean?" Eads demanded.

Jay hesitated and Hal Myers took control. "Rev. Eads, Brooke ended her relationship with your son because she found out he was gay," he said gently. "Now, you might already have known, but—"

"*Gay!*" Eads nearly shouted, half-rising from his chair. "Do you mean homosexual? I never heard anything so preposterous, so silly, so . . ." He sputtered to a halt, then said, "He was dating Brooke Yeager. A female. Doesn't that tell you something?"

"It tells us he was trying to hide his sexual orientation," Hal said. "The person he was romantically involved with was Aaron Townsend."

"Aaron Townsend?" Eads repeated faintly. "His boss? Or rather, former boss? *Romantically* involved?" Hal nodded. Eads looked deeply offended. "And how do you *think* you know this?"

"Brooke Yeager told us. Reluctantly, I might add. She didn't know, either, for a while. Then she caught Robert and Townsend in a compromising position. She was just as shocked as you are. Anyway, it seems your son was desperate to hide the truth. When Brooke found out, he was terrified she would tell people. That's why he was stalking her—to persuade her not to tell the truth. Obviously, she didn't intend to tell anyone—even *we* had to drag it out of her—but Robert seemed to go off the deep end about the whole thing. He just couldn't or wouldn't believe that she wasn't going to tell the world. Or you."

Rev. Eads stared at them. Then he simply seemed to implode in his chair, sinking down, looking half the size he had a few moments before, his eyes going dull, his face gray, his lips parting. Jay was on the verge of suggesting they call the EMS when Eads said at last, "Well, I guess that explains a lot about Bobby's behavior over the years. I don't know why I didn't see it. He probably needed someone to talk to and I let him down."

"I'm sure you didn't let your son down in any way," Hal said sincerely.

"He didn't feel free to be honest with me."

"Maybe he thought this was something he couldn't tell you for fear of losing your love."

"There is *nothing* Bobby could have done to lose my love."

"I'm glad to hear that," Myers said. He paused, then asked, "Do you think Tavell might have given Robert something to keep for him?"

"Something to keep?" Eads repeated emptily. "Such as what?"

"A letter opener."

"A what?"

"A letter opener. And a wedding ring, but we're more interested in the opener. Rev. Eads, we told you your son was stabbed to death. We didn't tell you with what. The murder weapon was a silver letter opener that had been given to Anne Yeager by her first husband. Brooke has positively identified it. It disappeared a few days before Anne's death, along with Anne's wedding ring from Karl. Obviously, Tavell couldn't have kept either in prison with him all these years, which had us really puzzled. Now that we've found out about the friendship between Robert and Tavell, I wonder if Tavell gave the letter opener and ring to Robert to keep for him."

"Why would Zachary take Anne's letter opener and ring?" Eads asked.

"Tavell was jealous of Karl Yeager. He didn't like the way his wife cherished gifts from her first husband. Anyway, he could have taken the things and given them to Robert to keep with some flimsy excuse a fourteen-year-old wouldn't question. Maybe he said he planned to hock them someday. The ring did have a diamond in it. Robert apparently liked Zach and might have been glad to do him a favor. Then Zach killed Anne, and Robert was left with the opener and the ring."

"That's not possible. He would have said something," Rev. Eads challenged.

"You said Robert was fascinated by the murder case. He might have held on to the items as macabre keepsakes." Rev. Eads glared at him. "Or, more likely, simply because he was afraid of being dragged into the whole mess. He was a kid, Rev. Eads. Kids don't always use the best judgment."

Rev. Eads seemed to ponder what Hal had just said. "I suppose it's possible. But if Tavell didn't have the letter opener, how could he have used it to stab Bobby?"

"Robert could have had the opener with him. Maybe he was planning to give it back to Brooke as a trade-off—'I'll give you your mother's letter opener in return for your silence about me and Aaron.' " Rev. Eads's face reddened with insult. He was about to protest, but Hal plowed on, his voice taking on a more soothing tone. "I'm sure such a thing wasn't in character for Robert, but he was desperate, and desperate people don't always act in character."

Rev. Eads seemed to disappear deep inside himself for a few seconds. Finally, he looked at them again and nodded. "Yes, he could have done something totally out of character because he was frightened. That must explain his behavior." He paused. "But if Bobby *did* have the letter opener, how was he stabbed with it?"

"Maybe Tavell confronted Robert in the alley," Hal said. "Robert sensed he was in danger. He pulled out the opener to defend himself, only Tavell was stronger and more skilled with weapons. He wouldn't want Robert raising some kind of alarm that would alert the surveillance police stationed in front and back of the apartment building."

"And so, to protect himself, Zachary wrested the letter opener away from Bobby," Rev. Eads finished slowly. "And then he proceeded to stab my poor son to death."

Jay watched in deep sympathy as Rev. Eads buried his noble face in his hands and began to sob.

# 2

Madeleine Townsend burst into Aaron's office, her color high, the light of anger simmering behind her dark brown eyes. Aaron looked up from his desk, startled. "Where were you yesterday?" Madeleine demanded.

"Home. Why?"

"Why? Because the Garden Club party was yesterday— the party where the white, pink, and cerise variegated rose was being named in Mother's honor. And you were *not* home! I called time after time."

"I had the phone turned off. I had a migraine headache and I went to bed. I forgot about the damned garden party. I suppose Mother's furious."

"To say the least."

Aaron sighed and tossed down his pen. "So what else is new? She's always mad at me. At least this time I gave her something to be mad about. I don't, however, know what *you* are so mad about."

"Aside from missing the garden party, you were supposed to take me out to dinner night before last and you didn't show up."

"I'm sorry. I forgot. Besides, I thought our plans were extremely tentative."

"You didn't even *call*!"

"Maddy, please lower your voice," Aaron said evenly. "Just because my door is closed doesn't mean the employees can't hear you at that volume."

"I don't *care* if they hear me. I don't care what they think of me!"

"Since when don't you care what people think of you? I thought your main concern in life was what people thought of you." Aaron took a deep breath. "Forgive me. I didn't mean that. I really didn't."

"You *did*!"

"Maddy, has something happened? Are you upset about something and taking out your anger on me?"

"I am upset about you and your increasing lack of regard for me!"

"What do you mean?"

Madeleine's usually soft voice rose. "I *mean* all of these social gatherings of Mother's are boring for me unless you're around, but lately you only show up half the time! I *mean* I count on you for a dinner out once a week, an evening at the movies or the symphony, an invitation to come over when you're opening one of your ridiculously expensive wines and downing it like it's some magic elixir. Most of it tastes like crap, actually."

"Maddy!"

"It does. I only pretend to like it. For you. I pretend for *you*. I try to look pretty for you. I try to act cheerful and charming for you, no matter how I feel. Everything I do is for you. You used to appreciate my efforts. Now you don't seem to know I'm alive!"

"Madeleine, please. . . ."

"Don't you dare try to placate me like I'm a child. That might work on acquaintances, but I've known you all my life. You were a selfish, careless, neglectful excuse for a boy and you haven't improved one scintilla as a man!"

Aaron stared at his beautiful sister for moment and saw a mixture of hardness and petulance in her face that reminded him of his mother. Maddy had become the center of his life ever since he'd wrecked the snowmobile on which she'd been a passenger and shattered her leg and hip. He'd been trying to make it up to her ever since then and he thought he had. After all, she'd seemed loving and forgiving. Now he knew she'd been acting. She hadn't forgiven him for anything and for the last twenty-four years she'd clung to him with the tenacity of a leech.

A leech? The word startled him. How could he possibly have such a thought? He felt overwhelmed by shame and was about to say something comforting, conciliatory, even tender, when Madeleine snarled, "You started ignoring me when *he* came into your life. You pushed me aside for that unsophisticated, sloppily adoring sycophant Robert Eads! Of *all* the men in the world to pick for a lover, why did it have to be him?"

Aaron was too stunned to speak. He had no idea Maddy knew about his homosexuality, much less his affair with Robert. How long had she known about his sexual preference? Exactly how repelled was she by it? Plenty, if the look on her face told him anything. He couldn't bear to see her disgust.

"I . . . I don't know what you're talking about," he said weakly. "Are you implying I'm . . . gay?"

Madeleine burst into bitter laughter. "God, Aaron, do you think I *just* realized it? I've known for years. And I don't care who you have sex with—women, men, animals!" Aaron's jaw dropped slightly in shock. He'd never heard his gentle sister speak harshly, much less with such venom. "What I care about,

Aaron, is that you stopped putting me *first*. I am your little sister that you crippled, whose life *you* ruined, whom *you* turned into an object of pity to some people and a freak to others. *You* did all of that, so you owe me. Instead, you pushed me aside for some pretty-faced young twerp."

Madeleine stopped, her face slightly damp and pink from rage, her eyes seeming lit by something ugly, almost savage. Finally, she drew an almost heaving breath. "I thought when he was gone, things would change. But they haven't. You're just as far away from me as you were when he was alive, and I *will not* stand for it!"

Aaron sat astonished as he acknowledged the acrimony his sister felt for him because of the accident. He'd been eaten up with guilt because of it since he was sixteen, and he'd heaped love and attention on Madeleine, hoping he could partly atone for what he'd done. He knew the exercise was useless where his mother was concerned. She never had and never would forgive him for "ruining" the beautiful girl she'd looked at almost as a valuable museum piece, not a beloved child.

But Aaron had thought Maddy loved him enough to forgive him. She'd been his shadow since she could walk again and she'd never acted happier than when she was in his company. Now he realized she felt he owed his entire being to her. She was to be his Alpha and Omega, leaving no room for anyone else in his life, male *or* female.

"Does Mother know about me?" he finally asked in a frail, frightened voice he loathed.

"Do you think you'd be sitting in that fine leather chair here at the agency if Mother knew? A couple of times she's had doubts about you, but *I* quashed them. *I* have kept you in her good graces as much as you can ever be, and it hasn't been easy. And she's not the only one. Brooke Yeager didn't just suspect. She knew. I could see it in her eyes when she looked at you *after* Robert's hasty retreat. Do you realize the damage she could do to you, Aaron?"

"Brooke would never do anything to hurt me. She didn't hurt Robert. She's not vindictive. She's kind and—"

"Oh, shut up, Aaron." Madeleine leaned over the desk and slammed her fist on the shining wood. Aaron had forgotten how strong her right arm had become from the years of lifting her whole body weight up on her cane. "You don't really know a thing about Brooke Yeager except that she's an attractive asset to the office and she has a tragic past. You don't know me, either. All these years you've thought I was fragile, vulnerable, the one in need of protection. Instead, *you* were the one in need of protection, particularly from your choices of lovers, and most especially from Robert Eads. You *loved* him, didn't you? *Didn't you?*"

"I don't know." Aaron felt sick. He didn't know how he'd felt about Robert. He didn't know anything anymore now that he was seeing his sister's true nature—the nature of a parasite. And then it hit him. She was a parasite willing to do whatever she could to rid herself of someone she perceived to be her rival. "The phone call and the letter threatening to tell Mother about Robert," Aaron managed. "Robert and I thought they were from Brooke, but they were from you, weren't they, Maddy?"

"You weren't being as careful with Robert as you had been with your other lovers. I knew Mother was going to find out. I was trying to warn you to be more cautious."

Aaron gave her a long, flat look. "No. That is not the reason. You called and wrote because you thought Robert meant more to me than anyone in the past had and you were jealous. You wanted to scare me into giving him up. And you hoped I'd think they were Brooke's handiwork because you wanted her out of my life, too." Madeleine didn't answer and an awful thought crept into Aaron's mind. Just *how* jealous had Madeleine been of Robert? Clearly, she wasn't the calm, stable woman Aaron had thought her to be. There was something deeply wrong with her beyond the injury to her leg. But how wrong? What was she capable of? Exactly how far had his beloved sister been willing to go to get both Robert and Brooke out of his life?

# 3

Brooke looked up from her desk to see Madeleine Townsend standing in her brother's glass-enclosed office. Her face was flushed, her usually perfect hair tousled, and she leaned so far over his desk she looked like she was going to collapse onto it. Brooke could hear voices coming from the office although she couldn't make out words. In her three years at Townsend Realty, she had never seen Aaron and Madeleine argue.

"Wonder what that's all about?" Judith Lambert asked, suddenly appearing in front of Brooke. Last year when Judith had dated Aaron, everyone had been surprised because they couldn't believe she was Aaron's type, even though they had no idea who *would* be Aaron's type. Ever since their much-anticipated breakup, Judith seemed to spend half her time watching Aaron's every move. Right now her blue eyes were bright with curiosity. With her extremely thin body and short, spiky haircut, she reminded Brooke of some kind of high-strung miniature dog that always seemed to be quivering with anxiety or excitement.

"I have no idea," Brooke said absently, turning her gaze back to her work. She didn't like Judith with her blatant nosiness and constant gossiping. Brooke knew that more than once she'd been the target of Judith's voracious curiosity and rumormongering, especially about "The Rose Murder." "Brothers and sisters argue sometimes, Judith. It's probably not a big deal."

"*That* brother and sister don't argue," Judith persisted, unfazed by the dismissive tone of Brooke's voice. "In fact, they're so close, it's weird. It used to drive me nuts when I was dating Aaron. Madeleine was *always* around. She'd arrive just as we were leaving for a date, and half the time Aaron would ask her to come with us. And she would!" Judith blew air hard out of her nose like a horse. Brooke half-expected her to snort and flap her lips. "Couldn't she tell he was just being polite when he invited her along?"

"Maybe she could tell he wasn't. Maybe he really wanted her company."

"When he was on a date with *me*?" Judith clearly thought the idea of a man not wanting to be alone with her was absurd. "No, there's something funny about those two."

"Oh."

"Honestly, I know what I'm talking about."

"Ummm. Okay."

"Mark my words. Strange. Peculiar. *Unnatural*."

Judith obviously had no intention of giving up no matter how uninterested Brooke acted. "Such as what, Judith?" Brooke finally asked bluntly. "Do you think they're not really brother and sister? That they are actually *married* and just trying to put one over on all of us?"

Judith drew back. "You don't have to be flippant and make fun of me!"

"You said they act odd together. I gave a suggestion as to why they might act odd. How is that making fun of you?"

Judith's laser blue eyes narrowed. "You think you're better than everyone here, don't you, Brooke?"

Taken aback, Brooke asked incredulously, "Why would you think that?"

"Because you're semifamous. Or should I say infamous? You got to be one of the players in the famous 'Rose Murder.' You got to testify at a murderer's trial and have your picture splashed all over the paper when you were just a kid. It's a wonder you don't charge for autographs."

Brooke tossed down her pen, swept up in a shaking fury. "You're absolutely right as usual, Judith. Having your mother murdered always gives one a sense of superiority. None of the rest of you in this office got to live through that lovely, fairy-tale experience. Just me. I'm the one people like you speculate about, gossip about, make up stories about. That certainly does make me feel a step above everyone here, especially you, Judith, with your absolutely humdrum, boringly normal upbringing. Now, will you please take your meddlesome, vicious, destructive self away from my desk before I run this pen straight up that beak you call a nose!"

Judith backed away from her, her mouth opening slowly. Everyone else in the office was looking at them, some in shock, some on the verge of laughter. Her flat cheeks almost as red as her hair, Judith accused shrilly, "I think you're as crazy as your stepfather!" Then she flounced away to the restroom.

As soon as she slammed the door behind her, a burst of applause broke out in the main room. In spite of her embarrassment at her outburst, Brooke couldn't help smiling a bit as one of the other Realtors, Charlie, exclaimed, "She's had that coming for a long time. Good job, Brooke!"

The office hoopla had drawn the attention of Aaron and Madeleine. Aaron rose quickly from his desk, brushed past Madeleine, and opened his door. "What's going on out here?"

"Judith chose the wrong day to pick on Brooke," Hannah said, beaming. "Don't get mad at Brooke. She was just trying to do her work. Judith wouldn't let her alone."

Aaron looked at all of them without a trace of emotion. Normally he would have either chastised everyone or insisted on having a private meeting with the two warring employees. This time he looked at Brooke and asked, "Are you all right?"

"Of course. I just blew off steam that I probably should have kept to myself."

"I doubt that," Aaron said. He looked around the room. "When my sister leaves and Ms. Lambert finally emerges from the sanctuary of the restroom, will someone ask her to come to my office?"

He looked like he was going to say something else, changed his mind, and returned to his office, shutting the door behind him. Surreptitiously everyone watched Madeleine begin talking again, loudly, as Aaron ignored her. After no more than three minutes, she turned and left his office, stopping to give all the employees a murderous look before she swept out the front doors as grandly as she could manage with her limp.

"Trouble in paradise," Hannah murmured.

Charlie made a droll face. "It's about time. I was getting sick of those two fawning over each other. Hey, Hannah, let's do a coin toss. Heads I tell Lady Judith she's being sent to the principal's office, tails you do."

"Okay," Hannah said hesitantly, then breathed in relief when the coin came up heads. "Looks like it's your job, Charlie." She turned to Brooke. "I have to admit, Aaron scares me."

"Don't let him," Brooke said. "He's mostly hot air."

Hannah smiled. "I wish I was as brave as you. I don't think anyone frightens you."

Brooke looked over at Mia's still empty desk and thought of the man who had brutally killed both Mia and Brooke's mother. I wish what Hannah said were true, Brooke thought. God, how I wish that were true.

# 4

Four o'clock, Brooke noted on her wristwatch as she climbed out of her car. She'd just shown a truly darling young expectant couple a house they wanted desperately, a house that would be perfect for them and the child who would arrive in two months, a house too far out of their price range. These situations happened every day, but this particular couple had gotten to Brooke, maybe because they looked like a young version of her own parents. She promised to talk to the owner about lowering the asking price and saw the hope flare in their innocent, smooth faces, which hurt her even more because she knew the owner had no intention of dropping the price by one dollar.

Tired and discouraged after her first day back at work

since Mia's murder, Brooke trudged into the office, stopped at the water fountain, passed by the desk of Judith Lambert, who gave her a truly vicious look, and plopped down on her desk chair with a slight groan. She opened a desk drawer and took out a couple of Hershey's Kisses for energy. She knew Aaron wouldn't mind if she went home an hour early on this particular day, but she was determined to stick it out although she was exhausted and the burn on her lower back stung.

Before she got the second Hershey's Kiss down, a tiny elderly woman crept up to Brooke's desk, clutching fearfully at her purse as if she thought someone might make a dive for it. Brooke tried to give her a reassuring smile, feeling that she already knew the woman's errand. She was right. The woman told Brooke her name was Amelia Gracen, she was eighty-six years old, she had been married for sixty-five of those eighty-six years, and she lived in the lovely Victorian on the corner of Shaw and Clifton Streets, a house with which Brooke was familiar.

Then Mrs. Gracen broke down and described her husband's death four months earlier. It seems he'd decided to climb up on the roof and adjust the satellite dish himself. "Damn fool," Mrs. Gracen said, then burst into noisy sobs she tried to hide in a dainty lace-edged handkerchief. "Our grandson gave us that dish for our wedding anniversary and I knew it was trouble the first time I looked at it. Those things aren't natural. Television antennas are natural, not those crazy space-age doodads. I always expected it to start spinning and send us right up to the moon, but Orville, that was my husband, was just fascinated with it and must have climbed up on that roof twenty times to 'tweak' it, he always said. Well, he tweaked it one time too many. He slid off the roof and splattered himself all over the sidewalk. Oh my God, what a mess he made, the old coot!" She sobbed some more into her handkerchief.

"I'm so sorry," Brooke murmured, unable to come up with anything truly comforting to say about such a gruesome accident.

"It served him right. He was the most hardheaded man I ever knew. Nobody could tell him *anything,* especially me. Well, I guess he learned his lesson that time." She sobbed some more and nearly blew a hole into the delicate material of the handkerchief. "Anyway, I can't afford to keep the house all by myself. I don't even want to. I mean, inside there are a lot of wonderful memories—we lived there forty years—but as soon as I step out on the sidewalk . . ." She shuddered. "Oh, lordy. You can still see stains on the sidewalk. For a little guy, he had enough blood in him to fill up a grizzly bear. And I swear, you can see a dent in the sidewalk where that hard head of his hit."

"Oh, how awful for you," Brooke mumbled, sympathetic and yet on the verge of macabre laughter.

"Well, my friend Inez lives in this nice little retirement community not too far from downtown and she says they just have a ball there with Canasta Night and Charades Night and those wonderful gospel singers that come on Sunday afternoons. So, I think I'll put up the house for sale and move there. Do you think that's terrible of me?"

"Of course not," Brooke reassured her. "I'm sure your husband would want you to be happy."

"I guess, but it doesn't seem right, me singing and playing cards and games when he's lying in his grave, all cold and alone. But if he'd just *listened* to me for once in his hard-headed life—"

"So you'd like to list the house with us?" Brooke asked before Mrs. Gracen could get started again on her husband's hard head.

"Yes, I certainly would, if you don't mind."

"It would be a pleasure." Brooke gave her a smile, offered her a cup of water, then handed her a few Hershey's Kisses.

"Oh, I just love these!" Mrs. Gracen said, ripping into the foil. "So did Orville. We'd eat a whole bag of them in one night." Then she cried some more.

By the time Brooke finished with Mrs. Gracen, she felt tired enough to fall out of her chair. Fifteen more minutes, she thought. Fifteen more minutes and I will have made it with honor through one whole day.

She had just begun to straighten up her desk when a young, jaunty-faced guy around nineteen entered Townsend Realty. He stood at the front of the room, holding a package, and called out, "Brooke Yeager? Do we have a Brooke Yeager in the house?"

"Yes, we do," Brooke said.

"Then *this* package is for you!" he announced grandly.

Brooke was amused by the young man's cockiness. He acted like she'd just won the lottery. Instead, all he handed her was a small box about two by four inches swathed in brown wrapping paper. She glanced down to see her name and the address of Townsend Realty printed in block letters, clearly done with a felt-tip pen. Then the return address caught her gaze:

Sunset Memorial Park
Charleston, WV

Brooke's heart beat faster. Sunset Memorial Park—the cemetery where her parents were buried. She had decorated the graves on Memorial Day.

The delivery guy held out a clipboard to her. "Just sign on line twenty-five and it's all yours," he said cheerfully.

"What company do you work for?" Brooke asked.

"Archway Deliveries. Been with them for almost a year now."

"Who sent this box?" Brooke asked faintly.

The guy tilted his head and grinned. "Well, it's either a joke or someone who lives in a cemetery."

Brooke gave him a long look and his grin faded. "Seriously, I mean who brought this box in and paid to have it delivered to me?"

"Oh, I don't know." The guy's smile wavered slightly. "Honest, I don't, ma'am. People come in, leave a package, and pay the manager or his wife, and they assign us to deliver it sometime during the day. Well, occasionally people want a package delivered at a certain time. That was the case with yours. My manager said it was to be delivered ten or fifteen minutes before five." He stared at her. "Is there something wrong, ma'am?"

"I just don't know who could have sent it."

"Guess you'll have to open it, then." The guy shifted impatiently from one foot to the other, looking slightly alarmed. "If you'd just sign the sheet here, Ms. Yeager. I hate to rush you, but I got another delivery to make before five or I'll get in big trouble."

"Well, I wouldn't want that." Brooke signed her name as if in a dream. The guy waited a minute longer, clearly hoping for a tip, then gave it up as a lost cause with the weird-acting woman on the other side of the desk. She was in her own world, not even thinking about how much he might count on his tips. He said sourly, "Hope you enjoy whatever's inside— *not*."

Brooke stared at the box sitting on her desk for what seemed an endless time. Finally, Hannah looked over from her own desk and asked, "What's wrong? Afraid there's a snake in it?"

"I'm afraid it's something worse," Brooke said, her mouth dry.

"Like what?"

This time Brooke didn't answer. She couldn't just keep staring at the thing. She had to know what was inside, even though every fiber of her being told her the contents were not going to make her happy. Not with that return address.

With trembling fingers, she loosened the tape and removed the brown wrapping paper as carefully as she would beautiful gift wrap. The paper fell away, exposing a small, white box. There was no label on the box, but Brooke instinctively knew it had come from a jewelry shop. It wasn't a new box, though. The corners looked slightly frayed, and one end had the yellowish tinge of exposure to sunlight.

Her breath coming slowly yet deeply, she gently took the lid off the box. There, on a bed of white cotton, lay a small gold wedding ring adorned with a tiny diamond. Even though she didn't have to look to know what was engraved inside, Brooke picked up the ring and slanted it so that she could see the names written in tiny script:

*Anne & Karl*

# eighteen

## 1

Brooke hadn't been able to rise from her chair. She asked Charlie to go out and get the surveillance cops while she sat at her desk, staring at the wide gold ring with its one-third-carat diamond. When she tilted the box slightly, she could see the engraving, but she didn't touch the ring.

It was time for Townsend Realty to close, but naturally the arrival of the ring disturbed the schedule. Charlie insisted on staying with Aaron and Brooke until Hal Myers and Jay Corrigan arrived. Hannah, out of concern, had offered to stay as well. Judith, out of malicious curiosity, wanted to stay, too. Aaron had sent both women home.

"I have some brandy in my office, Brooke." Aaron's solicitous tone shocked her. She didn't know he had it in him. "Would a little help?"

Brooke shook her head. "I think it would take the whole bottle to help, and then I wouldn't make a good impression on the cops. Thanks anyway, Mr. Townsend."

"Call me Aaron, please," he said, sounding as if he'd like to add "just this once."

"I'll take some brandy," Charlie volunteered, trying to lighten the mood.

Aaron answered stiffly, "If Brooke doesn't need any, neither do you. This isn't a party."

"Well, excuse me for living," Charlie answered, patting Brooke on the shoulder. He'd been patting it for ten minutes and she thought if he didn't stop, she'd scream.

To her relief, Hal and Jay walked in and Charlie immediately backed off, as if he might be reprimanded for touching her. Hal smiled at her easily. Jay looked tense and angry. "Don't anybody touch that ring!" he barked.

Brooke, Aaron, and Charlie all froze guiltily before Brooke said, "Sorry. I already did."

"Calm down, Jay," Hal said mildly, then to Brooke, "I'm sure there weren't any fingerprints on it anyway. Tavell's too smart to have left any."

"So I assumed as soon as I saw the return address on the box." Even Brooke noticed how tired and dull her voice sounded. "My parents are buried in that cemetery." Hal nodded. "It was delivered by a boy from Archway Deliveries. And I did a little police work on my own. He said someone dropped this off to either the manager or his wife and said it was to be delivered before five o'clock. The boy didn't see who left the package, but maybe the manager remembers."

"What did the boy look like?" Jay asked.

"He was around nineteen. Straight brown hair. Some acne. I think his eyes were blue."

"Nothing suspicious about him?"

"No. He was just impatient. And mad." Brooke managed a small smile. "I forgot to give him a tip."

Hal frowned. "Oh, the poor thing. Well, at least we'll know which one he is at the delivery store—the one griping about you."

Brooke smiled slightly. "By the way, the stinging on my

lower back is reminding me to ask if the lab found out what had been sprayed on me at the planetarium."

Hal looked into her eyes. "Good old-fashioned drain cleaner. *Strong* drain cleaner, as if it had come from the bottom of a bottle that hadn't been shaken. That stuff can be fairly corrosive, especially on delicate skin." Hal paused. "Are you sure the girl with the blond hair sprayed it on you?"

"I'm ninety-five percent certain," Brooke said grimly. "What I don't know is her identity or why she would be working with Zach Tavell. I know you're going to tell me it's probably for money, but I have a hard time believing a teenage girl, no matter how hardened by the world, would be stupid enough to trust a half-crazy-looking man like Zach who she *has* to know is a murderer."

Hal gave her a doleful look. "Brooke, you'd be surprised what some people will do for a couple of dollars. Unfortunately, she's probably one of them."

# 2

Brooke wasn't sure when Vincent arrived. She sat slumped at her desk, answering Hal's and Jay's questions while Aaron and Charlie hovered around, acting as if they were being an immense help, when she looked up and saw Vincent standing about a foot away. He gave her a long, slow smile, bent down to lightly kiss her cheek, and said, "Hi, Cinnamon Girl."

"Hi, yourself," she answered. "Do you have an alarm that goes off at your house every time I'm in trouble?"

"It's a whirling red light with one of those air horns like you hear at football games." He looked at the detectives. "Hi, Hal, Jay."

They both nodded as Aaron approached importantly. "I'm Aaron Townsend, owner of this firm. And you are?"

"Vincent Lockhart."

"A friend of Ms. Yeager's?"

"Obviously."

Aaron colored slightly at his stupid question. "Well, I just wanted to be sure. You can't be too careful, you know." Charlie looked at Brooke and rolled his eyes. "Are you involved in the case, Mr. Lockhart?"

"Not directly."

"His father was the lead detective when Ms. Yeager's mother was murdered," Hal supplied. "He's a friend of Brooke's. *And* he's quite a famous writer."

"Famous writer?" Aaron frowned; then his face lit with an almost sickening veneration considering his earlier near hostility. "Oh yes, I've heard of you. You've been on the *New York Times* Best Seller List a number of times."

"A few," Vincent said modestly.

"Well, this is most exciting." Aaron became aware of the detectives looking at his beaming face and quickly rearranged his expression into one of concern. "Of course, our main worry is Brooke. This madman who seems to be after her . . . well . . . it's just unfathomable." And then he couldn't help himself. "Are you going to write about it, Mr. Lockhart?"

"I don't think so," Vincent answered laconically. "I'm just here as Brooke's friend." He looked at Hal. "Are you about finished with your questions? Because Brooke looks like she could use a good meal and some time to relax, hopefully with me."

Hal grinned at him. "We're through questioning her. Whether or not she wants to go running around with you is up to her."

Everyone looked at Brooke expectantly. What she wanted more than anything at that moment was to leap from her chair, grab Vincent's arm, dash off into the evening with him by her side, and never look back. Instead, she tried for a restrained smile, controlled body movements, and said calmly, "Dinner does sound nice, Vincent. Thank you."

Later, as Vincent pulled out of the Townsend Realty parking lot and they headed into the six o'clock traffic, he asked, "Any place in particular you'd like to eat?"

"Somewhere out-of-the-way. Informal. Dark. Quiet."

"I know just the place. Music?" She nodded and he turned on the CD player. "Now relax. Forget about flowers and rings, beautiful lady, and just float to the mellow sounds of the Eagles, circa the 1970s."

"You sound like a deejay."

"But you're smiling," Vincent said. "It's working already."

They headed west and the sinking sun slanted directly onto Brooke's face. She put on her sunglasses, then leaned her head back and listened to "Peaceful, Easy Feeling," wishing she could slip out of her troubles and into the beautiful world of the song.

She realized she was almost asleep when Vincent announced, "Here at last." She opened her eyes and looked at a cozy log cabin restaurant overlooking the river. "Do you want to go in and have dinner, or would you rather curl up and take a nap in the backseat?"

"You don't have a backseat," she said groggily.

"I guess we'll have to go in and eat, then." He cocked his head and grinned at her. "You're the only woman I know who takes a nap after getting scared half to death."

"I'm one of a kind, all right. Maybe you'll put me in a book someday." She looked at him. "A book of *fiction,* not a book about 'The Rose Murder.' "

"I have no intention of writing about 'The Rose Murder,' " Vincent returned gravely. "That's the truth and I want you to know it for certain, Brooke. My interest in you has always been . . ."—he seemed to search for a word, looked away, then said lightly, "chaste as the driven snow."

"Oh, heck, that's what they all say," Brooke returned, acting disappointed. He was teasing her, and for the moment, she was glad. But she hoped, she *knew,* their relationship had grown beyond mere altruistic friendship. And in spite of everything, that made her happy. "Let's go in. I'm starving."

Brooke immediately liked the knotty pine interior and the

casual ambience of the restaurant. They passed a bar where a plump man gave them a friendly, "Evenin', folks," then moved on to a larger room with round tables and portraits of country scenes on the walls. A jukebox played softly in the background, and only about ten other people sat around, looking as if even a hurricane couldn't shake them.

"My goodness, this is a calm crowd," Brooke commented as they sat down.

"I don't think the people who frequent this place are looking for a rowdy, roadhouse atmosphere," Vincent said. "My parents used to bring me here until I was about fifteen and I decided I was too cool to be seen having dinner out with them."

"So they stopped coming and your mother stayed home to fix spoiled young you a fabulous meal."

"Oh no. They came anyway and left me at home with a frozen dinner. A particularly *bad* frozen dinner. That taught me I wasn't going to call all the shots, although I never backed down. I was as stubborn as they were."

"And you all turned out just fine." Brooke smiled. "Family life seems like fun."

"I think it's more fun in retrospect. When you're young, particularly a teenager, you usually feel totally misunderstood and abused."

Five minutes later, Brooke ordered a chef salad and an iced tea, until Vincent talked her into having a glass of Chablis instead. Afterward, she said, "I've drunk more in the last week than I have in the last year."

"I'm glad to hear that," Vincent said solemnly. "I was beginning to think you were a lush." She made a face at him. "Don't be so hard on yourself, Brooke. This hasn't exactly been a tranquil week. A couple of drinks to calm your nerves aren't going to turn you into an alcoholic."

"It's been more than a couple. Grossmutter absolutely forbade drinking. I think her uncle and grandfather were alcoholics, or maybe it was her father and brother. I can't remember. Anyway, she never kept liquor at our house, and if she saw me with a glass of wine in front of me, she'd either snatch it away from me or let me drink it, then give me a lecture on the evils of drinking."

"Well, you're a big girl now," Vincent said soothingly. "You can make your own decisions."

"I'll *have* to make my own decisions from now on. Not that my grandmother ever dictated to me after I became an adult, but she was always quick with the advice, and it was usually good advice." Brooke sighed. "I'll miss that."

"She's not gone yet," Vincent said gently.

"But she will be soon." Brooke took a sip of her wine, then said, "Well, aren't I the gregarious dinner companion? Tell me something funny to cheer me up."

"Something funny?" Vincent frowned, then smiled. "Remember our next-door neighbor whose wife leaves regularly for a couple of weeks, claiming she's never coming back and throwing her husband into a tailspin because the dope thinks she means it, so he offers her something great, like a diamond ring or a car, and back she comes? Well, looks like he finally caught on. He called her yesterday evening and told her not to bother coming back this time. Today she sent him a *telegram*—jeez, I didn't even know they had telegrams these days—and said she'd be back tomorrow and she loved him madly."

"Why the telegram?" Brooke asked, laughing.

"I suppose because if she called, he could tell her not to come or else listen to her message on the machine and not answer. Now she'll just appear on the doorstep, whisk him up to bed, and hope for the best."

"And maybe stop this stupid game of hers. What do you think gave him the nerve to give her the heave-ho?"

"Dad on the day they were watching the baseball game. He always thought the guy was stupid for letting her do this, but he was too polite to point it out to him. The tactful days ended with the Alzheimer's. Now he says exactly what he thinks."

"And this time, with a good result. I'll bet she doesn't try this trick again next year."

"No, I give her two before she thinks the shock has worn

off." Vincent looked at Brooke approvingly. "You're smiling, Miss Yeager."

"You were successful. You cheered me up when I thought it wasn't possible."

"I guess I'm just a miracle worker."

"You seem to be." She looked down at her barely touched salad. "Now if you could just find Zach."

"Maybe I overestimated myself," Vincent said. "I don't think I *can* find Zach. And I'm beginning to wonder if the police can, either, which is why I'm asking you again to leave Charleston. Brooke, he sent you your mother's wedding ring."

"I do recall that, Vincent. The ring that's been missing since the same time as the letter opener. At least Zach is polite enough to have returned all of Mom's things."

"I don't think being polite was his reason for returning the ring," Vincent said dryly.

"I know. I was being sarcastic. Or sardonic. Whatever—you're the master of words."

"Don't change the subject, Brooke. You *must* leave Charleston." She gave him a hard stare. "Okay, I'm going out on a limb here, but would it make any difference if *I* asked you to leave?"

"Why do you say you're going out on a limb?"

"Because I'm implying you care about what I want, that your safety is very important to me." He made a small huffing sound. "And *you* are changing the subject again."

Brooke's gaze dropped. Vincent had said he cared about her, not in those exact words, but his meaning was clear. And she did care that he cared. She cared so much, the feeling frightened her. But she could not tell him how much his concern meant. She'd spent too many years closed off, hiding her feelings, not letting people in, especially a man she'd known less than a week, a man who would probably take off and forget all about her as soon as the excitement was over. At least, that was what she told herself, although the look in his eyes said that's not at all what he intended to do. Still, if she let down her guard, she could only be asking for trouble.

"Look, Vincent, I don't mean to be harsh, but I've made

myself clear on this topic. I'm not leaving my grandmother. Period. Now, it's very polite of you to spend so much time with me, to express this much disquiet over my situation—"

*"Polite! Disquiet!"* Vincent burst out, his eyes flashing. "I think if you were a guy, I'd punch you!"

"Well, then, I'm glad I'm not a guy," Brooke returned, her voice remarkably calm in spite of her surprise. "To what do I owe that outburst?"

"To your patronizing attitude. I am *not* being polite to you. I am *not* disquieted by your situation. Good God, Brooke, why can't you believe someone cares about you? Because your father died and your mother was murdered?" She winced, but he went on relentlessly. "Well, I'm sorry as hell all that happened to you, but it doesn't mean you have to shut yourself away from everyone except your grandmother, dammit! You're being absurd!"

A young waitress appeared at their side and with a red face said softly, "Sir, would you mind lowering your voice?"

"Yes, I would," Vincent snapped.

The girl turned even redder. "Oh. Well, then I'm afraid I'll have to ask you to leave. You see, this is a family restaurant and the manager is—"

"Too much of a coward to come over here himself and tell me to shut up." Vincent took a deep breath. "I apologize to *you* for my bad behavior." He looked at Brooke. "I don't apologize for one thing I said to *you*."

"I'm crushed," Brooke returned.

Vincent tossed a fifty-dollar bill down on the table. "Keep the change," he told the cringing, crimson-faced waitress. Then to Brooke, "Let's go back to the car."

"No thank you. I will ride home with the surveillance police."

"Surveillance police?" the waitress wavered.

"Now you've scared her," Vincent accused Brooke. "If you don't go get in my car, the cops outside will think we've had a lovers' tiff and spread it all over headquarters. Would you rather have that than ride home with me?"

In a huff of annoyance, Brooke grabbed her purse,

marched with head high past the other staring customers, walked out into the warm summer evening, and climbed into Vincent's Mercedes. *Well, there's one restaurant I won't be able to enter again,* she thought, seething. In a moment, Vincent climbed into the driver's seat and they left the parking lot with a squeal of tires.

He did not put on any music. He drove too fast. He breathed heavily. At last he said sternly, "Brooke Yeager, you are the most stubborn woman I have ever known."

"You acted like a jerk back there."

"I haven't been called a jerk since the eighth grade."

"You're acting like you're in the eighth grade."

Vincent was silent for a couple of minutes. Then he said almost meekly, "I'm sorry."

"Fine."

" 'Fine'? Not 'apology accepted'?"

"I don't know yet if I want to accept your apology. Give me time to think about it."

Brooke expected him to keep pushing her, but Vincent just looked at the highway, his face set, his hands tight on the steering wheel. She wasn't quite certain why she was so angry with him. True, he'd caused a scene in the restaurant, but the scene was minor and in a place where she'd never been before and knew no one.

A thought hit her. Could the reason for her anger possibly be that she knew he was right? That he was being perfectly reasonable and she was acting almost like a reckless, mulish kid?

She stopped breathing for a few moments. *Almost? No. Exactly.* A slow flush crept up her face. She, too, looked straight ahead but said reluctantly, "I guess you think I'm a total fool."

"Not *total*."

"Oh. Thank you."

"Well, do you want me to throw you a line of bull to get back in your good graces or do you want to hear the truth?"

She paused, then finally said, "The truth, I guess."

"I don't think you're a fool. I think your judgment is

skewed because this bizarre experience hit at exactly the time you think your grandmother is dying."

"The time I *know* she's dying."

"Okay. You're probably right. But Brooke, the woman has spent most of your life trying to protect you. Do you think she put in all those years so you could throw it away just to be with her at the end? I know that sounds cold, but if she loves you as much as I'm sure she does, she probably couldn't think of a worse ending for both of you. You know her better than anyone does. Leave sticky sentiment out of it and look at the situation rationally. What would your grandmother want? For you to live, or for you to sit helplessly by her bedside while she dies, leaving you with a good chance of being murdered within the next few days just like your mother was?"

"You don't mince words, do you, Vincent?"

"I don't sugarcoat things, if that's what you mean. I say what I think. I didn't mean to offend you, but I don't apologize for anything I just said."

Brooke wanted to say something cutting, something to put this know-it-all in his place, but nothing came to her. She wasn't certain if that was because she was just too tired to argue anymore or if she simply was no longer mad. He'd made a lot of sense. She was beginning to think her own actions *didn't* make sense.

They rode in silence for miles. She hadn't paid attention to how far the restaurant was from her apartment building, but the trip back seemed to take forever in spite of the velvet warmth of the night. Somewhere along that drive, her anger at Vincent drained away. He'd been right. And he cared.

When they pulled up in front of the apartment building, Vincent finally turned to her. "Do you want me to walk you to your door or just let you out here?"

"I want you to come up and stay awhile," Brooke said softly. "If you want to, that is."

Vincent blinked at her. "I've been thinking you couldn't get away from me fast enough."

"You're very often correct, Vincent," Brooke said seriously, then with a smile, "but not *always*."

He stared at her for a moment, then returned her smile. "I'm glad that I'm not always correct. I'd really like to come up. And I promise not to lecture anymore."

"Good," Brooke said easily. "Because more lecturing could get you tossed down the stairs in a heartbeat."

"I'll keep that in mind, ma'am."

As soon as they entered the lobby, Vincent had the impression that a large parrot was darting at him. It turned out to be Eunice in a floating cheap green net and chiffon concoction apparently meant to be a negligee. "Have you seen Harry?" she nearly screeched at the couple in a high, tight voice. "Is he outside?"

Vincent, still taken aback by the birdlike creature in front of him, stepped backward and left the situation to Brooke. "No, Eunice, we haven't seen Harry this evening," she said calmly. "How long has he been gone?"

"Too long. I need to talk to him!"

"Did he forget about your insulin shot again?"

"Uh . . . yes. Insulin."

Brooke knew better than to suggest that someone else be allowed to give Eunice her injection. "Maybe he's doing something in the alley."

Eunice shook her head violently. "He won't go out there after dark since that Eads fellow got stabbed." Eunice rubbed her arms and Brooke saw that they were beginning to break out in a rash caused from nerves. Brooke also smelled scotch and clove cigarettes.

"Maybe he's in the basement," Brooke said. Eunice looked at Brooke as if she were crazy. "I just noticed a light flickering back behind you." This was a lie, but she didn't want to stand here for twenty minutes with a nearly hysterical Eunice Dormer. "There could be something wrong with a circuit, and the circuit breakers are in the basement."

"I'll bet you're right!" Eunice burst out. "He's not afraid of the basement. I'll go down right now and check."

Eunice headed for the basement door in a cloud of violent green. Brooke looked at Vincent, who raised an eyebrow at her and said, "I didn't notice a light flickering."

"Neither did I, but she's gone, isn't she? We just have time to get to my apartment before she comes back."

"Why, Miss Yeager, you wily woman!" Vincent laughed.

"What's she done now?" Stacy asked, descending the bottom of the interior stairs into the lobby.

"Successfully diverted Eunice Dormer," Vincent said. "Sent her to the basement in search of Harry."

"The *basement*?" Stacy echoed.

Brooke nodded. "She was desperate for her insulin."

"And romance, judging by that outfit," Vincent added drolly.

Stacy shook her head. "Those two are nuts. I wish Harry would *really* screw up and we'd get a new superintendent."

"Be careful what you wish for," Brooke said. "The next one might be even worse."

"I don't know how he could be." Stacy glanced between the two of them and a small smile, almost a smirk, appeared on her pale, taut face. "Have a nice evening, you two. Jay's working a double shift, so if you need me, I'll be right next door."

"We'll keep that in mind," Vincent said over his shoulder as he and Brooke raced for the elevator, hoping to avoid Eunice when she returned, with or without Harry. Brooke already had her keys out of her purse by the time they reached her door.

Elise ran to them, joyful as usual when her mistress came home for the day. "She'll need a walk," Brooke said. "I think there's some wine in the refrigerator and some Pepsi and Sprite. Fix yourself something to drink."

"No, you fix yourself something to drink," Vincent said. "I'll take out Lady Elise. After all, it's after dark. Besides, you don't really want to run into Eunice again, do you?"

Brooke let out a groan.

"I didn't think so." He knelt by the dog. "Want me to take you out for a change?" The dog licked his hand before he reached for the leash Brooke offered. "We'll be back soon. I promise not to run off with her."

"Sure you don't want to go down the fire escape to avoid Eunice?"

"We'll take our chances, won't we, Elise?" Vincent said. "Why don't you put on some music?"

Vincent had ordered Chablis at the restaurant, just as she had, and neither had finished their glass. After he'd left with Elise, Brooke filled each glass, then found half a can of relatively fresh cashew nuts and dumped them in a glass bowl. You can certainly tell I don't do much entertaining, Brooke thought ruefully. She had nothing else to offer a guest.

Well, she might be short on party food, but she had plenty of candles. They were festive, weren't they? Festive or romantic. But she didn't want to go for romantic. Or did she? Suddenly she didn't know and was baffled. An hour ago she'd been furious with Vincent. She'd felt like she never wanted to see him again. And now . . . She lit five scented candles and turned off all but one lamp with a low-watt bulb glowing beneath a pink shade. The flickering light threw the room into soft relief, and the scent of the candles helped hide the faint, odd smell Brooke had picked up on as soon as she entered the apartment—a faintly familiar smell. Cloves? Had Stacy been right? *Did* Eunice prowl and had she been in this apartment tonight? If so, she hadn't found the errant Harry.

Brooke pushed Eunice from her mind and concentrated on Vincent. He'd asked for music. She knew he liked rock— she'd heard him play it in the car—so she went through her CD collection and first pulled out Los Lonely Boys. No one could stay in a bad mood listening to them, she thought as "Señorita" came on. She knew the only other occupied apartment on the third floor was Stacy's, and she certainly wouldn't care how loud the music was as long as it wasn't classical. Brooke turned up the stereo, kicked off her high heels, and took the pins out of her upswept hair, letting it trail down her back. She was sipping wine and dancing by herself when Vincent returned with Elise.

He walked back into the apartment, stopped dead, staring

at Brooke moving gracefully around the middle of the living room holding a glass of wine. His mouth opened slightly in surprise. Elise barked at her, clearly shocked by this abandoned behavior. Vincent let go of the dog's leash, walked to Brooke, took her lightly into her arms, and quickly fell into the step of the sensuous music with her. He put his mouth beside her ear. "Does this mean I'm no longer a jerk?"

"Perhaps. It all depends on how well you can dance."

"My mother made me take dance lessons at Miss Lucille's when I was five. I was one of her best pupils and the star of the recital, I'm proud to say. Now. At the time, I thought my macho image was shot to hell. I believe I alternately pouted and cried in my room for a nearly a week afterward. Then there was a brief, regrettable disco period in my early teens followed by grunge when I hit California. Three years ago I learned salsa dancing."

"That settles it, then. Unless you're fibbing to me."

"I'm not." Vincent held his right hand against his chest. "Cross my heart."

"Okay," Brooke laughed. "I was much mistaken in my appraisal. You're not a jerk. You never were."

"I'm glad. I must say I have trouble keeping up with your moods, though, Brooke."

"Yeah, me, too. Chalk it up to my frequently being wrong, then able to admit when I am."

"You think you were wrong this evening?"

"I think I've handled this entire situation wrong. I should have left Charleston days ago. It just takes me a while to get things through my hard head."

The mention of a hard head sent her mind flying back to the last client she'd had before the ring was delivered—Mrs. Amelia Gracen, who claimed her husband, Orville, had possessed the hardest head she'd ever encountered, the man Brooke knew Mrs. Gracen would love to the end of her days. Brooke laughed slightly, both at the irony that the woman had cared so much for a man she'd found so flawed and also at the happiness the woman had found with him for so many years.

"Any reason for that laughter?" Vincent asked.

"Just my eccentric nature."

"I don't think you're eccentric."

"Is that so?"

"It is. I think you're naturally a fun-loving, optimistic woman who's been keeping all her hope and joy buried for a long time." Vincent leaned back and looked at her. "You might even be hedonistic."

"Fun-loving and optimistic, maybe. Hedonistic—well, don't get your hopes up." She smiled. "Drink your wine."

He looked deep into her eyes, his arms tightening around her. "I'd rather keep dancing with you."

"You can drink and dance, too. I am. And you should certainly be able to pull it off since according to you, you're one of the dance masters of the world."

"I didn't say *that*!"

"Close enough. Get your wine."

Vincent did as he was told. Elise sat on the couch, her tongue lolling happily as she watched Brooke and Vincent dance to "Nobody Else." The candles flickered as Vincent tangled his right hand in her long hair, gently pulled back her head, and kissed her deeply. She didn't pull away, but when the kiss ended, she whispered, "You've had too much to drink."

"I haven't had one sip."

"Do you kiss all the girls you dance with?"

"Not lately."

"And how long is *lately*?"

"Does it matter?" Vincent asked huskily. "You're the last girl I'm going to kiss tonight."

"And tomorrow night?"

"Tomorrow night, too."

"And the next and the next?"

His green eyes seared into hers before he bent his head, kissed his way up her neck to her ear, and murmured, "I think I'd like for you to be the last girl I ever kiss."

Brooke tipped back her head, her own burning glance meeting his. "I think I'd like that just fine."

Just before he kissed her again, he whispered, "My Cinnamon Girl."

## 3

Eunice didn't like the basement. She always told Harry she couldn't stand dark, dank places, to which he always replied accurately that the basement was not dank and it wouldn't be dark if she'd just turn on the fluorescent light panel at the top of the stairs *and* the one halfway down the length of the basement wall. True, at night the area got a bit dimmer before you reached the second panel. True, the basement was crowded with tools, utility supplies, the furnace, the dehumidifier, and all the locked cages holding storage for the tenants. However, if Harry could navigate the basement at three in the morning using only one set of lights when the furnace or the water heater clicked off, Eunice could certainly do it with both sets of lights when it was barely dark.

But Brooke had said there might be something wrong with the circuit breakers. That meant if they snapped off, so would the lights. So would the comforting hum of the dehumidifier and the water heater. At least, Eunice thought water heaters hummed. Maybe she was thinking of the furnace.

Oh, blast it! Eunice thought in a fury as she started down the stairs in her best negligee, the one she'd bought on sale for two-thirds off and thought made her look fetchingly feminine with its net and chiffon, even if the green was a bit bright for her sallow complexion. She hadn't meant to come into the lobby wearing it—people would think she was showing off—but she wouldn't don her faded chenille robe over her beautiful negligee, and a quick search for her winter coat stored during the summer months had proved fruitless. So, frantic to find Harry and tell him what she'd heard, she'd simply dashed into the lobby wearing net and chiffon. She hoped Brooke wasn't jealous. She liked Brooke.

At least she'd worn her thick, furry house slippers, so the cold floor wouldn't chill her feet. Of course, it was summer, so the floor probably wouldn't be cold, but with basements you never knew. After all, when she'd been "bad," Liz had locked her in their basement more than once, and no matter what time of year, it had always been chilly in there. And dank. And full of shadows even in midday. Eunice shivered at the memory. God, she'd hated that place and she'd tried hard to be a good girl so she'd never again have to enter a basement.

And here she was, looking for her husband in a basement at night. Eunice thought this was no better proof that the universe was vastly unfair and if there really was a God, he didn't like her. In any case, she was extremely mad at God, the universe, *and* Harry at the moment.

Eunice flicked on the switches at the top of the stairs, and three rows of fluorescent lights flared blindingly yet comfortingly. Thank goodness, she thought. "Harry!" she called from the top of the stairs. "Harry, I need you."

How wonderful it would have been to have heard, "I'll be right there, darling!"

Instead she heard nothing. Her anger level raised a notch. "Harry Dormer, if you're playin' some kind of game with me—well, you'd just better stop it right now."

Again, nothing. He wasn't down here. He probably never had been. Eunice was about to turn and leave the basement when something on the fifth step down caught her eye. It was a silver chain with something round attached. In a flash, she knew what it was. She scurried down and picked up Harry's beloved necklace—the silver chain bearing the pendant with the black widow spider encased in plastic. Eunice gingerly picked it up by the chain, looking at the spider splayed and forever frozen in some kind of acrylic. Horrible thing. Harry had *said* he won it in a card game, but she'd always believed one of his trashy girlfriends had given it to him during her bout of depression after their child's death. That's when he'd started wearing it, and he wouldn't give it up.

Well, he's given it up this time, she thought in victory as she bent down and tucked it in her big, fuzzy shoe. If he'd known it had dropped off his neck, he would have immediately picked it up and put it back on. Now he'd never find it because Eunice intended to destroy the hideous creation. But its presence proved one thing—Harry had come to the basement, and when she'd last seen him a little over an hour ago, he'd worn the pendant proudly against a tight white T-shirt.

"Harry, I know you're here!" Eunice yelled.

Once again, she heard nothing except the gentle humming of the dehumidifier. Nothing scary about the piece of equipment that kept the basement dry and pleasant-smelling. Nothing scary about the whole basement, in fact, she thought with spirit.

"Harry, if you're going to play stupid games and hide because you think I won't bother you here, you're wrong. I'm coming down!"

She waited a few moments for him to realize he was trapped; then she gave up. He didn't think she'd come after him, but that she was just making idle threats. Well, he'd find out!

Eunice descended the stairs without hesitation. She wished she had on hard-soled shoes so that Harry could hear the firmness of her steps. When she reached the bottom, she looked around. She saw some shelves with toolboxes, other shelves holding extension cords and drills, and more containing larger tools such as an ax and a hatchet. A selection of shovels leaned against one wall. She had never seen Harry use even half of this equipment and decided it must be left over from former superintendents/handymen who were more energetic than Harry. In fact, aside from the toolbox he carried around, mostly for show, she'd only seen him use the snow shovel on the steps at the front of the building, and only then after several tenants had complained. As for the tenants, they only came down here when they wanted to get something out of their storage cages.

Obviously, Harry wasn't dusting, oiling, and polishing the tools of his trade. He'd probably never even touched most of them. He wouldn't be working on the furnace in August. Eunice hadn't heard any complaints about the water being cold, so he wouldn't be fiddling with the water heater. The air conditioners were outside. What could he be doing?

Halfway down the length of the basement sat a small, enclosed space with a commode and a sink. Perhaps Harry was in there, Eunice thought, although the walls weren't so thick he couldn't have heard her calling to him, and he lacked any modesty—if he had been sitting on the commode, he wouldn't have cared if she stood right in front of him. But he could be using the enclosure as a hiding place. Eunice could just see him standing in there, ignoring her, maybe even snickering at his cleverness.

Furious over the imagined scene, Eunice marched smartly to the bathroom enclosure and flung open the door, her mouth already open for the beginning of a tirade. But the little room was empty. No Harry. No bulb burning over the sink. Just a dusty, dim little room badly in need of a good cleaning.

She stepped out of the space, looking around her without quite so much confidence. She'd passed the bright glare of the first set of fluorescent lights. Now there was only a soft glow. She could either go back upstairs or make herself walk to the opposite wall and turn on the second set of lights. Was the trip across the basement worth it?

Then she heard it. A sort of skulking sound at the farthest end of the basement, not like a mouse or rat—something much larger. A man! Eunice thought triumphantly. A man tiptoeing around in the dark, hiding from her! Harry, the creep! He was not only trying to avoid her; he was trying to scare her. Well, it wouldn't work because she was already more scared than he could make her with his stupid tricks. That's why she'd come down here in the first place—not for her insulin, but to tell him something was terribly wrong. She'd heard something that had seemed merely confusing at the time, then snapped into frightening focus as she was donning her lovely negligee—something so frightening, she didn't think she could go back upstairs without Harry, such as he was. But if he wasn't down here . . . well, she just couldn't go back upstairs alone, even if it meant she might have to sleep in this awful place.

Eunice swept across the basement, net and chiffon wafting out behind her, and touched the cold metal of the light switch plate. She flipped the switches, closing her eyes against the burst of fluorescent light she knew would follow. Except there was nothing. She kept her eyes closed, flipped the switches up, then down, then up, then down again. They weren't working. Brooke had been right. There was something wrong with the circuit breakers and it was affecting the lights at the far end of the basement. Well, she was certainly capable of snapping circuit breakers back into place. The only problem was that she couldn't remember exactly where the circuit breaker box was.

"Oh, hell," she said loudly, hoping Harry heard her and knew just how irate she was getting. Harry liked to tease her, he liked to get her about half-angry, but he really didn't like it when she was furious because she slammed doors for days and refused to serve a meal that was fit to eat. Harry needed to get the message that he'd better end his little game if he knew what was good for him.

She stood for a moment, trying to decide whether to keep looking for Harry or to go back to the bright end of the basement. There was an old couch there. Yes, it smelled moldy, but perhaps she could bear to sleep on it. She wouldn't feel so frightened in the morning and she'd go back up to the apartment and maybe even pack her things and leave if Harry had still not returned.

Abruptly, all the lights went off. Eunice stood absolutely still, too startled to be afraid for a moment, just surprised. She turned and took two steps, then realized she was headed for the back of the basement, not the stairs. She had turned the other way and started forward when she heard a deep voice murmur, "Eunice?"

She froze again. Then she realized the voice must be

Harry's. Someone had told him she was down here and he'd decided to give her a good scare. Well, he'd regret that impulse.

"Harry Dormer, turn on the lights this instant," she said harshly. The lights remained off. "Harry, this isn't funny."

By this time Harry should have been guffawing at the cleverness of his trick. But Harry wasn't laughing. No lights were flashing into brilliance.

And Eunice realized she was in trouble.

Once one of Liz's "boyfriends" had held Eunice down and pressed an ice cube against her neck. She remembered the pain that had shot into the base of her skull and down her spine. She had that same sensation now. She drew quick, shallow breaths because they hurt less. And she held perfectly still, as if whatever was trying to prey upon her might not see her if she didn't move. She wanted to close her eyes, but she didn't dare. Vision might be the only weapon she had at the moment. For nearly ten seconds she stood immobile as a statue and just as blind in the dark. She heard a tiny scraping noise, like metal against concrete. Then, slowly, her eyes adjusted slightly and she caught a glimpse of movement, something coming toward her, cutting her off from the stairs.

She swallowed hard and said in a small, trembling voice, "Just let me out of here. I won't say anything about this. I *can't* say who you are because I don't *know* who you are. And I don't care about finding out. I just want to go. Please." Nothing, but the movement seemed to be undulating toward her, and she still couldn't move. Her body absolutely would not cooperate with her brain's instructions for her to run, or even to open her mouth and scream. "Please," she whispered this time, her throat too tight for anything but a slight passage of air. "Please, don't hurt me. I won't say a word. I promise—"

Eunice was vaguely aware of arms being raised high in the air before her world exploded into a nightmare of brilliant colors and the sound of bone smashing. Something hot and blinding gushed over her face as she dropped to her knees, instinctively reaching for her head. For just a second, her hands registered that her head was not in one piece.

There seemed to be two sections with sharp edges, and in the middle a pool of hot liquid.

Eunice Dormer fell from her knees onto her face, the back of her head split wide-open, blood drenching the net and chiffon folds of her ugly green negligee.

# nineteen

## 1

Brooke sighed, rolled over, and reached out to touch Vincent. Instead, a wet nose pushed its way into her palm. Her eyes snapped open to face those of Elise.

"Why is it I keep going to sleep with *people* and I end up in the morning with *you*?" she asked, rubbing the dog's head. "Do I kick? Snore? Have horrendous breath?"

As the dog cuddled closer to her, she saw a note left on the pillow:

> Dearest Cinnamon Girl,
>
> Embarrassing as it is to admit, I had to be home by three. Dad has a tendency to wander after dark, or take out the car—he always manages to find the keys—and the next-door neighbor won't leave the presence of his precious wife.
>
> I'll call you in a few hours.
>
> VL

The first thing Brooke noticed was that Vincent hadn't written: "Love." But how would she have felt if he had written, "Love, Vincent"? Would she have believed he was sincere? Or would she have thought he'd merely jotted down "Love" out of habit?

"I'm doing way too much thinking without my morning coffee," she said aloud. "I need coffee and something deliciously sweet. If we had time, Elise, we'd walk down to the café for croissants, but I have to be at work in an hour. I barely have time to make it."

She was tossing off the sheet and quilt when the phone rang. Vincent, she thought, smiling. Then she looked at the caller ID readout. Charleston General Hospital. Her heart went cold as she picked up the handset, and after what seemed like an hour, but could only have been seconds, she learned that her grandmother had just suffered another massive stroke. She was still alive, but barely. Brooke had jumped out of bed and dressed in jeans and a blouse and was driving toward the hospital within fifteen minutes.

She was on the verge of hyperventilating by the time she parked her car in the hospital lot, bypassed the elevators that were all on other floors, and reached her grandmother's room. She had expected to see a gaggle of doctors and nurses gathered around Greta, the doctors shouting, the nurses scurrying like on television shows. Instead, only one nurse stood by Greta's bed, frowning as she wrote on a chart. Brooke tiptoed to her and whispered, "How is she doing?"

The nurse jumped. "My goodness, you scared me. Are you related to the patient?"

"I'm her granddaughter."

"Oh. Well, I'm afraid the doctor will have to explain her condition to you. I'll see if I can find and send him in as soon as possible. He just left the room about ten minutes ago."

The nurse left so silently Brooke couldn't even hear her crepe-soled shoes on the floor. She crept closer to Greta's bed, which at first appeared to be empty. Then she saw her grandmother lying on her back, her body looking as if it weighed ten pounds less than it had two days ago, her skin thin as parchment. The left side of her face was still pulled down, but less than the last time Brooke had seen her. Her eyelids were tightly closed. She seemed to be barely breathing.

Brooke took her grandmother's cold hand, feeling nothing except thin skin over bones. Greta used to complain about her big hands. "They look like a man's hands next to your mother's," she would tell Brooke. "But they are strong." Not anymore, Brooke thought, tears rising in her eyes. "Grossmutter," she said softly. "It's Brooke. Can you open your eyes?"

The eyelids didn't even flutter. Brooke squeezed her grandmother's hand. "Grossmutter, I love you. Please give me a sign that you know I'm here."

Brooke saw her grandmother's lips move slightly and she slurred out a word Brooke interpreted as "BAnI." Bunny. Greta's old name for her only grandchild.

"Miss Yeager?" Brooke looked up to see the doctor standing near her. She hadn't even heard him enter the room. "Would you mind stepping into the hall with me to discuss your grandmother's case?"

Ten minutes later, Brooke returned to her grandmother's side. The doctor had spewed a mass of medical terminology at Brooke, keeping his voice calm, his face expressionless, and his language nearly incomprehensible. But she understood. Her grandmother was dying. She might have a day. She might have an hour. But the end had finally come.

Brooke drew a chair up beside the bed and once again reached for Greta's hand. She began talking about all the fun they'd had together when Grossmutter, Daddy, Mommy, and she were young.

At the end of her story, Brooke laughed as if she hadn't a care in the world. She saw Greta's mouth move in a semblance of a twisted smile, and she lightly squeezed Brooke's hand. Encouraged, Brooke told another story of her childhood, then another, then another. She recounted all the holiday festivities of the past, the birthday parties, her learning to ride a bike, her starting first grade. After three hours, she noticed that Greta seemed to be responding less and less.

Every half hour a nurse checked in on them, took Greta's pulse, then smiled encouragingly at Brooke. "Won't you let me bring you a cup of coffee or a soft drink? We've all been catching bits and pieces of your stories in the nurses' station and they're charming, but you must be bone-dry by now."

Brooke hadn't thought about it, but she hadn't had so much as her morning coffee. She handed the nurse some money, which the woman tried to refuse, but Brooke wouldn't let her and asked for a can of Coke and a Snickers bar from the vending machines. Now there's a healthy meal, she thought. But her throat was parched and she badly needed a sugar boost.

After downing the Coke and candy bar, Brooke finally left for the bathroom. Under the less-than-flattering light she looked pale and haggard, mauve shadows under her eyes and dry, nearly flesh-toned lips. She applied some lipstick, then rubbed a little on each cheek for color. She'd called Aaron on her cell on her way to the hospital to tell him she wouldn't be at work today, and she had to admit that he sounded relieved after yesterday's drama. Now she dialed Vincent.

He answered on the second ring. "Brooke!" he exclaimed as she said his name. "I called you at work, but they told me your grandmother was worse and you were at the hospital. I didn't want to bother you. I thought you'd call me as soon as you got a chance."

"I could have called earlier, but frankly I didn't even think of it. She's had another stroke, Vincent, and she's not going to make it. I don't think she'll see the day through."

"I'm so sorry, honey," he said, startling her with the endearment. "I'd come and be with you, but Dad has a doctor's appointment this afternoon. They're going to do some tests and I need to take him—"

"I've been driving since I was sixteen!" Brooke heard Sam yell in the background. "I think I can get myself ten miles to the doctor's office! You act like I'm a kid, Vincent, and I won't stand for it, do you hear me?"

"He's having a bad morning," Vincent muttered into the phone. "Otherwise, I would have come ahead to the hospital."

"You're talking about me! I know it!" Sam boomed.

"That's all right, Vincent," Brooke said calmly. "There's nothing you can do. There's nothing anyone can do besides wait. I just wanted to let you know where I am and that I'm fine and . . . well . . . to thank you for last night."

"Thank *me*! Good heavens, that was one of the greatest evenings of my life."

"What was one of the greatest evenings of your life?" Sam asked loudly and querulously, obviously standing right next to Vincent. "Put that phone down. I need to check in at headquarters, make sure it's all right for me to take off to see this doctor. They might need me."

"You have your hands full," Brooke said sympathetically. "We both do. Take your dad to the doctor and I'll sit with Grossmutter. We'll talk later this evening."

Brooke clicked off the phone, stuck it back in her purse, leaned across the counter to look in the mirror again. "How am I going to get through this day?" she asked herself miserably. Then she took her hands off the counter and stood up straight. "The same way I did when Mommy died. One minute at a time."

Those minutes dragged throughout the afternoon as Brooke sat beside her grandmother. Finally, around five o'clock, Greta once again said something that sounded like "BAnI," sighed, and grew still. Frantically Brooke called for the doctor, but even before he told her, she knew.

Greta Yeager was dead.

# 2

The hour after Greta's death later seemed like a blur to Brooke. She kissed her grandmother's still face and, just like her mother had done to her so many years ago, whispered, "Good night, my angel," one last time. Later she talked to the doctor, who assured her everything that could be done for Greta had been done and told her with complete lack of emotion he was sorry for Brooke's loss. She filled out forms and notified the undertaker. By six thirty in the evening she was headed for home, glad that she'd missed rush-hour traffic. So far she hadn't shed one tear, but she felt like the least little annoyance might send her into a torrent of sobs. But she couldn't do that in the car, she told herself. She must concentrate on her driving and keep herself safe, because that was what Greta would want.

Brooke pulled into the apartment house parking lot and heard the reassuring sound of one of the surveillance cars' engine beside her. A window whirred down and one of the policemen asked, "Want me to walk you to the door?"

Brooke shook her head. "It's only a few feet away and we're right under a dusk-to-dawn light. I'll be fine, but thanks anyway."

She'd called Stacy from the hospital and told her of Greta's death. Stacy had wanted to come to the hospital to help in any way she could, but Brooke had told her the best way she could help would be to take Elise for the walk she hadn't had all day, and perhaps have some cold wine on hand.

When she walked in the lobby door, Brooke found Stacy waiting for her. Stacy wrapped her arms around her and hugged her tightly. "Honey, I'm so sorry about your grandmother."

"We all knew it was coming," Brooke said, trying to sound strong, trying not to cry.

"Knowing death is coming and having it actually happen are very different things, Brooke." Stacy drew away and scrutinized her. "You look absolutely exhausted. I took Elise for a walk and fed her. She's in our apartment waiting for you. We have wine and I made sandwiches. You look absolutely wiped out. Come upstairs with me."

Brooke looked around the lobby. Mrs. Kelso stood at a distance, staring at her. Brooke saw no sympathy in her face—merely curiosity. A couple of other tenants also milled around, one elderly man asking querulously for Harry.

Brooke, for one, was relieved to see that Harry was nowhere around.

"Did you call Vincent and tell him about Grossmutter?" she asked Stacy.

"I'm sorry. I forgot. You can call him from our place."

"I called from the hospital, but I got no answer on his home or cell phone."

Stacy shrugged. "Hard to tell where he is. Come on, Brooke. You need something to eat before you faint."

"One minute," Brooke said. "I want to check my mail."

She dug her key ring out of her purse, walked to the row of mailboxes on the lobby wall, and inserted a tiny key into hers. She had only four pieces of mail. The phone bill, a credit card bill, a magazine subscription offer, and a small white envelope bearing her name and address but no return address. Absently, she opened it and withdrew a card bearing a drawing of a small girl with long blond hair playing with a small, golden dog. She opened the card and read the short message:

> Brooke,
> But the day of the Lord will come as a thief in the night . . .
> You are next.
>
> Zach

"He always had such pretty handwriting for a man," Brooke said faintly as the world seemed to spin around her. "Mom always said so."

Stacy peered over Brooke's shoulder at the note she held in her shaking hand and gasped. "My God! I can't believe it!"

"He didn't print this one like the others. And he actually signed his name. He's ready to come out of hiding, Stacy. He's ready to come for me, whatever the cost. But not without a warning to scare the hell out of me, first."

"Yes. A . . . warning." Stacy drew a deep breath. "Come up to my apartment." Brooke stood stiffly, chills running through her body like an electric current. "Jay is upstairs.

We have to show this to him. Brooke, come *on*." Stacy pushed her toward the elevator. "Don't freeze up on me."

Brooke felt dazed as they rode to the third floor and Stacy led her down the hall to her apartment. As soon as she opened the door, Elise rushed toward Brooke, her tail flying, and Brooke knelt to hug her so tightly the dog let out a little squeak of surprise. Brooke felt tears pushing behind her eyes, but they refused to run down her face, releasing some of the pressure. She didn't think she'd ever felt so tired or so alone in her whole life.

Jay had been draped over the couch, watching television, but he immediately jumped up, as if sensing something was wrong besides Greta's death. "What is it?"

"Another communication from Zach," Stacy said tensely, "only this one was mailed, handwritten, and even signed. Look at it."

Brooke shakily held out the card. "I'm afraid my fingerprints are on the outside, but I didn't touch the inside. As soon as I saw that picture on the front of a blond girl with her blond dog, I knew who'd sent it."

Jay first picked up a tissue from a table next to the couch, then took the card from Brooke. He read it without expression and slipped it back in the envelope, which he wrapped in the tissue. "I have to take this in and log it as evidence. I'll call Hal, too."

"Jay, do you think Zach is holed up at the Holt Street house where he shot my mother?" Brooke asked. "After Mom's murder, no one stayed in that house for long. One or two years and 542 Holt Street was back on the market. I kept track. But this time, it's been empty for over two years."

Jay sat on a dainty armchair slipping shoes over his dark socks. "That neighborhood has really run down since you lived there. It's now a high-crime area. Maybe that's the reason for the quick turnover and recent desertion. Anyway, we searched the house after Tavell broke out of prison and again a couple of days later. There was no sign of him."

Jay stood up. "We might have located the car Tavell has been using, though. According to the airport, a silver Taurus with the license plate number 3R-1615 was put in long-term parking last week. The family is in Paris and will be for five more days, but the car is missing."

"Just like Vincent suggested," Brooke said. "Just like the scenario he used in his book. I wonder if Zach read that book?"

Jay opened the front door. "We're only certain the car is missing, not that Zach took it."

"Oh, he did," Brooke said with certainty, remembering the day at the café when she'd felt someone watching her and she'd seen an apparently empty silver Taurus parked across the street. "I'm absolutely sure that's the car he's been using."

# 3

After Jay left, Stacy gave Brooke a glass of wine and a chicken salad sandwich. The wine she wanted; the sandwich she did not, but Stacy insisted and because her stomach was rumbling, Brooke obeyed and ate it. The food tasted like cardboard, though. She couldn't really taste the wine, either, but she could feel the effects. As she emptied her glass, she felt as if the tight muscles in her neck had begun to relax.

"I'm pouring you another glass of that," Stacy said.

"I really shouldn't have two."

"Why not? Will it throw you into a fit? Make you explode?" Brooke managed a faint smile. "Just one more glass and you'll be able to unwind enough to sleep tonight."

To sleep, Brooke thought as Stacy moved around in the kitchen. Greta was finally sleeping. Brooke hoped it was a peaceful sleep. Greta's life had not been easy.

And neither has mine, Brooke thought. She'd never been one to wallow in self-pity, but so many people she knew had led happier childhoods, more peaceful young adult years.

"Drink this slowly," Stacy said, handing her a glass. "Do you want some music?"

"For once, no."

"That's out of the ordinary for you." Stacy smiled. "Conversation?"

"If you don't mind—"

"I will gladly keep my mouth shut. In fact, I will even bury my face in this new magazine I got today called *InStyle* full of things too expensive for me to buy. If you feel like talking, though, don't hesitate to drag me away from the splendor on these pages."

The apartment was almost unnervingly quiet without the music or television Brooke usually kept on for company. Elise lay beside her chair, breathing rhythmically and thumping her tail on the floor when Brooke reached down to touch her. The glass-domed clock Brooke had always admired ticked softly on an end table, and once in a while Stacy turned a page and sighed.

At last, Brooke said, "I'm going to leave tomorrow." Stacy looked up. "I'm leaving Charleston tomorrow. Grossmutter wanted to be cremated, have no ceremony and be placed in the mausoleum next to her husband. She's gone. All of her arrangements have been made. Meanwhile someone wants to kill me. In fact, he even warned me tonight that I haven't much time. I finally have no choice—no reason—to stay in this city."

Stacy gave her a long, measuring look. At last she said, "Thank God you're finally doing what you should have done a week ago."

"If I'd done it a week ago, maybe Robert wouldn't have been killed. . . ."

"Now don't go down that path." Stacy set down her wineglass. "I'll help you pack tomorrow."

"No. I'm going to the basement, get my luggage, pack, and leave tonight."

*"Tonight?"*

"I hate to admit this, but I'm afraid to stay until tomorrow. I know I won't get any sleep anyway."

"You don't want a nap now or . . . or to talk to Vincent?"

"A nap? I just told you I'm not sleepy. And I can talk to

Vincent later tonight. Or in the morning. What's the matter, Stacy? You act like I need his permission."

Stacy drew back. "His *permission*?" Stacy suddenly looked stern and almost offended. "I certainly don't think you need Vincent Lockhart's permission to do *anything*. In fact, I'll be glad when there's some space between you. I've never liked the way he just turned up when all the trouble started. But you seem so . . ."

"So *what*?"

"Attached to him. I got the feeling you wouldn't make a move without asking him first."

"You thought *I* wouldn't make a move without *asking* him first?" Brooke bristled. "Good heavens, Stacy, you act like I'm a little girl. I don't owe Vincent either explanations or his permission!"

"Okay!" Stacy held her hands up. "I'm sorry. I read the signals wrong." She lowered her hands. "If you're determined to get your luggage tonight, I'll help. If Harry were around, we'd get him to do it, but nobody has seen him all day."

"Oh God, don't tell me he finally ran off with that mistress Eunice was always so certain he had."

"That's probably exactly what happened. They're together on a Caribbean island right now, she in a bikini, he in a Speedo, drinking mai tais."

"Harry Dormer with his hairy shoulders and back, beer gut, and beautiful spider necklace wearing a Speedo." Brooke shut her eyes. "I think I'd rather be stalked by a murderer than conjure up *that* picture." She stood up. "If you help, I'll only need to make one trip to the basement. Thanks, Stacy."

Brooke made a hurried trip to her apartment and picked up the key to her storage cage in the basement. She kept it in an empty candy dish so she wouldn't have to add it to the collection of keys on her key ring.

"I hope Harry isn't messing around down here," Brooke said as they took the elevator to the basement. "I think having to put up with him tonight would just about tear it for me."

Stacy half-covered her eyes and groaned. "Wouldn't it, though? Especially with you collecting your luggage. He'd be full of questions." She paused. "And as a matter of fact, even *I* have one. Where are you going tomorrow?"

"I haven't decided yet. There are no relatives I can go to, although I wouldn't anyway. When Zach discovers I've left town, he'd no doubt track me to them. I could go to New York City, but that would be expensive if I plan to stay for long. Maybe New England. For some reason, I've always wanted to go to New England."

"You can go to Vermont and watch them make maple syrup."

"I don't think they do that at this time of year. Besides, I couldn't take the excitement," Brooke said dryly, then added, "although lately I think I've taken about all the excitement I can stand for a while."

The elevator jolted to a stop. "So much for smooth landings," Stacy said. "I think this old thing has about had it. That's why I usually take the stairs."

The doors creaked slowly open to pitch-darkness. "Oh no," Brooke moaned. "I forgot that the light switches are nowhere near the elevator."

"I didn't," Stacy said, triumphantly holding up a flashlight. "Always on my toes."

Stacy plunged ahead with the flashlight, shining it on the cool concrete floor, then flicking it around until she finally reached the far wall midway down the basement. "Shield your eyes," she called before flipping on the fluorescent tubes that lit the far end.

"I would like to know what genius forgot to put in a light switch panel beside the elevator," Brooke grumbled as she stepped out of the cubicle and headed toward the safety of blazing light. "Light switch at the top of the stairs, light switch halfway down the length of the basement. Nothing beside the elevator. Brilliant."

"Maybe Harry designed the building," Stacy said solemnly.

"I don't think so, unless he was an architect in 1922 when this place was built."

Every apartment had a wire storage cage, each approximately twelve by fifteen feet in size, with a door that locked. Many of the cages were stuffed full. Brooke's contained only her luggage, a box containing her artificial Christmas tree and another holding all the tinsel and ornaments, and a horribly old steamer trunk Greta had given Brooke when she'd sold her possessions and moved into the nursing home.

When Brooke had protested, Greta insisted. "You might need this on a trip," Greta had pointed out.

"A trip!" Brooke had cried. "What kind of trip? An ocean voyage on the *Titanic*?"

Greta had frowned, pretending to think. "*Titanic* is at the bottom of the ocean. Unsinkable. Ha! Pick something better, like the Love Boat. You'll find a handsome man on that trip and marry him."

"Not if he gets a look at this trunk that comes along with the bride. He'll think I'm a kook."

Greta had thrown back her head and laughed but still insisted Brooke take the trunk, which had originally belonged to Greta's grandmother.

Brooke used her key to open her cage door. Both she and Stacy stepped in and looked around. "I swear, Brooke, you have the neatest cage down here," Stacy said.

"That's because I don't have much to store." She glanced at the red luggage set she'd bought in a fit of extravagance last year. "Let's see. I'll take the upright Pullman, the port case, and the boarding bag."

"Only one upright bag?" Stacy asked.

"I don't want to be loaded down with baggage."

Stacy reached for the largest upright case. "How does Elise like flying?"

"I have no idea," Brooke said, picking up the other two smaller bags. "She's never flown before."

"I've heard that some dogs have to take a tranquilizer. Ouch!" Stacy had brushed against the steamer trunk and a sharp-edged brass fitting had pierced through the back thigh of her beige slacks. "Damn it. I think I tore them."

"Oh no." Brooke knelt down. Sure enough, the fitting had

slit Stacy's slacks and Brooke saw a drop of bright red blood beginning to spread against the linen. "I think you cut your leg, too."

"The leg will heal. The linen won't."

"Don't be silly, Stacy. Your leg is more important than your slacks. You might need a tetanus shot. I have no idea how old that brass is—"

She broke off and Stacy craned around, trying to look down. "What else is wrong?"

"Stains," Brooke said slowly. "There are rusty-looking stains where you brushed against the trunk."

"*Stains!*" Stacy sounded horrified. "Have I been wearing stained slacks all day?"

"No. The stains weren't there earlier."

"Rust. Dammit."

"Maybe it's rust." Rust was the most obvious answer, but fear fluttered in Brooke's stomach like a cold, dark wing. She touched one of the stains with her index finger. It wasn't moist, but it wasn't completely dry, either. The tip of her finger looked darker than the others. She held it close to her nose and caught a faint whiff of copper.

"Well, maybe the dry cleaner can get out rust," Stacy was chattering on. "If the tear isn't too large, maybe they can fix that, too. These aren't my favorite slacks, but they are fairly new."

Brooke sank from kneeling to sitting on the concrete. In spite of the fluorescent lights, she felt as if the room had dimmed. "Stacy, I don't think you have rust on your pants. I think it's blood."

"Am I bleeding *that* much? Do I need stitches?"

"Not your blood," Brooke quavered. "Older blood. But not old enough to be dried."

"What are you talking about?" Stacy let go of the bag and looked at Brooke's face, then at her slacks, then at the trunk. "Let's open it," she said finally.

"No! It's locked. I don't know where the key is—"

Stacy stooped down and looked at the brass fittings. "The

lock is broken." She placed both hands on the lid and began pushing upward.

"Stacy, don't!" Brooke almost shouted. "Don't open that thing!"

But it was too late. With a strong push, Stacy flung the lid back so hard it almost hit the side of the wire cage. She pointed the flashlight into the trunk, drew a deep, shaky breath, then whispered, "Brooke, we need to get the police. *Don't* look."

But it was too late. Brooke had staggered up and grabbed the flashlight. Now she stood gazing down into the trunk, down at what seemed to be yards of green net and chiffon, down at the white face of Eunice Dormer lying in a puddle of blood that looked like dark red sludge.

# twenty

## 1

After a moment of stunned, horrified silence, Brooke and Stacy turned and almost ran for the stairs. By the time they reached them Brooke was hyperventilating. Stacy went first, grabbing Brooke's hand and almost dragging her up the stairs. When they reached the top, Stacy slammed the basement door, pushed Brooke into a chair, and forced her head between her legs. "Breathe deeply or you're going to pass out," Stacy ordered.

Mrs. Kelso, who spent most of her time in the lobby, gaped at them. A haughty woman who found most of the world beneath her, she rarely spoke to either woman, but now she couldn't resist. "Is something wrong?"

"No, we always act this way," Stacy snapped. "Where's Harry?"

"I haven't seen him all day, the shiftless—" Mrs. Kelso, who finally realized Stacy had spoken to her with sarcasm, stiffly turned her back and walked away.

"The beginnings of a lovely friendship down the drain," Stacy said. "Are you feeling better?"

"I think I can get my breath, if that's what you mean." Brooke raised her head. "The police."

"You sit here. I'll run out and get the surveillance cops. That'll be faster than calling nine-one-one. Don't you dare move."

"I won't," Brooke muttered. "I *can't*."

As Stacy dashed out the front door, Brooke sat rigid, her hands clutching the chair arms. She closed her eyes. Immediately the image of Eunice, buried in folds of garish green except for her stark white face and mouse brown hair matted with blood, flashed behind Brooke's eyelids. She jerked and nearly jumped out of her chair. She felt as if she were in a nightmare in which she kept experiencing looking into the trunk at a woman's dead, bloodstained face. First her mother, then Mia, next Robert, now Eunice. How many more people would die before Zach Tavell could be stopped?

Stacy ran back inside, two policemen right behind her. "They've already called headquarters," she said to Brooke. Stacy motioned to the basement door. "She's down there," she said to the cops. "The cage door is open. You don't want me to go with you, do you?"

"No, ma'am," the other one said. "The more people present, the more chance there is of contaminating evidence. Could you keep other tenants from coming down, though?"

"I wanted to get Brooke back to my apartment as soon as possible. . . ."

"The detectives will be here in five minutes," the other cop said. "Then you can go. Okay?"

"Okay," Stacy said reluctantly. She turned to Brooke. "Can you hold up another five minutes or so?"

Once the initial shock passed, Brooke simply felt tired. Tired to her bones. "I'm okay, Stacy. I'm not a little kid, you know," she said, sounding exactly like a querulous little kid. She sighed, rubbing her forehead. "I'm sorry. You just seem so strong and in control and I'm piled in this chair like a sack of potatoes. I'm ashamed of myself."

"I'm not as calm as I act. Besides, I haven't suffered as many shocks as you have lately," Stacy said kindly. "And you make a very pretty sack of potatoes. If Harry could see you—"

Their eyes met. "Harry!" they nearly shouted together.

"Where's Harry?" Brooke asked Stacy, although she knew Stacy had no idea.

"I haven't seen him all day. Mrs. Kelso said earlier she hasn't, either." Stacy paused. "Those cages downstairs, Brooke. Harry has a key to each of them just like he does to all the apartments. Your key wasn't missing. The lock on the cage wasn't broken—"

"But the lock on the trunk was," Brooke said slowly. "You don't think *Harry*—"

"Harry what? Murdered Eunice? You think Harry, not Zach, murdered Eunice?"

"I guess not. It was just a silly thought."

"Maybe not so silly. Harry wanted to be rid of Eunice. If she was murdered in the basement of *this* building, the building where you live, where Zach has been hanging around, what conclusion would the police draw? That Eunice went to the basement in search of Harry—"

"She did. Last night. She seemed upset."

"All right. She went down in search of Harry and instead ran into Zach. That's what they'd think." Stacy nearly wrung her hands. "Oh, I wish Jay would get here. I need to tell him this."

"Tell me what?"

Stacy whirled around to find Jay standing behind her. She threw her arms around him. "Thank God you're here. In the basement. Brooke and I went down and we found Eunice. She's in some old trunk in Brooke's storage cage. The storage cage was locked, but there was an old trunk with a broken lock and Eunice was in there and there was so much blood. . . ."

Jay hugged her tightly, then gently pulled her away from

him. "We'll need to question you, but right now you both need to calm down. You're talking like at a machine-gun rate and Brooke looks like she's going to faint. We need some time to get this area secured, so Stacy, take Brooke upstairs. Do not drink to calm down. I'll need some very clear and precise answers in a little while. Hal should be here soon."

Brooke remembered garish red lights flashing against the night sky as men and women in uniforms poured through the lobby doors, all seeming to be talking at once. My, wouldn't Harry dearly love all this commotion, she thought distantly, then wondered where Harry could be. Had he done this to Eunice, hoping Zach would be blamed? Was Harry making preparations with that mistress Eunice always feared for flight to better places? Or had Zach gotten to him, too, just the way he'd gotten her mother and Mia and Robert and maybe Eunice? Brooke's stomach turned and she prayed she wouldn't be sick. She could not let herself be a nervous, nauseated little weakling, she thought. She had to be strong. It's what Greta would have wanted. That's what she had to keep in mind: what dear Grossmutter would have wanted.

When they went back to Stacy's apartment, Brooke decided to call Vincent to tell him about Greta, and now the horror of finding Eunice. Her cell phone showed that she had one unanswered call. It was from Vincent, and on the voice mail he sounded tense and hurried:

"Hey, Brooke. Sorry I haven't been able to get in touch with you. Dad usually takes a nap in the afternoon and I write. Today he sneaked out on me. He didn't take the car, thank God. Keys are on the seat, though. He *tried* to drive somewhere. I've been out looking for him all afternoon. Take care of yourself. I've got a bad feeling today. Sorry I couldn't be with you at the hospital. Uh . . . I lo—" He broke off. "See you soon, Cinnamon Girl."

Stacy, who had been hovering close enough to hear Vincent's message, looked at Brooke and raised an eyebrow. "Was he about to say, 'I love you' at the end?"

"I don't think so," Brooke said briskly, passionately hoping he *was,* also afraid he *was,* and finally depressed because she was certain he *wasn't*. "You could tell he's nervous about his father. Probably even he doesn't know what he was about to say."

"Uh-huh," Stacy drawled. "The only reason I can think of that an articulate man like Vincent didn't know what he was going to say is because he was unsure of how well his declaration would be received."

"I never knew you were such a sloppy romantic," Brooke returned, putting her cell phone back in her purse.

"I have my moments." Stacy grinned at her. "Well, we've had orders not to get rip-roaring drunk so we can be halfway coherent when we talk to the police, although rip-roaring drunk sounds like a wonderful condition to be in after what we've just been through."

"I agree," Brooke said with a shudder.

"So, since I don't want to humiliate my husband in front of his colleagues, especially Hal Myers, I'm going to put on a pot of coffee. Do you want decaf, or something with some kick?"

"Caffeine will make me more wired than I already am, but at the same time, my bones feel like they're made of rubber. Maybe some caffeine will put some life back into me."

Stacy disappeared in the kitchen and Brooke scooted out of her chair and sat cross-legged on the floor, pulling Elise onto her lap. She buried her face in the thick hair around Elise's neck, hair that still smelled fresh from her bath less than a week ago, and fought off the urge to cry. She couldn't say she'd really liked Eunice. Brooke had never even had a real conversation with the woman. Eunice was a perpetually agitated, suspicious, prying hypochondriac, but Brooke had felt sorry for her. She'd been plain, bordering on ugly, and not the type who could make people look past her physical deficiencies to see a beautiful soul, if indeed she had one, but Brooke sensed that Eunice's life had been a hard one, driving out any potential charm or attractiveness. And now her death had been hard, too. Not just hard. Horrifying. Brooke didn't want to think about it.

But she couldn't think of anything else. How had Eunice been murdered? All they'd seen was the body and an incredible amount of drying blood. They would find out soon enough, as soon as they talked with Jay, but no matter what the method, Eunice had looked shocked even in death. The attack must have been swift. They hadn't seen blood on the floor. Someone had been careful to wipe that up, although luminol and ultraviolet lights would certainly show the point of attack and the trail leading to Brooke's storage cage.

Brooke wondered when Eunice had been killed. No one had seen her all day. But Brooke and Vincent had seen her last night. She'd looked frightened. She'd wanted Harry. And she'd been wearing that god-awful green negligee—the one she still wore as she lay in Brooke's trunk.

Brooke jerked with realization. Eunice had come rushing up to her and Vincent in the lobby wearing the negligee just twenty-four hours ago. Brooke had wanted to get rid of her, so she'd directed her to the basement in search of Harry. When she'd gone downstairs, her killer must have been waiting.

Brooke stiffened as her thoughts spun in a mass of horror, astonishment, and regret. *She* was responsible for Eunice's death! "It's my fault," she cried. "It's *my* fault!"

Stacy raced in from the kitchen. "What's wrong?"

"My God, Stacy, I just realized that *I'm* responsible for Eunice being murdered. It must have happened night before last because she had on that hideous negligee and I sent her to the basement because I wanted to be alone with Vincent and she was murdered—"

Stacy held up her hand for silence. "Brooke, stop! You're not making any sense."

"Yes, I am. It makes perfect sense. The timing, don't you see? Zach was in the basement waiting for me and suddenly Eunice came flying down and saw him, so he had to kill her—"

By now Stacy knelt in front of her and put her hands on Brooke's shoulders. "You are not making any sense. Why would Zach be waiting in the basement for you? Were you supposed to go to the basement?"

"No, but he could have been planning to come up later. Or maybe he'd already been up here, almost got caught leaving the building, and dashed down to the basement to hide. Oh God!"

Stacy came close to shaking her. "Stop it! We don't even know if Tavell killed her."

"Who else?"

"Harry."

"Oh, Harry, that idiot! I don't believe it. He's basically a coward with a big mouth. He didn't kill Eunice and put her in *my* steamer trunk, clean up after himself, then just walk out of here. Even if he'd tried something so . . . so daring, he would have bungled it. You know it, Stacy. You *know* Harry!"

Stacy went quiet for a few moments. Her lids dropped over her gray eyes as she looked at the floor, clearly thinking about what Brooke had said. Finally, she answered slowly. "You could be right, Brooke. Not about being responsible for Eunice's death—if Zach killed her, how could you possibly have known he was in the basement?—but about her not being killed by Harry. He's just too much of a screwup to have pulled off something like this."

"So another person died because of *me*," Brooke nearly whispered, feeling too crushed inside to speak aloud. "Mia, Robert, now Eunice. Who's next?"

"According to that signed note you received, *you* are." Dismay flashed across Stacy's face. "I'm sorry."

"Don't be. It did say I'm next. But what if someone else gets in the way? Someone like you or Jay or . . ."

"Vincent?"

Brooke looked at her friend and nodded. "Of course I don't want to die. But I don't want anyone else to die, either, especially not because of me. I can't let it happen. I *can't*." Brooke let her arms drop away from Elise and stood up. "I'm leaving right now, Stacy."

"What about the police? They want to question you."

"They can call me. Besides, you can tell them anything I can."

"Where will you go?"

"As far as a jet scheduled for takeoff within the next few hours will take me."

"A jet? You're going to fly?"

"I can get farther much faster, wouldn't you agree?"

"Well, yes, but . . ." Stacy stood up. "Brooke, you don't have a flight scheduled."

"Flights leave all the time."

Stacy frowned. "Brooke, you *can't* leave right this minute."

"Why not? What am I supposed to do? Sit here for hours while the police do whatever they have to do downstairs, hold still for dozens of questions I can't answer, *wait* to be killed or for another person to be killed?" She shook her head. "I'm driving to the airport right now."

"No!" Stacy looked shocked, then blank. "No, it's not wise, it's not the right time. Wait until tomorrow."

Brooke reached for her purse. "I'll go to my apartment and get Elise's travel carrier. I'm not leaving her behind. Then I'll go down the back stairs and try to get past the sur-veillance guys. Maybe I don't even have to worry about them. They might be with the other cops in the basement."

"Wait!" Stacy put her face in her hands for a few mo-ments, then looked into Brooke's determined eyes. "You can't leave with only Elise and what you're wearing. You don't have enough money for a whole new wardrobe. I have a suitcase and tote bag in the bedroom. I'll get them and you can pack a few things. Then I'll help you down to the car."

Brooke came as close to a smile as she could at the mo-ment. "Thank you, Stacy. I don't know what I'd do without you."

"You're going to make me cry." Stacy grinned. "Now stop being sentimental and let's get going."

# 2

For the sake of speed, Brooke chose only Stacy's large suitcase and a boarding bag. They hurried to Brooke's apartment, where she tried to match outfits, although her mind felt so jumbled, she had a feeling she'd arrive at her destination with a conglomeration of wrinkled clothes, none of them comprising one decent outfit. She tossed cosmetics into a Ziploc plastic bag before stuffing them into the carry-on bag in case anything spilled. She opened a drawer and pulled out the two credit cards she usually never carried—she didn't know how much money she'd need—and finally urged a reluctant Elise into her pet carrier. After one final look around the apartment, Brooke announced, "I'm ready to go."

"Are you sure?" Stacy asked. "Don't you want to take one more tour around the place and make sure you haven't forgotten anything crucial?"

"Crucial things are sold at airports. All I want right now is to get away from this place."

"Okay. You take Elise, she'll feel safer that way, and the carry-on bag. I'll take the big suitcase."

Brooke went dry-mouthed with fear as they sneaked down the back steps—none too clean in spite of Harry's protests about the hard work he did keeping the apartment house in order. Stacy flipped off the lights before she opened the door and they stepped into the dark alley behind the brick building. After the door shut behind them, they stopped, surveying their surroundings.

"There's the surveillance cruiser," Brooke whispered.

"I see only one guy in it and he doesn't appear to have seen us."

"I would never have thought to turn off the light before we opened the door."

"Yes, you would have," Stacy said absently, peering at the surveillance car. "The other cop is probably helping in the basement," Stacy said.

"Whether there's one or two men in the cruiser, we can't get past it to the parking lot."

Stacy went silent for a moment. Then she said, "We can't *both* get past. But one of us can if he's distracted. I'll go up to his window and start talking. You go past on the other side. I'm afraid you'll have to make two trips in order to get all the bags *and* Elise, but I think I can keep him chatting."

"Are you sure?"

"Have you ever known of me to run out of things to say?"

"Well . . ."

"There's your answer." Stacy smiled, then turned serious. "I want you to put your stuff in my car."

"Why yours?"

"Because if they realize you're gone, they'll be looking for your car, not mine. Besides, that isn't even *your* car. It's a rental." Yes, Brooke thought, hers had been in the shop since Mia's death. "Tonight I'll drive you to the airport and I'll turn in your car for you tomorrow."

"*You'll* drive me to the airport! Stacy, Jay will kill you!"

"Jay will yell at me. Besides, as you're always saying, he adores me." She gave Brooke an exaggerated wink. "Don't underestimate my powers to soothe my husband's temper."

I'd never underestimate you, Stacy, Brooke thought as Stacy strolled over to the patrol car. The window must have already been down, because Stacy immediately propped her arms on the door and leaned inward slightly. Brooke heard the rumble of a man's voice, then heard Stacy giggle. Now was the time for the first trip.

Brooke skittered to Stacy's car with the large suitcase and the carry-on bag, opened the back door, piled the luggage on the backseat, then quietly closed the door. Skulking through the parking lot again, she saw Stacy still leaning in the window and heard the tinkling sound of her laughter. Brooke picked up Elise's carrier and once again made a dash for the car, trying unobtrusively to signal Stacy as she ran. She scooted onto the passenger's side and set Elise's carrier on her lap. "It's okay, sweetie. I hope in a couple of hours we'll be headed away from this place." The dog whined slightly, then licked Brooke's fingers through the wire door of the carrier.

Brooke's heart pounded as she waited for Stacy. Was she doing the right thing, just running off like this? Would it be better if she waited until tomorrow, made a reservation . . .

And gave Zach twenty-four more hours to get to her or kill someone else in his pursuit of her? And what if the police for some reason wanted her to wait another day? What if they demanded to know her destination and word that she was thinking of going to Vermont leaked out?

Elise yelped and Brooke jumped as Stacy hopped into the car and burst out, "Told you I could do it!"

"The surveillance cop had to see you get in this car."

"I was going to try telling him I just *had* to run to the drugstore—'I'll be right back,' 'please let me go,' 'I'll be back before my husband knows I'm gone,' et cetera. He was waffling, but I was sure he was going to say no. Then luck struck like a gift from Heaven." Brooke waited. "The cops inside radioed for this guy to come in and help them with something! I couldn't believe it. I told him I wouldn't leave. I walked back inside the building with him and when he went sailing off for the basement, I ran out here. Didn't you see me?"

"I wasn't looking," Brooke admitted sheepishly. "I got lost in my own thoughts."

"I can't believe it. One of my most daring exploits, and you missed it!"

"I'm sorry."

"Oh, don't be silly," Stacy said, starting her car. "I'm just kidding. I think I'm giddy, actually, pulling off this whole scheme."

"Maybe you shouldn't be involved in this, Stacy," Brooke said sincerely. "I can drive my car and you and Jay can pick it up sometime and return it—"

"Pick it up out of long-term parking when they just had a car stolen? They won't let Jay have it."

"He's a police detective, Stacy. He'll explain. Besides, he's going to be furious with you."

"It might take us days to get that car out of long-term parking, days you'd have to pay for. And I told you, I can handle Jay."

"He'll forgive little things, yes, but this isn't a little thing."

Stacy looked at her sternly. "No, this isn't a little thing. This is about your life, maybe about other lives, too. If I can't make him understand that, he can't understand anything and I don't care how furious he is."

Brooke sighed. "All right. I'm too tired to argue. Actually, I'm too frightened to wait any longer to get out of this city and too nervous to trust my own driving. So, if you're willing to take the chance . . ."

"I am." Stacy crept out of the parking lot with the headlights off. "Just chill out and leave this to me, Brooke. I'll get you where you need to be."

A quarter mile away from the apartment building, Stacy turned on the headlights. They were free, Brooke thought. Finally, she was on her way to freedom and safety.

"We're about twenty minutes from the airport," Stacy said. "Want some music?"

Brooke nodded and Stacy slid in a CD of Celtic songs, beautiful, lyrical, dreamlike. After the tension of the day, sitting beside her grandmother for almost ten hours talking, then the shock of finding Eunice's body, Brooke felt her eyelids growing heavy with fatigue. Slowly, she drifted off to the sounds of "The Moonlight Piper" by Carlos Núñez.

Brooke was dreaming of lying in her bed at the house on Holt Street, looking up at the stars her mother had painted on the ceiling, when she vaguely became aware of the car stopping. In a moment, Stacy was outside and opening Brooke's door. "Trip's over," she said.

Brooke blinked twice and looked at her friend, standing tall and grim-faced in the light of the full moon. Silence surrounded her. "Stacy, this isn't the airport," Brooke said groggily.

"No, it isn't."

Brooke struggled to sit up straighter in her seat, to get her bearings. She clutched Elise's carrier even closer to her chest, like a shield, on a primal level sensing danger. "Where are we?"

Stacy stepped aside and swept her hand almost grandly at a small white house, the house Brooke had been dreaming of, the house where Zachary Tavell had murdered her mother.

"I've brought you home, Brooke," Stacy said triumphantly. "I've brought you where you should have died fifteen years ago."

# twenty-one

## 1

"My home?" Brooke asked in bewilderment.

"Yes. I told you already. *This* is where you were supposed to die a long time ago."

Oddly enough, Brooke felt as if her heart were slowing, not picking up speed in fear. This whole scenario seemed unreal, and for a moment, she thought she was still dreaming. She'd dreamed about the stars on her bedroom ceiling. Now she was dreaming about the entire house. Except that Stacy looked so real and this experience didn't have the slightly fuzzy, dreamlike quality of the one before it. Brooke still couldn't quite believe that Stacy had brought her to what had once been known as "The House of the Rose Murder," but on the other hand, sharp points of realization as well as apprehension had begun to pierce her fog of confusion.

"Stacy, what are you doing?" She was surprised by the calmness of her voice. Not a quiver, not a break. "Why have you brought me here?"

"Because I'm taking you inside."

"Why?"

Stacy suddenly looked impatient. "Why, why, why? I've said we're here because we're going in. That settles it."

"Not for me."

"Will this help?" Stacy had been holding her right hand behind her back. Suddenly she whipped her arm around and held it out stiffly in front of her. In her hand, she gripped a gun. "This is a Smith & Wesson Model 36LS. I know that in terms of firearms that means absolutely nothing to you, but you're bright enough to know that it can kill you. You and your flea-bitten dog. Now get out of the car and march up to that house. And don't try to run or do anything you consider smart and heroic, because I'll be right behind you and have this gun pointed directly at your head."

This cannot be happening, Brooke thought as she clambered from Stacy's car, still holding tightly to Elise's carrier. When Brooke emerged, she didn't set the carrier back on the seat. She had a feeling Stacy would immediately shoot the dog if she did. Elise was safer with her. *Safe.* That was a laugh. No one was safe with her. No one ever had been, not even her own mother.

Brooke walked toward the house, glancing around slowly so Stacy wouldn't think she was getting ready to bolt. She knew the neighborhood had gone downhill over the last few years, but she'd had no idea how much. It had never been one of the nicer neighborhoods in town, but it had been neat and presentable in its modest way. Now, even with just the glow of the moon and the few streetlights that had not burned out or been broken, the area looked downright shabby.

As they neared the porch steps, Brooke noticed the cracks in the badly chipped paint on the little white house, the empty urns that used to hold cheerful red geraniums, the shattered globe over the porch light, a light that always used to burn in welcome to guests. Brooke wondered how long it had been since a live bulb had been screwed into that socket.

"Place has changed, hasn't it?" Stacy said suddenly. "It didn't used to be a palace, but it looked a helluva lot better than this. Fifteen years ago, that is."

"How do you know what this house looked like fifteen years ago?" Brooke asked. "You told me you lived in Ohio. Did you see photos of it in the newspapers?"

"I saw it in person."

"Oh," Brooke returned scathingly. "You were one of the tourists drawn to the spot of 'The Rose Murder.'"

"No." Stacy laughed softly. "I was hardly a tourist. Go in the house, Brooke."

Brooke hesitated, feeling as if she couldn't possibly take a step into that house with its horrible memories. Then she felt the barrel of the gun press against the back of her head. "I said, go in. *Now.*"

Brooke opened the door and took a step into almost total darkness. Almost. Enough light shone from the outside for her to make out the stairs—the stairs she had run down when she'd heard the shots, the stairs from which she'd seen Zach Tavell standing over her mother with a gun.

The house smelled stale. Brooke knew it had accumulated years of dust and mold and wood rotting from leaks that had never been fixed. But it also smelled of something else. Death. This house smells of death, she thought with a certainty she tried to quell. Anne Yeager Tavell had been murdered in this house fifteen years ago. It could not still smell of her death.

But it did, at least to Brooke.

"I made a few arrangements in here earlier today when I found out your grandmother was dying and I thought things might come to this," Stacy said casually. "We can't stand here in the dark and talk." Light flared beside Brooke and she realized Stacy had bent down and turned on a battery-operated lantern. "There, that's better, don't you think?" Brooke remained silent and Stacy's voice turned harsh. "I asked you if you thought that was better."

"Much better."

"I think so, too. Now for the others." Stacy stepped in front of her and smiled. "And don't think, Here's my chance! While she's lighting lanterns, I'll make a break for it! It won't work."

"I didn't. . . . I wouldn't. . . ."

"Oh, of course you would. Anyone would. It's just that anyone who did would end up dead. And our Brooke is too smart for that. So, you stand perfectly still while I turn on another lantern," Stacy said as she stepped backward, gun pointed at Brooke's face, stooped down, and turned on a lantern by the stairs, then repeated the process as she turned on a third lantern just inside the entrance to the living room. "Jay always says it's like I have eyes in the back of my head. That was an excellent demonstration, wasn't it?"

"Yes, I guess. . . ." Brooke ran her dry tongue over her parched lips. "Stacy, what is this all about?"

"They say some sisters can read each other's minds. But we can't. Maybe that's because we're almost stepsisters."

"Stepsisters?"

"Yes. My birth certificate says my name is Lila Stacy Cox. It should have said 'Lila Stacy Tavell,' but Zach wouldn't let my mother—her name was Nadine—put his name down as my father. She tried to tell me later that he was embarrassed because they weren't married, but I always knew the real reason. He didn't want any ties between us—between him and Nadine and me. He always figured one day he'd just take off and leave us with not even a connection on a shred of paper. And that's exactly what he did."

"Zach . . . Zachary Tavell is your *father*?"

"Yes. He was with my mother when she was really young. Some would say she was stupid, but she wasn't—just naïve." Stacy stood beside a lantern. The light shone up at her, emphasizing her height, her prominent cheekbones, the hollows where granite gray eyes burned down at Brooke with complete hatred. Brooke felt as if she were a little girl huddling in on herself as she clutched Elise's carrier even tighter, although it was becoming heavy and the timid dog inside was trembling with nerves. You tremble for both of us, Elise, Brooke thought, because I'm afraid to move.

She couldn't move, but she could still talk. If she talked long enough, then maybe something would happen. Maybe the entire police force would burst through the front door and . . .

"I feel that I don't have your full attention," Stacy snapped.

"I'm sorry. I'm so surprised. I don't know what to say, what to ask. Why don't you tell me everything that happened in your own way? I won't interrupt you."

"Of course not. You're too *polite* to interrupt, aren't you?" Stacy's voice became high and saccharine. "Ladylike Brooke Yeager. Such a pretty girl. Such nice manners. And the poor little thing had such a rough life, too. What a shame!" Stacy's voice deepened. "Well, you had an absolutely grand life compared to mine."

"May I set down Elise in the carrier? Then you can tell me about your life."

"Like you care about *my* life."

"I do," Brooke said, not sure whether she really cared, she was curious, or she was just stalling for time. It didn't matter, really. All she wanted to do was draw out this moment before the inevitable violence.

"All right, set down your precious dog. Honest to God, you treat it better than I was treated."

"How *were* you treated?" Brooke asked, moving slowly as she lowered the carrier to the floor.

"Not bad at first. At least I don't think I was. I mean, what does a baby know? But I've seen photographs of Zach with my mother. She was only seventeen when she had me. Just a kid herself, although she already had a baby before she had me. Someone else's baby, not Zach's. It died, though, right after I was born. Zach was in his twenties and had already been in some trouble. But Mom always told me he'd decided to straighten himself out with her help." She laughed harshly. "He just didn't want to marry her, even though she had his kid. After all, I wasn't her first kid. He didn't have any respect for her.

"But he was good to me," Stacy went on. "Mom said he 'doted' on me. I guess I was an amusement, something new in his life. And my mother was gorgeous. He was proud to be seen with her, proud to say that she was *his* girl because she was so pretty." She paused, her face hardening. "But when I was four or five, things began to change. He got restless. He had guys over all the time and they drank and played cards. Zach would get drunk and a few times, he hit Mom. She'd cry and bleed. . . ." Stacy stopped and the look of an old horror crossed her face. Then she went on. "But he'd never hit me. *Never.* Mom said he hit her because she got on his nerves and deserved it, but he wouldn't hit me because he loved me so much. But then one day, he just left. Not a word, not a note, nothing. He was just gone.

"Mom looked everywhere for him, but it was like he'd dropped off the face of the earth. And there we were, all alone." Stacy's eyes lost their sharpness—they seemed dreamy, as if she were lost in the past. "Mom's parents wouldn't have her back. She didn't have any friends—Zach didn't allow it. We got by on what she could make working at a convenience store, but she kept getting sick. She'd never been strong. So, naturally, she got fired from that job. Then another and another. Finally, in despair, she hooked up with some loser who promised to take care of us. She didn't care about him. She just wanted some financial security for me. And he just wanted her beautiful face and body. Well, he got it. He also got her hooked on heroin."

Brooke opened her mouth, but Stacy snapped, "If you dare say, 'I'm sorry,' I'll blow your head off right now." Brooke quickly closed her mouth.

"So, Mom's rescuer stayed with us for two years. Then Mom started showing the effects of her bad health and the lovely things heroin addiction does to your body. So out the door he went. Once again, no good-bye, not a thought in the world but for the woman he'd already begun seeing. I was seven by then. Mom tried to take care of me in spite of everything, but she was too beaten down. The heroin had taken control of her life, and she'd never been the same since Zach left. He was the love of her life."

Stacy smiled bitterly. "And you know what? Zach was the love of mine, too. Isn't that absolutely ridiculous? But he was my daddy. I had adored him. I was sure if he'd only come back, we could be a family again. He could make Mom well. He could fix everything. But I didn't stand a chance of finding him. Finally the state stepped in. They *did* locate Zach Tavell, but he claimed he'd only dated Nadine Cox a few times years ago and he said he'd never heard of Lila Cox. He asked if Lila Cox was Nadine's *sister*! They didn't do DNA tests in those days. So I was taken away from Mom, she was thrown into rehab, and I was sent to foster homes. Do you know what happens to a pretty little girl in a bad foster home? Oh, I know you were in one for what—two months? But I'll bet the father didn't find you, shall we say, sexually attractive. I had two of those before I was even ten. And when the wives found out, they blamed *me*; they hit *me*."

Brooke and Stacy both jerked when Brooke's cell phone rang, sounding like an alarm in the dark, musty little house. Brooke cringed, terrified the shock would frighten Stacy into firing the gun, but after the first ring she regained her composure. She stood motionless as the phone rang again and again. After five rings, it stopped.

"I'll bet that was Vincent," Stacy said, smirking. "Vincent Lockhart, looking for his . . . what is it he calls you . . . looking for his Cinnamon Girl. But you're only the girl of the moment, honey. He'll forget you as soon as he goes back to California."

"I know that," Brooke said meekly.

"Do you? I'm not so sure. You're not used to being forgotten, are you? Oh, you've had your little dramas, but they've always ended up with you getting even more love and attention than you did before they happened. But being forgotten . . . well, I think maybe that's worse than what happened to me over the years in some of those foster homes. Not all of the homes were bad, but I managed to get myself thrown out of the ones that were good. I guess I'd had the bad ones first and they . . . changed me. By the time the good ones came along, I didn't know how to act like a decent little girl anymore.

"But all those years—those years when my mother never got well enough to take me back on her own—I kept thinking of Zach. I kept thinking of what a happy family we'd had. I'm sure I changed things in my mind, made it sweeter, more loving, warmer, than it had ever really been, but I was certain at the time. So, I decided if I could find Zach, if I could tell him all the things that had happened to me and to Mom, he'd make it all right. He'd get Mom out of that place where they kept hopeless junkies. He'd make me forget the sexual assaults and the beatings, and we'd be a happy family again. I just had to find him. So when I was sixteen, I ran away from my last foster home and started my search." She paused. "It took me two years, but I did it. I found Zach."

"When you were eighteen you found Zach?" Brooke did some quick figuring. "That means you found him when he was married to my mother."

"Right. I've always shaved a couple of years off my age. Anyway, he was a respectable man then. He had his own little photography studio—he was always good at photography. He'd married a pretty widow with a cute little girl. He was living in what to me was a fine home. Meanwhile, Mom and I . . ." Stacy's voice broke as her head bowed slightly. Then she raised it again and glared at Brooke. "Do you know what discovering all of that did to me?"

"I can imagine," Brooke said faintly.

"No, you can't. Your father didn't voluntarily leave you, then deny you, then set up a whole new life. He died. Then along came Zach to save the day, Mom and me be damned." She sighed. "But in spite of how mad I was, I still believed he could save the day for us, too. I thought if he saw me, if he heard what I'd been through, what Mom was going through, he'd feel guilty enough to leave you and Anne and come back to his *real* family, his *real* daughter." She fell silent and stared past Brooke. "But you didn't, did you, Zach?"

# 2

Slowly, Brooke turned and saw a tall, extremely thin man standing about three feet away from her. His hair was more white than black, his face bore deep creases and the lids hung halfway over the dark eyes, and the lips were thinner, but other than that, he was the same Zachary Tavell she remembered.

Zach looked at Stacy, not at Brooke. "You knew I was here, didn't you?"

"Yes," Stacy answered casually. "The police searched the place after you first escaped from prison, but they gave up the last few days. I came back a few evenings ago and saw you pass by a window." Her cold gray eyes narrowed as they traveled up and down his tall frame. "You're sick, aren't you?"

For the first time, Brooke noticed in the strange lighting from kerosene lamps that Zach's pale face was covered with perspiration and his big hands trembled. "I think I got an infection," he said.

"From the gunshot wound. It was *so* stupid of you to try to get to Brooke in the Lockhart house."

"You were there first, remember?" Zach said to Stacy. "I was trying to keep you from doing something to her."

"How touching. You wanted to protect her?"

"I wanted to protect you, Lila," Zach said. "If I hadn't gotten in the way, they might've shot you. Might've killed you."

Stacy looked taken aback, shocked almost into tenderness. Then she hardened again. "Did you get any medical treatment?"

"I thought I could take care of it myself."

"Obviously you didn't do such a good job of it," Stacy said acidly.

No, but he's lived long enough to finish me off before he goes, Brooke thought. Except that nothing about this scene seemed right, especially Zach saying he'd wanted to protect "Lila" at the Lockhart house.

"I don't understand," Brooke ventured. "What's going on here?"

Stacy looked at Zach. "Do you want to tell her, or shall I?" Zach remained silent. "Well, I guess this is my show, then. Where did I leave off? Oh yes. I finally tracked down Zach. I must say, I'd hoped for a warmer welcome. Actually, he was horrified to see me. Even when I said I wouldn't make any trouble for him if he'd just get Mom out of that so-called rehab place they were keeping her and leave with the two of us. But he wouldn't do it."

"I was married," Zach said, his voice sounding raspy and weak.

"That was a technicality. Your responsibility was to Mom and me. Nadine and Lila. But he wouldn't even talk about it, Brooke. Can you imagine just washing your hands of your flesh-and-blood daughter and her mother like that? So I started applying pressure. I told him if he didn't do what I wanted, I'd tell your mother everything. Then he started to get nervous."

That's when things had begun to change, Brooke thought. Zach had never been warm to her, but at least the home life had been calm. Then Zach had started snapping at Anne, drinking again, picking fights over nothing. He'd been a nervous wreck, she realized now, terrified that "Lila" was going to ruin everything for him.

"I offered you money," Zach said to Stacy. "I offered you every penny I had to just leave. But you wouldn't. You even started sneaking into the house when Anne was out. You took things of hers." The letter opener, Brooke thought. The wedding ring. "I was ashamed of what I'd done to you and your mother. God, you'll never know how ashamed."

"But not ashamed enough to do anything to help us."

Zach bowed his head. "Not strong enough. I've never been a strong man. But I was trying to be a good man, and I'd taken a vow before God to stand by Anne and Brooke."

"How honorable of you after what you'd done to Mom and me," Stacy said sarcastically. She looked at Brooke. "I decided if you two didn't exist, my weakling of a father might do what was right. So I waited until one night when he was supposed to be in Columbus, being careful that he had an alibi, and I came in this house with a gun to get rid of both of you."

Brooke felt dizzy. Stacy was standing in front of her—funny, sarcastic, flirtatious, often lovable Stacy who had been her friend for over a year—telling her about how she'd planned to murder both Anne *and* Brooke. It didn't seem real.

"*You* killed my mother?" Brooke asked barely above a whisper.

Stacy smiled grimly. "Yes, I did. You should have seen the look on her face when she saw me standing in the living room with a gun. Zach walked in then. He started trying to wrestle the gun away from me, but I still managed to get off three shots. You were coming down the stairs. I could have gotten you, too, but we heard noises outside. I ran." She jerked her head toward Zach. "He *tried* to run, but your neighbors got him."

Brooke looked at Zach. "You mean *you* didn't shoot Mom? *She* did?" He nodded. "But you let yourself get convicted of first-degree murder."

"I'm not an unselfish man. I tried to get out of it with that story about the guys breaking into the house and me catching them. But that story fell apart. I still had one chance—to tell the police about Lila," Zach said. "I've got to admit I thought about it hard. But there must be a little bit of good in me, because I finally decided I'd already done enough harm. To Lila. To Nadine." He almost choked. "And Anne. My life was over, not that it ever counted for much anyway, so what did it matter if I spent the rest of it in prison?"

The cell phone in Brooke's purse began to ring again. Stacy smiled. "The persistent lover, no doubt. Did you have a date with him tonight?"

"No."

"I guess he just wants to hear the sound of your voice." Stacy's smile faded. "That thing is getting on my nerves."

"Then let me turn it off," Brooke said in a sudden burst of

inspiration. "Otherwise, it'll be ringing every ten minutes."

Stacy seemed to think this over. The phone rang on and on. Finally she said, "Do it. It's driving me crazy."

Quickly, before the connection was broken, Brooke reached into her purse, grabbed the cell phone, and pushed the ANSWER button. Then, before Vincent could burst out with a loud greeting, she said shrilly, "Is that better, Stacy? Will you stop pointing the gun at me?"

"For God's sake, Brooke, I'm only a few feet away," Stacy snapped. "You don't have to scream at me."

"I'm sorry. I'm nervous. I'm terrified."

"Then today is your lucky day." Thank God Stacy didn't have a soft voice, Brooke thought. She was certain Vincent could hear her. And, bless him, he hadn't blurted out a word, although she was certain he was listening. At least she prayed he was listening and hadn't hung up right before she pressed the ANSWER button.

Brooke began slowly. "Stacy, what did you do after that night after you shot Mom here?"

Brooke didn't know if they could trace cell phone calls, but she had gotten in the word "here." They were at the house where Anne had been murdered. Vincent didn't know where that house was, she thought, but the police would.

Stacy didn't answer for a few moments and Brooke was afraid she'd caught on to the trick with the cell phone. Brooke almost stopped breathing in fear that Stacy would simply shoot her right now. But when Stacy started talking, it was with the far-off quality of someone dredging up memories. "My better instinct was to get as far away from here as possible before Zach told the truth about me," she said. "But when he didn't come out with the story right away, I got this weird fascination about what he *would* do when things got bad for him. I wanted to see how long it would take him to break. But he didn't. Not ever. I couldn't believe it.

"After he was convicted, I stayed here. I'd made some friends among the 'working girls,' as they euphemistically call prostitutes. That's what I did to support myself, you know. I worked the streets. And I can tell you that I met some women who had twice the love and charity in their hearts as the so-called respectable women in the world. But then I met a guy who wanted to keep me for himself, so he put me to work in his store."

"Chantal's?"

"No, another one. I lost that first job after I met Jay. I actually fell in love with Jay, and my 'sponsor' didn't like it. Thank God Jay didn't do a background check on me. He can be so innocent and trusting sometimes. That's one of the things I love about him. In less than a year, we were married." Her voice turned acrid. "I had just the kind of life my mother always wanted, always deserved, but she didn't know it. I went to see her all the time, but the drugs and the depression had taken their toll. She knew my name and sometimes we could have something close to a conversation. Those times gave me so much hope. I thought somehow I could bring her back. I'd loved her *so* much." Her voice that had turned soft suddenly lashed through the room. "I loved her as much as you loved your mother, Brooke, although everyone thought Anne was worth that kind of love. They thought Nadine Cox was dirt. She didn't matter to anyone except me. She certainly didn't matter to you!"

Stacy jerked the gun in Zach's direction. He flinched but didn't take a step. He was gray, sweating profusely, and trembling. He's really sick, Brooke thought. And he didn't get this way overnight. For days he'd been hiding in this house, dying—this house that didn't have a phone.

"Stacy, the flowers, the notes, the packages. They were from you, weren't they?" Brooke asked.

Stacy smirked. "Sure. Except for that card you got in the mail." She glanced at Zach. " 'You're next,' it said. You put that in the mailbox at the end of this street, didn't you?" He nodded. "That was your only *real* communication from Zach. A warning." Stacy made a sound of disgust, then looked deep into Brooke's eyes and said at last, "You see, Zach isn't the one who's been planning to kill you, Brooke. *I* have."

"How long have you been planning this?" Brooke managed to ask Stacy evenly, although she felt tremors running through her body.

"My mother didn't die when I was eighteen like I told you. Christmas before last some lazy orderly let Mom get hold of something sharp and she slit her wrists. After that, I decided I *had* to kill you. I'd meant to do it fifteen years ago when I thought I could get my family back and make things right. You and Anne were responsible for that not happening. I made Anne pay, but you escaped me. After Mom committed suicide, I decided you weren't going to get away with it like you did the first time. It's a good thing I've been keeping track of you all these years. I even talked Jay into renting that apartment next to yours." She smirked. "I'm very thorough, Brooke. And very clever."

"All these years, she's been writing to me in prison," Zach piped up in his raspy voice. "After Nadine died, her letters changed. They were so full of hatred for me, but more for you, Brooke. I knew she was dangerous. That's when I started planning to break out of prison. I had to save her."

"Save *me*?" Stacy exclaimed. "Don't you mean save *Brooke*?"

"Her, too. But most important, to save you from yourself. You are my child."

Stacy burst into laughter. "Oh, your child! And you love me more than anything, right? God, Zach, they told me you'd gotten weird in prison, but you've gone right around the bend, haven't you?"

"Lila, I *do* love you. I guess I always did, only I was too stupid to realize it when I was young." He broke into a violent coughing fit. Brooke noticed that it sounded crisp, with rattling sounds that accompanied it, and wondered if he had pneumonia. When he regained control of the coughing, he brushed sweat out of his eyes. "Over the years I had time to think about what I did to Nadine, what I did to *you,* my baby girl."

"Shut up." Stacy looked at him with hatred. "I cannot stand to listen to you anymore."

Brooke—who'd been terrified of Zach for days—now feared that Stacy was going to shoot him. She didn't take time to analyze her feelings; she just acted. "Zach, did you go to see Grossmutter in the nursing home?"

He nodded. "Lila had said in one of her letters where Greta was. I didn't feel so bad then. I pulled it off, but Greta was too scared to listen to me."

Stacy scoffed. "That wasn't one of his smarter moves, but the cops told you he'd gotten even crazier."

"I wanted Greta to warn Brooke," Zach said almost pathetically.

"Not without watching your own back, as usual," Brooke snapped. "Why didn't you warn anyone else about Stacy?"

Zach's tired face fell into deeper creases. "I told you I was trying to protect her. I thought if you left town, Lila couldn't come after you because of Jay and her job. You'd both be safe. But, if I told the police about Lila, they'd check into her background and it would be all over for her."

"I see." Brooke looked back at Stacy. "And what about the roses?"

"They were from me, using the numbers off credit cards from women who came into Chantal's," Stacy said.

"And the girl in the church with the vase of roses?"

Stacy smiled. "A young working girl. I saw her standing on a corner one night in a skirt that barely covered her panties and a ton of makeup, but I could still see the resemblance to you. She was glad for the extra money. And she thought the trick, pardon the pun, was fun."

"What about at the planetarium?"

"Same girl. I told her the stuff in the bottle would just ruin your dress and give you a little sting." Stacy had been smiling. She stopped. "But when she saw you carrying on so much about the pain on the Clay Center steps and the ambulance arrived, she got scared. She wouldn't do anything else for me, but that little brain of hers went to work. She decided she needed some money to keep her mouth shut. She came to the apartment building. Jay wasn't home, thank God, and we had quite a scene. If I could have gotten her in the apartment, I would have killed her, but she was too smart for that. She just stayed in the hall, yelling about what she'd done on *my* orders, demanding more money.

"Right after she left, I saw Eunice leaving your apartment. She'd been snooping, just like I told you she did, and I *knew* she'd heard every word that little tramp had said. That's why she was so scared. So, I had to get rid of her." She smiled again. "Thank you for sending her to the basement for me, Brooke. I heard you tell her Harry might be there just as I was on the last two steps of the stairway coming into the lobby. She was already headed down just as you and Vincent were running for the elevator. You didn't even see me go toward the basement."

"And Harry?"

"I didn't do anything to him. I have no idea where he is. Sorry, Brooke, but I cannot be held accountable for Harry."

"Just Robert, Mia, and Eunice."

"Yes. Mia was an accident, I'm embarrassed to say. And Robert, ridiculous as this sounds, was a loose cannon. I came out to the car that night and I saw him trying to climb the fire escape. He was going to break into your apartment. I thought someone that desperate might have killed you, and I couldn't have that pleasure taken away from me. I'm so glad I had your mother's letter opener with me. I'd intended on using it as another scare tactic, but I think I ended up putting it to much better use."

"So what now, Stacy?" Brooke asked. "You shoot me and then vanish, leave your old life behind, leave Jay?"

For the first time, Stacy looked surprised. "I have no intention of leaving Jay. Or my *old life*. I'll just go back to the apartment building, tell Jay I saw you out in the parking lot talking to a man and then getting in his car. I tried to follow you. Coming in and telling the police would have taken too much time. He'll give me hell for doing something so reckless, but I'll cry and apologize and tell him how terrified I was for you, and he'll forgive me. And in a day or two, the police will decide to search this house again and they'll find your body." Elise let out a tiny whine as if she'd understood, and Stacy actually laughed. "And they'll find your loyal dog lying dead right beside you. I never did like that dog, you know."

"I do now," Brooke said dryly. "And what about Zach? Don't you think he'll tell the police what really happened?"

"Who would believe him?" Stacy asked. "Besides, they'll never find him."

"Never find me?" Zach repeated, his voice even weaker. "Where do you think I'm going?"

"I haven't quite decided yet, but don't expect any mercy from me. You lost your right to that a long time ago." Stacy tilted her head and looked at Brooke with eyes the color of a frozen pond. "Well, I'm beginning to worry about how long I've been away from the apartment building. I think it's time for this little drama to end."

Stacy took four steps closer to Brooke, putting her about three feet away. Then Stacy pointed the gun at Brooke's forehead. Their gazes met and held for what seemed to Brooke interminable seconds. Stacy didn't blink. Brooke tried desperately to hide her violent shuddering. She knew it was the end for her, but for some stupid reason, she didn't want to show Stacy she was afraid.

As if far in the distance, Brooke thought she heard a car door, and hope flared in her. Then she remembered. This was a neighborhood. A car had simply pulled in at another house and someone was getting out.

But Stacy heard the noise, too, and she stiffened. She held the gun absolutely still, completely deliberate, completely unflappable, and cocked it in her strong right hand. Brooke kept her eyes open but somehow managed to shut out the vision of Stacy and replace it with another—the memory of dancing by candlelight with Vincent in her apartment.

The gun went off with shattering intensity. Brooke heard Elise let out a howl of desperate fear in her carrier. Brooke waited for the pain. She waited for cessation of consciousness. She waited to hit the floor in almost the same place her mother had fifteen years ago.

Then she heard a groan. And she felt nothing. Abruptly she forced the memory of dancing with Vincent from her mind and returned to the scene in front of her—the scene in which Zach stood in front of Stacy, then fell toward her, his body stiff and straight as a board. Stacy raised her arms as his head hit her chest. She took a step backward and Zach crashed to the floor. Stacy gazed at him, then at her blood-drenched T-shirt, then back at Zach as if stunned. "He saved your life," she said in wonder. Then she looked at Brooke with more venom than Brooke thought a human's eyes could show. "He deserted me, but he gave up his life to save you. *You,* you sniveling, spoiled, weak little bitch."

Stacy raised the gun again. Lucky once, Brooke thought. Impossible to be lucky twice. This was it. She stood tall, refusing to close her eyes, this time thinking of her mother—her mother young and beautiful and laughing like when Daddy was alive.

The cocking of the gun again. Brooke went rigid. Then the front door slammed open and a man yelled, "Drop it!"

Later, Brooke was certain that at that moment, instinct had taken control of her. Without a thought, she sunk to the floor. Brooke put her hands over the back of her head, a gun went off, and she felt bits of sharp glass rain down. The bullet had hit the window behind her, she thought. She heard the male voice again: "Drop it *now!*"

One gunshot. Another gunshot. A high, keening sound from a woman, then a thump like someone banging against a wall.

"She's down!" The sound of heavy footsteps entering the house. Not one person. Not even two. A man ordering, "Stay back, sir." Someone running toward her. She cringed. Then strong arms closed around her body and kisses covered the hands on her head. "Brooke, it's Vincent. Everything's all right now."

Slowly, Brooke let her arms drop and looked up. Stacy slumped against a wall, her right shoulder and the wall drenched in a starburst of blood, the gun still held limply in her right hand. Then it dropped with a clatter. Hal Myers reached for the gun. Jay Corrigan reached for his wife.

Brooke immediately turned her gaze away from Stacy and looked into Vincent's beautiful green eyes. "Are you okay?" he asked.

"I . . . yes. I guess I am," Brooke mumbled.

"Thank God," Vincent said, pulling her close to his warm, strong body.

Brooke lost all track of time. First an ambulance arrived. Then another. Zachary Tavell was pronounced dead at the scene. Massive damage had been done to Stacy's shoulder by the shot of a .44-caliber pistol and she'd lost a lot of blood, but her vital signs were good. "She's going to live," the paramedic said to Hal.

"Good," he replied, trying to smile and looking at Jay. "Did you hear that, Corrigan? She's going to be fine."

But Jay made no response. In fact, he revealed no emotion whatsoever. He looked like a man in a daze. But Brooke understood his lack of expression. He was in shock. She had glanced up just at the moment he had been the one to shoot Stacy.

A paramedic came to Brooke and put a blood pressure cuff on her arm. "Where did you come from?" she asked Vincent.

"You have to be quiet, ma'am," the paramedic said as he placed the end of the stethoscope against the inside of her elbow.

Vincent spoke to her softly. "Dad was missing. I'd been searching for him for hours when I finally found him about two miles from the house. He'd fallen into a ditch and his leg was broken. He was in a lot of pain and totally confused, but he's going to be all right. After I got him to the hospital, I went to your apartment house to tell you what happened and I ran into all these cops and found out about Eunice. Harry wandered in from God knows where and fainted when he saw her. Broke his nose when he hit the concrete. I was in the lobby watching the cops question him and the paramedics trying to get his nosebleed under control when I called you. You answered, but I couldn't believe it when I heard what you were saying to Stacy. I held out the phone for the cops to hear, too. And here we are."

"Just in the nick of time," Brooke said weakly as the paramedic removed the cuff, then began tenderly touching her in the neck area and asking if she had pain, which she didn't.

She looked at Vincent again. "Stacy. She was Zach's daughter. She's been planning this for over a year. I can't believe . . ."

Vincent put his finger over her lips. "Don't think about it now."

She saw Stacy lifted onto a gurney. Conscious, Stacy looked over at her with those still-frozen gray eyes. "You ruined my life," she said icily. "You ruined my life, and Mia's life, and Robert's life, and Eunice's life, and—"

"Shut up," Jay said finally in a dead voice. "For once in your life, just shut up."

As they wheeled Stacy out, she never took that unnerving gaze off Brooke. At last Brooke dropped her head, unable to look at the woman she'd thought was her friend. "She's right," she muttered. "If it hadn't been for me—"

Vincent put his hand under her chin and raised it so that she was looking directly at him. "You didn't hurt anyone, Brooke. *Stacy* did. You are gentle, and kind, and strong."

She looked at him for a moment; then tears welled in her eyes. "How about funny?"

"You're a laugh riot."

"Pretty?"

"Not pretty, gorgeous."

"Smart?"

"You're an Einstein."

Brooke sniffed. "Well, I guess that about does it."

"Not quite." She looked at Vincent questioningly. He smiled, his teeth white against his tanned skin, his face only an inch from hers, so close she could feel his warm, sweet breath. "You're the most fantastic woman I've ever met and I love you."

From her carrier, Elise barked sharply. "And I love you, too," Vincent called before he pulled the carrier over, opened the door, and set an ecstatic Elise on Brooke's lap. "The two most beautiful blondes in the world. How could a guy help himself?"

# epilogue

Brooke opened her door at the same moment Jay stepped into the hall carrying a box. During the past week, she'd seen him only a couple of times in the lobby, but their eyes had never met. Now she was staring directly into his, and they were tired and bloodshot. He looked like he hadn't slept for a couple of nights in a row.

"Hi, Brooke," he said in a toneless voice, his old, quick smile missing.

"Hi." She swallowed, momentarily panicked about what to say. "I heard you were moving out."

"Yeah. This place is too big for one person." He shrugged and gave a short, sharp laugh. "That's not true. I'm trying to escape my memories."

Brooke nodded. "I understand."

Jay stared down the hall, then turned and faced her. "I've been avoiding you because I haven't known how to apologize for all the awful things my wife did to you. I just—"

"Don't apologize," Brooke interrupted. "It's not necessary, Stacy had an unspeakable life. She was sick. She didn't know what she was doing."

"That's what I keep telling myself, but it seems like an excuse. I just can't believe that I lived with her for years and had no idea. Until the last week, that is. I thought she was acting strange, but I was so caught up in what was happening to you that I didn't really analyze her actions as I should have. Still, I believed she loved me. Instead —"

"Jay, she *did* love you," Brooke said quickly and forcefully. "She wasn't incapable of love. She loved her mother, and she loved you deeply. I'm not just being kind. Hell, I certainly don't feel like being kind about Stacy. You have to believe me, though. She fooled me about a lot of things, but she couldn't fool me about her feelings for you."

Jay glanced down at the box in his arms for a moment, then back at her, his eyes looking slightly brighter, maybe from a sheen of tears. "I'll try to take your word for that."

"Good." Brooke hesitated. "How is she doing?"

"Her shoulder is healing as well as can be expected considering it was shattered. There's no infection. They say she'll be out of the hospital in a couple of days. Then it's off to jail. I don't know when the trial will be, but she doesn't stand a chance. As a cop I say she doesn't deserve a chance, but as a husband . . ."

"At least she's alive, Jay."

"Yeah," he said absently. "At least she's alive. I just wish your mother and Mia and Robert and Eunice were." He turned abruptly and walked away.

Brooke stood in the hall, wishing she could call out something comforting to him, but she went blank. Maybe because there isn't anything, she thought, feeling desolate for the good man named Jay Corrigan.

She watched Jay disappear into the elevator, then went back into her apartment. Vincent stood by the window in the living room looking down on the street. Elise sat by his side. "Pretty day out there," he said without looking at Brooke.

"Beautiful. It's hard to imagine that in a couple of months the days will be short and gray when winter is on its way." She shivered. "I hate that weather. I always have."

Vincent turned. "Me, too. It's why I moved to California." He glanced down at Elise, who seemed to have formed a strong attachment to him. "I have a suggestion. Let's not waste this gorgeous day. Let's go for a ride."

"In your convertible?"

"Of course."

"And take Elise?"

"Would you even consider leaving behind Elise with her passionate love of riding in convertibles?"

Elise looked at him, then at Brooke with what she would have sworn was desperate appeal. "I certainly wouldn't. I'll get her leash and my purse, and we're on our way."

Twenty minutes later they sailed down Kanawha Boulevard. Elise, ears flapping, sat on Brooke's lap wearing an expression of what Brooke interpreted as rapture. A bright late-August sun glinted off the Kanawha River running parallel to the boulevard. Several larger boats moved gracefully over the water before a speedboat cut a swath through the pattern, throwing up water as it roared by with skiers behind it.

"Elise looks like she'd like to be out there skiing, too." Vincent grinned as he looked over at the dog, whose ears had perked up in excitement.

"She's putting on a show. She'd be scared to death if you set her on a pair of skis."

Vincent pulled a face. "I believe someone once told me she'd be scared to death riding in a convertible, too."

"Okay, I was wrong about that one. But not about skiing."

"I'd have to see Elise's reaction to skis before I believe you. I'm not sure you know your dog as well as you think you do, Miss Yeager."

She stuck out her tongue at him and held Elise a tad tighter, afraid the dog was going to jump out of the car and head for the river to hitch a ride on the speedboat. Then an old memory popped into Brooke's head. "My parents rented a speedboat for a day and Daddy skied. I was only four or five and scared to death at first, but Daddy reassured me. Then Mommy skied, and within an hour, I was laughing and clapping and never wanted them to give back that boat."

"That's a great memory," Vincent said. "And someday, when you have a daughter who actually stands on *two* legs instead of four, she'll probably love skiing, too," Vincent said. "Not to mention that if she looks like her mother, she'll be a doll."

Slightly embarrassed by the compliment, Brooke began furiously petting Elise and asked, "How's your father doing?"

"Griping, grumbling, complaining nonstop, unsuccessfully trying to make my life miserable, but I'm so glad he's alive after that dive into the ditch, I think it would be impossible for him to get on my nerves. At least for another week." Brooke laughed. "He's mastered those crutches in record time. I'm not surprised, though. Whatever Dad set out to do he always did faster and better than anyone else."

Brooke waited a moment, then decided to broach a subject that might take some of the joy out of Vincent's face. "All we've talked about the last few days is me and Stacy and that whole drama. We haven't talked about yours." Vincent looked at her quizzically. "What are you going to do about your father? Put him in a nursing home here in Charleston?"

"He says no and I'm tired of arguing with him."

"So you're going to get him a twenty-four-hour-a-day caregiver?"

"No. He won't stand for that, either. So there you have it."

"Vincent, you can't just go back to Monterey!"

"Oh yes, I can," Vincent said. "And that's exactly what I'm going to do."

Shocked, Brooke stared at him with a slightly open mouth for a moment before she managed, "You *can't* do that! Look what happened to him last week. If he'd lain in that ditch all night, he could have died." Suddenly, she realized she had gone from shock to anger. "How can you even think of going off and leaving him?"

Vincent looked at her innocently. "Who said that's what I was going to do?"

"You said you're going back to Monterey."

"Did I say I was going back alone?" Brooke stared at him. "Dad has agreed that he can't go on living in that house alone, but he doesn't want to be stuck in a nursing home in Charleston, either." Vincent looked at her and grinned. "Brooke, he's coming back to Monterey with me. They have nursing homes out there, too. As a matter of fact, there's a really nice one just ten minutes away from my house."

Brooke realized she'd been holding her breath. She finally let it out. "Oh, thank goodness. For a minute there you had me scared to death about Sam, and also thinking you were a completely irresponsible jerk."

"And now what do you think?"

"Now I'm thrilled for Sam. I think the change will be wonderful for him. All he does is wander around that house he shared with your mother. It's too filled with memories. He needs fresh scenery."

"The same could be said for someone else, you know."

"I suppose that would be your subtle way of referring to me."

"Yes. Charleston has some beautiful spots and I know you've lived here all your life, but you have to admit it's not exactly teeming with wonderful memories for you."

"Well, no," Brooke said reluctantly. "But I guess I have time to make new memories."

"Here. All alone. No relatives. No friends—"

"Vincent, stop it!" she snapped. "You don't have to rub in the fact that I'm not surrounded by loved ones."

"Think you might feel better with at least two loved ones around?"

"Two? And just who would these two people be?"

"Dad. You do love Sam, don't you?"

She was silent for a moment. "Yes. I guess I do. I have since I was eleven and wanted to become his daughter."

"Well, I don't want you to become my daughter, but how about me?"

"You?"

"Do you have any tender feelings toward me? Well,

maybe 'tender' was too strong a word. Do you think you can stand spending some time with me in the future?"

"Spending time with you?"

"Brooke, you're beginning to sound like a parrot, repeating everything I say."

"That was a lovely compliment."

"I guess it didn't help my case, did it?"

"And what would your *case* be?"

"To talk you into coming to California, too. Specifically, Monterey."

Brooke looked at him in surprise. "You want me to come to Monterey?"

"You're doing it again. The parrot thing."

"I just . . . I mean . . . why?"

"Why do I want you to come to Monterey? To get a new start."

"Oh."

"And because I love you and I think you love me, too."

"You love me—"

"Brooke—"

"I'm sorry. Broken record. Parrot. Whatever."

They rode in silence for a few moments before Vincent said, "I *do* love you, Brooke. Am I right that you love me, too?"

She glanced at him, his black hair shining in the sun, his forest green eyes focused on her, their intensity belying the casualness of his smile. A nervous tension suddenly grabbed at her, as if trying to hold her back. For fifteen years she'd been so careful, so aloof, keeping her heart closed to everyone except Greta. Was it too late to change?

Vincent clicked the CD player. In a moment, the sounds of Neil Young's "Cinnamon Girl" filled the car. Vincent sped up. They seemed to be sailing above the ground, the river sparkling and glinting beside them, the sky bluer than she'd ever seen it. As the wind blew her hair and the warm sun touched her face, Brooke felt freedom wash over her. She didn't *have* to stay chained to the past. It wasn't impossible for her to hold a man's hand, to run in the night, to chase the moonlight, like the couple in the song. It just had to be with the right man. And as she looked at Vincent, she felt the heart she'd tried to close for so long open wide, open happily.

Vincent glanced at her again and asked with a mixture of hope and uncertainty, "Well?"

Brooke smiled wider, more freely than she had for years. She shook her long, loose hair, tilted her head to look at him coquettishly, and shouted joyfully, "I do love you, Vincent Lockhart! Take Elise and me to Monterey and let's live there forever!"